# IN THE
# FRAME

# IN THE FRAME

## LORRAINE AMRANI

NOMAD
PUBLISHING

# IN THE FRAME

## ACKNOWLEDGEMENTS

I would like to express my deep appreciation
to my husband Skip and son Sam,
who never once doubted my ability to complete my novel.

## DISCLAIMER

This book is entirely a work of fiction and, except in the cases of historical facts and personalities represented in the narrative, any resemblance to actual persons, living or dead, is purely coincidental. The publisher and the author assume no responsibility for errors, inaccuracies, omissions, or any other inconsistencies herein.

Published by Nomad Publishing in 2023
Email: info@nomad-publishing.com
www.nomad-publishing.com

ISBN 978-1-914325-25-0

## DISCLAIMER

This book is entirely a work of fiction and, except in the cases of historical facts and personalities represented in the narrative, any resemblance to actual persons, living or dead, is purely coincidental. The publisher and the author assume no responsibility for errors, inaccuracies, omissions, or any other inconsistencies herein.

CIP Data: A catalogue for this book is
available from the British Library

# CONTENTS

# PROLOGUE

## Paris, September 1940

It is now four months since the Nazis goose-stepped into the French capital. German tanks and soldiers fill the arrondissements, wielding their might as they take over every public building while graphically displaying a ruthlessness and cruelty made all the worse by their reckless indulgence in crystal methamphetamine, giving them a false confidence. Hard-wired on the Class A drug, they were turned into perfect killing machines, feeling no need to sleep or eat – just a relentless pursuit of the goal demanded by their superiors in Germany.

With the Occupation now complete, and the heels of the Germans on their necks, their systemic oppression saw far fewer Parisiennes sitting in the boulevard cafés, smoking, flirting, laughing, and meeting friends, as was the accustomed French way of life, while enjoying a glass or two at the end of their working day as would be the normal scenario on any given evening. Instead, it was now full of loud and vulgar cavalier German soldiers, off duty and riotously gratifying themselves on an abundance of French wines and beers to excess, while conspicuously intimidating any French mademoiselle who took their fancy.

The mood in Paris was despondent and subdued with apprehension and suspicion everywhere. Nobody knew what might occur next, from actual sadistic violence to mental abuse that preyed on them without reprieve. Many of the French had boarded up their businesses, and those who could, had took flight to the south of the country. The French Government had surrendered, and Vichy France was now officially known as the French state, or more aptly, Berlin's 'puppet' government; people knew who was really in control, and that was; Reichsmarschall and Kommandant of the Luftwaffe, as well as founder of the Gestapo; Hermann Göring. Once a celebrated ace pilot, hero in the Great War, and recipient of the distinguished Blue Max, subsequently reduced to making a living as a flying circus stunt rider; to him, it was the ultimate humiliation; but then came his cataclysmic union with Adolf Hitler that inspired his intrinsic narcissism.

A gunshot wound from a failed coup in Munich, fighting alongside Hitler had left him in constant pain; while being 'fed' with so much morphine by the surgeons, his addiction to the drug had begun. This pernicious dependence to opiates would never leave; forever to dominate, transforming his behaviour, physical body, and once fine looks. Now warped of mind, the unyielding thirst for the 'tyrant' of morphine resulted in his containment in a lunatic asylum for violent outbursts, paranoia, and deep-rooted depression, leaving him erratic, while always on the verge of physical destruction; this rapid decline gained mastery, as he became a danger to all.

The detention in the asylum was Göring's lowest ebb. Shame and desperation to get out of the hospital focused an unwavering determination that saw him leave the institution and begin a new life, something his strong and uncompromising personality had to attain. Discovering a reservoir of pure steel, Göring was now mentally where he needed to be, as he carried a conviction to see his heady rise to unchallengeable power within the Third Reich.

The vision of a preordained image had finally reached its destination; and he intended to take full advantage of what he believed was his absolute right.

The once much younger charismatic fighter pilot that had been Hermann Göring, was now long gone, as the new morally corrupt Göring was ready to be embraced by the Nazi Party, an organization that permitted him to exercise his greed and unrestrained influence.

The habitual 'fix' needed now, was to fill his world with as much wealth and luxury as was humanly possible, because, his ego demanded it, and his soul would accept nothing less. Göring had become a kind of vampire, always looking to satiate his lust for more and more. At last, the 'Master' of all he surveyed. And he wanted it all; nothing less would do.

But his new 'addiction' would unknowingly put in motion a series of events that would change the history of art forever…

# CHAPTER 1

## The Pillage of Paris

It was six in the evening and the curfew would start at eight. The hue from the autumn sun cast a cold harsh glow as dusk began to set. The Kommandant, Reichsmarschall Hermann Göring, was travelling in a large motorcade along the Champs-Élysées; his destination was the Louvre Museum, where he was to meet the head curator of the fine arts department, Professor Charles Jardin, as pre-arranged.

Along the boulevard a large crowd had started to gather; French men and women soberly watching their new 'masters' in a procession that proclaimed their full jurisdiction over them. The aggressive and deafening parade of high-ranking Nazis sauntered along in their shining automobiles – presumptuous, like all conquerors, emboldened in their invincibility as they eyed their newly captured territory.

Reichsmarschall Göring sat comfortably in his two-seater open-topped vehicle, taking in the full spectacle of the assembled crowd, when his pleasure was brought to an abrupt halt by his chauffeur hitting on to the brakes. Göring, instantly annoyed by the unexpected disruption, straightens his obese frame from the comfort of his car seat to ascertain what the hell was happening to warrant the driver's action, but quickly comes to realise it was from the loud fracas occurring up front. Göring, with predictable impatience immediately begins shouting, demanding to know what exactly was going on.

'Well?' he yells harshly at a German soldier who runs up to inform

Göring that a group of insurgents were causing trouble;

'Kommandant, they ran out from the crowd in a brazen attempt to attack us in our vehicles, throwing gasoline bombs, setting two of the vehicles alight, and firing shots from their guns!'

'Bring them to me at once!' Göring states without hesitation, 'I will show them a thing or two!'

The captured men and women were swiftly marched by several stern-faced German soldiers pushing them aggressively in the back with their guns up to the Kommandant. As they stand face to face with the Reichsmarschall feeling defiant, but foolhardy, Göring makes no attempt to question any one of them, as far as he is concerned any dissent to Nazi authority will not be tolerated under any circumstances. Without mercy he orders just the women to fall to their knees and bend their heads, 'So, you like to play with fire, do you? In that case, let's see if you like this?'

His voice was cynical and condemnatory. He then whispers into the ear of one of the German soldiers, who immediately obeys – with his hand gripping a can of petrol from one of their trucks, the Reichsmarschall instructs him to pour it liberally over their heads as he hands the soldier his own gold cigarette lighter. The Reichsmarschall was about to unleash hell on the now terrified captured women as he gives the nod to set light to their beautiful wavy hair. In an instant, an uncontrollable inferno of flames takes hold – the screams of agony and pain from such torture were unbearable, and soon, their now blackened charred bodies were so distressing, that the crowd, almost unable to believe what they were seeing are panicked into a shared mutual shock at the total viciousness of this man and his utter barbarity, immediately take flight in horror, scared for their safety. Göring, with malicious indifference, promptly orders the German officers to 'Shoot the rest of the agitators – at once!'

Göring, his hands balanced on either side of his huge expansive body, was momentarily amused while watching the crowd run, cowering that he may turn on them.

'Run away you snivelling little cockroaches, in case I come after you!' thrusting back his head as he laughs out loud to himself, feeling not a trace of empathy. The only thing he felt was a profound displeasure at the disruption in his day. Nonetheless, he was more than satisfied that he had dealt with the problem with such superb efficiency.

Brushing away the stray embers of the burnt remains from his smart uniform, he calls out to the German officer, 'Don't forget to clear away all the debris, we don't want any stench in our new city!' Struggling to climb back into the car, Göring immediately snaps his fingers at his chauffeur, 'Drive on, and get me to the Louvre. I do not wish to be detained here one moment longer, my time is precious, and I have a very important appointment – to view art!'

The tiresome elimination of trouble on the Champs-Élysées was not going to thwart any excitement he was feeling for his planned visit to the museum. As his chauffeur pulled slowly into the Louvre, the Reichsmarschall's enthusiasm was conspicuous. Stepping from his large, gleaming custom-built Blue Goose 540k Mercedes-Benz, a personal gift from his Führer, Göring stopped, enjoying an overwhelming feeling of self-satisfaction in his position as Hitler's most trusted senior Nazi.

.

# CHAPTER 2

## When Diplomacy is the Finest Art of All

Göring's typically cold, puffy eyes displayed a subtle hint of pleasure at the sight of the grand building of the Louvre Museum that somehow helped soften the dread of one of the most dangerous men in Europe. His solid built frame was partially concealed by a heavy woollen coat, dramatically draped over the broad shoulders of a large rotund body, covering his immaculate field grey uniform, decorated by so many medals they clashed for attention with the brass buttons stitched all the way down either side of the jacket. No detail of his image was overlooked, while his knee-high tan leather boots completed his resolute appearance; upon one hand he wore a large impressive radiant ruby ring of eighteen-carat gold, which accentuated his murderous stubby fingers. Göring's commanding and intimidating presence signalled absolute terror.

Overriding his personal concerns, the museum's Head Curator of Fine Arts, Professor Jardin, formally greeted Göring.

'Welcome to the Louvre, Kommandant.'

As the two men shake hands, Jardin feels a tightly squeezing pressure from the overpowering grip and duration of the handshake before Göring finally lets go.

Hermann Göring stared straight into the eyes, as was his habit, deliberately holding his sickly gaze to any recipient of his hand. Jardin found this very unsettling.

The Professor had given much thought about this moment. When he became aware of his impending meeting with Göring, he had decided, wisely, to let Göring take the lead in any conversation that would ensue, as the Kommandant was not the type of man you would dare to make small talk with. Jardin was quite aware that this was to be a time when all his diplomatic skills would need to be deployed if he was to survive the visit and his certainty of his survival was tenuous, at best.

The Reichsmarschall's entry into the Louvre was with a determined but almost relaxed swagger, displaying a confidence that reflected the Nazi domination over Paris. Göring, now feeling poised and on the threshold of fulfilling a long-held belief in his own greatness and destiny, was on an art looting bender, a lawlessness over which the French now had no control.

Jardin, dressed in his usual conservative manner, wore a navy-blue pin-striped double-breasted suit, while his brown horned-rimmed glasses were tucked into his top pocket, greeted Göring with all the heartfelt prudence he could muster, all the time mindful to maintain an attentive smile, ready for what was about to occur.

It had been requested from Berlin that the Reichsmarschall would like to see the Louvre's Old Masters. It was an all-consuming and overriding ambition of Göring's to get first pickings from the world-famous Louvre Museum and its unsurpassed art collection.

Jardin concealed his disquiet, along with a heavy heart and feelings of deep unease, directs Göring up the stairs to the main salon, 'This way Kommandant, s'il vous plaît.'

Proceeding along the famously polished parquet flooring to the sound of the Kommandant's entourage of minor Nazi officials strutting behind with their heavy boots reverberating like violent thunder around the grand chambers, every step allowing Göring to devour each gluttonous moment with hawk-like scrutiny, scouring the rooms, ready to pounce and hungry for his kill.

The chillier than usual autumn sunlight, begins to fade fast through the large sash windows, casting strange dark shadows that exaggerated the high ceilings and wooden relief carvings in the magnificent structure of the building, the rooms Jardin feels privileged to spend much of his working life in now seem to possess a noxious underbelly.

The Professor offers Göring the civility of a glass of Chateau Margaux 1929 – Göring smiles as he nods to the curator seemingly with approval.

'Why Professor, how fortuitous! You appear to have chosen one of my favourites, and a good year I believe?' Jardin concurs, 'Yes, I do believe so.'

When Jardin had learnt that the Reichsmarschall was intending to visit the museum he took it upon himself to discover what Göring liked to drink, as the need for a smooth visit was imperative and nothing less would do for this man who now has the fate of Paris in his grip.

The Reichsmarschall eagerly accepts the exquisite hand-crafted Venetian glass containing the dark red wine, as the Professor detects the hint of a smile manifest from his mouth.

'So, Professor, you will join me in a glass?'

Göring gestured to the open bottle on the Louis XIV mahogany gilt table in such a way that the offer to partake seemed more like an 'order' than a polite invitation. In any other situation, and with anybody else, a glass of Chateau Margaux would have been one of life's great pleasures; but this is not one of those moments. However, Jardin accepts the offer with an aversion; to drink with such a man is repugnant to him, but he had little choice. As the Professor sipped the wine, it was not the Chateau Margaux he was savouring on his tongue, but the piquancy of death soiling his mouth, smothering his taste buds.

Finishing his second glass of wine, Göring was now in a pleasant enough mood, with a smug self-satisfied grin on his face he slowed his pace through the museum's long, and seemingly never-ending grand gallery. The Reichsmarschall's enjoyment was the Professor's misery, this wide-awake nightmare had only one origin, and he was standing right beside him.

Inspecting each painting in turn, taking considerably more time to look at a very desirable and exceptional Vermeer, before moving on to a flawless painting of the Madonna and Child by Raphael, then a

15

Rubens, while eagerly seeking out one of his most admired painters, Albrecht Dürer, whose Portrait of the Artist Holding a Thistle, circa 1493, was without doubt one of the Louvre's most precious and rare works of art. The sight of it excited him greatly, a real coup for the Kommandant as he squealed with joy at the prospect of owning this particularly beautiful painting.

'Ah, yes, yes, indeed, truly wonderful, even exceptional, 'was his reaction to the Dürer, in fact, it was only second to the painting he sought most of all, the one that left the Reichsmarschall breathless with a childlike exultation.

The situation Jardin found himself in felt surreal, watching the Reichsmarschall almost salivate, displaying a greed the likes of which he had never seen before in any human being, was a sight utterly repulsive to the Professor as he pondered for a moment the thought that, if he were a psychologist, he may have had a totally different perspective and find the antics fascinating to observe, however, that was not the case, instead it was simply a grotesque demonstration of the very worst kind of human characteristic.

Göring prided himself on his knowledge, his 'expertise' and art connoisseurship, something he liked to demonstrate whenever the opportunity arose, enabling him to flaunt his refined taste in old masters, an obsessive display of superiority.

# CHAPTER 3

## "Everything You Can Imagine Is Real… I Dreamed of Owning the Mona Lisa" – Hermann Göring

It was time for Professor Jardin to make the formal introduction to the 'Cultural Symbol of France'. They both stood before the masterpiece – the glorious Mona Lisa, the young woman with a mysterious smile that had captivated and intrigued the world for almost five hundred years. A painting whose style and technique were so utterly unique that only Leonardo da Vinci could have imagined and had the brilliance of mind to execute it to perfection. The work transformed the art of portrait painting forever. With its bold originality, it had become the most desired and truly priceless oil painting in the entire history of Western art, and now it was to take its place as part of Göring's extensive private collection.

For Göring, this was to be his most valued and coveted art grab. He was now finally up close and personal, at last fulfilling what had been his dream since Germany began waging war across Europe.

With this one statement acquisition, the Mona Lisa would represent the epitome of his success.

'You know something Jardin,' Göring pauses long enough to make the Professor nervous, 'there seems to be wild stories flying around Paris that the Mona Lisa had been removed and placed in a safe house?' Göring's unrelenting stare at Jardin made him swallow hard, 'Really? How foolish, no, I had not heard those stories, which are obviously quite false because as you see she is here before us.'

The Professor almost choked on his words trying to seem ignorant of any such talk, stunned by the fact that the Reichsmarschall's spies had managed to gather such intelligence, Göring smiles in response to the answer, 'Um, just as well it was only gossip; because', as he leaned in closer to murmur in Jardin's ear, 'I would have hated to be in your shoes if she had not been!' These penetrating words filled the Professor with a feeling of trepidation.

Göring, fascinated by the depiction of the young female in the painting, turned to the Professor, 'So, who actually was the Mona Lisa?'

'In truth we really don't know, it was never conclusive, just that it was perhaps the wife or mistress of one merchant or another, but there is no proof or evidence to support that theory,' Jardin replies.

'Well, it is of no consequence, but tell me, has she ever needed to be restored in any way?'

'That is such an interesting question, Kommandant,' before the Professor could reply to the inquiry posed, Göring retorted like quicksilver, 'Yes, you don't need to tell me, I know it's an interesting question, do you think I am uninformed about art? Why are you so surprised that I ask you such a question? Well, what do you have to say for yourself?' Göring asks sarcastically. The Professor, taken aback, was now desperately searching for the right words, not wanting to displease him any further.

'No, not at all Kommandant, my sincere apologies if I sounded impolite in any way, I have heard how much knowledge you have of culture and fine art and genuinely admired what you asked,' he said, stumbling on his words.

'Do you think I have I have infinite time on my hands, Jardin? So please, when you can find a moment, I would like the answer to my question, which I am still waiting for, but then again, as it was so long ago that I asked you, I presume you have forgotten, therefore I will try once more; has it ever been restored?' Göring berated.

'Actually no, never, and, as you know, Leonardo da Vinci didn't produce that many paintings, some of which he never finished, so his catalogue of work is very small, and interestingly, he kept the painting of her with him, in fact he would never be parted from it, until his death – did you know that the painting was actually stolen from the museum in 1911 by an Italian, and remained hidden by the thief under his bed for two years? Fortunately, he kept it well protected', but before the curator could finish his story Göring interrupted him, 'Yet again, you think me uninformed, of course I know about that,' tutting in a scolding manner.

'Really, Professor, the Louvre should learn to protect their most valuable collection much better, it could have been lost forever – it's actually quite shocking to hear of such incompetence by the museum!' Göring's cynicism was jaw-dropping.

'I can confirm categorically that she has never needed to be removed from her original frame for any work whatsoever, she is intact from her conception,' Jardin assured the new owner.

'So, Professor Jardin, what is your opinion of this painting?' Göring asked the curator, eagerly waiting for the reply. Without any hesitation, Jardin's lucidity on the quality, history and beauty of the painting was immensely pleasing to Göring, who turned to the curator and loudly concurred, 'I agree with you Professor, you have a keen eye, almost as good as mine I expect! Well, no, that could not be possible. . . Even if I say so myself modestly,' Göring, pauses in thought as if struck by his own remarkable magnificence before he suddenly declares, 'You know Professor, I suddenly realised during our very intelligent conversation that I am quite the Renaissance Man – just like one of the great Florentine Medici's. I think perhaps you and I do have something in common, a love of fine art, and that I like, but don't let my compliment go to your head!' Göring's words, inferring that they might possibly have 'anything' in common, felt like an affront to the decent and respected Professor, who now just smiled meekly at Göring's blatant and transparent insincerity.

The Curator, who had studied Italian and French art, was more than qualified to offer Göring his expertise, not only on the Louvre's Old Masters, but as he had spent many years in daily contact with the

Mona Lisa, he felt a special bond with her.

Studying this painting was a life-long passion. So, he was more than happy to talk about her at great length. Then, suddenly Jardin realised how unprepared he was for the feelings of immense bereavement he was beginning to experience. The loss of this painting felt like a death.

Trying to contain his emotions before the Reichsmarschall took all his resolve. He was in a difficult situation, maintaining a level of decorum and diplomacy that the gravity of the situation demanded.

The words of affirmation concerning the authority of this immortal painting from the Professor were not only very flattering to Göring but had confirmed to him why this work of art was to take pride of place in his home collection.

This was a day that Reichsmarschall Hermann Göring, Commander-in-Chief of the German Air Force, an accolade bestowed upon him by Hitler for his victory over France, and the Curator of Fine Arts at the Louvre, Professor Charles Jardin, will always remember – but for completely different reasons.

France always viewed herself as the epitome of a civilized and sophisticated society, taking pride in its influence as the standard bearer of art, culture, literacy, and philosophy, where elegance and knowledge were reflections of the nation's deep-rooted history.

The prospect of a person such as Göring, whom Jardin saw as no more than an ignorant, but highly dangerous and unstable buffoon, taking possession of such a great work, was something the Curator was finding abhorrent. Göring, a man whose perception of himself as an 'intellectual', viewed this acquisition as his God-given rite of passage, an 'official ceremony' of critical importance, a landmark in his career and personal life. Now, the artistic rape of France had been set in motion.

When German soldiers began their Occupation of Paris, within days Jardin, as head curator, had wanted to remove the most valuable works out of the capital, with an idea of transporting them in ambulances to varied châteaux in Provence, but the museum instantly came under intense surveillance, with security checks of all movements in and out of the building and body searches at any given moment, so the opportunity of removing the artwork, which, would have been a colossal task under even normal circumstances, was now found to be impossible.

In anticipation of their invasion, Göring was already one step ahead. From the start of the Occupation, and even before Paris was fully aware of how things would unfold, the Nazi had drawn up his plans.

The Reichsmarschall, knowing what he wanted, and fearing it might 'disappear', dispatched a personal envoy with orders sent via Berlin from Göring himself to be hand-delivered. It was addressed to Professor Charles Jardin, Head of Fine Arts, Louvre, Paris, with a directive, stating, 'Under No Circumstances' was any part of the collections to be disturbed in any way whatsoever! And that NOTHING was to be removed. Signed Reichsmarschall Hermann Göring.

With consternation uppermost in his mind, Jardin immediately realised what was at stake. Nobody at the museum dared to upset this notoriously unpredictable man. Göring stated in his letter that Jardin would be personally responsible for the custodianship of the Mona Lisa, upon threat of execution not only of himself but of his entire staff. However, Jardin was acutely aware of the momentousness and consequential loss that this unique painting would entail for France, if not the entire world, because after all, this was no ordinary Old Master; it was a truly irreplaceable object. The burden was profound.

When the Professor first received his orders from Göring, he immediately put in a call to Pierre Guyon, Director of Musée National.

'Pierre, Bonjour, it is Charles, how are you? I was thinking it would be nice to meet up for coffee this afternoon at the Cafe de Paris, would you be free?'

'Oui, Charles, merci; that would be delightful, I look forward to seeing you later today.' They hung up their phones.

At 4.30pm, the two men greet each other and decide to sit inside due to the dampness of the afternoon. Before the occupation, the elegant Cafe de Paris was a place they would often meet to converse and enjoy each other's company, now with eyes everywhere, they would need to have their wits about them, because nowhere was safe or secure.

Charles Jardin tells Pierre about the contents of the letter from Göring, with its implications, and of his impending visit. That afternoon, the two men discussed the problem at great length, but realised all too soon the impasse they found themselves in, and the inevitable death sentence that would occur to their staff if they removed the Mona Lisa.

'There is a sensitive question I am about to ask you Charles – the thing is,' Pierre hesitated, 'I don't get a good feeling about this Phillippe Pétain – I don't want to put you in an awkward situation but, please tell me truthfully, what do you think of our new Chief of State of Vichy?' Pierre asked of his friend. Charles Jardin looked pensive as he sighed deeply, 'Well, I think he is duplicitous, we cannot be too careful where he is concerned, and I can't say I trust him on any level – he is a puppet of the Nazis, make no mistake of that, and while for appearance's sake he will stand up to them for the rights of France, don't be fooled Pierre, he is a difficult, self-interested, self-regarding man and you are right in your instincts not to trust him, that is why I didn't phone him with regards to the art collection, or Göring's planned visit; the less he knows the better!' Jardin stated with his knowledge of the Chief of Vichy.

Both Pierre Guyon and Professor Jardin agree that from now on they will keep Phillippe Pétain, the head of the so-called French Government, in the dark as far as possible. They were both working for the good of France, while Phillippe Pétain, they both believed, was working only for the good of Phillippe Pétain!

That afternoon in the Cafe de Paris, Pierre Guyon smoked almost an entire packet of cigarettes.

'Pierre, you look terribly thin; are you eating and sleeping?' Charles Jardin could see his friend was not really coping, 'Thank you, Charles, for your concern. I will be fine – we just have to get by as best we can under these desperate circumstances, what else can we do? It's all out of our control, everything is falling apart, who knows if France even exists anymore?' Guyon's words were true enough, and the Professor could only agree.

'Yes, I understand, everything is so volatile, we must be careful at all times,' the Professor echoed Guyon's sentiments.

They had to concede to their distressing predicament. Fully aware that it was now going to be impossible to remove the Mona Lisa as they had wanted, because the reality was, their hands were completely tied. France was one of the most important and well-respected countries in the world, but now it was broken, and the two men felt paralyzed; how could this be happening?

Jardin would have been ready to put his own life at risk for this altruistic cause, but he could not put the lives of his staff in danger.

With a determination to do something, and a sharp insight, the two men collude in a subterfuge, for what it was worth.

They resolved to set in motion low-level rumours that the Mona Lisa had been taken from the Louvre. This fabrication was to be accompanied by some staged photographs apparently showing the painting being removed by the French authorities to a safe and protected secret location. This propaganda would be totally discreet, shown to only a selected few who would use their influence to spread this information underground, confirming that the painting was safe and secure, buying them the time they needed. But in truth, only Jardin and Guyon knew where the Mona Lisa was really going. Today in Paris was uncertain and tomorrow nobody dared think about. Now was not the time for the French people to know the real destination of the Mona Lisa, the unbearable, and dreadful truth that her new home was to be in Germany. Just thinking about it made them both feel a deep sense of grief.

The daily survival and well-being of the French people were now of paramount importance, and the occupied Parisiennes had many important things to concern their every waking hour. The theft and plunder of their most treasured works of art and as such their very 'identity' as a people could soon be lost forever, but this was too much of a burden to add to what they were suffering right now.

Jardin consoled himself that one day she would return to her rightful place. However, sadly this thought was incompatible with the brutal truth of the times that both Paris and Europe were living in.

Now after the Reichsmarschall's private 'viewing', Göring was feeling utterly frustrated that he did not have sufficient time to view even more art, ensuring he got all the best pieces for himself, but he was wanted elsewhere.

'Professor, I will need to visit again – and soon, but for now I am ready to instruct you as to which paintings are the most important to me at this precise moment. I expect them to be crated up and ready to be collected tomorrow morning, after which they will be transported and loaded onto my private train. Your staff, I think, are going to have a busy night!' Professor Jardin nods meekly in assent.

'And now I must take my leave, as my business here is concluded... for the time being, viewing art, it seems, has given me an enormous appetite! I am in need of savouring your delicious French cuisine, which I must confess is almost as good as your fine old masters,' Göring remarked without a trace of irony.

'Therefore, Professor, I will send my agent Bruno Klein to see you tomorrow morning,' the Reichsmarschall briskly informed the curator. The legal transfer of 'ownership' of the paintings was imperative to Göring.

'Klein will come here to attend to the matter at hand; and I trust all the paperwork will be ready, signed, as well as witnessed by the time he gets here; is that understood?' Göring's manner was abrupt and to the point as he informs Professor Jardin of his requirements.

Momentarily off guard, the Professor turns to the Kommandant to ask.

'What time should I expect Herr Klein?' All at once Jardin notices Göring's face show an irritation that was unnerving, leaving the Professor quite perturbed.

'Professor, please,' his voice sounding vexed, 'as I have already informed you...in the morning! Is it really too much for you to pay attention?' he said with unmistakable sarcasm.

'I really don't want to have to repeat myself,' the Reichsmarschall replied with contempt. Jardin looked away now feeling well and truly rebuked. Realizing just how quickly his mood changes; it was a warning to the curator not to make any mistakes when dealing with this man or taking his seemingly pleasant mood for granted. He must always remain on his guard.

'And now Professor, until next time, I bid you a good evening,' Göring, not bothering to shake the Professor's hand, turned quickly on his heels, and started to take his leave from the museum. Jardin was relieved to see the back of him and his entourage.

Even though Göring was there to plunder the Louvre of its fabulous collection, the deed had to be done with utmost legality. It was truly ironic that a thief wants and demands it all legal and above board.

# CHAPTER 4

## The Ritz-Carlton

Hermann Göring, now on a tight agenda after taking longer at the Louvre than he had anticipated, nonetheless wanted to take a quick shopping detour to Cartier the jewellers to pick up a little 'something' for Emmy, his wife, before heading off to the Ritz Hotel on an unscheduled visit to see Günther Von Dincklage. All the luxury stores on the Palace Vendôme had been told to remain open and be on standby for a possible visit when suddenly Göring's eyes detected a very pleasing sight.

'Stop at once!' he yelled at his driver, who does instantly as he is told. Göring had set his sights on Fabergé.

His eyes lit up in wonderment as to what he might discover in this classy treasure trove of a store with so many possibilities, bewildered and chastising himself that he could ever have missed it before.

Göring, feeling instant excitement in anticipation that once inside the fabulous House of Fabergé, he had a lot of acquiring to do, huffed and puffed to himself.

'God, how could I have overlooked it?'

Delighted with the items of yet even more luxury, Göring, gathering up his harvest of anything and everything he could get his hands on, totally exhilarated, gets back into his car and orders his driver to take him onto Cartier.

With the Swastika flapping high above the Eiffel Tower, the sign of the Third Reich's total power and authority over France, senior Nazi officials requisition all the very best hotels of Paris, but for Göring, the only place to be was in the sheer opulence that was the Ritz.

Every night at the Ritz was party time as it became filled to bursting with the upper echelons of the German military being entertained by the maudlin tones of Edith Piaf singing out, pleasing the rowdy and contemptuous Germans, who would now spend each evening in its plush sanctuary. Young bellboys would appear on hand, always at the ready to appease the 'guests' of their every whim, while smartly dressed waiters attired in black tails would supply them with their voracious demands for the champagne to flow fast and freely.

The riotous gathering of the men, who were always invariably drunk on a cocktail of their own massive egos of grandiose self-importance while fully loaded on a mixture of strong narcotics, took the sadistic delight in cruelly treating the staff like they were just minions, as the enraptured Nazi throng gratified themselves with all the pleasures of Paris.

While everything inside the pampered world of the Ritz appeared normal, outside, the rest of Paris was devastated by desperate food shortages and widespread malnutrition. Beyond those doors of the luxury hotel, real life in the rest of France was swiftly descending into chaos, as a harsh and ruthless catastrophe befell the nation. Göring, avidly pursuing full comfort from the hotel's hospitality, took over an entire floor of the vast building, where his Imperial Suite was filled with priceless works of art stolen from Warsaw after a raid, including a Botticelli and a van Gogh, just as emeralds, sapphires and diamonds were scattered carelessly onto side tables with no regard as to their value, always aware that he could obtain more whenever he wanted to.

The Imperial Suite became Göring's gilded paradise, as every possible amenity was made available to him, and upon his personal instructions, the walls of the grandiose salons were covered with Versailles inspired pale blue wallpaper, the perfect compliment to the eighteenth-century mahogany furniture the elegant rooms demanded. The soft ambient light, dictated by the festoon of curtains matched the feather filled brocaded cushions sitting upright and neatly in place on the velvet buttoned sofas, as if standing to attention when in the presence of the Reichsmarschall himself. The hotel always decorated their suites to the highest of standards, with ample attention paid to even the smallest detail, so creating the high living to which their VIP guests were accustomed to, and demanded.

The closets in Göring's suite were filled to bursting with his many uniforms, along with his silk Japanese wraps, and bejewelled slippers. On his dressing table, his own personal face make-up and exotic perfume bottles displayed an alternative side to Göring of which most Germans were totally unaware, and upon the Art Deco mirrored table was a stunning Lalique topaz coloured glass bowl brimming with his morphine pills; always at the ready for when he required his next little 'fix.'

# CHAPTER 5

## The French Mistress

Gabrielle 'Coco' Chanel, a dark-haired ageing French designer, was engaged in a relationship with the Nazi, Baron Hans Günther von Dincklage, and was openly living with him in their suite at the Ritz. The Baron, personally selected by Joseph Goebbels, Hitler's trusted propaganda chief, was positioned as a secret attaché to Paris, answering to Goebbels personally on all matters regarding the goings on in the French capital, something that Chanel knew and was only too willing to aid and abet with all her extensive connections both in France and in England put at the disposal of the Nazis; so clearly, she had her uses. Coco Chanel, founder of an haute-couture fashion house, and undoubtedly a creative genius, not only fraternized with high-level Nazi officials, but decided to capitalize on her powerful connections to the of benefit her ever expanding business empire.

'Hello, who, exactly am I am speaking to?' Göring's Germanic voice said to the person on the end of the receiver.

'It's Madame Chanel,' she replied.

'Ah Coco, my dear, how are you?' he inquired, not wanting, or waiting for her reply before asking, 'Is Günther there?' She recognized his voice instantly, and even though she had never spoken to him on the phone before, Coco was immensely flattered that he had remembered her.

Chanel vividly recalled having been introduced to the all-powerful, magnetic Göring a few times when attending parties in Berlin with the Baron, and although she had never engaged in a conversation with him, it was her understanding that she had made a striking impression on both himself and his wife Emmy.

Restraining her excitable voice, she informs him that Günther was still at the embassy, 'But I am expecting him to return here quite soon.'

'Good, I look forward to seeing him,' Göring informs her.

'I will be arriving at the hotel in due course, but at this precise moment, I'm in Cartier, and I will be leaving here as soon as they have finished with all the gift wrapping, one or two pieces of exquisite jewels for my wife, oh yes, and I have also picked up one or two paintings that I am rather pleased with!' he laughs.

With his shopping now complete, Göring was eager to get to the hotel.

'And now I just want to relax and enjoy a pleasant dinner with Günther, and of course, with you, Coco, as I insist you will please join us, so give me a couple of hours to refresh and change for dinner and I will see you soon. I trust you can arrange that my dear, and, of course in the privacy of your suite's dining room?' Göring decided he was suddenly keen to get to know the world's most famous and talented woman of fashion. Coco was enthralled. To dine exclusively with Hermann Göring was a real triumph, and without any hesitation Chanel confirms in her smoker's husky French accent, 'I will be honoured to arrange dinner.'

'Excellent, I will be there presently,' Göring promptly hangs up Cartier's telephone.

Chanel's desire was now to impress the autocratic Göring.

Planning to go all out to make herself as appealing and irresistible as possible to such an important man; Chanel, possessed with an unsurpassed confidence of her potent beauty, marvelled at her own uniqueness, feeling invincible, she would not, and could not fail!

Coco was immensely excited at the prospect that Göring himself would soon be paying a visit to their suite. It was as if she had 'arrived' and was now in a position of influence. Chanel, who had been born to unwed parents from peasant stock, was a snob and a social climber par excellence. Her soul was composed of utter disdain for anybody who did not possess money, importance, or lineage, by reason of the fact they were of little use to her, and therefore of no interest whatsoever.

Chanel was notorious for enjoying the company of rich and influential men who desired to help fulfil her lofty aspirations, and the more aristocratic they were, so much the better – their marital status held no barrier to such conquests.

Coco would always use her selective charms to beguile those who could elevate her position and prestige, aiding her rise to the top of high society. Their gifts of money to invest in her fashion empire allowed her the freedom, independence, and power that she craved. For Coco Chanel, the Nazis represented the epitome of such qualities, and to her, Göring was the very highest manifestation within their hierarchy. A man she set her sights on exploiting to the full. That evening, as she pondered her entrée into his circle of influence, she smiled at her own remarkable cleverness, thinking to herself, 'little did he know what I have in store for him – after all, who could resist the one and only, the fabulous Chanel?'

Göring was soon striding down the hallway, quickly covering the yards of red plush carpet with his brisk arrival at their suite, while the Baron's personal manservant immediately opens the door. Göring was not to be kept waiting, even for the briefest of moments, the timely call from the Reichsmarschall's personal bodyguard to Günther's suite that his arrival was imminent precipitated this action.

The manservant at once formally announces the arrival of the Reichsmarschall. Now standing there with a deliberate saccharine smile on his face.

'Ah Madame Chanel, how are you this evening? And I must express most sincerely how delightful you are looking,' Göring tells her, totally disarming the Baron's mistress. Coco, with her grin so wide that she could not hide her yellow-stained teeth from too many cigarettes, couldn't contain her pleasure at seeing him.

Chanel was dressed in her usual stylish manner of a black chiffon evening gown, soft velvet gloves that reached to the elbows, all brought alive by a long strand of the most exquisite dazzling white cultured pearls of the purest quality. Her short jet-black dyed hair had been carefully coiffured hastily in her bedroom by the hotel's resident hairdresser, and bedecked with a diamond and emerald hair broach, a gift from a previous admirer. The trademark dark red lipstick left her face looking hard and washed out, but the doyen of French fashion was more than a little pleased with her elegant appearance. With the aroma of her perfume Chanel No 5 wafting throughout their suite, she felt alive, 'these are the days I was born for' she thought, in total adoration of herself.

'Kommandant, I am so privileged and utterly delighted to see you this evening,' Chanel declared as she welcomed Göring with her unfailing admiration. Her abundant effervescence of his presence was pure theatre, but, in such a controlled manner.

'Please Coco, you really must call me Hermann,' he said as he shook her limp bony hand.

'I insist.' Her charisma and beauty, she sensed, had triumphed yet again.

Tonight, Coco believed she had conquered and dazzled the Kommandant, which naturally came as no surprise to her, as she now considered herself on affectionate terms with this incomparable man.

Coco Chanel concluded that only victory was now on her horizon. But, while she was in the potent midst of feeling delirious with her new imagined standing at the heart of the Nazi party, Göring was not entirely as captivated with her as she imagined.

The Reichsmarschall was a man's man, and her flaunted feminine charms left him unmoved; his antenna had immediately gleaned her motives. Göring had not got to where he was by being so easily seduced, especially by such an obviously egotistical and cunning woman; not only did he find her transparent shallowness and blatant sycophancy distasteful; it was a character trait he actually found very unattractive in any woman, and, she was so clearly a well-rehearsed 'player'. To him this was a grotesque habit in any female, but, if she thought she could get the better of him, she was in for a shock, there would only be one winner, and it would not be Chanel. He also suspected she was a fellow morphine addict; the signs were all there.

They both possessed an insatiable desire for only the very best of everything, and neither was willing to settle for anything less, as he quickly identified her greed. To Göring it was evident that she was willing to sell her 'dark rotten soul' to the highest bidder for her own advancement, and she was, in his eyes, little better than a glorified 'hussy' up for sale. They were both supreme narcissists, but, unbeknown to her, he instinctively read how she conspired and manipulated, which gave him the distinct advantage; he did not buy into her charms for one moment.

In this deadly game between the two, Göring, whose intelligence was borderline genius, would prove to be Chanel's undoing. He did not trust her, or even remotely like her. No, it was Chanel who would be played, for now, at least. If she only but knew what little regard he truly had for her, Chanel's all-consuming self-love affair would have suffered a severe setback. Besides, the Kommandant always had the upper hand, knowing that she could be disposed of, if it ever took his fancy.

Hermann Göring was totally nonplussed as to what the Baron, who was quite a bit younger than Chanel, saw in her. Now, well into her late fifties, Chanel was painfully thin with a mannish appearance, but Göring would permit her to believe she was just ever so clever, at least for the time being. His thoughts as to how he may, or may not use her, entered his mind, as he watched her move, although he had his serious doubts if she was of any plausible use to him whatsoever, but tonight, he just may enjoy himself, totally at her expense of course!

He was determined to provoke her for his own personal entertainment, waiting for the right opportunity to present itself. But now, Göring had more pressing things on his mind than that of an ageing harridan.

# CHAPTER 6

## The Dinner

'Heil Hitler!' The Baron and Göring mutually greet each other. 'My apologies for not being here upon your arrival, but I was unfortunately delayed at the Embassy,' the Baron expresses his regrets to the Kommandant.

'Apologies accepted my friend, besides it allowed me the pleasure of getting to know the one and only famous, and dare I say, beautiful Chanel!' Göring was not only understanding of the Baron's late arrival, but it also allowed him to throw in a mockery of her, his own little private joke.

'Would you forgive me further if I go and change for dinner? I need to try and look as elegant as you, and may I say Kommandant, how much I admire your uniform, I understand that you design most of them yourself, is that one of your own?' The Baron knew just how to please his guest, which of course, the Reichsmarschall readily accepted with great aplomb.

Quickly returning to join his dinner companions, the Baron was acutely aware of just how much attention to detail and pride Göring took in his lavish uniforms. Thoughtful to this, and not wanting to out-do the Kommandant, the Baron with his natural stylish appearance knew this was going to be a tall order. Göring was extremely obese, and therefore, whatever clothes he chose to wear, did little to hide that fact, much to Göring's consternation, whereas the Baron's frame made him the ideal poster boy for the Nazis.

Günther was in his early forties, possessing a carefully styled mass of blond hair, which was swept back to one side, penetrating light hazel eyes, while his aristocratic heritage gave him a natural, almost regal presence, with a slim athletic frame that always guaranteed his clothes displayed an elegance and sophistication of which Göring could only dream; with his dashing Germanic good looks, the Baron turned every female's head wherever he went. But he was a man whom Göring personally liked, respected, and approved.

Now dressed magnificently in the sharpest black evening trousers, with a satin band down the side, coupled with a hand-embroidered maroon and gold smoking jacket, casually finished off with a silk cravat neatly tied around his neck, tucked into his crisp white shirt, gold cuff links bearing his family crest added a touch of nobility, and to complete his ensemble, leather, hand sewn Italian shoes, achieved his desired look.

The Baron's evening wear provoked a rare silence in Göring while he took in every minuscule part of the Baron's clothes, not missing a single stitch of his ultra-refined glamour and beautifully manicured fingernails, while relishing the heavenly delight of his cologne. Günther's striking appearance and good taste triggered in Göring envy and delight in equal measure, but without doubt he overwhelmingly admired the Baron to such an extent that he could not contain his pleasure.

'Well, now it's my turn to compliment you Günther! I must say, I like what you're wearing; it's quite striking, so well put together, I do believe you are setting a fashionable trend. Tell me, is it Italian inspired? And what is that wonderful cologne you are wearing?' Göring wanted to know every detail of the Baron's ensemble.

'I'm impressed at how well informed you are Kommandant, you really do have a deep appreciation of refined elegance! If you wish, I can give you the name of my very talented tailor, who, well let's face it, because he's Italian, has a natural flair, possessing the required artistic temperament; he does not make clothes, he creates a vision! Or, if you prefer, I can call and arrange for him to visit you personally in Carinhall at your convenience? I know he would be only too delighted. As for my cologne, it was created by Jean-François Houbigant.' The

Baron was only too happy to assist the Kommandant.

'Yes, yes, thank you Günther, do that, and as soon as possible.'

Göring was now squealing with delight – obliviously ignoring his own vast dimensions of stature, while happily consumed with images in his mind of looking as sleek as the Baron – 'Good, that's settled, get him to come to Carinhall; Göring's vivid imagination was in overdrive – the self-styled 'Caesar' excited by the prospect of a new wardrobe of hand-made Italian clothes. Alas, unfortunately he did not have the figure to go with it.

The Ritz butler pours drinks for the glamorous couple and their VIP guest from their well-stocked bar. Günther, picking up a silver box from the glass coffee table, offers Göring and Chanel a Sobraine Black Russian gold tipped cigarette, which they both accept as they continue to indulge in small talk for the next fifteen minutes, but now the Reichsmarschall has had enough of Chanel's draining voice, and besides, he was hungry.

'So, are we to eat or not?' he said in a rhetorical tone, his cutting remarks fully intended to sound like a scolding. Chanel quickly indicated to the servants, who at once open the double doors to their private dining room. Taking his seat, Göring admires the exceptionally beautiful wallpaper of silken peacocks, while he nods in approval of the impeccably laid ensemble that Coco had painstakingly orchestrated, as the pure white linen tablecloth was the backdrop for the Ritz monogrammed red and gold China dinner service, silver cutlery and late autumn blooming roses, all arranged and directed by Chanel. A table fit for their very important guest.

'Dinner is served,' the butler announced.

*Dinner Menu:*
*Duck melon, foie gras with jam and fresh mint Langoustine, raw*
*imperial caviar, and citrus mushrooms*
*Pork loin, with roasted potatoes and vegetables*
*Seasonal blackberries with crème caramel soft*
*meringue & almonds*
*Selection of the best French cheeses*

Sitting down to dine, Chanel was feeling nervous; never before had she entertained someone of such high status as the Reichsmarschall. She had no idea of what Göring would like to eat, so taking advice from the hotel maître d' she had chosen the menu.

He seemed genuinely pleased with her choice of food, and now feeling more relaxed that the dinner was to his liking, she could start to enjoy herself.

'For how long are you in Paris?' Günther enquired.

'My train must leave tomorrow, by early afternoon. My art agent Bruno Klein will telephone me as soon as the train has been loaded with the 'shopping,'' Göring tells them as they all laugh, fully aware of what he meant by this remark.

'I will travel to the Berghof for my meeting with the Führer, and my consignment will go onto Carinhall, after which I will be very happy to go home and see my goods unpacked for my inspection,' Göring informed them both.

As the dinner was coming to its seemingly premature end, Chanel's eagle eyes noticed some of the crème caramel on the Kommandant's trousers, which he had not noticed. Chanel thought this atrocious faux-pas must have occurred somehow during the serving by the butler; her insides almost shook with absolute rage. Chanel's natural instinct would have been to lash out, but the need to remain stoical and in full control was uppermost in her mind. Feeling there was no choice but to point it out to Göring, she took a deep breath as she uttered the words.

'Please forgive me for this appalling calamity, dear Hermann,' Chanel stated in a restrained fluster. Göring was actually feeling extremely amused at the sight of her grovelling for forgiveness; it was making the evening so much more enjoyable.

'Ah, please Coco, do not give it a moment's thought, it's not a problem, these things happen,' all the time Göring smiling at her with a wicked intent.

'Oh, thank you Hermann, you are just so kind,' Chanel said breathing a sigh of relief that he appeared so understanding.

'Now Coco, would you be kind enough to get me a cup of coffee?'

Göring asked of her, and the fashion icon immediately clicks her fingers at the butler for him to pour a coffee for the Reichsmarschall, when suddenly, Göring turns to the servant and signals for him to stop.

'Coco, dear lady, may I ask you, do you have a hearing problem?' Göring enquired, looking puzzled, she replies 'No, not at all.' 'Um... I see, then perhaps you have difficulty understanding my German accent?' Göring probed her even more. By now, Chanel started to feel somewhat confused and unsettled with the line of questions from the Reichsmarschall, 'No, of course not Hermann,' she insisted. Göring, turned his entire imposing body directly towards Chanel as they sat side by side at the dinner table and stared boldly into her black eyes as he stated with a hard cold indifference, 'You see, when I ask you to get me a coffee, then you get me a cup of coffee, do you understand me now, my dear Coco? Therefore, perhaps you could perform that simple task!' Göring's intention to humiliate her in front of the watching servants was complete, while knowing full well his insult would be spread all over Paris by the attendant listening ears.

The Baron just looked on, cool, unruffled and totally nonchalant.

'Now I have enjoyed my coffee, I think it is time the Baron and I adjourn to his study for cognac and cigars,' Göring said with a firmness that was not to be questioned. The Kommandant looked to Chanel, 'I feel sure you will now want to retire to bed, as you are looking quite tired, and I don't want to deprive you from your much needed beauty sleep.' His stinging comment with more than a hint of ridicule bore deep into her insecurity.

'I would like to thank you for a splendid dinner, for being such good company, and for the wonderful entertainment you provided me with, which I so enjoyed! But now Madame, goodnight!' Göring's words were not open to challenge.

The Reichsmarschall's jarring termination of their evening was an obvious snub, and she perfectly understood his meaning, which was that he did not want to see any more of her that night. In fact, if she only but knew Göring, had decided he did not want to see her again... ever! Chanel's sense of superiority was the foible that he used to cut her down to size. Her cringing and fawning manner throughout the dinner had left him feeling nauseated, not from the food, but from her. With those departing words, Göring and the Baron headed for the other salon, firmly closing the door behind them, which left her thoroughly out in the cold and not privy to any of their conversations.

Coco not only felt rejected, she had been rejected. And it was wholly intentional, a slap in the face, something that she had never experienced before. She did not take kindly to being excluded, it did not suit her one bit.

She was more than a little concerned that the Baron had not tried at any point to come to her defence, but she then comforted herself with the rationalization that he was simply not able to question Göring, so she quickly dismissed any notion that he didn't care about her; that, she thought was simply not possible.

'Looking tired?'

What did he mean? She was taken aback; Chanel was not used to being spoken to in such a supercilious manner. She was confounded by Göring, he had been so polite, so attentive. Then he seemed to change, but why? She couldn't read him, and this made her feel very unsettled.

Chanel always had the upper hand in dealing with people.

Contempt for others meant their opinions counted for nothing, with Göring however, it was extremely disturbing; she hadn't seen it coming, so with her confidence taking a serious nose-dive, Chanel didn't take kindly to the fact that she had to concede she was out of her depths with a man she couldn't wrap round her fingers.

But worse still, she had not imagined the dinner would end so soon, and that riled her, now fuelled by a heightened temper burning inside like a bottomless pit needing to erupt, she inwardly exclaimed, 'What the hell had happened? What had gone wrong? Could her grand plans for advancement be in jeopardy?'

Now, as paranoia rushed through her veins, she ruminated over the drastic situation. Never for one moment did she think it could possibly be anything she had said or done! That was simply preposterous; after all, she had been the perfect hostess; she had been interesting, informed, witty, and, of course, she displayed her immense intelligence. So, the idea she had done anything wrong was a thought that would never have crossed her mind; she was the Grand Dame of Haute Couture.

She was Chanel!

This was not how the evening was supposed to have turned out. Her mind racing, she was tormented with why and how the course of events had turned so sour. Suddenly, her focused conclusion was because of the food stain on his trousers, 'Ah!' she placed her hand to her head, as if she had had a vision from God, 'that must be the reason!'

Consumed in thought, she lit up a cigarette as she paced up and down beside the fireplace, then, at that precise moment she became aware of the servants clearing away the remains of the dinner, she stares long and hard through the double doors leading into the dining room at the hotel waiter who had served the food to Göring. She puffs away before instructing him to come into her sitting room. As he enters, she calmly asks him his name. Unaware of any problem, he replies.

'Henri, Madame.'

'Um,' Chanel snorts out loudly in contempt.

'Well, Henri, can I ask you this, do you know who our guest was this evening?' she asks him icily.

'Oui, indeed Madame,' he replied. Walking slowly over to Henri, she is now so close he can smell her bad breath; then, with the full force of her venom she spits into his face, before taking a long drag on her cigarette and blowing the smoke directly over him. He stands there as her thick slimy drool streams down his cheeks, his eyes look straight ahead, while not daring to speak, unable to move until he is dismissed, feeling mortified.

'You disgust me,' she screamed.

'Get out of my sight you loathsome, hideous, vile and pointless excuse for a human being!'

Henri had not the slightest idea why this had happened. She had not told him, because Chanel explained herself to nobody. Before he left, and holding his dignity intact, Henri bowed his head, 'Goodnight, Madame.' Chanel picked up the telephone. The next morning Henri, a father of four and with fifteen years of devoted service at the Ritz, was fired.

# CHAPTER 7

## Göring and The Baron

As Günther and Göring entered the study, the Baron informed the staff they are not to be disturbed. The Chinese porcelain table lamps emitted a soft glow through the red silk shades, it felt warm and inviting, with a distinctive personality of its own, the hand carved wall-to-wall mahogany cabinet was filled with his varied collection of tomes, it was a man's domain, masculine but not austere, the aroma of cigars and old leather from the deep buttoned sofa filled the air, a comforting smell, it was a room that Göring found particularly pleasing. The strong character of the study suited its owner well. The decorum gave way to a haven of peace, that once inside, left the outside world seeming a long way away.

The Baron offers Göring a large cigar which was gladly accepted.

'I have a bottle of Grande Fine Cognac, which was distilled in 1865 and bottled in 1932, would you like to try it?'

'Yes, indeed I would, you have such a fine palate,' Göring commended his host. Günther opened the bottle and poured out two large glasses. Handing the brandy to his dinner guest, Göring admired the superb shade of the vintage liquid before the two men toast in equal vigour to the large photograph of the Führer that hung proudly on the wall behind the Baron's desk.

Sitting on the sofa and at ease, Göring was more than intrigued to know something.

'Tell me Günther, I am curious, how do you find your house-guest?'

referring to Chanel. Günther stares calmly at the cognac warming in the palm of his hand, before slowly exhaling on his Cuban cigar while his eyes then watch as the smoke disappears into the air, the Baron, contemplative for a few moments before he answered the Kommandant, replied.

'Yes Kommandant, I really do understand what you are asking, believe me, I ask myself this all the time, but, let me just say this, as you know, I have breeding, and I have heritage, but Hermann, she has money! Need I say more?' They looked at each other, knowingly, and laughed out loud.

'Now Günther, we have things to discuss; as you know I have been extremely busy in Berlin, I have a lot of responsibilities and my time here is short as I have been ordered back, and it is imperative that I return tomorrow by early evening. Our bombing over Britain is at a crucial stage. But now I have to discuss the Führer's plans with you, and I need to emphasise that it is of great urgency. Here I have his orders, that must be put into action, and without any delay,' Göring begins to explain.

'As you are aware, since our war began, over three hundred thousand of the most prominent and richest Jewish families have left Germany and Poland, taking their vast wealth with them,' Göring's narrative tone began to grow more hard-line, as he continued, 'By fleeing to France, they foolishly believed the French would be able to protect them and their money!' From nowhere the Kommandant's temper exploded into a fury with his voice growing louder as he began to shout.

'The Führer will not tolerate this! These orders are his expressed wishes, and to be obeyed at all costs,' as he slammed down his fist against the arm of the sofa.

'This must end!' Göring, momentarily rattled, realising he had lost control of his own emotions, quickly moved to compose himself.

'Therefore Günther, I am going to entrust you to oversee an 'Expropriation' decree. This will allow for the following: seizure of all private property by a public agency for a purpose deemed to be in the public interest and authorized by the German government to take.' Göring instructed the Baron, 'You will have all the necessary power to appropriate and confiscate all works to include the following: paintings, furniture, money, bullion, jewellery, gold, furs, bonds, coin and stamp collections, first edition books - the rest of their books you must burn - and any other item not mentioned here you deem of monetary value. This list is quite exhaustive. Look Günther, I needn't tell you…take it all, oh, and don't forget to check the teeth.' The Baron looked uncertain as to the Kommandant's meaning, 'The teeth?'

'Yes, the teeth, Günther do you not realize just how much gold they hold in their mouths alone? It's really quite incredible the lengths people will go to hide their money!' The two men smiled at each other, but the Kommandant was more than confident that the Baron knew precisely what the regime was after.

'You will go systematically from house to house, leaving nothing unturned, every part of the building must be searched thoroughly, you have unlimited powers, so use as much torture as required. I personally find that this is the most efficient method of inducing obedience,' he stated in a matter-of-fact way, 'so deal with any resistance by firing squad, if necessary entire families; make an example of them; besides, where they are going, they will have no need for such possessions,' Göring stated, confident that the Baron would undertake this mission with his usual thoroughness.

'All Jews in Europe will be under our jurisdiction. From then onwards they are to be processed and numbered by means of a tattoo and sent back to Germany by train… they will be forbidden to take any personal luggage with them.

They will be divided into two groups; the men will be separated from their families, who will then be further divided into groups of those capable of work, and those who cannot. Then, their circumstances await them. The women and children will stay together for the time being, until we have decided their fate! We will inform you to which camps they will be sent. Understand Günther, this operation is absolutely vital to our need for an extensive labour force, so we require them to be dispatched at once. This will be the course of events until we have concluded what is to be the final solution for

the Jews! And Günther, there are to be no exceptions, and no mercy!'
The Führer's decree was final.

'All the artworks seized are to be catalogued. A museum is
being commissioned by our Führer which is to be built in Linz, the
birthplace of our great leader, and will house all the finest works,
becoming a showcase to honour our great nation; a museum the likes
of which has never been seen before. I know he will appreciate your
dedication and loyalty in this cause,' Göring informed the Baron of
the Führer's master plan to make Germany the artistic and cultural
capital of Europe, displacing France.

'Before I take my leave, the security at both the Louvre and Musée
d'Orsay is paramount. Emmy, my wife, greatly admires the French
Impressionist paintings, so the Musée d'Orsay is next on my list. I
need to take home on my next visit some of their charming works,
which I know she will adore, therefore, Günther, my orders are
for around the clock surveillance, which must not be contravened,
nobody is allowed in or out without a thorough search. If anybody
attempts to try and remove anything, you know exactly what to do.
Accordingly, make sure everyone is fully aware of my orders.' Göring's
request was crystal clear.

The Reichsmarschall's obsession with owning art bordered on
the fanatical; his mission was simple, to amass the biggest collection
possible, but there would never be enough to satisfy his mammoth
appetite.

'I tell you something Günther, I do not trust these French, they
will covertly try to remove the works if they get half a chance, even if
it were to costs them their lives.'

As far as he was concerned, the art belonged to him now, and to
him alone.

It was gnawing away at the Reichsmarschall that he hadn't had
sufficient time to get his odious hands on all the priceless works of art
that Paris possessed before Hitler.

One thing was certain, he would be making many more visits to
Paris

'Günther, you must do whatever it takes to look after my interests.'

The Baron had no qualms about obeying the directives of Göring.

'Kommandant, consider it done. It will be my absolute pleasure,' Günther reassured him.

'Good man, I knew I could rely on you. Goebbels chose the right person for Paris.' The Kommandant was delighted to have found a kindred spirit in the Baron.

Enjoying their evening together immensely, they decided to have one more drink. With business out of the way, Göring, unable to contain his delight, wanted to tell Günther about the new acquisitions he had obtained earlier that day. The Baron smiled warmly, 'I have heard so much about your magnificent home and your amazing art, which I understand is probably the most extensive, and the best, private collection in the world! Your reputation as an expert is well deserved,' the Baron flattered Göring, who swallowed up the compliments with complete ease.

'Thank you, my dear friend, and yes, I think you are correct in that assumption.' The Kommandant was delighted with such praise; it made the perfect end to a profitable day.

Aware that it is now very late, feeling fatigued and really quite intoxicated, Göring rose to leave the comfort of the Baron's study, 'I will bid you goodnight, Günther.' The two men shook hands, 'And I would like to extend an open invitation for you to visit me, and soon Günther, very soon. I really would like you to advise me more on my wardrobe, I think we understand each other; we are both men of exceedingly good taste, therefore, it is our duty to present an image that will exhilarate the German people, don't you agree?' Göring's admiration for the Baron was boundless.

'And above all, I want to show you personally my breath-taking collection, it's truly a sight to behold,' he states, without a trace of modesty.

'Heil Hitler!'

So, on a natural high, Hermann Göring took his leave.

Looking forward to his bed and the next day when he would see the Führer. Then subsequently onto his home, where he was always at his happiest.

But, more importantly, he could finally introduce the Mona Lisa to his pride and joy and her new dwelling place, Carinhall.

# CHAPTER 8

## The Agent Provocateur

B runo Klein, a man of no shame or moral conscience, had much in common with his client Göring, where each in turn would feed off the other's greed. Klein, a naturalized Dutch art dealer, had originally been a German Nazi banker. The short dark haired, portly thirty-seven-year-old was married to a Jewish woman, something that Göring conveniently overlooked; even to the point that Göring had made her an 'honorary Aryan' but only because the art dealer was useful to him. Göring knew that Bruno Klein had numerous connections through his wife to many of the wealthiest Jewish families who owned some of the most desirable collections that were ripe for the picking.

Right from the beginning of the war, Klein had started to appropriate their possessions for his most valued client. Using menacing tactics, the works of art owned by his wife's friends were procured, whereupon they would be given the choice between selling and signing away their family heirlooms to him at rock bottom prices, or, at his coercing, be just inclined to 'gift' them; otherwise, they may come under suspicion with the authorities, which they knew to mean the Gestapo. Most Jewish families, terrified for their own safety, would readily hand over the rights to their properties in the belief that it would extricate them from a far worse outcome; in reality, this would not be enough to save them from their perilous situation that would become increasingly more dire. Klein felt no remorse in seeing them deported to concentration camps to die of starvation, be used as slave labour, freeze to death, or ultimately, to be gassed.

Bruno Klein would by any means necessary obtain their reserve of treasures for his political friend Göring, proving his worth as the perfect henchman.

At exactly 9am the following morning, the art agent arrived with armed German officers in attendance at the doors of the Louvre. If Jardin thought Göring was a tricky customer, he had not bargained for the odious little man who was standing before him, with all the appearance of a hood from a gangster movie. Wearing a black leather trench coat, belted at the waist, failing to disguise his stout chubby body, Klein's pock-marked skin and greasy dandruff hair, had immediately made the Professor feel quite repulsed.

Jardin was not used to dealing with someone like Bruno Klein, in fact, he had never even met someone to compare to him. The Professor was totally unaccustomed to types such as Klein, and felt completely out of his depths.

Jardin asked himself, how can this man possibly be an 'art dealer'? The Professor had expected someone more cultivated. Right away, he comprehended that these individuals were just bourgeois philistines with no real love of art, to them it was just about money and reputation. The Professor suddenly understood that they were coming from two different ends of the social spectrum; where he loved art and it was his whole life, these men were just ignorant opportunists exploiting the war to further their unquenchable lusts and nihilism.

Stomping into the Louvre accompanied by a pack of armed German soldiers, Bruno Klein followed the curator up to where the 'merchandise' was located.

Irked by the effort needed to climb the stone steps, leaving his fat body short of breath, Klein angrily barks at the Professor, 'So, where are these paintings that are to go? I want all the paperwork of legal transference, stating the title, the name of the artist, and furthermore, that those paintings named, now belong solely to the Reichsmarschall Hermann Göring, which have been gifted on this day from a grateful French nation!'

Having hurriedly worked with lawyers throughout the night, Jardin confirms to Klein that, 'Yes, I have the documents here in this file and most of the paintings are crated up over there, but we have still more to do,' Jardin points them out to him.

'What do you mean, you have more to do? Um, I do not like the words I am hearing, they displease me, in fact they displease me a great deal, actually, I hope I have misheard you. Well, Professor? Unless I am mistaken from my good friend the Reichsmarschall, all the paintings should be ready to go. Is that not the case?' Klein stated without blinking.

'You were told what was needed to be done, and by when,' displaying his glaring annoyance, Klein's mouth screws up tightly, so annoyed he is about ready to blow! Jardin, seeing Klein's dark personality emerge, tries to explain, but instead begins to stammer from his developing unease –

'Sir, I am sorry they are not all already, we have been working non-stop through the night, but because the paintings are so old and most are very fragile, we needed to take a great deal of care and time not to damage them, that's why it has taken us longer than we anticipated.'

'What..? Do not joke with me, as you will find to your cost that I don't own a particularly good sense of humour!' Klein shouted into the face of the Professor – a sound that rebounded around the museum, bouncing off the now semi vacant walls.

'Do you think I have time to waste on your incompetence – well? The Reichsmarschall gave you a simple enough task to perform and it appears you have not managed to carry out his orders... That is the trouble with the French, you don't pay attention to the details – whereas we Germans do! And that is why we now have your country in our hands!' As Klein gloated and threw around abuse, Jardin had no choice but to just stand there allowing this ghastly man to mock him and his country, not wanting to risk his wrath any further, mindful of the staff in his care.

'For your information, the Reichsmarschall has a very important meeting early this evening, so, tell me Jardin, how do I explain to him if his cargo is not on board? Or, maybe you are trying to deliberately sabotage this mission in an attempt to undermine me in his eyes?

Well, answer me, what do you have to say Professor? Please explain this to me,' Klein, hard-nosed, went on and on berating him.

'No, Herr Klein, not at all,' Jardin at pains to calm the moronic behaviour of the man, but to no avail.

'Do I need to remind you of just who I am? Well, Jardin, nothing to say for yourself? Then let me inform you of this... I carry the authority of the Reichsmarschall, who in turn carries the authority of the Führer, do I make myself clear? You irrelevant little representative of the Louvre! You were given a simple enough task and you have failed; the paintings need to be ready and they need to be ready now!' The art agent was not interested in excuses... of any kind.

Klein immediately instructs some of the soldiers.

'Take those out and start loading them onto the trucks,' while he slyly gave a nod to the rest of the Nazi officers who move in closer, as they stand over the workers in an intimidating manner. Jardin quickly turns to his young staff and tells them.

'Come on hurry, you need to work faster,' but their hands were now painful and bleeding from the sharp splinters coming from the roughness of the wooden crates, making their job harder, slowing them down considerably.

Their tiredness was overwhelmingly evident, then, unexpectedly, without warning a young girl, overwrought, stood up and screamed at Klein in an emotional hysterical outburst, 'Why are you doing this? Do you not realise these paintings are very delicate and need to be handle with the greatest of care?' A visibly stunned Klein stopped in his tracks and turned towards the girl – 'What did you just say? Are you talking to me?' Without thinking her naive irrational protest continued.

'We need to take our time, they are hundreds of years old?' Suddenly, in a flash, the grave enormity of her words brought her back to her senses, shocked by her own reaction, realising what she'd just said, she threw herself on his mercy.

'I'm sorry, so very sorry, Sir. Please... please forgive me, I'm just so tired I didn't mean what I said,' the young girl begging him on her knees, but it was too late – Klein bursts into an onslaught of aggression.

'Forgive you?' Klein cruelly laughed out loud.

'You want me, to forgive you? So, you say you are sorry! Well I don't believe you. I think you are lying, and I think you knew exactly what you were saying! You are not sorry.' Now seething mad, he demands to know, 'Just who do you think you are to question me?' His look decidedly burns into her young face, declaring, 'you are of no benefit, and just so everyone here understands me, I will demonstrate exactly what I mean.'

Jardin knew all at once, how much danger the young girl had placed them all in.

'Sir, she is just exhausted and not thinking straight,' Jardin pleads the young woman's case, but sadly realises his defence of her is useless.

Klein is stubbornly unmoved by Jardin's pleas – Göring's agent has no interest to her emotional state of mind. Looking around the museum at the staff, Klein calls to one of the young men to come over to him – 'Hold out your hand, the young man does as he is told as Klein places a revolver in his palm, the cold unfamiliar feel of the gun is making him feel afraid, but that feeling is quickly replaced by sheer horror as the art agent orders him to shoot the girl!

'What..? What?' The young man cannot fully take in what he is being told to do, he is shocked and frozen to the spot.

'Sir, please no… I cannot, no, please don't make me do this,' he deplores of Klein, but the young man's protests fail to sway the agent, who is now more than determined to show his willingness to impose any measure of authority he desires. Klein's temper flares into overdrive shouting at the young man.

'Are you stupid or just willing to defy me? – I said shoot her – No?... You don't think you can do it? Well, then let me tell you this – if you don't shoot her, I will put the gun to your head and pull the trigger myself... And then I will do the same to every one of your colleagues here! DO YOU UNDERSTAND ME? So, do it!' Klein yelled at him again – the young man with tears streaming down his face points the gun, trying to steady his trembling hand, then, aghast as he feels the sheer pressure of Klein's large hand tightly grip his arm forcing him to raises his aim, no, place your aim higher and shoot her in the head, it's much more lethal, very precise' Klein said indifferently, the young man could hardly find any life-force in his fingers to literally execute Klein's orders, 'Come on, I have a busy day ahead of me, so don't waste any more of my valuable time, do you hear me...?!' He was screeching his vile words into his ears.

'This is your last chance to save everyone's skin, so get on with it – NOW!'

The loud noise of the gun-shot ricocheted around the museum – it was all done. With just a single shot, the young girl's life was no more.

'Excellent – see, that was not so difficult, was it? Now with that out of the way perhaps we can finish the task at hand without any more interruptions...Unless of course anybody else has something they want to say? No?... Well then get back to work,' the art agent exclaimed – Klein had shown a disdain worthy of any Nazi follower. The museum staff were traumatized at what they had just witnessed by the gruesome inhumanity inflicted to their friend – with their feelings on hold, they resumed the packing as ordered in a trance like state, doing what was needed in order to survive. Klein's callous disregard for an innocent life was what it had now come to.

'Professor – you are very lucky, I'm in a good mood today, next time perhaps you might not be so fortunate!' Bruno Klein's raw smile at the Professor seemed to distort his acne-scarred face, that truly revealed his despicable inner being.

As the art agent and the German officers take their leave, the Professor looks at the lifeless body of a lovely young girl lying in a pool of blood on the wooden floor of the museum.

The Professor's staff are dazed, disorientated and silent with fear, he tries to console them and it takes every fibre of his being to do so. They are just young men and women whose lives are never going to be the same again. The Professor can't imagine that since the Louvre had been built it had ever seen a day like it; a dark day for France. Now, unable to hold back his own emotional torment, it was time to say goodbye to the woman he had come to adore, the Mona Lisa, as she was about to board the Kommandant's private train taking her to Germany, and her new home... Carinhall.

# CHAPTER 9

## Carinhall – Home is where the 'Art' is.

In 1934 Göring built a palace. The lavish interior was filled with images of his late first wife, his 'unforgettable Carin'. Göring had always been in awe of her natural gracefulness, charm and wit. In his eyes she could do no wrong. Carinhall was named in her memory. When she died at the age of forty-three, he had a mausoleum built within the home. Göring never lost his love for his immensely beautiful and adored aristocratic first wife, Carin. It was his intended desire to be laid to rest beside her in the crypt.

And now as his power grew, visions of an ever more grandiose home had increased; with the full approval of the Führer, no expense was to be spared to build a home on a massive scale, one that would accommodate his vast collection of art and antiquities.

A home fit to entertain Foreign Heads of States, Industrialists, and Ambassadors on behalf of the Führer to raise money for the Reich and influence those in power. With the seclusion Carinhall offered, Göring could now escape into his own absurd world of hedonism, allowing him indulge in a life of pure fantasy.

Göring's new marriage to Emmy, much to her delight, guaranteed her the lofty position as 'first lady' of the Third Reich, she had much in common with her high-profile husband, notably, both were conceited, vain and full of their own self-importance. Emmy, once a stage actress in her younger days, was now a middle-aged woman with a stout motherly figure, dark blond mousey hair styled into a bun at the back of her head, a woman who could not be described as especially attractive, let alone beautiful, but her penchant for expensive clothes did manage to give her the semblance of grace and elegance.

The huge oil painting of her husband's first wife looking young and delightful hung over the ornate fireplace in their main drawing room, and was the first thing she saw each day upon entering the vast room where it dominated; she knew her husband didn't love her in the same way that he had loved Carin, but then again, Carin posed no real threat. Emmy was a pragmatic woman who adored what she had, aware of her status, fabulous wealth and a life at the very heart of the Nazi inner circle, a position in life that most women would just die for.

Therefore, she had no complaints if her husband was prone to reminisce over a dead woman, after all, it was she who was still alive and enjoying the fruits of her husband's success. She was now Frau Hermann Göring, the first lady of Germany. And that was something she never let anyone forget.

# CHAPTER 10

## The Berghof: A Dressing Down

On his drive to the Berghof, home of the Führer, and in between thinking of what else he wanted to possess for his fabulous home and his charming conversations the previous evening with Günther, Göring was speculating as to why the Führer wanted to see him. He was somewhat perplexed, because Hitler had known and approved of his visit to Paris, so he pondered as to exactly why he was now ordering him to return almost immediately.

Göring had wanted his duration in Paris to last several days, allowing more time for some relaxation. He had been looking forward to enjoying his suite at the Ritz for a bit longer, but then after his phone call from the Führer's office instructing him to come back at once to attend tonight's meeting, everything had become a rush, and if he was honest, it had vexed him considerably, and he wondered why it could not have waited.

However, the Führer must have his reasons, but as far as Göring was concerned there was to be a meeting the following week where they were all coming together for their Council of War briefings, so why was he recalled home, and literally 'ordered' to be at the Berghof tonight?

Finally arriving at the mountain retreat after his rushed but rewarding trip to the French capital, Göring is feeling relaxed and happy but somewhat tired as he gets out of the car, wishing he was already home, instead of finding himself at the Berghof. A grand residence by any means, but it paled into insignificance compared to the imposing home of Göring, which he had acquired with the Führer's consent on the proviso that Göring and his wife take on the formal duty of hosting on behalf of the Nazi party. Emmy, now officially the 'first lady', a role at which she excelled, except, she had now taken her own importance too far, creating a rift between herself and Eva Braun, Hitler's young mistress.

Emmy openly despised Eva, a young girl half her age and with none of the experience and sophistication of Frau Göring.

Never missing an opportunity to put her down and snubbing her publicly along with the wives of the other top Nazi officials, who treated her with contempt, because in their eyes she was of no importance, due to the fact she was not married to the Führer.

This animosity had left Eva feeling isolated and depressed, she had self-harmed and twice attempted suicide. Hitler was concerned for the state of her fragile young mind, but what concerned him even more was the scandal that would emerge if it ever became known by the public about their relationship. Hitler was paranoid in wanting to hide Eva because he had vowed to dedicate himself to the German people, promising them that he had no time for a wife and normal family life as he was exclusively devoted to the German Fatherland. As this was his pledge, keeping Eva a secret was an absolute necessity. But tensions between Eva and Emmy had reached a breaking point, as the young girl was no longer prepared to put up with it.

Now at last, she had found the courage to confront Hitler with her outpouring of misery at the hands of the other women, who she stated Emmy Göring as the ringleader, feeling untouchable as the wife of one of the elites. Eva had burst into Hitler's study with her deluge of grief; it was a gamble, having no idea how he would react, but she was unable to take any more of Emmy and the other wives' jealousy and spitefulness. She was utterly miserable, lonely, and felt wretched. Her impassioned hysteria had angered the Führer, who became visibly disturbed and uncomfortable. He had no genuine empathy with the young girl and found this unstable side to her personality difficult to cope with; in fact, it quite disgusted him. He did not need or want such difficulties and distractions in his life. But Hitler realised angrily that if Emmy Göring was disrespecting Eva, then she was disrespecting him as well. And that was an altogether different matter. That he would not tolerate.

Hitler decided he had had enough. Emmy Göring needed to know her place.

The issue had been fermenting and festering within him for days. Hitler was put in a dangerous state of mind. He would not countenance this situation for a moment longer. Eva would be treated with dignity and respect; this he demanded. Now, fully aware of what she had been suffering, the Führer would ensure this maltreatment of her would come to an end or else there would be a high price to pay, for Göring and for his wife.

The Berghof was the Bavarian home of Hitler away from Berlin. The mountain retreat was where he preferred to be, but it was a place full of shadows and tensions that became obvious from the moment any guest entered the great hall, which was Hitler's favourite room, one he had designed to his most exacting requirements. A carpet of the brightest red, chosen by him as his favourite colour, that any guest who received a personal invitation would encounter. The imposing fiery glow reflected Hitler's dominate personality, just as the stark white walls emphasised his cold ruthless streak, while the low wood-panelled ceiling gave a temporary protective impression, although it was a sheer impossibility to feel at ease standing within close proximity to the Nazi leader.

Hitler's manservant welcomed the Reichsmarschall. Taking his coat, he invites the Kommandant to accompany him to his master's study at the other end of the great hall. Knocking on the door of Hitler's private domain, he received no reply. The servant waited a few moments before knocking again. Göring was now beginning to show signs of impatience, nonetheless, they were both too aware of the Führer's habits not to realise that they would have to wait.

Finally, after some considerable moments had elapsed, a harsh infuriated voice echoed from the room.

'Enter.' Hitler had given the order to go in.

Göring, who had naturally been in the study many times before, was always careful to remember his place, any impatience would vanish once in front of the Führer, all trace of irritation replaced by humble obedience to his Master.

Now shown into his study, the most robustly crafted furniture that Hitler so admired was there as his befitting choice, no sign of opulence would exist for the leader, whose austere personality was more than apparent from the surroundings; apart from the Austrian landscape paintings of one of the Führer's admired artists, Adolf Ziegler, which hung proudly on the rosewood panelled walls, with only hand-made Persian rugs complimenting the solid wooden floor, could be described as luxury. It suited him well.

At the far end of the excessively large room was Hitler's desk, where details and orders of the war sat waiting to be issued. The unusual red marble fireplace, a gift from the Italian fascist leader Mussolini, burnt fiercely. The wood produced such intense heat it could be felt as soon as the Reichsmarschall entered the room, Göring noticed immediately the logs spitting out ash all over the legs and feet of the Führer, who did not even flinch, standing with his hands tightly clasped behind his back, staring into the wild untamed furnace as if hypnotized. Hitler's stature looked small and almost insignificant against the vastness of the fireplace, but all too soon Göring felt instinctively hot, and it was not a result of the mass of burning wood, but from his leader whom Göring could sense was on the verge of self-combusting, such was the frenzy searing inside him. The leader was famous for his fiery temper, but this was to be a whole new level of anger, and one that Göring had never witnessed before.

The Reichsmarschall wisely hesitated before stepping any closer towards him. There was a long, awkward and very deliberate pause; minutes seemed to pass, then all of a sudden and without turning towards Göring, Hitler exploded into a tirade – his castigation of fury towards the Reichsmarschall was so violent, its hostile energy permeated every inch of the room with his powerful voice so formidable it filled Göring with utter trepidation.

'How dare your wife speak down to Eva! How dare your wife

show her such disrespect. How dare she humiliate her in front of the other wives? I will not permit this kind of conduct! DO YOU UNDERSTAND ME, Göring? DO I MAKE MYSELF CLEAR?

'If you don't deal with your wife, believe me, I will do so!' Hitler's screeching and incendiary words went on and on as he repeated himself over and over, not stopping to take breath, his anger was off the scale, his face red and inflamed.

'Every good German wife and mother should know her place, and that place is behind her husband, that is her duty, she should not meddle in things that do not concern her,' Hitler continued.

'She would be wise to remember her position in life; but it is apparent that your wife is ruling you. Tell me Göring, are you afraid of your wife?'

Then all of a sudden came a calm restrained tone from Hitler, so much more perilous that all his blood curdling shouting as he states with still coldness, 'I like your wife, she has been a good hostess many times, but, Göring, if your wife is unwell, and needs to go somewhere for a rest then that would be understandable. That could be quickly arranged,' the Kommandant knew only too well what the Führer meant by 'a rest' – it would have been to commit Emmy to an institution until she learnt to 'toe the line'. Göring had seen Hitler angry on many occasions, but never was the anger directed towards him.

'My profound apologies,' then Göring hesitated, before unwisely stating to the Führer, 'Do you think maybe that Eva could have imagined this? I'm sure Emmy wouldn't do something like that to Eva, maybe you should talk and reason with her, if she is over emotional?' All at once he knew that he had gone too far.

'Who is this person in front of me that speaks as if I need his counsel? Who are you to advise me?' Hitler stared at him in such a way that he felt all his self-worth drain from his body. Göring understood this was a rhetorical question, to which he dared not reply.

Never before had Göring felt such uncontrollable fear welling within him, he could hardly speak a word, such was the deep and wounding shock he was feeling.

'I will of course deal with this immediately as a matter of great urgency, and you have my complete assurance this will never happen again.' It was all that Göring could offer his Führer.

Hitler's mood was stubbornly undiminished. Göring, realising he should not remain any longer, turned to make his exit, but before he could reach the door to make his overwhelming desire to get out of the room, the Führer issued a stern warning to him.

'And one more thing, don't overestimate the power of your importance, because, Kommandant, if you cannot manage your own domestic situation, how can you be trusted to control the Luftwaffe?'

The Führer's final words cut Göring as sharply as if the leader had just struck a knife into his heart. The foreboding reminder from the Führer of his tenuous position within the Nazi hierarchy, made the Reichsmarschall know exactly where he stood, and that it was Adolf Hitler who was the ultimate supreme head, and only he who would have the last word.

'Heil Hitler!' Göring saluted his leader, and with that he took his leave, feeling utterly disgraced, diminished, and betrayed by his wife's totally unforgivable behaviour.

He had gone to the Berghof that evening at the request of the Führer, but this was not what he expected would be on the agenda when he arrived. All that Hitler was concerned about that night was Eva Braun, and that demonstrated to Göring the profound and deadly seriousness of the situation.

Göring left Hitler's Mountain retreat that night full of suppressed anger towards his wife. His waiting car was ready to drive straight to Carinhall. A showdown with his wife Emmy was now waiting for her on his return.

# CHAPTER 11

## 'What did you buy me in Paris, dear husband?'

By the time he arrived home, Emmy is already in bed asleep, but the long drive to Carinhall did nothing to quell his unease, in fact quite the reverse, as he had had the time to think over everything that had occurred and his seething resentment to Emmy was growing stronger inside him; as he neared Carinhall his feelings were now too much for him to handle, he knew there was only one way he could deal with the shattering effect on his dignity. He immediately went into his study and locked the door behind him, where in his desk his morphine was there ready and waiting for him; morphine was his friend and darkest hell in equal parts. Downing a very large brandy in one gulp, Göring sat in his chair and rolled up his shirt sleeve, slowly to inject himself and wait for the drug to kick in, which is almost instantaneous. Then came the relief, his anger vanishes, the desired quest for unconsciousness, a euphoric oblivion, nothing else mattered at that precise moment. Tomorrow was another day.

Emmy sipped her hot morning tea from the bone-china tea service laid out in the breakfast room, gracefully wearing her dusty pink silk dressing gown, trimmed with an abundance of ostrich feathers, planning her day ahead while going through her correspondence.

'Marie, did my husband return home last night?' she asked her maid.

'He returned home in the early hours this morning, Madam,'

Marie replied, hesitating in her response. Emmy was looking forward to welcoming her beloved husband home, she was more than a little excited as she wondered, exactly what wonderful gifts had he brought for her on his trip to Paris? He never returned home empty handed, maybe it was some new diamonds, emeralds, or rubies? She didn't really care what he got for her just as long as it was big, expensive, and she could flaunt them before the other wives. Emmy loved nothing more than when she inspired envy in the other women, it simply made her day. She hoped he would join her soon, as always, she was eager to hear all about his visit to the Berghof. Emmy assumed he had slept in his own bedroom, not wishing to disturb her as was his habit when-ever he arrived home late. Her husband was always so thoughtful.

'Tell Robert to take some coffee and freshly squeezed orange juice up to my husband's room,' she instructed the maid.

'I believe he spent the night in his study, madame,' the maid told her mistress. Emmy froze with that news, knowing immediately what that meant; lightening up a cigarette, her anxiousness to see him had now somewhat diminished, replaced with fear that things must have gone rather badly.

'What exactly could have happened?' she wondered.

She felt a tension wash over her, well aware of her husband's fragile and unstable ego, her nervousness was well placed, she understood that the bombing missions over London were not going as well as they had wanted and planned for; this must have been a cause of friction between Hermann and Hitler.

However, in spite of that she would reassure and console him. At that precise moment her train of thought was abruptly interrupted as the door of the breakfast room was flung wide open as her husband stormed in, 'Leave', he screamed at the maid, holding the door open for her to exit immediately, as she did so, with an almighty force, Göring slammed it firmly shut behind her.

Emmy was now scared by her husband's behaviour, standing rigid with his stiff angry stance, his eyes like a wild rabid dog.

Emmy begged her husband, 'Hermann, whatever is wrong? Tell me what has happened.'

Without warning, Göring uttered a vile litany of abuse from his mouth.

'You have disgraced me with the Führer, your humiliation of Eva has put me in a perilous situation. Do you know what you have done?' Göring screams at his wife. Emmy, without thinking, tries to defend herself.

'I didn't realise how upset she was, but I don't think Eva was treated that badly, and considering her delicate situation we could have behaved far worse, and besides, she is twisting everything entirely out of proportion, trying to make me look bad with the Führer, just to gain his attention because he ignores her most of the time, and if he really cared so much about her, he would have married the girl and given her the respectability that she craves so much; it is Eva who is the jealous and vindictive harlot, not me!' said Emmy, trying desperately to find a convincing reason for her treatment of Eva.

Göring can no longer endure anymore of these words from his wife, as he yells at her, 'Enough, just shut your vicious mouth up! Do you honestly think I will believe your lies over that of our great leader? Do you think he has time to have to deal with this kind of idiotic nonsense?

'Do you really expect me to side with you over this?' his voice full of cynicism, 'Are you really so stupid, do you know nothing? Tell me, did I really marry such a foolish woman? It is not your place, it's not within your function as my wife to behave in such a manner, you will not act towards Eva this way anymore. It is your duty as my wife to respect me, and respect all my wishes. That is only where your obligation lies, you do not meddle in my affairs, and you will be ill-advised to differ from that! And furthermore, on this you will comply, there is no discussion, do you understand me? That is final.'

Without warning, Göring struck her across the face with the back of his hand and with such force of retribution, it knocked her fully to the floor. Blood began to run from the corner of her mouth where his large ruby ring had caught her face. Emmy's degradation was complete, her treatment of Eva Braun had been malicious, and it had compromised her husband's standing with the Führer. His wife's resentment of the Führer's mistress had threatened their position.

'I'm sorry, I'm so sorry,' Emmy sobs through her tears, 'Please forgive me, I went too far, I will obey you, it will never ever happen again, let me make amends, please Hermann,' Emmy appealed to her husband, as she grovelled on the floor clasping onto his leg, imploring him to give her a second chance to put things right.

'Ugh!' he shrugged her off, 'I think a woman's tears dry very quickly.' Göring's cutting remark showed that his wife's sobbing and distress did not cut much ice with him.

She had potentially all but ruined his reputation with the Führer, and this meant more to him than almost anything else in the world, and something he would not forgive in a hurry.

Emmy was now beyond distraught, the knowledge that she could have been so utterly reckless, filled her with a dread that cut her down to size – it had achieved exactly what the Führer intended, putting Frau Göring firmly in her place. This new feeling of humbleness was a lesson she would not forget.

She enjoyed a good life, and this made her realise how close she could be to losing all of her privileges that she had become so used too, even to the point of becoming blasé.

She had taken it all with such a sense of entitlement. Emmy was smart enough to know that the Nazi party was an utterly ruthless organisation and would tolerate nothing that stood in the way of the goals of the Third Reich, and that nobody was more important than this dream. Their desire was to win at any cost.

She could see her husband's volatile temper slowly subsiding.

'You must understand what is critical here, so let me explain this to you, and you must also understand this once and for all. I will never allow you under any circumstances to put me in this situation again – ever! Emmy, you of all people know what it has taken for me to achieve my position. You see, you need to comprehend, our Führer is destined for the greatest of all victories. He will be remembered forever and the name Hermann Göring will take pride of place beside him in all the history books. Germany is glorious again, like that of ancient Rome, the legacy of our great Fatherland will live on. You are my wife and I love you, but don't ever make the mistake of taking my good and kindly nature as a given, even for you my dear. You must appreciate I am just far too important.'

Göring had spoken. And Emmy had heard.

# CHAPTER 12

## The Price of Atonement

Emmy was apprehensive but excited. Looking forward to the grand affair they had both organized. More than anything Frau Göring wanted to make amends to her husband and heal the rift she had caused between him and their cherished leader. So, it was decided to hold a lavish house party, inviting the Führer, all the Nazi elite and of course Eva Braun, that would go some way to that end. Emmy knew she had just one chance to get this right, she would need to go out of her way to welcome this young woman and let Hitler know how things were going be different for Eva from now on. Emmy was well aware that how she behaved and treated Eva tonight would convey a strong message to all the other wives present, who, like sheep, would now have to follow her lead.

Hermann Göring also needed desperately to make reparation with Hitler. They had not spoken since the night of the Berghof, and nothing was of more grave concern to him than to make amends.

This matter must be put to rest as soon as possible. He had spent many nights thinking of how best to atone to Hitler, finally, his decision had been reached, he would make the ultimate sacrifice and give to his beloved Führer one of his most prized and rarest of paintings, the one by Albrecht Dürer that he had just acquired from the Louvre. This would be his gift, and at the same time he could display to everyone his most cherished possession above everything he owned, the Mona Lisa by the greatest artist of all time, Leonardo da Vinci. This was the pinnacle of his art collection, and now, the more he thought about it, the more it pleased him.

'Yes! A brilliant idea, ingenious', he thought, 'Everyone will see just who I am, and with no expense spared the finest of feasts will be served here in my magnificent home, Carinhall. It will be a night to remember!'

While Berlin was in the grip of constant nightly bombing raids by the RAF, the Nazi inner circle headed to the plush home of the Reichsmarschall. The fanatical disciples looked forward to the indulgences he always laid on for them. Once inside his glided palace he would pamper, amuse, entertain and spoil them. Hermann Göring really knew how to throw a party. Carinhall permitted, and Göring provided, all they needed for their ever growing, large and very disturbing egos and appetites.

Göring stood in front of his full-length bedroom mirror, taking his time to delight in fully admiring himself dressed up in a uniform by one of his favourite tailors, a Viennese named Tiller. With the flamboyant off-white uniform, encrusted with diamonds on the lapels and an impressive military cross sitting spectacularly around his thick neck and double chin, the Kommandant was feeling more than a little pleased with his reflection, as his valet stood holding out a purple velvet cushion with dozens of rings for him to choose from. Taking a minute or two, he decided to wear a gold and black onyx ring that bore his coat of arms.

'Tell me Robert, how do I look?' he asked of his manservant,

'Magnificent, Sir, like a Greek God,' Robert replied in admiration for his master. Göring, walking towards the full-length mirror to take an even closer look at himself, replied.

'Excellent, yes, I do believe you are quite right.' The Kommandant spoke without a trace of irony.

'You know Robert, I do love splendour so much, and I believe I will be the best dressed man in the room tonight. Now, for the finishing touch, fetch me my new French cologne, the Fougère Royale by Houbigant, such a lovely gift from Günther,' Göring was full of his own worthiness.

The Reichsmarschall, who loved nothing more than entertaining on a lavish scale, finished drinking his Remy Martin Louis XIII cognac that Robert had poured from his bedroom drinks cabinet and headed off to Emmy's room to see if she was ready to greet the guests who would soon begin to arrive.

Wearing a rose gold pleated and draped evening dress with garnet velvet accents by a new young French designer named Christian Dior, Emmy was feeling regal as Germany's leading society hostess. It was imperative that the evening be a huge success for the Görings, who would do their upmost to ingratiate themselves again with Hitler and with Eva. Tonight, had no room for mistakes.

'My dear, you look divine!' Göring was delighted with his wife's choice of gown, Emmy, mutually compliments her husband on his evening attire as they walk together down the wide staircase arm in arm, in a grand show of unity.

No matter how much money Emmy spent on her French haute couture clothes, she could never out-do her husband as the flamboyant peacock, she knew full well that everyone's eyes were always on him, whenever he entered a room his larger than life extrovert personality and outlandish outfits filled the space and demanded attention; he was forever the talking point, even if occasionally he was the brunt of a joke at some of his more extravagant clothes; he took this in his stride because there was nothing he liked more than to be the centre of attention.

And as long as everyone understood his dominance and utter control within the Nazi party, he couldn't care less what they thought; he knew just who he was, and that satisfied him.

'I am feeling sick with nerves at seeing the Führer and Eva tonight,' Emmy confesses to her husband.

'And so, you should be! You should also be very thankful that our great leader has accepted our invitation, what if he hadn't, do you think about that? What would we have done then, um? But you put us into these circumstances and now we must crawl to win back his favour, so tonight, I suggest you use all of your charms; you were once an actress, so act!' Göring gives Emmy her cue.

Each high-ranking Nazi was formally welcomed by Reichsmarschall Göring and Frau Göring before making their way into the long gallery, whose walls were covered with the very best of art the world had ever produced. Canapés, along with the finest perfectly chilled French champagne, were served by young maids in black and white uniforms, while valets hired for the evening handed out Dutch cigars to the men, and if they required anything more their requirements would soon be catered for. A trio of violinists played classical German music discreetly which created a relaxing sophisticated tone for the evening's soiree.

The Göring's wait anxiously by the entrance to their home for their guests of honour. As the armoured plated convoy of Mercedes Benz cars slowly navigates the torched lit gravel driveway, the Reichsmarschall glances at Emmy, his steely look a cool reminder to what her sole task is this evening, and she is under no illusion of what was expected of her. Emmy knew her place, and what would befall her if she was to step out of line again.

As Adolf Hitler and his young mistress Eva Braun enter Carinhall, they are greeted by the Göring's. Their very important guests were more than a little cool towards their hosts, which was exactly what Emmy had feared, but knowing what was needed of her, she conjured up all she had to demonstrate the warmest of welcomes; one that could have melted an iceberg.

Emmy embraced Eva, kissing her on both cheeks.

'Eva darling, you look absolutely wonderful, such a beautiful gown,' Emmy gushes. Looking fresh faced and delightful in her crimson satin dress, with a dark brown mink stole thrown around her youthful silhouette, provoking any envy the wives felt would have to be buried deep within them from now on.

'Come along and let us join the other women,' Emmy took Eva by the arm, as of now, she is one of them, accepted, and at last, an equal. Eva would be recognised by all the wives as the companion of the Führer and given all the due respect that he demands. No longer will she have to endure the distress inflicted by their snobbery and cruel vindictive behaviour; all the wives will henceforth go out of their way to acknowledge her and make the young woman feel the centre of attention for fear of any repercussions. Göring and the Führer watch on approving of the welcome that Emmy and the other wives have now adopted to the young woman.

Hitler turns to the Reichsmarschall, 'Good, I want this matter settled, it is crucial for me that Eva is happy. I do not need these female problems. I do not have time for the irrational behaviour of hysterical women, we have important work to do. Now, enough said on the matter,' the Führer was direct with his words, Göring knew there was no more to be said, the subject was now closed.

Hitler pulls Göring aside, 'At the end of the evening I want to speak to you all, there are issues that need our due diligence; requiring the utmost speed and efficiency,' he informs the Kommandant, 'Yes, of course, I will inform all of them and gather everyone in the sitting room at the end of tonight's entertainment,' Göring replied.

Although he sensed the tension between them lessening, Hitler was by no means going to make it easy for him, but Göring was confident the Führer would appreciate the lengths to which he had gone to make reparations. He prayed this evening would dispel any remaining ill feeling the Führer was holding onto.

The small talk and pre-dinner champagne reception in the long gallery where the retinue were gathered had now concluded and diners were being shown to their seat in the formal dining room.

At the top of the table, for the first time ever, Eva was placed symbolically next to Hitler, an undeniable affirmation of her place within the inner circle, at his side as his chosen companion. This arrangement finally puts the subject to rest permanently. The Führer can now enjoy the evening.

The entire Nazi high command were gathered at Carinhall to delight in the hospitality that Göring had laid on for them, and, for the night to go well, it was pivotal that Hitler's strict and bland dietary regime was adhered to. Göring had arranged that the chef from the Führer's favourite restaurant, Osteria Italiano in Munich, come to the estate and personally prepare his food, nothing would be overlooked this night.

The presence of the guest of honour meant the dinner was going to be a more sobering affair than Göring would usually have enjoyed himself, nonetheless, this would not prevent the hosts from displaying their fabulous wealth to the utmost.

The ostentatiously laid out table would have put the Ritz Hotel, Paris in the shade. The fine Sèvres porcelain dinner service had been commissioned and designed by Göring and carried his family crest; the plates and dishes were decorated with a gold leaf pattern influenced by his love of hunting. This was accompanied by the dazzling brilliance of the silver cutlery, only to be outshone by Florentine cut and faceted crystal glasses with a gold rim decorated by a rich floral design, also stamped with the family coat of arms. Understatement was not in Göring's nature.

The subtle light radiating from solid gold candelabras complimented the ambient surroundings, a perfect setting for the prominent, all powerful and most feared men in Europe.

As always, when in the presence of the Führer, it was acknowledged and understood that at mealtimes there would be no smoking at the table, and any talk of the war was utterly forbidden, the only subject permitted for discussion would be art. Nothing made Hitler happier than when he was talking on this, his favourite of all topics.

Hitler picked up the gold leaf printed menu to peruse his forthcoming meal, which satisfied his unsophisticated palette.

### Dinner Menu at Carinhall:
*Barley soup*
*Pasta and tomato with bell peppers*
*Liver dumplings with pork sausage and potato Trout in butter sauce and seasonal vegetables*
*Chocolate tortes*
*Apple cake*
*Selection of cheeses*

Now with the dinner finished, Göring requests his guests to join him in the long gallery for an evening spectacular. Knowing of Hitler's love of music, Göring had sent for Max Lorenz, the Führer's favourite tenor from the Berlin State Opera, to perform an aria from Wagner's opera Rienzi.

The Führer was utterly delighted with the gesture from the Kommandant and enjoyed the entertainment immensely.

However, the evening was not yet over. There was one more offering the Reichsmarschall had up his sleeve that would be the perfect end to the evening.

Göring, taking to the floor, makes his announcement.

'I would like to thank Max and the magnificent Berlin Opera House for their wonderful performance here this evening,' to which the appreciative audience applaud, 'furthermore, I would like you all to join me in the main drawing room where I would like to offer the gift of a rare painting as a gesture of my devotion, admiration and total loyalty to our great leader, also to see a little painting I have added to my own collection,' Göring, betraying a sly smile on his face, invites Hitler to join him. Taking the lead, they head off from the long gallery towards the drawing room, all the guests follow in anticipation, where, presented in their full glory within the elegant room, a backdrop befitting such beauty, were found Göring's two most coveted paintings, each sitting on easels in their antique frames.

The reputation of these two titans of the art world, needed no introduction, as everybody in the room knew the 15th Century Albrecht Dürer portrait of the Artist Holding a Thistle, and of course, the 16th Century painting by Leonardo da Vinci of the Mona Lisa, was enough to capture the audience's immediate awe and attention.

Standing there, quietly staring at the two masterpieces, Hitler took in each and every brush stroke of the paintings; several minutes had now passed, and still there was no reaction from Hitler, and although everyone there knew just how much their leader loved art, nevertheless, Göring was on tenterhooks.

'Sublime, just sublime, I knew it would be beautiful, but I must say that I had no idea just how magnificent it would actually be.'

Hitler's words were music to Göring's ears, he had wanted to please the Führer, and this was the response he had hoped for.

Göring's smug grin was as wide as his face permitted; but the Führer's next words were not expected. Hitler turned round to address all the attending guests, 'Firstly, I would like to thank our hosts for the dinner and the splendid evening of entertainment, and I am most happy to accept the wonderful gift you have presented me with here this evening. This, I think, will take pride of place in my own collection, which I must admit is nowhere as extensive as yours, Kommandant!' Everyone roared out laughing in agreement.

'But I must say, I am more than a little surprised, my dear friend, that you have chosen to bestow upon me the wonderful Mona Lisa, and not keep her for yourself! Such a gift, such unselfishness, I must say, I am almost speechless!' Hitler expressed to the gathered.

Göring just stood there looking stunned – his earlier self-satisfied smirk was now frozen solid on his face, his eyes fixed, unable to even blink, his body so rigid with shock, it felt like rigor mortis had actually set in. He was on the verge of hyperventilating when Hitler turned to the party and laughed out loud, and, in an exceptionally rare moment, the Führer displayed a comedic sense of humour, seldom witnessed, as everyone realised that Göring had become the butt of the Führer's joke.

'For goodness sake man, breathe,' Hitler tells Göring, 'I am extremely pleased with the Dürer.' The Führer is speaking with great aplomb, '...and besides Göring, why on earth would I ever choose an Italian painter when I can have a great German painter!' The whole room burst into near hysterical laughter, highly amused by the absolute rarity of their leader making a joke.

'And besides, it would have been an insult if you had given me a gift that was damaged!' the Führer teased him even further.

'Damaged?' The Kommandant looked puzzled.

Hitler repeated himself, 'Yes, Göring, damaged, can you not see, what is wrong with your eyes? Look here,' and with a closer inspection, Hitler pointed out where a piece of the frame on the Mona Lisa was broken off, not much, but sufficient to cause displeasure to the Reichsmarschall, which would have instantly provoked a sulking mood were it not for the presence of his guests.

It must have happened at the Louvre when they were packing her into the container, and, although Göring was feeling more than relieved that the Führer was content with the Dürer, nonetheless he was now perturbed by the damaged frame. First thing in the morning arrangements will have been made for it to be repaired; and without delay, a sense of urgency was now all prevailing to the Reichsmarschall.

# CHAPTER 13

## Circle of Evil

Himmler, Heydrich, Goebbels, Ribbentrop, Speer, and the rest of the top Nazi officials were in attendance.

When you receive an invitation from Göring, you simply do not refuse. As they all filed into yet another of Göring's comfortable sitting rooms, Hitler sat in the chair beside the fire looking pensive.

Alongside him was one of the Reichsmarschall's favourite Alsatians, appropriately named Baron von Zieglerhoff; the Kommandant's dog naturally needed to reflect the well-bred image he had of himself.

All members of the gathering were quiet. Nobody would dare to speak unless permitted to do so by the Führer. There would be no small talk at this meeting. Hitler was about to address the ensemble of the chosen ones.

'We are in an unprecedented era of bringing victory to our people, our success will be assured because of our superior intelligence and attitude. Our great strength we all carry within us is our attention to detail – the elements of any success come down to scrutiny, consideration and due diligence to every aspect of what we set out to achieve. But we require more funds, our war-chest must be filled, this is now crucial for our victory. Therefore, I want a lot more pressure put on those greedy industrialists who are always bragging of their immense wealth, and Göring, I trust you gave the Baron my orders when you were in Paris on your little stopover, for him to act, without delay?' Hitler quizzed him.

'Yes, all your orders will be implemented to the full, with immediate effect,' Göring reported back to the Führer.

'Good, that is what I like to hear, prompt and positive action.

'Now, I demand new ideas to come forthwith for raising more taxation, and Göring, as far as the art is concerned, I know I can rely on you to apply your very effective methods of procurement, but Kommandant, leave some of the best works of art for our own proposed Führer Museum!' Hitler's remarks cut into Göring's sensitivity and guilt over his gluttonous desire for artworks, as he witnessed the smirks of some of his embittered rivals resonating around the room, all eyes were now on him as he felt their resentment surge towards him. Was it Hitler's intention to try and make him look a fool? He couldn't be sure, but Göring did not like it one little bit.

Was Hitler making another of his all too rare jokes at his expense? Or informing him in a sarcastic jibe that he was fully aware of what he was up to, with his tendency to acquire for himself as much of the best stuff as he could. But in no uncertain terms he was being warned that, 'enough was enough!'

Göring was fully aware that the Führer cut him a lot of slack with his grab of the art; even though Hitler had passed a law making it mandatory that he, as the Führer, was granted first choice of everything they acquired, somehow though this didn't seem to occur. However, it seemed that Hitler was making it known that from now on, he would need to relinquish a lot more of his spoils than he was clearly presently doing. Göring heard what he was being told in no uncertain terms in full sight of everyone.

Continuing with his sermon, Hitler told them.

'The rest, that so-called modern art that pollutes our museums, with its puerile corruption and debased, vile, repugnant, odious, degenerate trash, has brought art to its lowest ebb, while those profane perverted so-called artists that deform the heart and soul of the youth in our nation, will be no more!'

On this matter, Hitler's words were akin to a Holy Commandment. His fists clenched with intense anger, the Führer's ear-splitting screeching and impassioned diatribe magnified his temper that informed every one of his furious frame of mind. His tightly twisted face where his passion for traditional art and his utterly uncontrolled loathing for anything other than the classics was evident for all to witness. Absolutely nothing inflamed Hitler more than talk of modern art, it was his weakness that tormented him every day of his life. Hitler's dream of becoming a classical artist himself had failed miserably, and that Jewish artists like Chagall, Kandinsky, and others had been chosen over him to attend the prestigious art academy in Vienna had long driven his hatred and obsession. Victory through war was the way he would validate himself and show his obvious superiority that all in the art academy had failed to appreciate.

Composing himself, Hitler continued,

'However, there are ignorant, backward fools out there who are vacant of mind and willing to pay for it, so we will sell it to the ignoramuses! It is fundamental that our efficiency in this matter is strictly adhered to,' Hitler's mood was defiant, his words felt like poetry to his high command, 'The fulfilment of great tasks entail the bearing of great sufferings, we are all here today because of the monumental injustices done to this great land. Our painful memories of those transgressions done to us in the Great War drive us forward today. Let us never forget it was the Americans, French and the English that brought our country to its knees. That abhorrent Treaty of Versailles delivered years of poverty, struggle and humiliation to our proud nation. But our time has now come; it is here, and it is today, we will never surrender again like before – EVER!' The strength of the Führer's words pressed deep into every Nazi in the room.

'At the present time, the United States of America has no desire to come into Europe. They are, I believe, just playing a waiting game, wanting to leave Britain to defend itself for the time being at least. Our spies in Washington keep us informed and the Americans are just sitting back and watching very closely. Nevertheless, if anything changes that threatens them and the United States does enter the war, everything will become much more challenging.' As Hitler's mood darkens even more, the atmosphere becomes tense.

'Operation Barbarossa is the code name for what will become our next, and the most critical, phase of our strategic plans.' Hitler now stared at each one in turn, intensely, his powerful intimidating look made each one of them extremely nervous, as they anticipated what was to come next.

'I intend to invade Russia in the next few months!' This audacious suggestion was a resolute command from the leader.

Hitler's announcement stunned them all, and for Göring, this was not something he had anticipated or wanted to hear from his leader.

The Nazis had successfully invaded several countries across Europe, Austria, Poland, France, Czechoslovakia, Luxembourg, the Channel Islands and many more. Göring knew they needed all their men and financial resources to maintain their iron-fisted control over those territories if they were to win the war, therefore, invading Russia, to open up a conflict on the Eastern Front was a madness, a monumental misjudgement on the grandest scale.

The air battle over Britain was already in trouble and not going at all as they had predicted, so, to even consider this new operation was suicidal. The Reichsmarschall thought to himself that Hitler was slowly sinking into a state of madness; this course of action was pure recklessness, it was as if he had utterly taken leave of his senses. But nobody would ever dare risk a word of dissent. Although most members of the Nazi party knew it would present them with the direst challenge, many relished the opportunity to manoeuvre their own ambitious plans up in the scale of command. Göring felt contentious of the impending foolhardy plan, but he could sense all too quickly how they all covertly eyed one another, each trying to figure out what every man there was really thinking, always looking for the weakest in the group to oust for their own promotional advantage, each in turn would cosy up to the Führer to flatter him in the hope of more advancement and favour. Their constant jealousies and petty rivalries meant that you would keep your misgivings and any doubts about any course of action to yourself for fear of your own position and safety. Göring, fully understanding the precariousness of this situation, knew of the need to keep his own counsel.

As the most catastrophic of all situations would go forth, nobody dare speak out for fear of reprisal.

To fight Europe on one front was enough, but to plunge Germany into fighting on the East with Russia was going to be an impossibility that would stretch their resources far beyond breaking point. Everyone in that room knew the truth, but nobody would dare to speak of their trepidation about their Führer's military intentions.

And now on that night, the gravest of plans to invade Russia was cemented in Carinhall.

'Our time has arrived, and we will never submit to failure, our quest is total domination – we are the only pure race and be it the Third Reich or the Fourth Reich, we will conquer, we will be triumphant, the world will know the glory of our Superior Aryan Race,' Hitler was fully consumed by his decision.

'Now, as your Führer, I demand that urgent contingency plans be executed down to the smallest detail. Göring, see to it with immediate effect that the production of our aircraft is ranked up to full capacity, nothing must be left to chance or overlooked, this will strengthen our resolve. It is not in our Germanic character to be unprepared, but we must always plan for every eventuality.'

The Führer's voice now takes on an evangelic tone that enlivens the captivated audience of his men

'I will tell you here and now, never in world history has there ever been a power as mighty as Germany is today, the challenges we faced after the Great War must not be the destiny of our youth. Now our future will no longer be denied, and peace will not come to the world until Germany takes her rightful place as the true leader.' The Führer's words, ferocious with deliberate intent, instil his men with ever more fervour

'Germany will be jubilant and glorious, and we will have absolute power! Our conviction, courage and self-discipline are what make us unique among men, and all of you will become heroes in our great Deutschland.'

Hitler's voice was loud and vociferous, his face flushed with emotion, his ideological mind, uncompromising and hard-line, remains undiminished, as his men, addicted to their demi-god and his orations, applaud louder and louder for their leader.

To this audience his beliefs were like a potent narcotic, and they couldn't get enough, each now feeling intensely high, as if drip-fed on his megalomania.

His moronic mass of followers raise their voices in rapturous cheering to the Führer.

'Sieg Heil! Sieg Heil! Sieg Heil!' The devil and his disciples were united in the quest for their birth-right.

Their holy grail, a belief in a pious nobility, where they were heirs to a perceived greatness, and on a crusade that would know no limits, for themselves and mankind.

# CHAPTER 14

## The Undressing of the Mona Lisa

Emerging from an agitated half sleep, Göring sits up in his four-poster bed, pushing back the quilted bedspread he reaches out to his side table, picking up the phone beside him, he calls down to his valet, 'Robert, come up to my room and bring my coffee,' the Kommandant slammed down the phone feeling perturbed. He had endured a restless night with little sleep. The damaged frame on his precious painting was still bothering him, and he would not rest until it had been restored to a perfect condition.

However, on his mind even more was the meeting the previous evening with the Führer, and his planned military operation. It was alarming Göring no end. For the first time since invading Europe, he was beginning to feel a real sense of unease about Hitler's intentions. Göring's dominant and personal instinct was to secure his personal future. His extremely opulent lifestyle was something he needed to preserve and defend. Now, for the very first-time, doubts about his leader's tactics had seriously begun stirring in his mind; this was unexpected and unsettling. Göring had always known Hitler to be volatile and unfathomably complex, but his behaviour had now passed the point of no return.

Since they had conquered most of Europe, the prospect that the party should even contemplate the implausible notion of any failure of their mission was of a totally alien concept, and it was surely sedition to entertain such doubts.

But what if the outcome was not what they had planned? Yes, they will be the undoubted winners in their course of actions, of this there is no question, but, as the nagging doubts started to prey on his mind, Göring's pragmatic nature toyed with the idea that it would soon be every man for themselves, and it does no harm to plan for all and any eventuality, after all, had that not been on the agenda the night before when Hitler decreed that they plan for all and every possibility?

As this introspection simmered away, Göring realised just how much he had become addicted to yet another drug; that drug was his grand lifestyle. It represented who he was to the outside world. His adored home and wealth were now non-negotiable, this had become essential to his very existence, the Reichsmarschall knew he could not now conceive of living a life any other way. He would do whatever was necessary to maintain his pleasure palace and high status.

Göring's delusions of grandeur were now dominant. His continued well-being and enviable lifestyle would need serious preserving. These realisations greatly steered his train of thought which was halted abruptly, 'Yes, come in Robert' Göring yelled through the door, 'Run my bath, and put out my No 9 uniform while I have my coffee,' he ordered his valet. All of Göring's extensive wardrobe of uniforms had to be numbered, so the valet never made the mistake of laying out the wrong garments or annoying his master with minor unnecessary questions.

The Kommandant, who had a photographic memory, knew all of his uniforms in detail, as he had painstakingly designed everyone to his exact requirements. Whenever he arose in the morning one of his first waking thoughts would be his attire, with the aim of dressing in a style that would captivate and enhance his personality and mood for that day.

Göring was more than satisfied with the previous evening's events in the sense that he was finally back in favour with the Führer.

But for the moment, his mind must focus on finding the right man to restore the frame of the painting. Sitting in his study and giving it some thought, he decided to put in a call to his art agent Bruno Klein who had collected her from the Louvre and arranged delivery to Carinhall. During the quick phone call, Klein reassured the Kommandant that he would contact a master craftsman he knows personally in Berlin and arrange for him to arrive early next morning at Göring's estate.

'Good, I will expect him first thing tomorrow morning.' Göring hung up the receiver.

As expected, the restorer arrived early at Göring's home clutching a large, well-used artisan's bag full of the appropriate materials. His manservant, Robert, leads him to his master's study, where he stands patiently, if somewhat apprehensive.

After a tense hour-long wait, the great man opens the door, standing in the hallway, Göring proceeds with an in-depth appraisal of the frame restorer's skills, know-how and craftsmanship, as he quizzes the man intently.

The Reichsmarschall was feeling totally flustered about the repair, the very idea of the Mona Lisa sustaining any damage in the process of being removed from her frame was making him feel not unreasonably anxious.

'You have been recommended to me by my art agent, Bruno Klein, who speaks very highly of your work, and I am told I can trust your skills. Is this true, are you absolutely proficient at your craft?' Göring interrogates the artisan, who feels more than compelled to give the Reichsmarschall the answers that he wants to hear as he quietly responds, 'I was apprenticed from the age of fifteen for seven years in Berlin, from there I went on to work in many international art museums for another twenty years before I established my own studio workshop, where now I only undertake the finest of repairs,' the restorer reassured him, 'Um,' was Göring's only response to his answer, as he paced up and down; he knew full well that whoever he employed on the repair, ultimately, he would have to put his trust in them.

Göring now had to make a decision, 'So, seeing as you have been sent by Klein, and I trust him, therefore I will trust you, but, and I warn you now, don't disappoint me...' Göring imparts the artisan with his customary unflinching stare, a look it would be perilous to ignore. At that instant, there was no mistaking the warning.

'Well, what are you waiting for? You can't do the work standing out here, go in,' Göring urgently ushered the restorer into his study, 'Now come here and let me show you what I want repaired.' The restorer drew a sharp breath from the shock as he became aware of the deed presented to him. This was not something he could have possibly ever conceived or imagined being asked to undertake. Even under normal circumstances, it would have been a daunting task to repair the original frame that carried with it such a work of iconic provenance, but doing this work with Göring present in the room, the restorer closed his eyes, thinking to himself.

'Dear God, what ever have I let myself in for?' His thoughts agonised him with the possibility of what would happen if it does go wrong and he damaged the frame even more, or worse still, damaged the actual painting itself. And although the restorer was more than up to the task, even if it is such a special and unique undertaking, nothing was guaranteed. He tried to stay calm, the need for a steady hand was paramount to perform this intricate work. A thousand thoughts were now racing through his mind at once, he wanted to beg the Kommandant to find somebody else, but he knew that he cannot suggest this, the task was a certainty, not an option. He was trapped, contained in a room with Göring strutting up and down beside him, he had no choice but to hold his nerve. The restorer understood perfectly what was at stake if he failed to deliver what was demanded by the Nazi watching his every little move.

'I have had a large table set up for you over by the window, there is plenty of light so there is no room for error, it must be perfect.' Göring walked over to the other side of the room, taking the Mona Lisa from the easel he carried the painting like a newly born baby, with utter gentleness as he crossed the floor and carefully placed it on the work sheet, 'Isn't she wonderful?' Göring asked, seeking admiring confirmation from the craftsman.

'Yes, I have to agree with you, she is beautiful, may I congratulate you, Reichsmarschall.' 'Yes, indeed you may.' Göring was always content whenever he is admired for his impeccable taste.

'Now, I will allow you to take her out of the frame, understand you must take the utmost care; no damage can occur, you realise she is very delicate, proceed with caution and go slowly. Do you appreciate just how privileged it is to be given such a commission?' 'Yes, indeed, thank you, Reichsmarschall, I am humbled you have chosen me.' The restorer thought to himself, if only he knew that I would rather be a thousand kilometres away right now.

With Göring overseeing his every move and action, the restorer began to examine the frame, where he discovered on closer inspection some hairline cracks and slight warping of the poplar wood that the Mona Lisa was painted on as a result of humidity over the centuries, which was brought to the attention of the Reichsmarschall, who simply shrugged his shoulders and told him to continue. With painstaking care the restorer began to tease her from the wooden gilt frame, when, to the utter astonishment of both Göring and himself, there appeared hidden between the painting and the back of the frame several pages of an old letter. Looking dumbfounded, Göring asked him, 'Have you encountered this kind of thing before, finding a letter in the back of a frame?'

'No, Reichsmarschall never, this letter must have been placed there at the time it was originally framed, I can tell you quite categorically that I know when a frame has had the back off, removed or been previously restored, I know exactly what Renaissance frames are like and I know when they have been opened up for any reason, and this one has not been touched since the day it was put in place.' The restorer was also just as bewildered and intrigued by the discovery. The Reichsmarschall stood for a few minutes looking puzzled, but all too quickly his umbrage comes to the fore.

'Well, get on with what I brought you here to do, we don't have all day to ponder on this matter,' he orders the restorer.

Taking the several pages of the letter over to his desk, he puts on the lamp to take a closer inspection, but to no avail, as he soon discovers that the writing on the paper is unintelligible to him. Feeling frustrated, Göring furiously begins tapping his fingers on his desk. Exasperated, with the thought of yet another problem to find a solution too, 'Damn it, I want to know what it says, and I want to know it now!' he thought.

Flinging open the study's double doors, the Reichsmarschall's yelling echoes throughout Carinhall as his officers react immediately, running up the long gallery as fast as their feet will take them to attend to his needs, whereupon he screams.

'So, what kept you, do you think I have all day to wait?' Admonished they stumble out their reply, but he has no time or interest in an answer.

'Go and find Bruno Klein and bring him back here, now! Well, why are you still here? GO!'

'Yes Kommandant, at once,' the officers replied as they depart, praying that they find him and fast.

At last, after waiting for more than six long hours for the Gestapo officers to locate Klein, his art agent finally ambles casually into Carinhall in an unfazed manner.

'Göring, my friend, how are you? So, what can I help you with?' Klein asks.

Without any of the usual formalities, Göring's irascibility is in overdrive, as he orders Klein:

'Come here and look at this, tell me, what do you suppose this is all about? It was found hidden in the back of the frame of the Mona Lisa.' Klein peers diligently at the letter, and light-heartedly teases Göring, 'Our dear Mona Lisa is certainly not making your life easy, is she?'

'Well, in all honestly, my friend, I really don't have any idea what this could possibly mean. Though I know of an academic with an impeccable reputation, his name is Dr Otto Becker, and his knowledge of Leonardo da Vinci's work is without question of the highest regard, should I contact him for you?'

'No, just give me his address and I will send my men to collect him first thing in the morning,' the Reichsmarschall answered.

Göring was now on a quest to uncover the mystery contained within the frame that was as old as the lady that it had been displayed in for so many centuries.

# CHAPTER 15

## Of Grave Concern

Bang, bang, bang – bang, bang, bang. Dr Otto Becker awoke from a deep slumber with a violent jolt to his body system, 'Was he dreaming? What was all that noise?' Needing a few seconds to gather his thoughts, he saw it was still dark and a quick glance at the clock next to his bed saw it was only five in the morning, 'But there it was again, now even louder'... bang, bang, bang. Becker realised it was from the door of his modest apartment that the noise emanated, he heard a stern voice instructing him to open at once.

Dr Becker grabbed his checked woollen robe and hurried down the dark passageway, 'Perhaps there was a fire?' were his first thoughts as he went to open the door, but to his utter shock and bewilderment standing there were four Gestapo officers. He immediately felt a surge of fear, 'What could they possibly want with me?'

'Are you Dr Otto von Becker?' one officer asked, 'Yes, that is me,' the Doctor looked puzzled.

'Then get dressed, we have orders to take you to see Reichsmarschall Göring at once,' they informed him, asking, 'Do you know Bruno Klein?'

'Well yes, I have met him a few times in a professional capacity, but I don't really know much about him,' the Doctor explained.

'Are you sure it's me you want? I am just an academic, a scholar of Italian Renaissance art,' the Doctor stated to the stern-looking Gestapo officers.

'Yes, quite sure, now stop wasting time and get dressed,' the Gestapo officer now sounding rattled, 'I have been informed by the Kommandant that he wishes you to transcribe some paper, so bring anything with you that you may need to complete this task,' the officer impressed upon him.

Dr Becker returned to his bedroom to dress himself.

Wearing an early morning grey stubble as there was clearly no time for shaving, he reached for his crumpled well-worn suit and braces that were casually draped over the bedroom chair, a sign of his utter disinterest in clothes. Mumbling to himself as he looked for his overcoat, scarf and hat to protect his ageing bones against the biting winds of the untimely early snowfall. On the floor next to the bureau sat his old brown leather attaché case that possessed all that he needed for the task that awaited him.

'I am ready,' he quietly told the Gestapo officers waiting in the corridor.

'Finally, then let us go now, we have a long drive ahead, and I know the Kommandant is anxious to see you.' The no-nonsense attitude of the Gestapo officer was all too obvious.

There was no conversation in the two-hour car journey, something Dr Becker was relieved by. At last, they arrive at the home of the Reichsmarschall.

To Dr Becker, Carinhall had a macabre atmosphere, intensified by the dreary grey skies. As he got out of the car, he was filled with apprehension. He knew of Göring's reputation, all of Germany was aware that he was a most frightening man with a low tolerance level. Now desperately hoping he will be able to fulfil exactly what was required of him to Göring's complete satisfaction.

'Ah, Dr Otto von Becker, a good family name, at last, thank you for coming,' Göring welcomed him. Meeting the Kommandant seemed like his worst nightmare, had become a reality. Even though Dr Becker was a German, he was not in favour of Germany's invasions and occupation of neighbouring countries, and many of his oldest friends were Jewish; but he kept his intense distaste for the Nazi regime a closely guarded secret, and known to him alone, as these days you could trust no one, not even members of your own family.

Dr Becker was a man of learning and a man of peace. He did not subscribe to the Nazi propaganda machine and still had vivid memories of the Great War and knew this bloodshed would not bring glory to Germany, only destruction and suffering. As they shook hands, Becker could sense immediately how toxic Göring's forceful personality presented itself, 'Have some hot coffee Dr Becker to warm yourself.'

Göring seemed polite, enough to put him somewhat at ease; though being in the presence of the Kommandant was a daunting experience which he hoped would be over as soon as possible.

'You are probably wondering why I have sent for you? So, let me explain; I have several pages of a letter that I believe is from the Renaissance era which I need to be transcribed, and I have it on good authority that this is your area of expertise. Am I correct in this?' Göring asked double checking his credentials.

Dr Becker was now starting to feel less anxious as he realised that it was nothing more ominous than a transcription.

'Yes, it is my field of study, and of course it would be my pleasure,' he assured the Kommandant.

'Good,' the Reichsmarschall was more than eager for him to get started, 'Sit here at the small table by the window, I will be over there at my desk if you need me, I will not be leaving the room, do you understand?' Göring was keen for him to begin; his eagerness matched his curiosity.

'Yes, of course, I will start at once.' Dr Becker was more than excited to transcribe the pages on the table, an opportunity to see original Renaissance papers were rare, and one which he relished with utter delight, he was itching to start to reveal the secrets of the past.

As he held the old and delicate looking paper, he instantly recognised its provenance, and the author of its writings; he suddenly gasped as a feeling of total elation washed over him; he looked over towards the Kommandant as he jumped up from his chair like a spring chicken.

'I cannot believe what I have here in my hand! This is truly incredible, this is without doubt the most thrilling day of my life! Reichsmarschall, I have here the writings of Leonardo da Vinci; this is exceptional, extraordinary, his handwriting is quite unmistakable' he exclaimed as he showed the Kommandant how the genius wrote backwards, a mixture of Italian and Latin

'It is quite confusing what he did, and makes it impossible for the untrained eye to read,' the Doctor explained.

'Are you absolutely positive it's the writing of the great master?' Göring was thoroughly excited too but wanted to be undoubtedly sure.

'Yes, completely, totally, without any hesitation whatsoever, and I would stake my life upon it. I feel privileged and honoured to do this transcribing, and will get to work at once,' Becker said as he sat back down at his table.

'Excellent, now get started Doctor.' Göring was now even more hungry to know what they might discover from the great master da Vinci's handwritten letter.

But, more interestingly, why on earth had Leonardo hidden the letter in the back of his painting? What would this letter reveal to Göring?

After considerable time spent studying the letter, Dr Otto Becker took off his glasses and put down the small mirror and magnifying glass that he had been using to enlarge the words written in such a bizarre and incredibly small way, so typical of the old master; only by now his exhilaration has dissipated.

He now sat slumped in the chair trying to comprehend the implications this discovery revealed. Leonardo described and documented so many things during his lifetime; from science and nature, human anatomy, war machinery, architecture and so much more, but here was the voice and the heartfelt expressions of the man bearing his soul. These words were unlike anything he had ever written before. Leonard da Vinci was speaking only a short time before his death, so this proclamation was his final truth. And there was absolutely no doubt at all about the authenticity of the letter.

Now consumed with dread, these truly shocking revelations written in the letter by the hand of Leonardo penetrated deep into the core of his being. It seemed almost impossible to believe, but he had read it for himself. However, now thinking about it, the Doctor could see that it was a truth. He understood the Italian polymath, whose rebellious and unconventional nature was there for all to see. And now this secret would stun the world if it was ever to be known.

'Have you finished, Becker?' Göring enquired.

'Yes Sir,' he quietly replied.

'Well, give it to me,' Göring demanded, holding out his hand. The academic handed over the transcription to Göring who sat back down at his desk, eager to learn what the Doctor had discovered.

As he studied Dr Becker's transcription rigorously, the lack of response in Göring was puzzling, and the deep silence in the room Dr Becker thought spoke volumes. The Reichsmarschall sat absorbing the enormity of what was presented before him, but didn't respond to the findings, which greatly concerned the Doctor, it made him feel extremely fearful.

Göring then asked the Doctor.

'You say you are an expert in this field?'

'Yes indeed, I have often been required to work in the Uffizi Gallery in Florence, and the Louvre, Paris, with Professor Jardin.'

'Ah, so you know the Professor?' Göring was surprised to learn.

'Yes, he and I have worked closely together on many occasions, as we are considered two of only a handful of people who are experts in our field,' Becker confirmed.

'Can you translate the writing on these pages into French and English?'

'Yes, that is not a problem.'

'Then go back to your table. I want copies of every page in each of those languages, and of course German, at once!'

'Yes, of course,' he followed the Kommandant's instructions and got back to work.

Becker's anxiety grew minute by minute, as he detected the tense atmosphere in the room, this feeling confirmed as he handed over the translated copies of the letters to Göring, who now made no eye contact with him.

'Thank you for your assistance, you are now free to leave, excuse me while I go and arrange your journey home.' Göring advised the scholar.

'Free to leave? Had I been a prisoner, if only for a few hours?' Becker thought to himself.

As Dr Becker puts on his coat, he looked at the two dogs sitting contentedly by the fireside, they look at him, as he realised, they had picked up on his scent of pure fear; their ears stand to attention, on full alert. His longing to leave was now almost choking him.

'Let me come with you to the car. I could do with some exercise,' Göring joked. The Doctor gave a weak smile, trying to join in with the forced humour. Walking down the thirty metre long gallery that displayed so much of Göring's seemingly endless collection of art, all that Becker was conscious of was the thumping of his heart which seemed to be beating so loudly he was sure the Kommandant could hear it, as vast quantities of pure adrenaline pumped through his veins, he felt like they could actually burst at any moment, all the while trying to hide the beads of sweat rolling down the sides of his face; the feeling of impending doom fills his body.

'Was it a premonition?' he prayed that it was just his imagination running out of control.

It felt like the longest walk of his life. Traipsing along beside Göring with his German shepherd dogs running beside him was now finally over as they reached the front door. At last, to leave this dreadful place and the shattering secrets he had unearthed.

'Goodbye Dr Becker, Heil Hitler,' Göring said.

'Goodbye Kommandant, Heil Hitler,' Dr Becker replied.

The academic hurried his way to the waiting car, breathing a deep sigh of relief, when suddenly, in that moment, he knew his certain fate; the noise that informed him was the click of a luger pistol – a sound that dispatched a deadly bullet through the back of his head. The brains of the brilliant scholar were splattered on the ground; his vibrant red blood spurting without restraint onto the white snow – a scene as poignant as the secret he had just uncovered – and would now take to his grave.

# CHAPTER 16

## Invitation for Afternoon Tea at The Ritz

D r Becker's transcription of da Vinci's letter was running vividly through his mind. Göring's thoughts were juxtaposed with a torment, he didn't know if he was enraged, amused, or just shocked; but he was certainly frustrated; and his thoughts divided.

He was so deeply engrossed in the quandary of the handwritten decree from this revered artist, it provoked a blinding headache for which Göring quickly reached for the usual opiates to ease the pain.

After a while the relief from the morphine allowed him to take a step back from his swirling thoughts. With an acute awareness illuminating his mind, he could see clearly what he needed to do, and that was to apply cool hard logic. Göring understood intuitively that revelations of this magnitude could have different outcomes, depending on the circumstances in which they were to be used. So, now the question was, 'How could this knowledge be used to his advantage?'

Göring's razor-sharp mind started to come into focus, and it all became as clear as crystal. The Reichsmarschall smiled with malice, he felt not only amused, but more than a little audacious;

'Um, this discovery was indeed timely.' The defencelessness of France was his leverage, not that he needed any, France was already under his rule, but, if he was looking for advantage in the game of war, then surely this disclosure was perfect!

'Robert,' Göring called his valet,

'I have decided to make an impromptu visit to Paris. We will leave early in the morning, so make the usual preparations.'

'Yes Kommandant, at once.' The shrill of the telephone interrupted his ruminations.

'Ah, hello dear Günther, you must have been reading my mind as I was just about to call you myself, I am visiting Paris tomorrow and I want you to arrange for the Chief of the State of Vichy France, Philippe Pétain, the Director of the French Musée National, Pierre Guyon, and the Curator of Fine Arts at the Louvre, Professor Charles Jardin, to come to the Ritz Hotel tomorrow for 3pm, and I mean 3pm, on the dot. Tell them,' he paused briefly, 'Tell them they are invited to take afternoon tea with me!'

Göring's Machiavellian grin crossed over his face, amazed by his own cleverness, cunning and just sheer brilliance, 'Umm,' he thought to himself, before he swiftly hung up the phone, without bothering to enquire as why the Baron had rung in the first place!

It was just after lunchtime when the Reichsmarschall arrived in Paris. The heavy rainfall did not dampen the spirits of the Kommandant as his entourage of cars pulled up outside the Ritz. The red carpet was as usual in place for his expected arrival at the hotel.

The sycophantic general manager, always eager to attend to his every whim, grovelled to ensure the Kommandant's exacting requirements had been carried out to his precise specifications, knowing there was never any room or excuse for incompetence. Göring never expected anything less than five-star treatment.

'Can we arrange for luncheon to be sent to your suite, Kommandant?' the general manager enquired.

'No, I have dined perfectly well on my train, however, I am feeling tired, so I will retire for a few hours, and I do not wish to be disturbed,' Göring replied in a brusque tone.

'Of course, Kommandant,' the manager quipped obediently.

His imperial suite was always ready for him at a moment's notice. The interior design suited his aesthetic tastes perfectly, no detail was overlooked to please him, from his own personalised well-stocked bar to an abundance of perfectly arranged flowers in every room; the scent of the bloom was so delightful he stopped to smell them while appreciating the harmonious display, as he looked at himself in the wall mirror of the room.

The handmade dark Belgian chocolates quickly caught his eye, as he immediately took a fancy to picking up several and stuffing his mouth, giving not a thought to his constantly expanding waistline. With the Grecian-style silver bowls overflowing with the freshest of fruits, it was the definition of French sophisticated charm.

'Robert, I'm going to take a nap, I have guests arriving at the hotel at three o'clock, therefore wake me at four, when I will require some coffee and freshly squeezed orange juice, before I take a shower. Oh, and Robert, lay out my clothes, today I will wear my dark blue and gold No 4 uniform, I think? Yes, that one will be perfect for my mood today, I'm feeling somewhat regal, and just a little mischievous. Now, arrange to have afternoon tea ready to be served in my salon at five forty-five sharp,' Göring gave Robert his exact instructions.

'Sir, do you mean you want me to wake you after your guests arrive at the hotel?' Robert wanted to make sure he precisely understood the Kommandant's instructions.

'Yes, you heard what I said quite correctly,' Göring took delight in explaining to his valet, 'They will be seated downstairs in the hotel lobby, where they will wait, and then wait some more, and I intend to keep them waiting, until I decide to send for them,' he smiled at Robert.

'Yes, indeed sir.' Ever faithful Robert was more than happy to comply with his master's wishes.

Sitting in the foyer of the Ritz Hotel the three invited guests apprehensively wait to be called up to Göring's Suite to take afternoon tea. An innocent and charming ritual in itself; but somehow the invitation seems more ominous, if not rather peculiar. Now, looking at each other puzzled at this sudden and surprising request of the Reichsmarschall, the three men confide in one another and find that they have no idea of the reason why he wants to see them.

Unlike Professor Charles Jardin and the eighty-four-year-old head of Germany's 'puppet government' Vichy France, Philippe Pétain, who constantly fiddled with his monocle, Pierre Guyon had never met Hermann Göring. Guyon, a handsome chain-smoking dark haired forty-five-year-old, looked more like a French Humphrey Bogart than the Director of the Nation's Museums.

Guyon, plainly edgy at the prospect of meeting Göring, looked to the fatherly figure of his friend Jardin to reassure him, although, the Professor, drawing on his personal experience, was sadly unable to steady Guyon's concerns. The three speculated momentarily on why they had been summoned; but to no avail as the Professor retorts, 'We will find out soon enough.'

That afternoon, like any other, the Ritz was full to bursting with rude, boorish German officers, accompanied by attractive young women as they partake in the grand custom of high tea, of which the hotel was famous.

Waiting for their audience with Göring was now becoming immensely tiresome, but any feelings of disquiet are diplomatically concealed. The appearance of Robert, who meets them in the hotel foyer, is a welcome relief.

'Gentlemen will you please follow me, the Kommandant has requested I escort you up to his suite.' The general manager, much to Robert's annoyance, is more than a little eager to make his presence felt, was on standby at the elevator as he ushered them into the lift. Robert took great pleasure as he informed him that his assistance was not required. Robert jealously guarded his very important job as personal valet to the Reichsmarschall, and woe betide any man who tried to muscle in. It was now almost five forty-five, after being kept waiting for nearly three hours, finally they will be taking tea with Göring.

Robert opened the door to the Imperial Suite and guided the men into his master's grand salon; a room of palatial proportions with the highest of ceilings. The magnificent pure white Carrara marble fireplace took pride of place in the centre of the rococo styled salon where museum pieces sat comfortably alongside pilfered old masters placed around the room to reflect the spirit of its illustrious occupant.

The head butler at the Ritz arrived and skilfully steered in the tea trolley laden with dainty thinly cut sandwiches of smoked salmon, rare roast beef, and the finest ham, while the dazzling jewel-shaped petit fours sat mouth-wateringly on the fine bone china tea service. Then, all at once the man himself made his grand entrance, gushing at the men like they were long-lost old friends.

'Ah, gentlemen! How lovely to see you all, I hope I haven't kept you waiting too long? Please sit down and make yourselves comfortable, so glad you could find the time in your busy schedules to come and take tea with me,' Göring's insincerity was repugnant. His contempt for them was unmistakable as they look at each other knowingly, thinking, 'As if we had a choice!'

'What a refined custom this is, don't you think? Such a civilized ceremony – but then again, France is such a cultured nation, isn't it?' Göring was on top form as he strides across the room towards the huge double French windows that looked out onto the elegant Place Vendome. He opened the windows fully.

'I see the rain has finally stopped. Do you know, I really believe I can actually breathe in the French culture, no, really, you may laugh at my remark, but I sincerely believe that even the smell of the rain is like a fragrant French parfum, it's in the air, you can almost taste that sophisticated allure that France has, it's really quite seductive you know, but here I am telling you all something you already know.' The three men sat almost aghast as they dutifully listened, fully absorbed by the Reichsmarschall's poetic musings, as if suddenly bewitched by this man.

'How beautiful Paris is, and I really do appreciate your fine architecture, especially with our Swastika flying so proudly over Paris. Well, it adds so much more! What is it you French say? That certain, Je ne sais quoi! Our German flag really seems to give it that little extra, something that was lacking before, that's why I love this country so much, and you may even be a little surprised that I have chosen to take you into my confidence with my feelings, because I trust you all with my openness!' Göring's malicious jest left them cold. The men were at pains to smile through gritted teeth to amuse the Reichsmarschall, even though they could hardly understand his true point, or his warped mental thought processes.

'You see my friends, and it's here that I have to make a confession to you all when I say that it's all about your art.'

The three men looked more than a little confused by his strange rambling words, 'Our great fatherland has much sympathy for your country, yes, of course you may disbelieve that, but it's true, we know how much weight you carry on your shoulders to protect all your artistic accomplishments, and we understand your struggles. You only need to look back at your Revolution to see how far you have come, and just how much the French appreciate all things of beauty, I mean, it is the very fabric of France itself. And, furthermore, let me tell you that Germany, and even the Führer himself acknowledges your intellectual and enlightened ways; why do you think we never bombed Paris?' Göring laughed out loud at his own tedious joke. While the three men squirmed in their velvet and gilt chairs, too afraid to laugh and too afraid not to.

# CHAPTER 17

## 'Blackmail is such an underrated occupation, don't you think?'

'Now gentlemen, Charles, may I call you Charles? I feel we are now old friends, and Monsieur Guyon, I would be honoured if you allowed me to call you Pierre? And of course, dear Philippe; we need no formality here, and furthermore I would like to say just how relaxed I feel in our cosy circle, so we should be at least on first name terms. On this I know you will concur with me?' The men, sat upright, and in total silence, just nodding in agreement while Göring continued to relish the sound of his own voice.

'Mon Dieu, as you French would say, what engaging company you all are, and what fun we are all having!' Göring's words, laced with sarcasm were cutting, as he mocked them brazenly with his monologue of a conversation, laughing openly, as if he were sharing a private joke with just himself alone.

'Now, with all this talk of art, I am trying to remember why I invited you all here this afternoon? Now, let me think, what was it? Ah, yes, now I remember, I'm getting forgetful in my older years! It was very amusing, and I feel sure you will find it too. You see, I was presented with something very interesting the other day and I wanted to share it with you. Charles, I do believe you are familiar with the work of Dr Otto von Becker?' Göring posed the question to Professor Jardin.

'Yes, indeed, we have worked together many times,' Charles Jardin confirmed this fact, as the Kommandant pressed him further.

'And you respect his work?'

'But of course, without question, he is a most accomplished academic whose work is exemplary, he is, and I put this modestly, like myself, an expert on all the workings of Leonardo da Vinci; we have dedicated our entire lives in this field of study,' Charles Jardin readily answered.

'Excellent, excellent, I like what I am hearing, therefore Charles, I will allow you to be the first to read this,' as Göring produced a copy of Leonardo da Vinci's letter transcribed into French by Dr Becker.

While the Professor started to read the transcription, Göring affirmed that he was ravenous and started to mimic licking his lips at the sight of the beautifully arranged abundantly filled tea trolley, without hesitation he began gorging himself with relish on the delicious French pastries.

'No, no! This is simply not possible, it just cannot be!' Charles Jardin protested most vehemently as he took out a handkerchief from his trouser pocket to mop his brow, as he began to tremble.

'You say no, why no Professor? Um? Tell me, can you give me one good reason why it cannot be possible? Did you ever believe it was possible that France would be occupied, well? I think I have made the point – nothing is impossible! Anyhow as you see, it's there in black and white, the words of the great man Leonardo.

'Do you doubt the transcription of Dr Becker? Or even the words of da Vinci himself?' Professor Jardin shook his head as he looked down to the floor, dispirited.

'No, I don't doubt the words of either man, not for a moment. I trust Dr Becker, and if this is what he transcribed, then these words are the truth.' By now, both Guyon and Phillippe Pétain are obviously baffled by Jardin's response and desperate to know what it was that he has just read that made him react in such an extreme and emotional fashion.

'May I, please?' Pierre Guyon asked to see the letter; as he reads through every descriptive word from the transcription, he began to feel numb, finally Philippe Pétain removed the letter from the still hand of Guyon. Pétain absorbed the contents, then suddenly stood boldly upright as if springing out of his chair protesting furiously, 'This is utterly preposterous! What is the meaning of this? Are you trying to humiliate France even more?' Pétain was unwisely showing his anger towards the Kommandant. Göring's eyes started to narrow unnaturally with annoyance at the head of state.

'Sit down, Pétain! Don't get above yourself, you seem to forget whom you are addressing, and let me remind you, I don't think France can be humiliated any more, do you Pétain? Unless, of course, the truth of this, what shall we call it, this 'predicament' for want of a better word, was to come to light? Then maybe your high and mighty claims of such an illustrious 'artistic heritage' might be a thing of the past, and then what will France be? And if you are too stupid to figure that out, I'll tell you where France would be, it would be considered a laughingstock, isn't that the expression? So, I suggest you take it upon yourselves to think carefully and restrain your petite bourgeois intellect before you make any unwise decisions.' Göring's barbed words were now echoed loudly in their ears.

The three men were now stricken with a feeling of sickness.

'Come gentlemen, your tea is getting cold, or should I order a fresh pot? I don't want you all to go home hungry, I mean what sort of host would I be if that were to happen? And besides, it really is quite delicious, you must try some.' Göring enjoyed watching the contortions on their tormented faces.

'So, now you have all have had a chance to see for yourselves this 'amusing' letter? And who would have thought that from da Vinci? He really was such an intriguing, enigmatic man in so many ways, may I add modestly, not unlike myself! However, that aside, I feel sure you all have your own thoughts on the contents, what do you have to say, Charles?' Göring directed his first question to the Professor, who took a few moments to compose himself before responding, 'Kommandant, this letter is a truth, of that there is obviously no doubt, and naturally I am, well, I cannot find the words to express my thoughts, but yes, I am stunned to the core of my very being, and I cannot in all sincerity deny its validation; the shock is indescribable.'

Jardin turned to Guyon who nodded.

'Yes, I agree, there really is nothing I can add to what Charles has said, except to say I am confounded, but then again, Leonardo was ahead of his time, more than we could have imagined; we thought we knew him, but it seems not. I wonder if we will ever see a man like da Vinci again?' Pierre Guyon glanced over to look at Göring, who was stuffing his face with French crème pâtissière. Guyon thought it was doubtful.

The Chief of Vichy France, Philippe Pétain, asked of Göring, 'What would you like us to do with this information, Reichsmarschall? After all, you now have the painting, as you know she is the most famous symbol of all time, the pride of the French people, so what is the point of this meeting and what do you want from us?'

'Professor, Pierre, isn't that such an amusing question that Phillippe has asked me? Well for now gentleman,' Göring stopped to pick up the china cup and began to sip his lapsang souchong tea, 'Ah, so refreshing,' after a long and deliberate pause he replied, 'Absolutely nothing.'

Göring astonished the three men with his reply, he then stated with determination, 'Well, except for you all to put your signatures to the documents I have here with me which states that you are all fully aware of this transcription and the original da Vinci letter, and furthermore, that you're all compliant in covering up this discovery from France, which you have read on this day in the presence of the current legal owner of the Mona Lisa: The Reichsmarschall Hermann Göring. Each one of you will have your own signed copy of this, which, I must advise you to take great care with; I don't need to tell you of the enormity of the damage if it were to fall into the wrong hands, and all this came to the attention of the world. Now, for the foreseeable future, and to all intent and purpose, no more will come of this, it will only be known by us. Naturally, it buys my silence for obvious reasons, and it will never be known outside this room; I don't think it would benefit anyone at this point in time for the truth to ever be known, do you?' Göring told the three men.

'So, you want to blackmail us?' Pétain sounded more than

exasperated. Göring tutted in an exaggerated manner, 'Blackmail? That sounds just so dramatic Pétain, you really need to calm yourself, you are not young anymore, and you make me sound so squalid,' the Kommandant's mood descended to a darker place. Pétain's ill-considered retort had been unwise as Göring, clearly annoyed by it, declared to his guest, 'I am The Kommandant Reichsmarschall Hermann Göring, and I don't need to use blackmail to get ANYTHING I want! You should be on bended knees thanking me, so, I caution you as one friend to another, but I am growing very weary now of your inane attitude, which I will put down to your advanced years, but you would be prudent to mind your own deliberation Pétain, be warned!' The three men knew only too well that the Reichsmarschall was not playing games but was deadly serious.

'Nevertheless, I do see the absolute quagmire of a mess which you find yourselves in; your reputation would be in tatters; you are, as the Yanks say, 'between a rock and a hard place'. So, you see, and from my own personal perspective, one must always think of all eventualities, we never expect our house to burn down but we always have an insurance policy. And this is just my own personal insurance, therefore gentlemen, be under no illusion, I will use this if it is deemed necessary, make no mistake. However, as I have said, this will never amount to anything because we are all men of honour here, and besides, as we have no intention of losing the war, it's all just purely academic!' Göring quickly reminded them.

'So, with this hanging over your heads our interests are as one; food for thought, eh? Now gentlemen, please don't look so worried, they say it's not good for your health! Shall we now finish our afternoon tea? After all, that is what you came here for!' Göring said with aplomb.

# CHAPTER 18

## The World Could Have Been
## So Very Different...

'Thank god that is over,' Pétain moaned.

'Yes, utterly diabolical, it could not have been more hideous,' Guyon declared as he reached into his jacket pocket for his packet of Gauloise. They all agreed how intensely they had loathed the mockery of their so-called civilized afternoon tea

'At least Pierre you have never had the displeasure of ever having met him before, and been subjected to his mercurial personality, unlike Professor Jardin and myself, it was a sheer debacle that had been spiked with his threats, and even though he protested vehemently that he had no need to blackmail anyone. It was, as the Americans would say, a 'shakedown' – he made it blatantly clear that he wanted us to know exactly the shocking revelations he had uncovered, and how he would be prepared to use them if ever he had a need to. That was of course the whole point of all this nonsense today. It was a total farce that he found highly amusing, while enjoying rubbing our faces in it, not to mention his utter contempt for France,' Pétain stated, mocking the Kommandant's double dealing game-plan. Now each clutching their copy of the transcription from Göring with the 'evidence,' each knowing they had to hide the truth, there was simply no alternative.

They agreed instinctively that they all badly need a very stiff drink, and quickly headed off to the Ritz bar.

Now that the hotel afternoon tea ritual was finished, and it was still too early for evening diners to arrive, thankfully the Ritz was fairly quiet. Finding a secluded corner in the famous bar they were reassured that the room was nigh on empty, allowing them to discuss what had just occurred without prying eyes. Guyon indicated to the waiter, 'Three cognacs please, no, actually make those three very large cognacs.' They sat at their table deflated by the afternoon's course of events

'God, I feel grim, and totally undermined as a Frenchman; we have now been squashed into a vacuum of inconsequential nothingness,' Guyon wallowed, feeling emotionally drained after his encounter with Göring.

Raising his voice far too much, were Pétain's headstrong exasperations are wilfully dangerous.

'He is a complete madman, a moronic, demented despot, a fascist with autocratic pretensions... An absolute idiotic clown!' Pétain's pent-up ravings started to pour forth.

'Madman or not Pétain you should keep your voice down,' Guyon instructed him – but it seemed the aged military head of state for Vichy France was not willing to listen.

'I am too old to be told how to behave and what to think. This is outrageous. I won't take this from him, and, I intend to burn my copy! As the Head of State for Vichy I have rendered to the Nazi authority and their fascist lunacy for the safety of France, but he pushes us too far!'

Pétain's quick temper showed no signs of abating. Guyon, a measured and well-grounded man, was now feeling utterly infuriated with Pétain's thin-skinned introspection and self-absorption, and felt it unworthy of his status, a position Guyon believed in. Pétain was honour bound to rise above the provocations in order and keep a cool head in the dark and painful times they were all facing.

'I know, and I understand how you feel, believe me, but listen to me, Pétain, just be quiet and mind your words. Your loose tongue will get us all killed. You know exactly what happened on the Champs-Elysée. You should conduct yourself with much more caution, considering this dreadful situation we find ourselves in,' Guyon was visibly angered by Pétain's reckless behaviour.

'Yes, of course. I know of the torture those young men and women on the Champs-Elysée; all of Paris knows what happened to them, how he had them set alight, he is insane, unhinged, and that other butcher at the Louvre, his so-called art agent Klein. Yes, yes, of course you are right Guyon, I am so sorry, please understand my fervent, over demonstrative and improper conduct. I am old enough to know better.' Pétain looked sheepish at being pulled up by Guyon on his lack of composure. Phillippe Pétain conceded to Guyon.

'I think we could all do with another cognac,' Pétain called over to the waiter to bring them another round of drinks. In the quiet luxury of the Ritz bar, after several glasses of fine Napoleon cognac the desired effect helped ease the dilemma they faced. The scholarly Jardin was thoughtful in his approach.

'If, and in the probable dismal circumstances we never get the painting back, then truthfully none of this will matter as nobody else but each of us and, of course Göring, will be any the wiser, and all the time he has the Mona Lisa he won't want anyone to know either. We don't know what will become of any of us or what the future will hold as we don't possess a crystal ball.' The Professor stated a matter of brutal fact with deep sorrow.

The smooth easy taste of the alcohol was a very small respite from the despondency Pierre Guyon was beginning to feel.

'Professor, how do you feel about the painting, the Mona Lisa, now we know the truth?'

Charles Jardin contemplated, and reflected for a few moments.

'I understand what you are saying Pierre. You're asking me, do I still love the painting exactly the same now as before this knowledge came to light? I say this to you both, if we had discovered for instance that the Mona Lisa was, let's say a fake, or a forgery, then yes, I suppose my feelings and opinions would have naturally altered. However, thankfully, at least that is not the case, because of course it was painted by da Vinci, the situation we find ourselves in is far more complex and has cast a huge shadow over the masterpiece. You see our dilemma. We are damned. If by any stroke of luck, she was to be returned to the museum, and we all, knowing the truth but said nothing, I don't know what I would do under those circumstances, lying to the French people in a cover-up? On the other hand, when we had her displayed in the museum, before she was stolen by Göring, everyone who came into the Louvre would walk pass all the other works of art and head straight to see her. She carried that unique aura that no other piece of art has. She's irreplaceable, and was absolutely vital to the French economy. You cannot calculate her value; you have to remember that the Mona Lisa is France, the main attraction, people loved and adored her. So, if we did ever get her back into the Louvre, what then? Lie, or deceive France of their cultural heritage? But, for now, and as things stand, one thing is crucial. We can never let it be known publicly what has gone on here today. We have no choice but to lie. At least that buys us time. We must protect our own reputations, because if any of this ever came to light, we will be finished, never trusted again. The French people would not appreciate the underhand deal that occurred here today. Quite frankly, it's all a huge mess, and, there is something vital to remember my friends, art, is all about just one thing, and that is perception. Delicate and finely tuned, but ultimately built on sand, nothing more! So, reveal this, and that whole mystique would evaporate; and the Mona Lisa would be no more, she would cease to exist! Therefore, we cannot, we must not, and we will not, allow our hearts to rule our heads. So, we are duty bound to deceive in order to protect France. And ourselves. Does that answer your question, Pierre?'

Professor Jardin, still debating their quandry with Guyon and Pétain, went further with his belief, 'If you think about all of Göring's arrogant tactics, then you should both ask yourselves, what's really his motive? And I'm convinced it has exposed something much deeper. We don't know what's really going on in Berlin, but Göring is either not as confident as Hitler is on the outcome of this war or if the Reichsmarschall still retains a strong desire to continue with the fight. Maybe he's not as committed as the rest of the Nazis. Think about it. He wouldn't be doing this if he was, would he? No, I believe he is looking to the future, when he may just need to cover his own skin. Göring may need a way to negotiate his way out of any potential crisis that may crop up down the line, and he now has the perfect weapon with this da Vinci letter; and to give him credit, as much as it pains me, he has played a good game, because in those circumstances, we would need to cover our tracks, and we would have to play ball with him. We would be left with no choice, there is just too much at stake. What do you both think, do you agree with me or not?'

As Jardin appealed to both men for their response, Pétain and Guyon nod in agreement.

'So, if the painting stays in Berlin, then that is that, it's out of our hands. If, however, Göring finds himself in a situation where his back is against the wall, he will come out fighting and use any means at his disposal to secure his safety and maintain his extravagant way of life, which he won't relinquish easily, and that is where the blackmail element comes in, we give him a free pass, immunity from any war crimes, and a comfortable life in exile, or he would divulge all. You know I really don't believe he is as anywhere nearly as ideologically committed as Hitler is. No, I believe Göring is much more pragmatic, insane probably, but, a pragmatist, and also far too greedy, he delights in the finer comforts of life; a fact he clearly demonstrated this afternoon.

'No, my friends, Göring's only desire is to look after number one, don't fooled by anything else,' Jardin speculated as to the Reichsmarschall rationale, and state of mind.

Pétain interrupted Jardin with an idea: 'What about if we were to offer Göring something else in exchange for getting the Mona Lisa back?'

Jardin couldn't contain his amusement at the suggestion, 'I'm sorry for laughing Pétain, I would like to say that's a very good idea, but I stood next to Göring that day in the Louvre and witnessed the man almost foaming at the mouth. I kid you not, he was actually salivating. It's not something I've ever experienced before, so, I cannot imagine him accepting that proposition. That is a non-starter.'

'Göring is a very devious man, and we shouldn't miscalculate him. He knows the true value of art; he might be an abomination of a human being, and ignorant on many things, but he's also smart. And besides, Pétain, how precisely would that solve the problem with the truth of the Mona Lisa we all are now in receipt of, tell me? That genie is now well and truly out of the bottle! Even if we were to ever get the painting back, and we could just simply replace her as if none of this had ever happened. We cannot forget the ticking time-bomb hanging over our heads all the while Göring possesses the original da Vinci letter, and until that is destroyed it could explode in our faces if it ever got out into the public domain, and I cannot see any way we could get our hands on that! Do you?' Jardin sighed.

Pétain moaned again.

'I am surprised by your words, Jardin. I think you have given him more credit and sophistication than the monstrosity of a man deserves, but I do see your point about our situation.'

Jardin, now looking through the prism of an evening spent partaking of too much drink, offered them some words of wisdom:

'Phillippe, Pierre, let me say this to you both. Look at the value art actually has, and why we are all sat here tonight in despair. After all, in reality it is merely a small piece of wood or canvas with some oil pigments laid upon it, or a lump of marble carved into a statute,. But when you dig a little deeper, then you find so much more. Just ask yourselves these questions: What is it that remains left behind and remembered when any civilization collapses? It is the art of course. What does every nation desire for its own prestige and cultural stature above rivals? The art of course. What is it that people travel all over the world to discover? The art of course. What is it that every wealthy person wants to acquire? The art of course. What is it that we are talking about here tonight? The art of course. Thus, what is the richest currency in the world? The art of course. Now, do you understand? Göring is everything you say he is, and more; but one thing is certain, he really does know art's true value. A perception that carries its own unique mysticism that people want to own and be close to. He is clever, very, very clever.' Jardin's summary of the meaning of art brought home to them just how much worth it truly carried.

Jardin's penetrating shrewd insight continued, 'None of us can predict what, or if, we have any future here in France under the rule of the Third Reich. Let's hope and pray that for once history does repeat itself. The Germans lost the Great War. Maybe they will lose this one too!'

The Professor, now sounding philosophical, asked them, 'Does it ever make you think, that if only a young Adolf Hitler had been accepted to study at the Vienna Academy of Fine Arts, which had been his deeply felt dream, then perhaps the world would now be a very different place! Goodnight gentlemen, I will leave you with that thought.' Sardonic words from the old man.

After an evening of far too many large cognacs, the Professor, now unsteady on his feet, attempted with unwitting dignity to make his way to the exit, while his two remaining companions sat awkwardly in each other's presence for several minutes before they made their departure.

# CHAPTER 19

## 'I had a good run...'
## Hermann Göring
## How the Mighty had Fallen

### Germany, early May 1945

With the Russian Army hot on their trail towards Obersalzberg, Officer Max Page-Hamilton, along with a small convoy of American troops was the first to arrive at what remains of the last home of Hermann Göring.

'Hey, guys listen, I've just heard on the radio how that fat dude, Göring, has been taken into custody. They said he was all dressed up in his monkey clothes,' the American G.I. shouted out to the other boys down the line of the trucks who had been dispatched there in the hope they would find some of the looted art before the Reds arrived.

'And now he's gonna finally get his comeuppance and not before time!' All the guys chortled.

'So, this is what's left of his place? Let's have a quick smoke first then we'll start searching through to see if there's anything we can rescue.' The soldiers, having a well-earned break from the long drive, began the usual army banter among themselves.

'You know what that Göring did to his last place? The screwball only went and blew up his mansion, what a jerk, some place called Carinhall, they say he'd heard that the Soviets were advancing and didn't want them finding him, so he loaded up as much of the art and gold as he could onto his private train then fled here to yet another one of his grand estates. Now, finally, thank the Lord, at last everything has fallen apart for those goddam Nazis! I've heard it's been reported in Berlin that Hitler and his Dame blew their brains

113

out a few days ago! But then again, there were other stories saying the bodies they found were burnt and therefore unrecognisable, and that they had managed to escape to make their way to South America? But now we've got Göring; and let me tell you that son of a bitch, well he ain't going nowhere, except to find himself at the end of a noose!' The soldier's news has the rest of American G.I.s all sniggering, united in their contempt for the man they have all come to despise. The once feared and ruthless Reichsmarschall Göring of the Third Reich.

'I'll start looking around to see what I can find,' Officer Page-Hamilton informed the American soldiers.

'Yes, Sir, we'll just take five minutes then we'll join you.'

The G.I., looking at the shambolic mess, shook his head despondently, quietly observing to Max with a resigned indignation, 'Doesn't it make you sick to the stomach when you stop to think about what those psychopathic 'ratzies' have done?' The soldier's comment was accompanied by him lighting a Lucky Strike American. He wasn't at all wrong.

The final home of Göring had been massively damaged by allied bombings, parts of the huge complex was completely ruined, but a large section remained intact. Walking through the stillness of the wreckage that was one of Göring's grand houses, Max felt a shiver run through his body, acutely aware that he was treading the same ground of this demonic man.

Max Page-Hamilton, an historian, specialised in Italian Renaissance art, in particular the works of the holy trinity of the geniuses that were Michelangelo, Raphael and of course Leonardo da Vinci. When Max volunteered to work for the Monuments Fine Arts and Archives, also known affectionately as the Monuments Men, he was assigned as a Special Officer for the headquarters of the Twenty First Army Group. At the age of forty-five, Max, who had suffered an injury during the Great War, wanted to contribute in any way he could, so he signed up to the MFAA, which comprised an unlikely platoon of museum curators, art scholars, historians and architects, who were brought together on a mission to safeguard and preserve the monuments, churches, and art that symbolized to the world 'all that we were fighting for in Europe.' Never imagining he would find himself in this situation, alone, aware that each of his steps followed those of Göring. Max could easily visualise the large shadowy figure dominating the space, such imagery of the notorious man was chilling.

While searching through the detritus of remains he started to think about Hermann Göring. Max, the historian, was naturally both fascinated and repelled by the man as he tried to imagine what went on in a mind like his, what actually possessed him to do the things he did? But he knew it was impossible to ever begin to fathom, he would never be able to comprehend that level of catastrophe, avarice and pure gluttony. Perhaps ultimately there was nothing to understand, maybe evil was just an entity that exists without reason in a void. The depth of the Nazi atrocities would have put Satan himself to shame! The first thing Max sensed about the place was just how soulless it seemed, with just the essence of Göring's insanity remaining, along with an air of his self-induced grandiosity that had once ruled absolutely.

The Reichsmarschall's home had been stuffed to the rafters with stolen art. Sculptures, paintings, tapestries, gold, books, the hoard was endless. As Max wandered around the burnt-out domain, his heart sank at the destruction of all the beautiful pieces of art that were now lost forever. The Nazis' scale of greed was an obscenity the likes of which the world had never seen before.

Max became aware that he could see at the far end of the preposterously large proportioned home, which he calculated must measure in excess of well over two hundred feet, what appeared to be some rooms still standing. Making his way towards them, he grew excited and started to climb over whatever obstacles were in his way, eager to get there before the American soldiers did; then to his disbelief, he was utterly amazed to come across what had obviously once been Göring's study. It had remained almost untouched, with just one of the walls down and one of the windows blown out along with a section of the ceiling that was partially down, but otherwise miraculously intact, merely covered by thick layers of rubble.

The first thing he noticed was the Reichsmarschall's desk and chair. Standing in front of it, Max ran his hand over the well-used leather chair removing the dust as he did so; the seat still contained the deep imprint of its owner, Max smiled to himself at the thought that it just might be still warm from hosting Göring's famous large backside. Within the silence of the study, he sensed he could feel the lingering ghostly presence of Göring, his stubbornness refusing to let go – it was strangely uncanny. Max decided to sit in Göring's chair; it creaked, he closed his eyes and tried to visualize just what it must have been truly like to be in the presence of the Nazis. The harrowing vision suddenly began to feel so real and disturbing as images came flooding into his mind, he needed to abruptly turn his consciousness away from the stark imagery he had started to invoke. Max quickly dismissed these thoughts as he turned his attention to the piles of papers strewn across the desk that had just been abandoned. The documents were all written in German, but Max immediately grasped that these papers would be invaluable and needed to be collected as vital evidence for what was to come, as the remaining Nazi prisoners who would now inevitably face trial. They would be crucial for governments to investigate and for historians to use as reference when they documented the events in their historical accounts of World War II. But what Max had not bargained for was the unmitigated horror of seeing the carnage of mass murder that lay on the desk beneath all the scattered papers: the black and white photographs of men, women, and children of all ages held in the concentration camps. The skeletal malnourished bodies and hollowed out faces were the only remaining sign of individuality that belonged to them. The utter despair they carried in their eyes was beyond anything anyone could have ever imagined. Those images were now fixed into his mind. It was impossible to believe that such a level of torture had existed, even harder to grasp exactly what the Nazi regime had been capable of doing to other human beings. Evidently, it had sunk to a level of perversion and wickedness that was completely incomprehensible. He was still sitting in Göring's chair in a daze while trying to gather his thoughts at what he had just seen, when, out of the blue, he stopped this thought process, as suddenly, from the corner of his eye he detected something. Max froze to the spot momentarily, unable to turn his head and not believing quite what he thought he had seen, thinking surely it must have been a trick of the light.

But no, it wasn't! My god, it was the Mona Lisa as bold and brilliant as life itself.

There, all alone on a remaining wall she hung untouched, except for a light patina of dust. While the house around her had all but fallen, she had survived, unruffled, seemingly without a care in the world.

Looking at the painting he sensed how her eyes seemed almost to focus on the viewer, and in that moment, Max was transfixed by the famous enigmatic smile and by her calm transcendent beauty. Encountering the Mona Lisa at that very moment was a timely reminder of just how much the beauty of art is a vital lifeline to the soul. It was just what Max needed after witnessing the haunting photographs on Göring's desk. She was the perfect antidote to his dispirited mood.

Taking the masterpiece down from the wall, Max felt something on the back of the frame. Turning the painting around he found an envelope that had been lightly stuck onto it, 'What's this?' Lifting it off carefully, Max found it was closed with a red wax seal, and, making an educated guess, Max supposed it to be Göring's crest that was emblazoned on it.

'Um, well that's certainly an interesting find. I wonder why it's there?' Max thought to himself, feeling overwhelmingly intrigued. Holding the letter in his hand, his mind went quite blank with indecision, not knowing quite what to do. He began to interrogate himself, unsure whether to open it or hand it in to the authorities

'But which authority? Who exactly should have it? I suppose the French, after all, it's behind the painting rightly owned by the Louvre, but then again it has Göring's seal on it, and as the Americans now hold him in custody maybe they should have it?'

There was no name or address on it, so perhaps not them?'

Feeling utterly conflicted about what to do, he realized the only way was to open and see if he could read the goddam thing, and maybe it was not that important in any case, he thought.

'So, let's have a look at what it's all about and to where and who it belongs. After all, we have been at war for a long time and we can't always play by the usual rules, and maybe it is no big deal anyway! But if it's all written in German...?'

However, the prospect of breaking the Göring seal, Max had to admit, made him feel elated. Was he about to reveal its potential enigma? It reminded him of his childhood when he would go on one of his many treasure hunts in the local woods with his school friends, hoping to discover a hidden cache of any kind as all little boys love to do. The excitement of the moment of discovery had never left him

'So, let's break this seal and see just what's what,' he said to himself. Then, as he read through the many handwritten pages, while not understanding the German, the French and English pages were all too clear. He could not quite believe what his eyes were telling him. Max frowned, he was dumbfounded and in a state of disbelief. After a few moments of feeling well and truly stunned, Max suddenly realised the enormity of the discovery, and that he had become privy to probably one of the most extraordinary secrets in human history. Thoughts were uncontrollably rushing into his mind, but predominately the single most important thought was, 'What the hell should I do now?'

Before he could think over the dilemma any longer, he was abruptly interrupted.

'Hey Max, where are you?' Hearing in the distance the G.I.s calling out to him, he quickly concealed the letter inside his jacket

'I'm over here; you should come and see what I have found,' Max called out to the men. They yell back:

'Yeah, well come and see what we have found too! We've located a tunnel crammed full of the art stuff. Where are you, Max? We need to get outta here and fast! The radio has reported that the Russians are closing in, so let's move it!' The men shout as they make their way towards Max whom they found in Göring's study.

'Crickey, Max, what the heck have you got there? Holy cow, that goddam kraut looted just about everything! Let's take her and the rest of the stuff and go, now.' The men moved fast to grab the stolen art and leave. A confrontation with the Russians was not on their agenda...well at least not for that day.

# CHAPTER 20

## The French Connection

The phone rang in the office of the Director of Musée National. 'Yes, speaking, this is Pierre Guyon.' The voice at the end of the line informed Guyon that the Supreme Allied Commander of the Allied Expeditionary Force, also known as General Dwight D. Eisenhower, wished to speak to him. Guyon was, to say the least, a little surprised to receive such a phone call.

'Bonjour Sir. Oui, merci beaucoup. Comment allez-vous?'

'Pardon? Could you speak a bit louder, I am having trouble hearing you... Oui, what... What? Excusez-moi? Really? Are you positive, Sir?' Guyon could hardly believe what he was hearing. Feeling absolutely ecstatic, Guyon leapt out of his seat in an excitable state, 'On the 6th May? Oui, Mon Dieu. Are you sure? This is just the very best news. Merci beaucoup, General, merci,' Guyon's words of gratitude somehow felt totally inadequate.

The poor telephone connection between the two men required Eisenhower to raise his strong American voice to an almost shouting pitch.

'Yes, yes,' the General laughed. 'You have most certainly heard me correctly. It's all quite true. It was found in the home of the Reichsmarschall Hermann Göring. The painting was discovered by a Brit, Special Officer Page-Hamilton. He is part of Monuments Fine Arts and Archives, an art historian, so the guy knows his stuff. Anyhow, the other good news I can tell you is that his report informs us that the Mona Lisa is just fine and dandy. In fact she's in perfect condition, which is a miracle, if you knew the conditions under which she was found. So Pierre, I have requested that Officer Page-Hamilton personally returns the painting to you at the Louvre within the next few days,' the General was delighted to inform him.

'There is something a bit delicate, perhaps a little awkward that I need to inform you of General. You see when we lost the painting, at that time it was decided not to inform the nation as we felt that the French people were suffering enough and we didn't want to add to their woes or dishearten them any more than was necessary. Likewise you were also unaware that...' Eisenhower immediately interrupted him.

'Yes, you kept it quiet! You know, Guyon, you really should have told us about that,' making his feelings clear in no uncertain terms that the Americans were not amused by this secrecy over the theft of such a global treasure, and France's most precious possession.

'Yes, of course in hindsight you are right, but at the time, and I confess in our panic we concocted a ruse around her disappearance to allow us time, although, looking back now, how we thought we were going to get out of that situation. Well, our reasoning and rationale was not well worked out. It was short-sighted of us, perhaps? But there you are, war makes you do irrational things. So you see, no one was any the wiser that she had actually been stolen, as Professor Jardin had personally crated her up to be dispatched to Berlin, and of course the museum staff were kept in the dark, totally unaware of any of this. And as the Louvre is not yet open to the public, as we are still without so many of our paintings, we have been dreading the day when it would finally have come to light that our most prized masterpiece was lost to the nation,' Guyon self-consciously confessed to General Eisenhower.

'Heck don't worry about that now, Pierre. I was made well aware of the subterfuge you and Professor Jardin tried with your so-called game-plan! However, may I suggest, Pierre, that you stick to your chosen career in art and that you never pursue the profession of a spy!'

The General, who was in good form, laughed at his own joke.

'So, Guyon, what you are trying to say is, that the Louvre and the National Museum would like all this to remain a state secret?' Guyon confirmed they would be very grateful for that outcome.

'Oui, that is it exactly, General.' Pierre Guyon breathed a sigh of relief knowing that Eisenhower understood, even as it occurred to him that the Americans must have been covertly bugging their office and home telephones, as he and Jardin were the only two who knew about their original plan for the Mona Lisa. He now wondered what else they might possibly know!

'Anyhow, all that is over, and the good news is the painting is on her way back. Now it seems that Nazi Göring has been asking to meet me. He had the audacity to send me a letter describing his ideas of rebuilding a post-war Germany, offering me his full co-operation, as if I need that, stating he would be willing to take on the task, this joker has more front than Bloomingdale's! He also mentioned that he has some information that the world should know about. Can you believe the nerve of this guy? It's almost laughable, if it weren't so serious; I mean, really? Here he is, a captured war criminal, sitting in a cell, but deluded, completely wrapped up in his own grandiose self-importance, actually thinking he still has bargaining power? Well, hell yes, I'm sure there's a whole lot the world wants to know about; and in due course, they will, when he stands on trial. He can shout his big mouth off and tell everyone about the Nazi's devastating and near total destruction of Europe, those concentration camps, the millions of Jews that were murdered, experimented on, tortured, and displaced, and about the theft of so much of the art; and God knows what else? But, for now, well, he can go take a flying leap, I have no intentions of meeting with this monster, he's just trying to do or say anything he can to save his rotten neck! And I don't wanna hear any cock and bull stories from his mouth, he can quit all his belly aching, and for his information, he can go rot in hell as far as I am concerned,' the General was most emphatic.

'Perhaps, General, he has some information or knowledge of critical importance to tell you?' Pierre Guyon was now on a fishing trip trying to assess if the General had any more information relating to the Mona Lisa, it was a bit of a long shot and as soon as he said it, he regretted the question, realizing that it sounded a very stupid thing to say. Fortunately, the General just retorted back.

'Such as? No, the guy is just trying to wing it; what's he gonna tell me? Does this jerk really think there is anything he can tell me that will now change what's coming to him? The Germans are finished – it's over, and there is nothing he can say that is going to alter the fate that awaits him, it's a done deal! I'm Dwight D. Eisenhower, General of the Army; the trouble is, this man is still acting like he's Reichsmarschall of the German Luftwaffe and making demands. No, Pierre. As I have already made very clear, Göring is now just a common criminal, and this General does not talk to criminals, of any kind! So, he can quit his whining, if he's got anything, he wants to get off his chest, they can tell him to go see the chaplain for confession!' General Eisenhower found the thought of Göring squeezing into the confessional box highly amusing as he laughed out loud sharing his army humour with Guyon. Eisenhower went on to explain his views further: 'Look, Pierre, we all went to war to protect our freedoms and democratic way of life, which, as you must understand is about our laws, history, culture, and our economic ambitions, it's that structural core that anchors and keeps it stable, and, goddam, to keep it a decent civilized society. Now we've got one hell of a mess to sort out, beginning with building confidence and morale again in people that will allow us to get up and running. This is an enormous task that awaits all of us,' Eisenhower sighed.

'So, Pierre, make sure you take care of her now, and don't let anyone else get their thieving hands on her – the Mona Lisa, that is! I will be sure to swing by and pay her a visit whenever I get over to Paris, France, she is, after all, the star of the show!' Knowing of the sheer magnitude and gravitas of this very special painting, the General had taken the time to put in a call to the Director of National Museums personally.

Guyon reached for a cigarette to calm his emotional outburst of joy and the sheer relief from all the stress of getting the Mona Lisa back. Also, it was not every day you speak directly to the Supreme

Allied Commander of the Allied Forces on the phone!

Pierre immediately put in a call to his good friend Professor Jardin to inform him of the intelligence he had just received, and who from. That Hermann Göring had been arrested by the United States Allies and the Mona Lisa had been found, would, he knew, be music to the Professor's ears.

The Professor was lost for words but equally as delighted as Pierre 'Mon Dieu', was all he could say as he sat back in his chair almost unable to assimilate what Guyon was telling him. Guyon quickly detected Jardin was a little choked up.

'I never ever believed this day would come. Now we can just put her back to where she belongs, and nobody but us will be any the wiser! This is such a burden off our shoulders, it has been preying on my mind all the time,' Jardin said. Guyon was well aware of the toll this ordeal and the personal responsibility had taken on the ageing professor as well as the guilt and trauma from which Jardin still suffered after the murder of the young girl that day in the Louvre instigated by Bruno Klein when they were packing up the art works for Göring. It haunted him.

'But tell me Pierre, did he say anything about this British Officer finding da Vinci's original letter and the transcription? Or did you mention anything to him?'

'No, I never actually asked him anything directly, I did try and pose a question to him, but with no success, it wasn't that easy, after all Professor, I was not really in any kind of position to say to him, 'Oh, by the way General, did you by any chance come across a transcription by Leonard da Vinci uncovering a secret?' But Eisenhower did tell me that Göring had been demanding to have a private meeting with him, insisting that he had something that the Americans and the world would find exceedingly interesting, but the General told me he had refused point blank to have any kind of talks with Göring, believing it was all a ploy by the Reichsmarschall, and Eisenhower was having none of it,' Guyon informed the Professor.

'What could have happened to da Vinci's letter and the transcription done by Dr Becker? Do you think we have still got a problem hanging over our heads? Do you suppose Göring even still had it when he was arrested? After all, if you recall that was the point of that afternoon at the Ritz, with his threats of blackmail if he was ever in such a situation that he now finds himself in. You know, with his back against the wall, and it was how he would survive the situation?' Guyon could hear the anxiety in Jardin's words.

'Professor, rest your mind, please. It's now been nearly five long and arduous years since that dreadful meeting at the Ritz with Göring, and to be honest, I never believed for one minute that the painting would be returned. Let's face it, neither of us did! So, quite frankly, I just got on with living and surviving the war.' Guyon claims stoically.

'But, Pierre, you know what he had. It was explosive, but it seems he hasn't revealed or said anything. Don't you ask yourself why?' The Professor contemplated suspiciously, not quite believing their good luck in having the painting returned without any of the consequences that they had for so long dreaded.

'Charles, listen to me, literally anything could have happened to it. Eisenhower disclosed to me that Göring had ordered the Luftwaffe to bomb his home Carinhall until it was completely raised to the ground when he knew the Soviet Army was making its way to his estate in an attempt to capture him. The Reichsmarschall knew he was on borrowed time, so had to get out as quickly as he could with his wife, daughter and an assortment of relatives and servants, and somehow managed to escape by road in a fleet of cars, while his S.S. officers loaded up his private train with at least some of his looted treasures to flee to another of his grand homes. So you see, Professor, while he was preoccupied with saving his neck, he was unlikely to be in any position to worry about bits of paper in those critical moments, and besides, who knows what his state of mind was by then? But it's more than probable that the letter was destroyed with the bombing of his home. Now, don't you think that is the most likely thing to have occurred?' Pierre Guyon's explanation was more than plausible, and most likely probable

'The General also told me that when they captured Göring, the only possession on him was an American Smith and Western Revolver which he thought was quite ironic! And now that dreadful man that conspired with the Nazi's, that traitor, whose name I can barely bring myself to utter, Philippe Pétain, is completely out of the picture. We never trusted him, and we were right not to. Anyway, General de Gaulle will make sure that he stands trial for treason, make no mistake there. All de Gaulle wants is his head on a platter, and from what I have heard, Pétain is now just a broken old man in very poor health, and even quite senile. Nobody would believe anything he has to say. Besides, remember he burnt his copy from Göring; if he goes to trial and is found guilty then he would surely be sentenced to death.

So, as you see, we have nothing to fear from Pétain, which only leaves Dr Otto von Becker, and you told me that over these past few years he just seems to have disappeared. But let's be realistic about what potentially happened to him, after he did the transcribing for Göring. Do you really believe he would have just let Becker live with that knowledge? I doubt that very much!' Guyon was adamant in his assessment.

'No, I think, finally, we can breathe, do you realise we are now the only two people on earth who know the truth? And we are not going to reveal anything. So, stop worrying yourself any longer.

Thanks to God this problem, like the war, is over; it is behind us, the painting is coming back, and as for the 'secret', Charles, what secret? Pierre told his good friend and partner-in-crime:

'All that was now a whole lifetime ago!'

# CHAPTER 21

## A Brush with Fate

Three days later, Special Officer Max Page-Hamilton was on his way to the Louvre Museum, accompanied by the Mona Lisa and several armed guards to personally deliver the painting to Professor Charles Jardin and Pierre Guyon, at the behest of General Dwight D. Eisenhower.

While being driven through the arrondissements of Paris, it brought to his mind exactly how many years had passed since he had last been in the French capital. While studying art history at Cambridge University, Max had become utterly consumed with the idea of becoming a painter, believing that if he immersed himself fully into the only place in the world where anyone truly serious about becoming an artist in the 1920s, Montmartre, then, as if by magic, he would, by a process of osmosis, achieve his dream of critical artistic success. Max's father, a successful criminal barrister, had wanted his only son to follow in his footsteps and be called to the Bar, but never for a single moment could Max conceive of that possibility. His Victorian father had been totally opposed to what he believed was a reckless, not to mention immature and preposterous notion that would end in inevitable failure, and he had implacably refused to support him financially if Max decided to go ahead with his ridiculous plan, repeatedly pointing out all the pitfalls he was likely to encounter. Max, hedonistic and with the inexperience of youth, was stubbornly convinced that he could not fail, and with a headstrong determination, decided to take the plunge and live his dream; although, after having been cosseted within the confines of the segregated and rarefied world of Cambridge for three years, he was hardly prepared for the tough, inhospitable existence, and far from romantic environment in which he would soon find himself.

The world of French Impressionism, Italian Renaissance, and philosophy he had read about in his history of art textbooks, bore little resemblance to the Parisian life he revered; instead, it was now a city that had been ravaged by the Spanish flu pandemic and the First World War. Sadly, this France was a million miles away from the imagined country he had long dreamt about.

Even after all these years, Max did not like admitting to himself that his father had been proved right. Remembering that period now generated mixed feeling about some of the difficult, often violent, and downright troubled friendships, he had formed during his time in Montmartre. Max had truly exposed himself to the authentic, but depressing life of being a struggling artist, and how it really was a world that was alien and remote from any semblance of comfort, or normality on any levels, as opposed to his idealized vision. It was a way of existing that had over time worn very thin. The excitement and sheer naivety he possessed on his arrival quickly vanished, only to be replaced with the harsh existence of abject poverty. Living in a squalid, damp room with its peeling paint, exposed rotting floorboards, little or no heating, and hungry for most of the time, as he competed for scraps of food with the abundance of sewer rats that seemed to enjoy dwelling in his tiny studio, while always owing money to Sennelier, the art suppliers. His once sanguine contemporaries, who had been living a similar existence for much longer than Max, seemed to be just about clinging to a veneer of sanity, mostly consumed with despair, whilst becoming hopelessly addicted to a concoction of cheap wine and plenty of hashish, before finally being seduced by a potent and lethal combination of absinthe laced with deadly opium, chasing the dragon, hastening their rapid decline, as they sought to blur out their impoverished way of life and complete lack of success; but remained unwilling or unable to abandon their chosen path and crawl out of the pit they were all immersed in. Finally, Max woke up to the terrible plight he found himself ensnared by, seeing the destructiveness of the life, as he witnessed how it had dragged a succession of his friends down into the depths of permanent melancholy, and, although Max was glad that he had given it his best shot and tried his hardest to capitalise on the glamour of Paris, he had not been able to find his own true painting style, which was an absolute pre-requisite for any decent gallery to take on an artist.

Now, Max was facing up to a stark truth, which was to get out while he still could. However, he remained committed to spending his life within a creative environment, but no longer as a starving painter. He decided there must be other routes to pursue that could allow him to continue in the art world, curating, restoration or becoming art dealer, all this would need some serious thinking. Now in his mid-twenties, Max knew time was not on his side if he wanted to establish himself in a career. He could not afford another error of judgement.

On a warm evening in June 1925, considering his options, he obsessively wondered what on earth might be that elusive, enigmatic ingredient that enabled an artist to succeed. 'Just what was it?' he asked himself again. His sense of failure was like a body blow, and, although he knew logically it was the correct thing to do, emotionally, he still had to come to terms with this fact and accept the painful truth that his career as an artist was going nowhere.

It was while sitting in the crowded and noisy smoke-filled atmosphere of Au Lapin Agile in Montmartre that night, making his sorrowful plans to return home to London, that none other than Pablo Picasso breezed in. A larger-than-life personality that demanded you take notice of him, he sat down on the table next to Max, and ordered himself a bottle of Bordeaux. The acclaimed man, still carried the strong aroma of turpentine on his work clothes, consisting of shorts that displayed his tanned legs, a frayed navy-blue and white striped jumper, an old pair of tatty canvas sneakers, boldly spattered with oil paints of all colours that it resembled an artist's palette, still wet from his day of painting. Picasso was totally oblivious to the fact that he looked the very epitome of what a true artist was – and without even trying. After striking up a conversation, Picasso revealed to Max that he had just left his studio after finally finishing a new work that he had decided to name, 'The Three Dancers'. Max felt privileged, knowing that he was probably one of the first people to be told about the painting and its title. He knew that Picasso worked in Montmartre, but in all the time he had lived there he had never previously seen him. Now invited to share another bottle of wine with him to celebrate his latest painting, Max knew that this night would be etched into his mind forever. Picasso, who lived with his Russian ballerina wife in a much more expensive and exclusive part of Paris, informed Max how he still rented his atelier in Montmartre, as he loved its bohemian feel, the vibrancy, and above all the earthy mix of the crowd who worked, drank and fought as they survived their daily battles. To Picasso, all this was a constant source of inspiration. Pablo, who loved the raw energy of life among real people, openly confessed to Max that he liked to live life as a poor man…only with money! He revealed that 'mixing with the rich, was not a guarantee of intelligent conversations, imagination or wit!'

It was during these exchanges of ideas with the animated Pablo Picasso about art, naturally, and life in general, that Max witnessed a side to the artist he had not expected. When the talk of politics reared its head, it was like a red flag to a bull, and all too quickly exposed Picasso's fiery passionate character.

But, to Max, the revelation of the artist's strong personality was a tour de force. Picasso's unflinching, dark, determined and uncompromising eyes revealed a man who would have been triumphant in anything that he put his mind to. He possessed an inner confidence and unyielding gravitas that Max had never witnessed before, as the artist's spellbinding persona left him knowing in no uncertain terms that he was sitting in the presence of a genius – a new 'Old Master'. When Max woke the next morning with the worst of all hangovers, he just wanted to get back to London, and to a more stable way of life. He had finally seen in Picasso, that indefinable, innate quality of what it really took to be a great artist, and he knew more than ever that he did not have those traits in him. It was a quality you were born with, and no amount of wishful thinking could alter that harsh fact. Picasso would never realise that this chance encounter had more than likely saved Max from a life of hardship, and debt, not to mention probable insanity. Fate moves in unimaginable ways.

# CHAPTER 22

## 'Is concealing the truth, a lie?'

Now arriving at his destination, Officer Page-Hamilton's mind quickly shifted gear firmly back to the present, fully focused on what he has been tasked to do.

'Bonjour, Bienvenu. Comment allez-vous?' Pierre Guyon and Professor Jardin greeted him warmly.

'Bonjour, Monsieur Guyon. Bonjour Professor Jardin, très bien, et vous?' Max asked of them both.

'Bien, merci beaucoup – Alors, s'il vous plait, shall we proceed to my bureau or office as you would say,' Jardin smiled as he indicated the way. The two French men were plainly eager to receive the property and quickly take possession of their precious cargo.

Max was thankful to be finally relieved of this heavy responsibility, happy he had managed to get the masterpiece there without any mishaps along the way.

'Please, Officer Page-Hamilton, we would be delighted if you would join us for a celebratory glass of wine, it's nearly lunchtime, so not too early!' Before he could reply, Jardin immediately began pouring them all very full glasses from the bottle of wine on his desk.

'Oh, well, er, yes, indeed, thank you, that would be very nice.'

'Please, take a seat,' Guyon said, pointing to a chair. Max perceived, that, despite their pleasant smiles, there was a constrained atmosphere that seemed awkward and uncomfortable. He guessed it was now only a matter of time before they began to question him about the circumstances in which he had found the Mona Lisa.

'Naturally, Pierre and I are very keen to know more about what happened when you found our painting, so, would you be kind enough to, please, enlighten us? And, um, well, was there anything else that you may have discovered along with the painting, perhaps relating to it?' The Professor finally managed to come to the point of what he really wanted to know. As both men sat staring intently at Max, watching, waiting, and ready to quietly dissect his response, they were desperate to see if he had something to hide. And he had. Max began to feel decidedly hot under the collar, as he sought hard not to give himself away.

'Here it comes', Max thought to himself, 'it certainly didn't take long for their inquisition to begin! And, they had only given me one large glass of wine – that's certainly not going to be enough to take me off guard, he thought to himself. But this was something Max had rehearsed.

'Of course, gentlemen, naturally you want to know all the details of what occurred on that memorable day as I stood in the remains of Göring's home. So, Professor, Monsieur Guyon, I have written a full and comprehensive report that I have brought along with me today,' Max said as he handed over a file containing everything, well, nearly everything. As Professor Jardin took the file, Max could tell straight away from their reaction that they felt short-changed, as it was fairly obvious that they had wanted to probe him and try and trip him up, suspecting that he must know a lot more.

It was a risky strategy, as Max wasn't sure if he could trust himself not to confess what had really happened that day, once he was in the tight grip of their questioning. Max had never been able to lie, so this situation was pure agony, and he realised that if they began to interrogate him, that would be that, his resolve would vanish, just as he now wanted to vanish. If they only knew just what was being concealed inside his jacket pocket, he feared they would personally bring back the guillotine. The art of deception certainly did not sit well with Max.

Before their scheduled meeting, Max Page-Hamilton had spent

the last three nights without much sleep, with his mind in constant flux, worrying about what he should, or shouldn't, do about da Vinci's letter. Fully aware that it was far too important to destroy and pretend it had never existed, even if that would have made his life a lot easier, he knew he didn't have the moral or ethical right, or even want to contemplate that notion. Although his scheduled meeting at the Louvre was 'classified' as all three men were made privy to that fact by the Americans, therefore they were forbidden to ever acknowledge their meeting had ever occurred, it made him wonder if, during their meeting he could just simply hand over the letter and put an end to it, knowing that all of them would be duty bound from talking about it. Surely, that would be fine, and the right and proper thing to do, would it not? Max played out the scenario in his mind, as he tried to foresee what their reaction would be if he had just handed over the transcription and original letter.

They surely would be pleased, even grateful. He had thought of nothing else for the past three days and was now beginning to curse the day he had ever found it. If only this letter had been about science or nature which were the usual subjects that the old master penned, then that would have all been quite straightforward and everyone would have been delighted to have discovered some new material from da Vinci

'But, oh no', he thought to himself, 'it had to be this bombshell! Why me? All that rubbish you dream of as a kid about wanting to find treasure. Blimey, if we only but knew what a burden finding it truly was!' As Max recalled the motto, 'be careful of what you wish for.' The rhetorical question to himself was now a waste of time and no help at all.

'And, as for that cunning old Nazi, Hermann Göring, what a mischief-maker he was. He had really put the boot in by making sure that it was all laid out clearly in the greatest of detail, the whole nine yards, as the Americans say! Göring had well and truly set them up with their signatures glaring out like beacons from the bottom of the page of the full transcription taken from da Vinci's original letter. That was solid, undeniable proof of their co-conspiracy. There was no way they could deny they did not understand what they were doing and what was going on. Of course, whether or not you deem they had a choice; maybe yes, maybe, no? Probably not! But the evidence of their intended deception was compelling. Was it morally, right?' Max had sympathy for the two men and did not envy the position they had found themselves in, but it is what it is.

Therefore, all things considered, neither man would ever under any circumstances reveal the truth, it would bring about Jardin and Guyon's certain downfall, and whatever else it would unleash in its wake. No matter how many times it circled around his mind, this bothered him tremendously, likening it to feeling like a thief. Having possession of something that did not belong to you, but aware of how precious this new knowledge that had come to light was. Now, although he felt obliged to preserve these sacred words, he was in spite of that still torn in two, as he struggled with the idea of who rightly owned this new insight into one of the world's most famous polymaths and geniuses.

Gripped in a state of indecision, Max prepared to leave for his meeting. Putting on the jacket to his uniform he suddenly stopped in his tracks; 'Of course, how stupid can I be?' In that instant, he knew without any qualms that his life, and perhaps the life of his family would be put in certain danger if he gave Jardin and Guyon the transcription and letter, as there would be no way he would be allowed to quietly walk away knowing this secret and just simply be allowed to get on with the rest of his life

'No, that wouldn't happen; they couldn't take that chance'. In that instant, his indecision evaporated as he wondered why it has taken him so long to come to the obvious conclusion.

'What are your plans now?' The Professor asked Max, who had just finished his drink.

'Actually Professor, I am leaving today to return home, back to London and my family,' Max explained, as he placed down his empty glass onto the polished desk and picked up his hat.

'Well, we both wish you a safe journey, and thank you so much for saving our Mona Lisa for France.' Professor Jardin exclaimed as he showed him to the door, as the men shake hands and bid each other a fond farewell. Max knew, without a doubt, they didn't believe his account, it was written all over their faces, it was as if they could see straight through his subterfuge; but what could they do? There was nothing, they had no choice but to accept his account of events, so through gritted teeth, they just had to smile politely and seem grateful.

One decision Max had taken was, upon returning to London, his very first action would be a detour to his bank, Coutts on The Strand, and immediately place the da Vinci letter and transcription into a safety deposit box, where, it might just remain undisturbed for a very long time

'Maybe this conundrum will lay dormant for another five hundred years? By then, perhaps it will no longer matter. At least, it will no longer be my problem! In the meantime, although I am not a religious man, I will pray to find a way to do right by da Vinci; for now, however, it's in the lap of the gods.'

Max breathed a huge sigh of relief as he made his way out of the Louvre. Stepping onto the Rue de Rivoli, he eagerly soaked up the beautiful spring day, then realised he was just a ten-minute walk from the Ritz, he intuitively started making his way there, understanding just how pivotal the hotel had been in this whole narrative he felt drawn towards it, and the ugly truth of what had occurred in that fine domain had come to light. Max, ever the historian above all else, wanted to see inside for himself, and possibly experience a sense of just what those walls had been subjected to during its Nazi occupation.

Walking into the imposing hotel, he became fully aware of just why Göring had loved the place so much, 'how could you not?'

'Bonjour Monsieur, may I help you?' the Maître d' enquired

'Bonjour, I'm afraid I have not made a reservation for lunch, but as it is my last day here in Paris, as I am returning to London, I would be extremely grateful if you could possibly find a table for me?' Max politely asked at the reception desk.

'D'accord, one moment, I will check. Monsieur, this way, s'il vous plaît.' Max followed in obedience. The calm ambience of the inner sanctum was a true delight, it seemed that the hotel had wholly managed to overcome the notoriety of the darkest of eras that had borne witness to the deadly Nazi regime, whose time there was spent filled on a panacea of high-octane drug taking, drunken debauched parties and, not least, deranged political intrigue that had driven the world to the brink of destruction, and a home, not only to Göring but the sinister Head of the SS, the cold-blooded killer Heinrich Himmler when he was in Paris, whose twisted personality had been even more terrifying than that of the Reichsmarschall Göring.

'Are you ready to order, Monsieur?' the waiter enquired as he studied the French menu, fortunately posing no problem for him.

'Oui, I would like to start with the melon, followed by Canton de Rouen Vendôme, Petite Pois Francaise, and Selle de Volaille aux Artichauis, and a glass of Chateau Cheval Blanc 1939,' Max informed the waiter of his choice.

'An excellent choice, Monsieur,' the waiter commented. While waiting for his lunch to be served, Max began to examine the evidence of the situation he found himself in. He had over the years picked up quite a lot of knowledge from his legally minded father, whose many criminal cases he had often discussed over dinner, so, he knew how to consider, probe, assess, and scrutinize all the facts.

Obviously, this had penetrated Max's thought processes, which he now put to good use. Mindfully, Max began to consider who really was the antagonist in this drama

'Göring? Naturally, surely that was the obvious answer, but was he really? da Vinci had started all this in the first instance, let's not forget him, not quite so innocent; are his hands really clean in this momentous affair? Or are those two French men, Jardin and Guyon, really the villains, who should hold up their hands to their crime, borne out of a passion to protect their cultural heritage and self-importance, remember, both were ready and prepared to dismiss the moral seismic eruption that telling the truth would undoubtedly have done!'

The waiter offered Max the dessert menu and he decided on Biscuit Glace Viennois, coffee, and a glass of Vintage Port. Taking the da Vinci letter and its transcription from his pocket, Max read it through once again, and without any doubt at all, Leonardo da Vinci, that most progressive of men made his intentions absolutely and emphatically clear, even though, at the time, the old master had no idea whether it would ever come to see the light of day? But now it had.

'L'addition, s'il vous plait,' Max picked up his cigarette case and lighter and headed towards the door to begin his journey back home to his wife, Amy, and young son, Howard.

Even now, after all this time, it seemed that the imperative was to annul the expressed wishes of da Vinci. Perhaps the nefarious art world always was, and always will be, dominated by morally corrupt men out for their own ends, and not, ultimately working for the sake of art. This, from his own experience, the great Leonardo had understood only too well.

And that the artist is merely a bystander to their creations.

# CHAPTER 23

## Time to Tell

*New York City, October 2017*
*It is now seventy-two years since the 'secret'*
*had been interred into a bank vault*
*in London by Max Page-Hamilton.*

I t did not take more than a few minutes before the driver started uttering every profanity he could muster with the speed of a machine gun out of his window, aimed at any vehicle that got in his way, 'For goodness's sake man, will you calm down, I want to get into the city in one piece if you don't mind!' The cab driver's fare demanded while he sat uncomfortably in the back of the iconic yellow taxi, clinging on for dear life. As Sir Howard headed into Manhattan from the airport, he felt more like a hostage than a passenger – thinking that this combative style of driving would not have been out of place in a Roman gladiatorial arena. It demonstrated the complete contrast between the more relaxed polite nature of London's black taxis and the friendly banal chatter from most of the cabbies. It was easy to forget about the vast differences between the two cities after being in London for the past few months, and, if he was honest with himself, as he was getting older, he had found it harder to deal with the frantic pace the city demanded with such relentless intensity. Nevertheless, Sir Howard knew he commanded a great deal of respect on the lecture circuit in the US, which he had to admit, he did genuinely enjoy. His depth of knowledge on Geopolitics was in high demand, something not necessarily open to him as much in London. So, for the time being, it would remain his home.

Now with darkening black clouds gathering over New York, it certainly didn't help lift his spirits as he prepared for the responsibility he was about to impose on his unsuspecting daughter. He knew the time had come to disclose to Francine a burden he had been putting off for several years, but now he could no longer rely on any more delaying tactics. His late father, Max, had given him carte blanche as to when he felt it was appropriate that she should be told of his bequest to her. Sir Howard had spent his time in the UK thinking of how he should handle this matter. He had gone to London for two reasons, one was to collect from the bank a sealed letter that was now in his briefcase; and the other, well he didn't want to dwell on that for the moment.

He himself didn't even know the full extent of the weight that he was to impose on her shoulders. Sir Howard, had often been baffled by the fact that his own father would never really tell him exactly what it was all about, just a few hints here and there, but never did he reveal the quintessential point of it all. It was only upon his father's death, that Sir Howard, going through his estate had remembered his instructions for his only grandchild, along with a cautionary letter. Events had finally necessitated that time was of the essence, and besides, she was now married, even if he was less than pleased with her choice of husband, whom, Sir Howard thought of with great suspicion, not because of his background of once being a Wall Street trader during the time that had to lead the world to the point of financial collapse, after all, everybody wanted to make money, and it would be hypocritical of him to suggest otherwise, having himself invested for years into stocks and shares, no, that was not the reason, he just didn't trust him, which Sir Howard put down to having a combination of worldly wisdom, and an acute sense of judgement, nevertheless, he was smart enough not to interfere with her personal life. Sir Howard reasoned that as his daughter was now one of Christie's top fine arts curators, a position that carried a great deal of prestige, responsibility, and authority, which spoke highly of her character and ability to cope with major decision-making, within the international multi-billion-dollar business, therefore, it was surely an intelligent assumption that she could cope with this conundrum he was about to entrust upon her, at least that is what he told himself. Whatever the case, the task had to be carried out, it was not his choice to make. Her grandfather had wished her to have the letter and it was not up to him to deny her this, even if he had his profound reservations.

'Should I phone or just message her?' he pondered

'Hello, Francine, I have arrived back home, and although I know you are extremely busy today, I need to see you, could we, therefore, arrange to meet, say at 1.30 at the Metropolitan for lunch? Let me know before midday if you can be there, and I will get them to set a place for you.' He quickly sent off the message before he could change his mind. He deduced that now she was going to be so busy with the upcoming auction, she would not have the time to dwell on the legacy that he was about to bestow on her.

'Welcome home, Sir Howard, I hope you had a pleasant trip?' the doorman to his apartment block greeted him.

'Hello, Seamus, thank you for asking. Well, it was interesting, shall we say. And how are you keeping, my good man?' he responded in kind.

'Oh, you know, I'm fine, just as long as the old legs keep me going, you won't hear me complaining!' he jested. Sir Howard liked Seamus, who was still working a twelve-hour shift, six days a week, because, although approaching seventy he simply could not afford to retire. The polite banter between the two men was one of mutual respect. Sir Howard always found time to chat and display jovial politeness towards him, after all, you don't become a diplomat without the ability to get on with just about anybody. Sir Howard made sure he went out of his way to show his appreciation for the way Seamus looked after him and Francine, and would duly show that at Christmas time by always giving him a very generous bonus, unlike most of the ultra-rich inhabitants of the exclusive co-op apartments, who would rather pull out their own teeth than indulge in any small talk with members of their staff, who were only there for one precise purpose, which was to keep their daily lives running smoothly, so felt no need to interject with any trite conversations that didn't interest them, or, would be of no benefit to their gain or existence, and, if any member of the staff got so much as a five-dollar bill at Christmas they could count themselves lucky. Fortunately, Seamus had developed a thick skin, it was the only way to handle being so undervalued. Sir Howard knew only too well of the hot-tempered personalities of most of the other residents, and God forbid any employee who could be fired on a whim if any of the detestable owners had a fit of temper because they got out of bed the wrong side that day. This bad treatment of the staff Sir Howard found repulsive. But he knew this kind of personality only too well. They were just the type of people he had had to deal with throughout his career, and, no matter what part of the globe Sir Howard had been dispatched to, you would always find them, basically, they were just megalomaniacs, whether they were dictators or even democratically elected leaders; the so-called elite, those privileged few who could make other people lives an absolute misery on a whim just because they could. Sir Howard's lifetime ability to get on with people had never failed him, as he had been exceedingly well trained. Having spent his entire career in the midst of such mortals, he finally arrived at the conclusion that they were deeply psychologically flawed human beings, whom all suffered from the same affliction, one that had no cure – a disease called greed.

But he lived in the same building as them and was therefore always polite. And, from time to time, he would attend their dinner parties, as it was always entertaining to just sit back and watch them scrambling to achieve one-upmanship over each other, aside this, Sir Howard had the remarkable ability never to allow their pernicious temperament to rub off on him. It was as if he had been inoculated against their poisonous venom, so he could just observe as their spectacular vanities put on a show that could rival Broadway, he would just rise above it all with complete ease and indifference, all the while thinking, this would be the perfect material for a block-buster novel that would certainly make the number one slot in the New York Times bestseller list

'Now there's an idea,' he amused himself with the possibility.

Seamus followed Sir Howard up in the elevator with his suitcases, 'Can I do anything else for you, Sir?' he asked.

'Yes, actually, I need milk, French bread, and some blue Stilton cheese. I would be very grateful. I am off to meet Francine for lunch soon, so I will freshen up and be on my way. If you could just put the milk and cheese into the fridge and leave the bread on the kitchen counter that would be perfect?' Sir Howard asked him pressing a hundred-dollar bill into his hand. Seamus knew he was getting a very big tip from this elegant British gentleman.

# CHAPTER 24

## Charm – His Hidden Weapon

Highly confident while attractively reserved, the impeccably dressed thirty-eight-year-old English born, Dr Francine Page-Hamilton, lived with Adam Faris, her new art dealer husband of nine months in the same apartment building as her father on Park Avenue Upper East Side; one of the most desirable addresses in Manhattan, but, whereas Francine and Adam's apartment was fairly modest, her father, Sir Howard's large plush apartment, enjoyed the luxury of a balcony where she and her father had enjoyed many breakfast times together when weather permitted. His vast library was well-used by his daughter for her ongoing research as an art curator. The comfortable antique-filled home could be considered quite grandiose.

Francine, having inherited a substantial amount of money from her adored late grandfather Max when she was twenty-one, had, on the advice of her father, bought a property as an investment in the same grey stone-clad 1930s Art Deco-style co-op building.

Now with her marriage, she had left the apartment of her father and moved into a much smaller un-modernized address several flights of stairs down. It was to most people, and Francine herself, a beautiful place full of charm, still retaining its 1930s feel, with three good-sized bedrooms, two bathrooms, an original fireplace in the light-filled sitting room, and an eat-in kitchen; 'What more could you require?' She considered herself very fortunate, and, although it had required some updating, as the previous elderly owner had done no work on it for many years, she loved its ambience and the fact that she could keep an eye on her now ageing father upstairs. However, Adam was of the opinion, so it would seem, that it would 'do for now 'and of course, they would need to hire a professional interior designer to make the most of it, which he said would vastly increase its resale value when the time came for them to upscale. While Francine had been hoping for something a little less predictable than the clinical unhomely magazine appearance, that seemed to be de rigueur of every newly designed apartment in Manhattan, her desire for the much more cosy, personal touch, was something Adam found terribly unsophisticated and unbefitting to their lifestyle and growing prosperity. After much ado, he had worn her down with his determined mindset, and reluctantly Francine conceded, feeling exhausted by his stubbornness, thinking, she would learn to live with it and besides, 'That would make life easier – wouldn't it?' It was beginning to become the norm now for Adam to get his own way. Maybe such a whirlwind romance and marriage had not been such a wise decision after all. Slowly it had begun to occur to her, she didn't really know him at all well, but she supposed it was due to the fact that, as a New Yorker, Adam, had a much more urgent attitude to life than she did, aware that her English persona was more genteel, and she had lived up until now at a much slower pace of life, mostly with her nose in an academic textbook, pursuing her profound knowledge of French and Italian art. On living as a married couple, she now sensed it was going to have to be her that would need to be the flexible one, not for one moment did she get the impression that Adam would ever be so accommodating to her. She was resigned to the belief that over time this would gradually change, it was still early days, and they needed to both fine-tune their new situation.

When Francine met Adam Faris, he had been running his own Contemporary Art Gallery in Brooklyn for nearly eight years. Where once he had been trading stocks and shares, now he was trading Modern Art to the new young rich of Manhattan and Greenwich Village, which consisted of a whole new breed of social media influencers;

those with daddy's money, and lots of the young and talented tech guys who loved the idea of becoming 'art collectors' and who would spend their free time trawling the galleries most weekends, picking up large abstract oil paintings to hang above their sofas in their newly acquired loft apartments, which would give them something to brag about over dinner to their equally rich acquisitive friends, who all revelled in the status symbol of the cultured, desperate to capture the glamour of an instant personal heritage that wealth alone could buy.

Business was good, but Adam had still not managed to make that leap into the bigger league. Faris knew it was vital to get his hands on the right products to sell, which meant acquiring some seriously important 'names' in Warhol's limited-edition prints – a small Picasso drawing, or even a Richard Prince; in fact, anything that carried the kudos to become a serious contender. He knew the likelihood of that was light years away, but he required those essential famous artists' autographs, the desired signatures that were so in demand, those were the guys that would make him rich. There was only one thought that consumed his every waking hour, and that was, he needed money to make money

'How could he square the circle?' Francine had been invited by a friend to an art exhibition of a new young emerging artist Faris was trying hard to promote, after being introduced, the two of them hit it off from the start, which was surprising, as they had come from completely different backgrounds. The term 'opposites attract,' is an old saying that turned out to be somewhat true in their case. Adam Faris was seemingly utterly taken with her perfect English accent, while Francine was fascinated by the fast-talking, obvious flair of Faris. With his ostensibly easy-going ways, she felt like she had known him all her life, and when he invited her out to dinner after the art exhibition, little did she realise that within two months they would be making plans to be married. It never entered her mind that Adam was anything other than what she believed him to be, that his kindness, listening skills, and charming likeable nature were anything other than amazing; how happy she was too have met him.

Unlike Francine, Adam's career path had been far from an easy one. The harsh reality of surviving the mostly ruthless atmosphere of New York, was at times, brutal. While Faris had tried his hand at many unsatisfying jobs, he was now utterly sick and tired of just getting by to pay the rent; he wanted far more from life and was determined to get it.

Always restless and eventually bored with every kind of work he undertook, Faris finally accepted the only way to make the kind of money he craved was on Wall Street. This conclusion was great, however, identifying where he needed to be was the easy part, the difficulty was getting himself behind one of the desks. But to Adam, this was a challenge he was ready for; as he told himself, 'What the heck have I got to lose?' So, with a steadfast determination and a single-minded tenacity, Adam got what he set out for, which of course, came as no surprise to him because when Faris set his mind on a project, he was more than prepared to pursue the matter to its desired and required end. Now he had his size ten feet firmly placed on the coveted floor of an investment bank, and after a baptism of fire, he hit the ground running, impressing everyone in the casino culture atmosphere with his sheer calculating, 'take no prisoners' attitude. It was as if he had been cloned with the DNA of a 'kill or be killed' belief system. Within a short space of time, he was seeing the green shoots of dollar bills growing rapidly in his bank account, as he reaped the financial rewards that he obstinately believed were vital to his desired way of life – while discovering himself to be a natural-born salesman. All too soon the exclusive hand-made suits were followed by the expensive cars and the mid-town apartment, not quite Upper East Side, but he knew his arrival there was imminent, just a matter of time.

That was in 2007. His fast and heady rise into the fabulous world of money now beckoned.

# CHAPTER 25

## In the Midst of Chaos is Opportunity

### September 2008.

In less than a year, the Global Banking Crash had wiped the ground from under the feet of Adam Faris. The burgeoning career was now gone as fast as it had arrived, and, although initially depressed, he soon snapped out of a despairing way of thinking, seeing the experience as fortuitous, providing the chance to try something entirely new. Faris was not the sort of person to let any kind of failure hold him back for too long, due to an unshakeable self-belief and conviction that something would turn up. There was no possibility he would succumb to defeat, that was not how any determined, edgy, self-respecting New Yorker would allow themselves to think.

Working among the testosterone-driven herd mentality that was endemic on Wall Street had allowed Faris to develop a resolve of granite. It was social Darwinism at its finest. Nobody on Wall Street was there to do good for mankind, altruism was not a word that would ever be heard on the trading floor. To every single individual who worked there, money truly was their god, and the only thing worth worshipping, it was the be-all and end-all, nothing else mattered. Faris did not have either the time or the patience for sentiments, except when it could be used to his advantage. Having been in the midst of traders, investment bankers, and hedge fund managers every day, Faris saw how their bonuses could match, even exceed, those of some small economies in the developing world, affording them fabulous homes in Manhattan, estates in the Hamptons, priceless art collections, private jets and much more. These guys enjoyed real, rock-solid power, the type of power where the President, the most important person in the Free World would make an annual pilgrimage to your lavish home on the Upper East Side in pursuit of financial contributions to help fund their next election campaign with their hands out begging. The rich traders would dangle any politician like puppets to be played, all the while extracting as much clout as possible for any future pay-backs, feeling ever so clever, superior, and goddamned important. That, he discovered, was what money allowed, and nothing else was so gratifying. Adam soon grasped that these particular types of men had clawed every inch of their way to the very top by any means necessary, legally or otherwise, it really didn't matter, so long as it was effective. Possessing principles was a belief system that they did not care about, or even need to contemplate. And if there was one lesson that he would take from his time on the trading floor, it was that you never give up – you must be ready to take chances, no matter what the circumstances. And now whatever it took he was prepared to do it.

Forty-year-old Adam Faris was tall, with thick, almost black straight hair, combed backward it conveyed a polished preppy look, he was most definitely the epitome of a 'charmer,' with an extrovert and ambitious, perhaps too ambitious side to him that was deeply disturbing to Francine at times. Her father had cautioned his daughter not to rush into marriage and wait a while, advising her to get to know him much more; but, totally out of character for Francine, she plunged headlong in, seeing in him all the outward dazzling shine and joie de vivre that she believed herself not to possess. Little did she realise what Adam really saw in her, which was his chance at really making it. To him, Francine was a piece of cake; he could conceive of no problem in wrapping her around his manipulative fingers; she was most definitely a great catch. Not only was she extremely well accomplished and privately educated, but her father was an ex-ambassador with connections in the White House and the British establishment, not to mention several homes on Park Avenue, London, and the South of France. Indeed, he thought he had hit the jackpot and could not believe his good fortune, so he had no intentions whatsoever of passing by this chance. Like so many others before him, Adam had discovered that after years of trying to make a good living in New York, life never got any easier, at times it could only be described as savage, the relentless competition was fierce, and it was completely terrifying to look behind you, as there was always someone younger, more talented, and willing to be paid less, to do the work that you did and possibly do it better. Having tried his hand at banking, he now saw his main chance in the unregulated Wild West which was the global art market. Adam was more than attracted to the dubious underbelly that surrounded it.

Many so-called art dealers, who were really little more than criminals, actually gave him such a natural high that he did not always need to snort a line of white powder to achieve the same sense of excitement, which was just as well, as Francine had no idea of his propensity for that particular kind of indulgence.

The banking world had brought him into contact with so many shady characters, that it felt like a natural habitat to him, liking the dangerous underhanded tension it brought with it. Faris was brilliant at being duplicitous, his 'charisma' was the result of an uncanny ability to read people, telling them exactly what they wanted to hear, feeding their egos without any suspicion, knowing precisely what he was doing, but they never detected, and that included Francine, but, he could not deceive her father, who had met some of the world's most politically notorious and difficult personalities, was much more adept and attuned to knowing what his potential new son-in-law was all about; an insight that made Sir Howard deeply uncomfortable and concerned. Trusting his well-tuned instincts, Sir Howard tried in vain to convey this sense to his normally down-to-earth, well-adjusted and pragmatic daughter, without wanting to sound too prejudiced, but, for all his trying, it just seemed to fall on deaf ears as Francine would smile, telling him not to worry so much. Alas, all too soon both men knew that Adam had won; achieving a 'hostile takeover' of Francine's mind as the marriage went ahead.

Now Faris was finally living on Park Avenue, confirming entirely his belief that he fully deserved to be lodged there – something that complimented his sense of entitlement. But to him, this was only the beginning of his inauguration into the high stakes of New York's fascinating, uber rich society, while his new, talented and very successful wife, Francine, would be the key to opening all the doors.

# CHAPTER 26

## Leonardo...The Chosen One

Francine's grandfather, Max, had doted on his only grandchild, and when she showed keen interest in art at a young age, he had encouraged her all the way. Both sharing a love of the classics, she followed in his footsteps by attending the same university to gain her degree and a master's in fine arts, culminating in her doctorate with her thesis, The Psychology of The Mind of a Man Who Was The Myth Called Leonardo da Vinci. Francine had no idea just how in demand she would become. Her successful career began to emerge while curating the Landmark Exhibition of Leonardo da Vinci held in London in 2011. To her complete surprise, she had been invited by the National Gallery in London to try a long shot and bring together for the first time ever, a collection of da Vinci's paintings. Francine understood it would be difficult, if not impossible. As this had never been done before she knew it would involve a massive uphill battle that would require months of delicate patient negotiations with the various institutions, which would no doubt be a minefield to say the least, mostly because of the potential damage that could incur during the transportation of the artwork, not to mention the probable jealousy among the professionals because they had not thought of doing this before themselves. Then there were the enormous insurance costs involved, plus the security measures; in fact, the list of obstacles was many. But her tenacity paid off as it went on to become an international phenomenon, an unparalleled performance for both the National Gallery and Francine, that would lead to her now unsurpassed career in her chosen profession.

It was a rain-drenched New York Monday morning in October, and Francine was heading toward Christie's, located in Rockefeller Plaza, for the first meeting with her new team. Going through the doors of the renowned auction house always gave her a sense of excitement; now at the top of her game, she would often pinch herself that she had been one of the lucky ones, able to do exactly what she wanted and get very well paid into the bargain. This was something she never took for granted.

'Oh, that's just wonderful! I knew I shouldn't have worn it!

Still, it's my own fault,' she thought to herself as a car driving far too fast and too close splashed dirty muddy rainwater from the sidewalk all up the back of her off-white French-style Macintosh, as the driver then had the nerve to blast her with his car horn, even though it was all his fault! It seemed that whatever the time of day, there was always just so much high-level tension about to break out in NYC, however, the speed and aggression of people pushing past her as they juggled their umbrellas like weapons didn't bother her that morning, as she had far more important and exciting things on her mind.

Fully concentrating on what was ahead of her, she was aware that this was going to be big. But just how big, nobody yet knew. The price it would fetch would be reflected in the absolute rarity of Leonardo da Vinci's paintings, which were in total less than twenty in existence. With interest pouring in from every corner of the globe, the upcoming auction, dubbed the 'Sale of the Century' by the media, would be taking place in a few weeks' time, and there was an enormous amount of work still to do in preparation.

Francine vividly recalled the very first time she had laid eyes on Leonardo da Vinci's Salvatore Mundi, in London in 2011. She had been listening to an evocative Nina Simone song, 'I put a spell on you' on her iPod, when from nowhere she felt a strong, volt-like shock of electricity charge right through her body as the hair on the back of her neck stood to attention. It was not something she was likely to ever forget. Staring into the eyes of da Vinci's The Saviour of the World, the painting had truly cast a spell on her. Francine had over the years seen and studied thousands of paintings, but this was unlike any other oil on canvas that she had ever come across before.

The sheer, unequalled depths of perception and consciousness the eyes of the man in the painting conveyed, were, without question, beyond any words. It was as if Jesus Christ himself had actually been present in the room when da Vinci had created the masterpiece – what other explanation could there have been for the artist to have managed to capture the pure, unquestionable force of personality that the painting possessed? It went far beyond divinity, it must surely be the nearest you would ever come to being in the presence of God himself. It was as if Christ had chosen to be metamorphosed in the studio of His chosen creator, that being Leonardo da Vinci, a man like himself who had also been born to a young mother and risen from the humblest of beginnings. There was an undeniable and natural affinity between the artist and the subject. Closing her eyes in the silent empty basement of the National Gallery, where the Salvatore Mundi painting had been undergoing its thorough cleaning before the London exhibition, Francine could actually imagine herself there in the studio of the painter in renaissance Italy, quietly unobserved, standing in a dark corner of the room watching the development literally take place, while becoming aware of the subtle smells from the ground pigments and lavender spike oil, as the flickering candlelight threw shadows on the cascading abundant ringlets of the multi-coloured tones of the hair of Jesus, and the soft sounds of Leonardo's brushstrokes as he imprints his vision, listening as they spoke of their early childhood was utterly gripping, but, most surprising, was the laughter and fun they enjoyed together; it had never occurred to her before that Jesus even had a sense of humour. In the future, if she ever thought of Christ, the image in her mind now would be of him laughing at da Vinci's brilliant wit and entertaining mischievousness, which must have been quite a respite for Jesus from his usual travails. She had always possessed the ability to transport herself into these situations; this experience was nothing new to her.

She had grown up with this gift since childhood. As an only child of a globe-trotting British diplomat, she had needed to rely on herself for company most of the time, this led to her developing an almost heightened supernatural imagination, to such an extent that now she thoroughly enjoyed being on her own. But, of course, with such a lucid imagination, she was never truly alone.

# CHAPTER 27

## The Selling of a Saviour

'Hi, everyone, and good morning. Well, I'm pleased to see that you all look keen, and, I expect, you probably all feel the same as me; that is, lots of excitement and anticipation as to who the painting will be sold to. And although I shouldn't say this, so I state here that it is 'without prejudice'. She laughed, 'I would not be disappointed if it was bought by a museum, or a very generous benefactor here in New York, but, of course, we are totally impartial, and our goal is to facilitate our client to obtain the highest bid, and naturally the best commission for Christie's! This, as you all know, is an exceptional painting, to say that it is a rarity is an understatement, and this auction will truly be a once-in-a-lifetime event, the likes of which you will probably never witness again in your careers, so enjoy the process, unless of course, the Mona Lisa ever comes up for sale, then all bets are off! The media will be out in full force, however, you are all professionals, so I am fully confident that you will be consistent in all areas of potential client confidentiality, which is a must. Under no circumstance give out any information as to any of the potential buyers, as privacy is sacred and an absolute to Christie's reputation, and please, don't get caught out, as they are gagging to know whose names are in the race. Therefore, I'm issuing you all with mobiles that you will use only for this event to communicate with each other, do not give out this number to anyone, as we need to maintain total security. So, as of today we have a month long public viewing, commencing at 12 noon today but at 9 am thereafter. We are anticipating huge crowds, in fact, I wouldn't be surprised if you started seeing them queuing around the block daily. I don't know if any of you are aware of this. Still, back in 1963, the then-First Lady, Jackie Kennedy, had the fantastic good fortune of getting the French to send over the Mona Lisa for an extended showing in Washington and here in New York, and just so you get some perspective on the interest that da Vinci can create for the public, the Metropolitan Museum had over one million people attend the viewing. So, as you can imagine security will be extremely high. You will all be issued with the names and photos of the team that will be on guard around the clock. If you have any suspicions, let me or a member of the security team know at once, don't take any chances.

From now on, you can expect to be inundated with calls from potential buyers, both private individuals and international institutions, who feel they may have a chance to bid, but let's face it, there are going to be only a handful who will be in the running. Even though there is no reserve price on the painting, it most certainly won't be going to anyone without the very deepest of pockets! At 10 am I will be holding a press conference to give them some basic facts. 'Oh, and I believe I'm on the front cover of Time Magazine this coming week,' she said pulling a slightly embarrassed face, 'as they have done an article on me with regards to the sale. So, that's all the talking we will be doing to the press until after the evening sale on the 15th of November. Now, the fun begins. Thank you all, let's get to work.' Francine's good humour and prep talk put her staff on top form for this unprecedented and thrilling event.

Switching back to her personal mobile, she could saw a message from her father. She was very surprised to hear from him, and responded immediately.

'Yes, of course, I can meet you for lunch, but you must be tired from the flight. What if I cook for us this evening, and we can really catch up? Is everything fine with you?' She responded back to him.

'I'm fine, and thanks for the offer, but I really would prefer this lunchtime,' he texted her back.

'Okay, I'll see you then,' she responded, as she thought that it was not like him; 'he never normally contacts me at work, and especially this week, I wonder why? I guess I will find out in a couple of hours.'

# CHAPTER 28

## No Such Thing as a Free Lunch!

It was still raining as she made her way to her father's private members' club, The Metropolitan, on One East 60th Street. The high black and gold wrought iron gates were complimented beautifully with its white columns on either side, which gave a formal tone to the building, informing everyone of its grand importance. It most certainly represented 'old money' and, only for those that could afford its fee, which she believed was quite considerable; but she knew her father enjoyed meeting his friends there for lunch most days, where they could withdraw into one of the smoking rooms and spend several hours each day putting the modern world to rights. Within the hallowed walls, it was all so easy to feel lured, beckoned into a realm of your own thinking, insulated, that's what the club did to you, once inside, reality no longer really existed out there, and you could forgiven if you forgot it was the twenty-first century. The beautiful angelic murals that glorified the top half of the marble-clad walls, provoked an almost religious experience, comparable to being within a cathedral, just as the extravagantly designed staircase could easily persuade your senses, that you actually were in such a domain. With no clocks anywhere, time there was literally suspended, deliberately, which was quite nice when you are all but retired, and it made her father happy. Besides, she occasionally enjoyed the benefits, one was holding her recent wedding reception in the grand ballroom.

'Good afternoon, Dr Francine, so nice to see you, your father is already in the dining room; please follow me,' one of the attendants said to her.

'Thank you, and please, just call me, Francine,' she smiled at him. In the distance, she could see her very distinguished-looking father seated in his usual place, as the waiter leads her towards the table; the restaurant was a quiet moment away from her very hectic morning.

Francine was extremely pleased to see her father back home and gave him an enormous hug.

'Hello, my dear, thank you for finding the time, today of all days, so tell me, how did your morning go, smoothly I hope?' he asked her.

'Yes, surprisingly well, just inundated with enquires from the media as expected, and, as I left to meet you, people were starting to arrive to view the painting, so we got off to a good start. It's actually nice to get away for a breather, as this morning was enjoyable but stressful. Anyway, enough about me, how was London, I'm not even sure why you went so quickly, you never told me the reason?' His daughter asked him as she picked up the menu.

'Well, let's order our lunch and I will tell you, but first, have you switched off your mobile? You know the club rules!' Sir Howard reminded his daughter.

'Sorry, I always forget the antiquated rules of this place! There, all done, I've turned them both off,' she teased.

'You need two phones now? Oh, good grief,' her father tutted as he rolled his eyes.

The formality of the dining room that overlooked a large terrace was something her father was all too used to, whereas for his daughter most days her lunch would consist of a quick bite to eat at her desk, washed down by a diet coke.

'Shall we order?' Sir Howard said to Francine as he indicated to the waiter. They both decided to have the soup of the day for starter, followed by beef tenderloin fragranced with rosemary and seasonal vegetables, and while Francine ordered a side serving of their delicious truffle-infused French fries her father declined

'Now, about London, what was the reason for your sudden decision to go? You normally head off to the South of France for the summer, and why did you want us to meet up here today? We could have just seen each other tonight when I got back home.' As her father was about to reply, the waiter brought over the soup, patiently waiting for him to go before he began to disclose to her his reasons.

'Before you start to worry, let me reassure you that I am absolutely fine,' was his opening line, to which she immediately put down the soup spoon she was about to use

'What?' Suddenly she felt scared, and her face drained of colour.

'No, no, it's okay, really. You see, at the beginning of June, I went for my usual annual health check-up, anyway, they found a suspicious mole on my back, after they did a biopsy, the tests came back showing it to be malignant, so I decided to go to London for a second opinion, and went to see my man in Harley Street, where they confirmed the same findings. Fortunately, it was discovered in time and promptly removed thankfully it had not spread any further, so I'm very lucky. They also ran another full MOT on me, and now I just need to go back every three months for the time being so that they can keep an eye on me, so you have no need to worry on that score. I'm afraid Francine, that these things happen as you get to be as old as me,' he said teasingly to her as he tried to reassure his daughter, who was becoming visibly more upset. It brought it home to her that apart from a few distant relations in the UK, he was all she had left of her close family, her mother had died when she was only five years old, so Francine was raised by her father and grandfather, Max.

'You should have told me, I would have come to London with you. Are you sure everything is quite okay now?'

'Yes, absolutely. I wouldn't tell you that if it weren't so, now put that out of your mind.' He reassured her once again.

'However, this health concern has made me face up to something I have been putting off for several years,' her father paused, Francine looked bewildered about what he was trying to say, 'While I was in London, I went to my bank to collect something that is rightfully yours, it was left to you by your grandfather, with the stipulation that I gave it to you when I deemed you were ready,' he told her.

'Ready? Ready for what?' she asked.

'Well, that's the question, which is the difficult part for me to answer quite frankly. Anyway, some of this you have always known, like, for example, you knew your grandfather was one of the Monuments Men based in Germany during the war, and something your grandfather was naturally very proud of,' he reminded her.

'Well, it's connected to his time there, apparently? Do you remember when he told you he was instructed to go to Paris at the personal request of General Eisenhower, to make a special delivery to the Louvre Museum?' Sir Howard tried to explain to his bewildered daughter, who was now beginning to look completely baffled as to what on earth he is talking about.

'Yes, I remember him telling me that particular story, but whenever I asked him what he had to deliver, he would just say, 'One day you will know' and that was that. I could never manage to get any further, so finally, I just gave up asking and forgot all about it,' Francine concluded.

'Actually, my dear, I have a cover letter here from him that possibly explains everything. I really don't know, it's all a bit of a mystery! Anyway, instead of me trying to explain something that I really don't understand myself, it's probably better if you just read exactly what your grandfather wrote. Then perhaps we will be somewhat the wiser. So here you are,' he said, handing the letter over to her.

Francine began to read the words that her grandfather had written down all those years ago in anticipation of this day.

# CHAPTER 29

## My Dearest Francine

*I*have bequeathed to you a sealed document, that your father,
as 'caretaker' has kept in our family bank vault. This cover
letter you are now reading will set out exactly what you will be
undertaking, which I must warn you carries with it a significant
obligation should you ever decide to break open the seal. If in those
circumstances, you do endeavour to take that course of action, then
you will become privy to a predicament that I did not have the
courage, or perhaps intelligence, to resolve. I made a discovery while
I was in Germany, which haunted me for the rest of my life, because
of the dilemma that this secret had brought with it. There was not a
single day that went by, when I didn't ask myself what was the right
and honourable thing to do? And I'm sorry to say, I never found the
answer, evidently. I just came to an impasse, because of the nature
of this secret, which is not only highly complex, but I fear extremely
dangerous. I won't go into it here, but, in all seriousness, I believed
at the time, that I was literally protecting my life, and that of my
family from those with a vested interest in it remaining hidden. If
you decide to go ahead and break the wax seal, you will understand
why I was afraid of many powerful forces. But, and I must emphasis
to you that life was very different then back in 1945. You need to
imagine what it was like at the end of the war; Europe was a
parlous state, having been ravaged into a near abyss by the Nazis,
people were broken, families wiped out, destruction lay on every

street corner, the most critical thing then was to rebuild Europe. If, at that time, I had divulged what I knew, and had proof of, it would have been devastating then. However, after all this time perhaps you will be able to see this with a fresh perspective? You may ask, why then, did I simply not destroy it, if its revelation was to prove so disruptive? It's only when you read it for yourself, you will come to know the answer to that question.

But, from my reasoned belief, there are only three options that I can see for you: The first is you destroy it without reading it, therefore, saving your conscience from any decision. Secondly, you can read it and reveal to the world with all the dire consequences that it will bring about. Or thirdly, you read it, and, like me, you leave it lying dormant in a safety deposit box, maybe for another five hundred years, or even perhaps for all eternity?

You may wonder, or even curse me, as to why I have placed this burden on your shoulders, and left this fate to you? The answer to that is simple, it's because there's no one else I could trust. I saw over the years how your interest in art grew into a tenacious dedication to da Vinci's work; you came to understand the manifold genius of the man. Yes, my dearest Francine, it is about Leonardo. And I will warn you, it concerns the shocking truth about the Mona Lisa. In all his thousands of pages of writing, Leonardo never wrote anything personal about himself, he was an intensely private man, that was until he penned this, whose authenticity is more than evident by his distinctive handwriting. Also, and more importantly, you will know quite clearly from his letter, that it was his 'expressed' desire for this absolute truth to be revealed to the world one day.

The only people who ever knew about this, as yet undisclosed truth, are now all dead. They were, Pierre Guyon, who was the Director of National Musée Paris, Professor Charles Jardin, Head Curator for Fine Arts, at the Louvre, Paris, Phillip Pétain, head of the puppet government of the Vichy regime, who was later

164

*charged with treason in France, and lastly, the notorious Nazi, Kommandant Reichsmarschall Hermann Göring, and of course me. Each of us had our reasons for wanting to either destroy, blackmail or hide the truth.*

*And now the baton has passed on to you. Perhaps, you will succeed where we have all failed.*

*Your ever-loving Grandfather,*

*Max Page-Hamilton.*

Suddenly, she gasped with shock and disbelief, before spluttering out loudly:

'Hermann Göring?'

'Ssh, Francine,' Sir Howard told her to keep her voice down as fellow diners turned around, tutting in unison under their breath, aghast at her outburst. As to whether their disapproval was because of the name of the infamous Nazi, or at what they perceived as simply bad table manners, unbecoming of the club, it was not clear; but knowing the snobbery of the Metropolitan, it was probably the latter.

Sir Howard's summary was to the point, and obvious, 'As you see for yourself, my dear, now we have both read the prelude to this strange intrigue, I must confess, I believe we are both none the wiser! Except to say, that it's obviously something very damning, not to mention possibly incriminating, to perhaps an institution, or a government, or even individuals? So, "that is the question" as Shakespeare once said! Sorry, I couldn't resist that one. Joking aside, what's your interpretation? After all, you know da Vinci better than most, what do you think he could have had hidden up his sleeve?' Sir Howard asked Francine.

'I don't have the foggiest idea, and, like you, I'm also none the wiser, it all sounds so obscure. So, all we know is that it concerns da Vinci and the Mona Lisa, but what on earth could it be?

165

I just can't imagine. I'm racking my brains already, but nothing springs to mind from all I know of Leonardo and his history, or the Louvre where it hangs, come to that. But, something grandfather unearthed, was so extreme, and so damaging, it caused him to be scared for the rest of his life; then to hide this 'secret' away for so many years? His warning to me was clear-cut, and as much as I want to know. I don't want to know, because, to be honest, I'm quite scared to discover what it is, I mean, if my grandfather was afraid, then maybe I should be too! It almost feels dreamlike, but as my neck now feels so tight with anxiety, I realise it is no dream! You know something, this morning, I woke up excited and jumped out of bed with so much energy about the upcoming auction, but now, I just feel this enormous gravity weighing me down, I mean, what am I supposed to do?' her question was of course rhetorical.

Her father listened patiently as he allowed his daughter to unburden herself; 'It's strange, you know because when I was studying art history, I was always so intrigued by Hermann Göring because of his part in the almost industrial, and systematic, theft of art in Europe. From what I could understand, he was such a caricature of himself. Little did I know then that he would be making such an impact on my life. Grandfather never mentioned anything about Göring over the years. Whenever I asked him about what had happened during his time in Germany, he would only speak about how they would find valuable treasures, that were returned back to museums, galleries, churches, and some to private owners, nothing whatsoever about Göring, but then again, whenever I asked him about his war days, he would just brush it aside most of the time and change the subject, saying it was such a long time ago. Now it's all starting to make sense; his coyness, those avoidance tactics about whatever it was he had discovered and didn't want to be reminded of,' Francine mused away to herself.

Giving a big sigh, she summed up, 'I need to give this a lot of serious thought; I really don't know what to say or think. After all, it's not really your run-of-the-mill kind of problem, is it? This mystery is certainly, well, unusual, to say the least. I'm completely bewildered. But if grandfather was not being dramatic, and if it's really something of such significance and magnitude, then how can I deal with it right now? I have just got so much on my mind at the moment because of the upcoming auction, which I really need to focus on, as the eyes of the world will be on us, I cannot afford to make any errors, plus there is your 75th birthday to arrange in the next few weeks. So, can we just let it rest for the time being?' She asked her father.

'I can see how stressed it is making you already, and there's no need to put yourself under a time constraint; let's face it, whatever it is has gone unresolved for nearly five centuries; I think a few more weeks will make no difference whatsoever!' her father's opinion was obvious when she thought about it

'Yes, of course, you're quite right,' Francine took a few moments to pause for thought while holding the letter from her grandfather, 'So, exactly where is the actual sealed document now?'

'It's in our wall safe at home unless you would prefer me to put it into my bank vault?'

'No, that's quite okay, it's secure in your apartment,' she confirmed his decision.

Francine folded her napkin and stood up, 'I really have to make my way back to the office, this lunch has lasted much longer than I had anticipated.' Her father, ever the gentleman, rose from his seat to kiss his daughter goodbye.

'This must have been something of a surprise, but try not to worry yourself unduly, it's quite possible that your grandfather just may have either exaggerated or misread whatever he believed he found. When you are ready to go ahead and see what it's all about, you know the sequence to the safe, you don't need to ask. Now, I'm off to the reading room for a couple of hours to take a nap, I can feel the jet lag kicking in, and later Eugene Dempsey is coming here for dinner, so I won't be returning back to my apartment until quite late. Oh, and by the way, I am flying again on Thursday to Washington, I have been invited to attend a reception to welcome the new Ambassador at the British Embassy, taking place on Sunday evening. I will return home Tuesday or Wednesday evening, depending on whom I meet up with,' Sir Howard told her as she was about to leave.

'Okay, that will be nice for you, catching up with everyone, and just in case I'm busy and don't see you before you go, please give everyone at the Embassy my regards, and enjoy your afternoon's snooze.' Seeing his eyes almost closing with tiredness, Francine gave her father a peck on both cheeks before leaving him to take his shut-eye. Slowly digesting her thoughts, she walked down the staircase and into the lobby where the door was held open for her, 'Have a nice afternoon', the young man said as she made her way out and back into the real world.

That cocooned feeling the Metropolitan always gives, can, if you are not careful, make you almost disorientated. Francine was grateful that the afternoon sun was beginning to appear between the tall buildings, at least that was something nice. As much as she respected the ethos of her father's club, it could very easily be seen as a bit of a throwback, and from time to time, it felt a bit overly stuffy, or perhaps she was just feeling a little too sensitive. Now out on the sidewalk, she could breathe, even if it was only noxious traffic fumes, it felt refreshing. Walking at a slower pace than the passers-by, her mind was in somewhat of a flux. Francine understood that she needed to interpret all that had occurred over lunch with her father, yet, with so much occupying her thoughts at this particular time she didn't have the spare mental energy to give it the attention it required and rightly demanded of her.

Turning left, she decided to go into Barney's Department Store, located just a few yards past the Metropolitan, seeking out a frivolous distraction from the lunchtime revelation. Although she really needed to get back to her desk and start replying to the dozens of messages that were now coming through as soon as she had switched her mobile back on. Gazing up from her phone momentarily, Francine stopped abruptly, 'Could this day get any weirder? she thought to herself. On the other side of the street, she spotted her husband Adam with Konrad Gray walking into the fashionable restaurant, Avra Madison

'What on earth was he doing with Konrad?' Who just happened to be one of the biggest Art Dealers and Investors in New York, and certainly one of the major players internationally. Seeing them together immediately redirected her thought process and she decided to give Barney's a miss after all, and instead, she started making her way back to Christie's. Work she deemed was the best cure for what ails you, rather than shopping.

# CHAPTER 30

## Invitation to the Penthouse

Francine and her father had known Konrad Gray and his wife, Millicent, for several years. The two of them lived in a duplex penthouse apartment that was a staggering twenty thousand square feet within the same co-op building. If ever a man could be described as strange, then Konrad Gray was that man. He always reminded her of the old British film actor, Christopher Lee, who was world famous for his portrayal of Count Dracula. Konrad appeared to be in his mid to late sixties, and was an exceptionally tall man with black hair, slicked back and going grey at the sides. His oddly shaped eyes conveyed an all-knowing look, which was really quite peculiar and did not help to offset his distinctive appearance, which was exaggerated all the more by his eccentric style of dress that looked like it came from another era altogether. Quite simply, he gave her the creeps, and she would avoid him at all costs. Her gut instinct told her to give him a very wide berth, although, she had to be honest, he had never actually been anything other than charming, in a ghoulish kind of way. Her father found him amusing, as he told Francine, 'If you think Konrad is weird, think again, you really don't know what strange is until you have met some of the people I have, they would make Konrad seem almost tame by comparison!' And, according to her father, he was quite the raconteur; whenever Sir Howard attended one of his dinner parties, Konrad would keep everyone thoroughly entertained with his unusual stories, so seemingly, he was a very intelligent man and extremely knowledgeable on many subjects. Nobody really knew just how he had acquired his vast fortune, and it was believed he was a billionaire. Konrad had cultivated quite an enigma around himself, along with a reputation for being a difficult man, if not downright rude, to most people who did not hold any interest to him. Francine had always held the belief that he had something to hide, and, in the few discussions she had had with her father about Konrad, Sir Howard always concurred with her that he probably did.

Adam, seeing his wife's bag on the glass hallway table, called out to her as he opened the door.

'Hi,' she greeted him back before noticing he was clutching a bottle of expensive champagne.

'What's that all about?' she asked, looking curiously at him.

Adam, grinning, couldn't contain himself any longer.

'If I play my cards right, we just might have a lot of celebrating to do! Because you will never, ever, believe, whom I had lunch with today?' he said, eagerly waiting for her to ask him. Responding in jest, she said.

'Um, can I take a guess? Let me think?' She paused for effect and asked 'Could it have been possible with Konrad Gray?'

'What, how the hell did you know that, I mean, who told you?' she laughed.

'Nobody told me, I saw you both going into Avra Madison, I'd just finished having lunch myself with my father at the Metropolitan, and as I was walking towards Barney's, I saw you both, and I must say, I was somewhat surprised,' she told him.

'You were surprised? Then consider my surprise when he came into the gallery, I was totally stumped, I mean, you just don't expect an art dealer of his importance to literally walk in off the street, and let's face it, you really can't imagine him in Brooklyn at all, it's just not his style! It must have been completely out of his comfort zone I would have thought. Although his chauffeur was outside, and ready to whisk him away from all the grime and graffiti at a moment's notice.' Adam went on, 'I've only met him once, and that was so brief it really didn't count, when your father invited him and his wife to our wedding reception, but I never spoke to him, I don't think he even really noticed me? Anyway, he never said a word, nothing, just looked around at the paintings for a while, then coolly, without any expression on his face, asked me if I was free for lunch! Me? Free for lunch, with Konrad Gray are you kidding me? I thought to myself, yes, of course!' Adam was animated with excitement at what he perceived as his good fortune.

'So, tell me, what on earth did he want?' Her curiosity was whetted. 'Well, you are not going to believe this, and hard as it might be to consider, but over our lunch, he was talking about making an investment into my gallery, God, really…you know, I was literally speechless. That would be amazing, don't you think? It could up my game overnight if Konrad invested. With his name and backing it would allow me to get some really good pieces, and, it would generate some awesome publicity, just imagine, I could get to do Art Basal, that's the place to be and get yourself noticed, moreover, finally taken seriously – as you know everyone who is anyone all go to Art Basal, it's the Mecca of art.' Adam's exuberance was almost childlike, but his outburst was not contagious, questioned why his wife didn't respond in kind, her obvious lack of enthusiasm was not to his liking, seeing her display a cool reserve on his seemingly good news really got under Adam's skin, and his back was up, finding his wife's aloof attitude annoying, it was almost as if she was putting a dampener on his potential good fortune, and, it was not something he needed or wanted. Francine, sensing his hostility, tried to give Adam her cautioned reasoning.

'If it's genuine, that will be incredible, but aren't you just a bit curious about why he would do that? After all, he's not known for his generosity, quite the contrary, but if it's on the level, it will be a very exciting opportunity for your business,' she just wanted Adam to keep his feet firmly on the ground and read the small print, so to speak, before he got carried away with the idea of partnership with Konrad. Adam's mood darkened swiftly, 'You know what Francine, I actually don't need your advice, or permission for that matter, I'm perfectly capable of making my own decisions,' his cutting remarks left her silent and somewhat taken aback, 'Also, just to let you know, we've been invited, along with your father if he's around on Sunday evening, to a celebration in Konrad's penthouse, as his wife Millicent has just been given a seat on the board of the Museum of Modern Art, an invitation which I gratefully accepted on our behalf, what do you have to say now? And by the way, we will both definitely be going!' he informed her, insinuating that she had no say in the matter. Feeling fairly stung by his overreaction, Francine decided to rise above his petulance, reminding herself it was because he wanted the gallery to grow and succeed, and she had to concede to the fact that it did seem on the surface, and for whatever his reasons, that Konrad was interested in Adam and his gallery, so she would need to give them both the benefit of any doubts that she harboured.

'I wonder if I'm being overly cautious?' She thought, beginning to doubt her initial skepticism

'Maybe I had been a bit harsh, even judgemental?' Now feeling guilty, Francine tried to lighten the mood by joking about Millicent.

'Wow, at last, you really have to admire her perseverance, she's been trying to worm her way onto that board for years, it appears now, I guess that their many charity fund-raising dinners have finally paid off, Konrad will be delighted that at last she finally managed it, adding a touch more kudos to their lives, something he likes so much, hence the extravagant champagne reception. It's well known in the best circles that Konrad is desperate to be seen as a philanthropist in the city of New York in one way or another, and he won't be content until he achieves that ambition, so pushing his wife into anything that will enhance his chances are so much the better, but goodness knows how he intends to do that because you really need to do something exceptional to obtain that level of recognition in this city. I think he sees himself in the same way as other past great names, like say Andrew Carnegie or the likes. Anyhow, he's definitely out to secure his legacy.' Francine declared.

'You shouldn't underestimate him; you never know, he just might pull something out of the hat and surprise everyone, the guy is determined, and I admire him,' Adam stated bluntly as if he knew something she didn't.

'Actually, my father won't be able to attend because he is going to Washington on Thursday and won't be returning until either Tuesday or Wednesday evening,' she informed Adam.

'Oh, I see. So just us then? And how was lunch with your father?' he asked her.

'Actually, he has been unwell, he had a bit of a health scare and that's why he went off to London to see his own doctor there. Luckily, he's now on the mend, and he…' she stopped herself and quickly pulled back from telling him about the reason for the lunch and the news her father had presented her with, concerning her grandfather's bequest.

'And? Go on, he what?' Adam asked, waiting for her to finish the sentence she had started.

'Oh, nothing, just that he's happy to be back and said he needs to take a bit more care himself. I left him in his club to take a quiet nap, you know, he was starting to feel the effects of the overnight flight from London, that's all.' Francine told Adam without going into any details of his health, dismayed by the fact that her husband didn't even bother to ask her what had been wrong with him and whether was he fully over it.

It was quickly revealed to her that she had no desire to impart to Adam any of the conversations she had had with her father during their lunch. Somehow, she instinctively knew not to divulge any of the details to him. It was strangely unsettling to treat her husband in this way, but she trusted her instincts.

# CHAPTER 31

*'We are such stuff as dreams are made on'*
– **William Shakespeare**

It was nightfall, and the flames from the fire gave a dusky appearance to the cold, stone-floored room, while the heavy maroon velvet drapes had been pulled together to help keep out the worst of the winter. She could see pottery dishes filled with food placed on the long wooden table, then noticed the beautiful chairs in the dimness of the candle-lit room where, to her trepidation, she saw someone, almost motionless in dark clothing, just sitting quietly, so so quietly, she knew then that they had been watching her wander around the room, suddenly a hand indicated for her to come closer, then a soothing, but a commanding voice said to her.

'Come, sit down next to me, you seem troubled?' The young woman who spoke seemed so familiar to Francine, but she couldn't quite place her, Francine's confusion provoked her to ask the seated woman.

'Who are you, do I know you?' The seated woman insisted she takes a closer look.

'Now, do you recognize me?' With a sharp intake of breath, she suddenly knew. It was now all so clear, how could she have failed to recognise those eyes, the dark thick hair and that perplexing smile that revealed the woman to her.

'It's you. Is it you? You're the Mona Lisa!' Francine declared her total astonishment.

'Yes, I am,' she said. Francine was overcome, feeling utterly confounded, even emotional, 'Tell me, am I dreaming?' she asked the Mona Lisa.

'I don't know, do you suppose you are dreaming?' Mona Lisa asked her back.

'What exactly do you want from me?' Suddenly, without any warning, a voice with authority spoke to her – it was him, Leonardo da Vinci himself.

'Francine, look at me, you must do it, because nobody else will,' he commanded of her.

'What is it you want me to do?' she asked.

'Open the letter and read my words, and don't let anyone make you believe any differently; the contents will reveal everything, and above all, don't be afraid, we will protect you.' The words coming from da Vinci were starting to fade into the distance.

'But how, how can you protect me? You are both dead!' she screamed back at them.

'Wake up, Francine, wake up,' Adam said, shaking his wife from her deep sleep

'Who is dead, who are you talking about?' Adam asked his startled wife.

'What? Oh, nobody, nobody is dead, it was only a silly dream,' she told him.

Or maybe it was the beginning of a nightmare? It just seemed all too real. Her exhausted mind was overwrought; she needed more sleep but was too afraid to close her eyes again in case the ghosts of Leonardo and the Mona Lisa paid her another visit.

# CHAPTER 32

## The Birthday Present

The queues at Christie's had exceeded all expectations. Each day, the viewing public would come and stand in front of the rarest of all masterpieces by Leonardo da Vinci and left completely in awe after seeing, 'The Saviour of the World', otherwise known as Salvator Mundi. On the fourth day of the opening to the viewing public, security had been waiting by the entrance for Francine as she arrived at the auction house.

'Dr. Page-Hamilton, could you come with us? We need you to take a look at the CCTV,' one of the team told a surprised Francine.

'Yes, of course,' she followed them upstairs, where they began to show the footage of the past few days.

'There, look, see that guy? Well we have flagged him up as he has been in to see the painting every day. He comes in and stays quite a long time, longer than anyone else. Just might this be an issue of concern? He has to queue for at least an hour each time, and we thought that might be a little unusual, don't you think?' the security team asked her.

'Yes, I agree, it needs checking out, it could be a potential problem' she told the men. Francine was obviously aware that, although they want as many people as possible to get reasonably close to the painting and enjoy the experience, it has been known before that on the rare occasions someone will try and cause damage to the work, maybe in search of instant fame, or because they are mentally unstable, you can never be entirely sure, but she had to agree that it might pose a threat.

'What would you like us to do about this situation?' the security officers asked her.

'Well, we don't want to make a big fuss if it's nothing; leave it to me, I will go down, check it out and speak to him myself,' she replied. Looking concerned, they asked.

'Do you think that's wise?' thinking of her personal safety.

'Yes, I'll be fine, just keep a watch, obviously if anything happens, or I indicate to you to come and intervene, then do so, but let me go and see first,' she reassured them.

Walking towards the young man whom she thought appeared to be probably in his late twenties, looked like most young guys, casually dressed in jeans and polo shirt, with a mass of unruly brown hair, additionally, she couldn't help but notice that he did look a bit down at heel, and thought that a good wholesome meal would not do him any harm. Taking a minute or two to observe him from a few feet away, she quickly realised just how intensely he was scanning the painting; 'Was he taking just a bit too much interest?'

'Hello, I am Francine Page-Hamilton, one of the curators here at Christie's, and I couldn't help but notice that you seem to like the Leonardo da Vinci painting; I see you have been here every day since we opened,' she told the surprised visitor.

'Yes, you're quite right. Is that a problem? I come straight here after I have finished my night shift, and I will continue to come here every day until the sale, because, after that, I will never be able to see it again' His honest reply took her by surprise.

'No, of course, that's not a problem, you are very welcome, especially if you have been working all night, then to stand in line for your turn shows such dedication. Is it the painting you particularly like, or da Vinci himself?' she was now curious as the conversation continued.

'Well, to answer your question, I don't think you can separate the two, can you? But in this particular portrait, it's the softness of light that just emanates from the face of Christ; look, see for yourself, just how his eyes are almost human, they bore right into your soul;

I really think he can see right through you, which is intriguing and scary, don't you think? For me personally, it seems that after just a few seconds of staring at Christ, you actually forget that it's a painting, it's as if he is in the room with you; anyway, I would just love to figure out how da Vinci achieved that effect'. His hypothetical flow of words was not what she was expecting at all. From his description of the painting, her next question was going to be obvious.

'Are you an artist?' but she didn't need to wait for the answer, because she knew it was going to be affirmative.

'Yes, I am, what made you ask me that?' he said.

'I just guessed, tell me, are you represented by any of the galleries?' she quizzed him some more.

'No, no, I'm not,' he now seemed embarrassed, going red in the face.

'I've never approached any, and well, to be honest, I don't really know anyone in the art world, as I'm self-taught. You see, I didn't attend art school, so don't have those types of connections, anyway, it's all a bit out of my league – I have been trying social media, you know Facebook, Instagram, that kind of thing, but it has limited appeal, you can get some attention, but it doesn't lead anywhere; plus you need so much time to dedicate to it, the time I just don't have the luxury of at the moment,' he told her. For no apparent reason, she felt sorry for him; there was an openness and a sincerity about him, which reminded her of the stories her grandfather told her of his time in Paris when he had tried to become an artist, how he witnessed so many of his friends' lives destroyed by drink and drugs, many driven to the brink despair by their passion for art; his stories over the years had made an indelible mark on her memory.

'Would you like to go and have a coffee?' she asked him, she even surprised herself with this. He looked at her somewhat taken aback by the offer.

'Okay, sure, why not? That would be nice,' accepting her invitation.

'Let's go outside, there's a pleasant enough diner just over there,' nodding in the direction of the Breakfast Bar cafe. Ordering their coffees, she asked him if he would like to get something to eat.

'A bagel, pancakes, or perhaps some eggs?'

'No, I'm not hungry, but thank you,' he told her.

'I'm going to have some, so keep me company, you've been working all night, you must be starving, and besides, it's on the company credit card, so don't worry, it comes under reasonable expenses!' she convinced him to help himself to a full breakfast, while she just opted for eggs benedict.

'Well, you have me at a disadvantage, as you know my name.'

'Oh yes, sorry, I'm Hector, Hector August,' he replied.

'Well, Hector August, if that doesn't sound like the name of an artist, I don't know what does!' she said to his amazement. They both laughed.

'Do you have any photos of your work on your mobile I can look at?' she enquired.

'Yeah, sure, of course, here you are,' he said handing her his mobile.

'Wow, these are really good. I mean seriously good!' she had presumed, without any justification, that he would present her with the usual large abstracts to view, but she was wrong, he did not present her with that, 'These are truly wonderful, I really like them, you have managed to paint in a classical style, which I love, but with a completely fresh, new and exciting dimension that makes them amazingly contemporary,' Francine was enormously impressed by his work.

'Do you really think so?' His modesty and lack of confidence in his own work were unjustified.

'I must admit, I am staggered, you're really very talented,' studying them quite intently, she asked him, 'Do you sell any of these paintings?' she asked the question because somehow, she had a strong feeling that he didn't.

'Well, no, not really, I don't know how to sell myself,' he told her. Now, Francine wanted to know just how serious he was about his art, as she asked him.

'Tell me, how often do you get to paint? The reason I'm asking is that if you really want to be taken seriously, you must give it all your time. It takes total dedication if you really want to succeed. You can't play at it. That's the price you have to pay,' she said without wanting to sound harsh.

But she was completely unprepared for his answer.

'Unfortunately, I do not paint as much these days as I would like to. You see, I'm a night porter, I work from midnight until eight in the morning, then I go home to take care of my mother who is very ill, she's got lung cancer and it is in the final stages, then there are the groceries to shop for, and the chores to do around the house, you know that kind of thing, and for the last few days I've been coming to the auction house straight from work before going back home; it's the only bit of time I get to myself these days.' His story was not what she was expecting to hear. Hector went on, 'You see, we no longer have any medical insurance, so all my money goes towards medication for my mother, food, rent and to pay for someone to be at the house during the night while I am working, she can't be left alone, and I'm all she has to help her. Besides, she's my mother, and I want to help her,' his plight was sadly compelling.

Francine now understood the terrible situation he was in.

'You know, Hector, I really like this particular painting and would love to see it, is it for sale?' She didn't want to presume it was.

'Yes, it's definitely for sale,' His spirits were lifted immediately by the prospect of a sale.

'You know, looking at this, for some reason it reminds me of The Battle of San Romano by Paolo Uccello,' Francine commented, he was completely amazed by her comments.

'Goodness, you certainly know your art, because that's exactly what inspired me, most people today wouldn't even know that name,' he was very impressed.

'Look, could I come and see your work?' She was keen to arrange a viewing as soon as possible.

'Sure, what about later on this evening, say around 7.30?' he asked her, and, as they swapped details, she confirmed the time was good for her.

'I have to go now, so I will see you later. Enjoy the rest of your day,' she told him. Thinking now that she had better go and explain to

181

the security team who were probably wondering what had happened to her when she walked off with their potential troublemaker. She couldn't help but laugh to herself at the way the encounter had turned out, which was so different from what she had been expecting. Wary of his motives, suspecting he was going to be a problem; instead, it turned out he was going to solve her quandary about what to buy for her father's seventy-five birthday present.

'How wrong can you be?' she thought.

'God does move in mysterious ways.'

# CHAPTER 33

## Drive-by Viewing

'Can you please wait for me. It may be a while but I will give you a generous tip if you do?' Francine asked the cab driver, who readily agreed as they pulled up outside Hector's home.

The house, like the entire neighbourhood, looked very run down, but although the fence needed repair and the porch light was broken, the fact that someone had recently planted flowers in the many pots of the front garden was reassuring. The door was swiftly opened as soon as she rang the bell.

'Hi, please come in,' Hector welcomed her, obviously glad she had turned up; he was desperate to sell one of his paintings; any money he could get would go a long way to help pay for his mother's numerous needs. Francine walked through the dim shabby hallway, where she noticed an oxygen tank that was obviously his mother's, a blunt reminder of his situation. At the back of the house was a small room that Hector used for his studio, and where he stored his artwork.

'This is the one you particularly wanted to see,' he said, pulling it out from behind the others.

Standing back from the painting to take in its full effect, she was overawed by his ability.

'It's beautiful, this is remarkable, and I have to say, it's so much better than the photos you have on your mobile, which don't do them any justice at all! How did you manage to obtain that almost translucent quality? And that look on their faces; it's unique; you have developed your style, which is the hardest thing to do as an artist; in fact, this type of painting would look fabulous in some of the up-market hotels in Manhattan; you really must get these paintings out there and see.' She was nearly tempted to tell him that her husband had a gallery; and maybe she could introduce them. But Adam had already warned her not to interfere in his work, so she instantly put that idea out of her head.

'What are all those other paintings over there?' indicating towards a corner, 'Can I see those as well?' She had spotted what seemed like a large number of canvases that were stacked against the opposite wall under a cover of some old blankets.

'Oh those, I copied many of the old masters from books, you know to teach myself how to paint,' he explained as he began dragging them all out. Francine's eyes widen.

'You really did all these? What have we got here, a Titian, Picasso, da Vinci, of course, Caravaggio, van Gogh, Klimt, and so many more? Is there any artist you can't imitate? From what I can see every brush stroke is done to perfection, it's astounding, how long did it take you to gain this level of competency, Hector?' she was fascinated.

'I just really wanted to paint like the old masters, and there was no way I could afford art school, besides which, they no longer teach traditional painting styles anyway, so I just went to museums, bought books, and then just studied their techniques until my eyes actually hurt. I think I succeeded because, for some unexplained reason, I really believed I could achieve it – in fact, I had no doubt whatsoever; it was not due to any arrogance, just from sheer perseverance, like it was meant to be, maybe some of the old dead artists felt sorry for me and gave me a helping hand. Funny though, no matter how much I tried I was never able to copy Michelangelo or Degas, it was as if neither of them would cooperate with me, but then again, I never liked the personalities of either of those guys, so maybe that was why.' Hector stated this bashfully.

Her comments about his painting skills were very welcome to

him. 'Thanks so much it's not that often, if ever, that I get that kind of encouragement.'

'I think that's because you're not showing your work off to the right audience; if you did, you would get a different reaction, just like I reacted, and I would very much like to buy this, so can we agree on a price?' she enquired. Seeing him shuffle his feet in awkwardness when she mentioned money, she decided to take the lead and help him.

'I would be willing to go to, say, $5,000, would you accept that?' He looked genuinely stunned. 'How much? Yes, certainly, that would be fantastic, are you sure?' he asked her, he could not believe what she was offering him.

'Hector, lesson number one, don't undersell yourself. This is a great piece of art, it's a big canvas, and think of the number of hours you have spent on it, plus the materials, and don't forget, it is unique, I can assure you, there are many people in the art world getting paid far more money, for doing a whole lot less!' and she was right. Now needing to wrap up the transaction, she asked, 'Before we conclude our business, would you be able to deliver it as it's quite large and I won't be able to take it with me in the cab?'

'No problem, I can borrow my friend's truck, but not until Sunday afternoon, would that be convenient?' he asked. That suited her perfectly, 'Yes, absolutely, that will be great, and I will pay you then? I will inform the doorman to let you come up to the apartment, here's my address, and thank you. I better go now, as I have a cab waiting outside. So, I will see you on Sunday.' Both seemed happy. Francine was delighted with the unique gift she had procured for her father, while Hector was delighted with his first-ever sale.

# CHAPTER 34

## Sunday Afternoon

'What time did you say that guy was coming over with this painting you had gone and splashed out on? How much did you say it was again, $5,000? Do I need to remind you not to talk to him for any longer than is necessary? We must get ready for Konrad's party, and we don't want to be late, do we? It's vital that I make a good impression on him. I really can't understand why you didn't ask me for a painting for your father, if that's what you wanted to buy for him. For god's sake, Francine, I do have a gallery full of them, remember! How does it look if you go shopping elsewhere?' Adam said in his normal sarcastic tone, annoyed with her, but then again, these days he was always annoyed with her over something.

'The thing is, the type of work you have in your gallery, well, they are a bit too modern for my father's tastes, he is just not into contemporary abstract art. Let's face it, he is somewhat old school,' Francine tried to explain tactfully to Adam, who didn't seem to care or try to understand.

'And I hadn't set out to buy a painting for his birthday, it just happened by chance,' she said almost apologetically, tiptoeing around his delicate sense of self.

'Perhaps your father should try and widen the scope of his taste somewhat!' Adam had another unnecessary dig at her.

'Really? Why should he try and change what he prefers, just to suit someone else? He knows what he likes, so I really don't understand what you are saying, because correct if I'm wrong, didn't you say to me only the other day, that you'd just love to get your hands on a Picasso, a Dali, or Warhol, to sell in your gallery? Let's face it, they are not exactly cutting-edge artists of today, are they?' Francine argued back.

'No, but they are blue-chip. Those names are brands, and brands that are now worth billions, as you know only too well, that's why I want them. And look who's talking! You're about to auction off one of the biggest brands on the planet; your idol, the one and only, the precious Leonardo!' Adam continued on in a thoroughly juvenile manner as he delighted in criticising her taste in the classics, 'So this artist you've found, where is he showing? Which galleries are carrying his work, if he is so good, he must be in big demand?' her husband said with disdain. Francine hesitated in her reply, knowing her answer would just provoke his overbearing attitude to continue, 'Well, actually he's not represented anywhere at the moment, he's an unusual guy, unassuming, modest even, not the normal brash full of themselves types, I've even a suspicion that he's a borderline genius, as he can literally replicate any style of painting, right down to the finest brushstroke, and the colours are exact, it's really quite remarkable; in all my years in the art world I have never seen that before, you see the fakes come through all too often, but his level of mastery is very rare.' Adam's unexpected brash outburst of laughter was just about as nasty and sarcastic as he could convey before his words revealed his true sentiment.

'Really? Christ almighty, maybe I should forget about wanting Konrad's investment and just get this genius friend of yours to whip me up a few Picassos, and a couple of Chagalls, which shouldn't be much of a problem for him, if he is that damn good!' Adam's petty spitefulness was blatantly obvious to her and was starting to become a tedious aspect of his personality; it was now coming to the point where she could hardly be bothered to argue back.

'I simply cannot begin to fathom how you can dismiss his work without even seeing it, or even talking to him?' Francine voiced her dismay at his attitude.

'Okay, okay, fair enough, I will look at his work, and if it's suitable and good enough for my gallery, then maybe at some point in the future, I could give him a try. Now, as I've said over and over again, I need big names to pull in the big buyers, my interest in trying to promote mediocre emerging artists started to bore me a long time ago – trying to flog their stuff with very little return, putting up with all their nonsense about not being inspired and such rubbish, most of them can't get out of bed in the morning and produce either the quality or the quantity that I'm looking for; what is more, there are just too many of them, on every street corner, most are totally unoriginal; a day in and day out, I see the same old stuff, they are okay for the young collectors who don't know anything about art, you can talk them into buying it if you give them enough of the banter, but older clients with more class and the money, they know a thing or two and want the real deal.' Adam was perfectly right on this matter. Francine knew exactly how the art market worked, even though her career was in a different sector, she was fully aware of how incredibly hard it was for any artist to make the grade, which meant working very hard and, more importantly, finding your own unique style that becomes recognizable, and much more importantly, saleable. That was a bitter truth and not something she could argue with Adam about.

The intercom went off.

'Good afternoon, I have the gentleman you were expecting here in the foyer, shall I send him up to the apartment?' Seamus asked.

'Yes, please, send him up, thank you, Seamus.' She looked over at Adam standing by the window, and it was obvious that he was still sulking, 'He's on his way, can we stop this arguing? and please, Adam, be nice to Hector, he's got it really hard at the moment, his mother is terminally ill, try and have a bit of understanding for the guy,' she appealed.

'Hello, Hector, nice to see you, please come in,' he hesitated, straight away she could sense he was ill at ease, maybe it was because of the address, she thought

'This is Adam, my husband. Adam this is Hector,' the two men shook hands.

'So, you are Hector? My wife has been advocating your talents to me, so, let's see what we've got here?' indicating to the young artist to remove the bubble wrap from the painting. Adam took several minutes to study the work before giving any response. To Francine's relief her husband began nodding his head in a positive manner, 'Well, it appears that my wife was right, you're really very good, unfortunately at the moment I'm not looking for any new artist to represent in my gallery,' Adam exclaimed to the young man, who was surprised by his statement, as he replied to Adam, 'I didn't even know you had a gallery.' Adam didn't believe him and firmly believed that he was being manipulated by his wife into displaying Hector's work; and he didn't appreciate that, not for a moment.

'Really! Well, well, you do surprise me, so you had no idea?

Sorry, what did you say your name was?

'Hector, Hector August, sir,' he replied firmly. It was more than obvious to him that Francine's husband was being condescending, seeking to make him feel intimidated and awkward, the only reason he didn't just leave was out of respect for Francine, who was giving Adam a look of pure anger that was obvious to Hector, who became aware that he seemed to be caught up in their personal crossfire.

Francine knew what Adam was doing, pulling rank on someone who was down on their luck, facing hardship and emotional challenges, all the time looking down his Upper East Side nose at this polite young man. It was on occasions like this that she wished she could resort to a pettiness that he would understand if only to remind him that it was only with her money that he was living the lifestyle that he now felt was his God-given right. And she bitterly resented the fact that it was just not in her nature to be vindictive, even if he really did deserve it.

Adam began making his way over to the door of the living room, indicating without any tact that it was now time for Hector to leave, 'Well, thanks for delivering the painting, but we are due to go out, so I'm going to have to conclude this meeting but, hey, if I hear of anybody looking for some great work, then I will be sure to pass on your name; do you have any business cards, Hector August?' Adam's remarks were so cutting that Francine had to do everything to contain herself, but she was inwardly furious and totally embarrassed.

'I will show our guest out.' Francine took her new friend's arm, guiding him into their hallway

'I'm so sorry about all that, I want to apologise for my husband's behaviour, I can't think what's got into him, I'm not making excuses, but you see, we really do have to go out tonight, as Adam has to see a potential investor for his business, and I think he is a little nervous about the meeting, and that's probably why his behaviour is, well, what can I say, a bit abrupt.' She felt awful about the disgusting way her husband had behaved and sorry for how it must have made Hector feel; it was completely uncalled for.

'No, that's fine, don't think any more about it,' he said, seeing her discomfort at the way the whole meeting had gone. She knew he must have found it humiliating, but it was Hector who was now showing the kind of manners she knew Adam was more than capable of displaying, but only when people of wealth and influence were around. Hector had neither of these desired attributes.

'What? What the hell was that all about? Why on earth did you treat him like that with absolutely no respect? I just don't understand your attitude, it was all just so unnecessary, and really quite vulgar, I just can't believe what I just witnessed,' Francine, was now livid.

'You're taking it all a bit too seriously, aren't you? Look, he has to understand the art world, it won't do him any good if he believes, or is under any illusion, that he can just show a few photos, do a bit of Instagram and Facebook, and that then qualifies him to waltz through the door of any prestigious gallery, and they'll accept his work on the spot, because, honey, it ain't gonna happen, and the sooner he realizes that fact, the better!' Adam's calculating words did nothing to restore her mood; on the contrary, they made her feel even more offended.

'Maybe, you should think twice before judging so quickly; after all, somebody once gave you a break on Wall Street, didn't they?' She threw back at him in an offhand way.

'Yes, very true, they did, but then, I just guess I had the talent that somebody was sensible enough to recognize.' Adam's smugness displayed his obvious pleasure in confirming his own special abilities. She was about to quote the adage, "self-praise was no recommendation," but, she could see that the remark would have been entirely lost on him.

Francine was feeling totally drained by the tense atmosphere.

'I'm going to take a long soak in the bath before getting ready to go to Konrad's,' she told her husband, marching out of the room, not waiting for or wanting to hear any response. Looking through her wardrobe as the bathtub was running, she decided to wear a figure-hugging, emerald-green velvet dress that she had bought from Bloomingdales purposely to match the diamond and emerald drop earrings that she had inherited from her grandmother, Amy. The dress had no sleeves, but fortunately, her arms were still tanned from the summer. Picking out some black suede, sling-back high heels, she could see that her shoulder-length dark chestnut hair needed to be worn up, hoping it would give her the look of a young Audrey Hepburn in Breakfast at Tiffany's. Laying the dress out on the bed she was confident she had made a good choice. Now her bath was ready, she wanted to escape for half an hour, adding a few drops of lavender essential oil she hoped it would balance her chakra, or whatever it was that needed balancing. The hot steaming water had helped to soothe her until she walked back into her bedroom. There, laying on the bed was not the dress she had put out, but an entirely different one. She was confused; had she just imagined she had put out an emerald-green dress or not? At that moment Adam walked into the bedroom, and seeing her bewildered expression, stated without any apology that he had changed the green velvet dress for a black dress; utterly devoid of sensitivity, he told her, 'I prefer that one; you do want to look good, don't you? Personally, I think that the green one is a bit dated, that fashion has long since passed! Sometimes, Francine, I really don't think you always make the best of yourself.' His smile was callous.

All she heard from Adam was the word 'I' – it was just about him and what he wanted.

'Who is this man I'm married to? I really don't know him at all, do I? Francine was beginning to see only too clearly that her husband really was a wolf in sheep's clothing. She recalled to mind one of her friends at university, Bella, who always told her to be wary of men who were just a little bit too charming; they were the ones not to be trusted; stay well clear of them, at all costs. How true her words had turned out to be if only Bella had been around when she had first met Adam to remind her of that cautionary observation. It seemed the idea of the handsome, charming, and dynamic art dealer, Adam Faris, was far more appealing, than what was the reality of the man. She had been well and truly taken in by him. However, her personal antenna was now on high alert, needing to be vigilant, but this time no amount of his pizzazz and fake charisma would blind her to the true facts. Her father had told her to wait, and it had been the first time she could ever remember that she had not taken heed of the advice from his wealth of wisdom, and now this was the result. The honeymoon period, if ever there was one, was well and truly over. Walking up and down their hallway in his new Tom Ford grey suit and white shirt, looking for the umpteenth time at his Tag Heuer Vintage watch, a wedding present from Francine, Adam had become more and more disconcerted by his wife, knowing full well that they should have arrived at the party at least thirty minutes ago. Finally, Francine emerged from their bedroom, she could see his turbulent mood and impatience had been pushed to the limit, which was not only due to her being late, but, that she had dared to disobey him by not wearing the outfit that he had personally chosen from her wardrobe, and instead was wearing the green velvet number that he thought was not only unstylish but downright dowdy. He realised that it was too late to pick a fight, that would have to wait for later; now they had to leave.

'Tell me, have you made us late on purpose? Are you trying to deliberately sabotage my possible investment with Konrad? I mean, how long does it really take to put on a frock and slap on a bit of makeup? Why the hell does it require almost the entire evening for you just to make an appearance?' He snarled, almost shouting at her as he quickened his pace down the corridor towards the elevator, telling her to hurry up, 'God, what is he going to think of me now, being this late? We only live a few floors down and it would appear to him that I can't even be bothered to show him the respect of being punctual, everyone else will have arrived for the champagne reception, everyone that is, except us!' She didn't bother to respond to these abrasive words, but something did strike her quite profoundly. She was becoming aware of a growing rebellious streak that was starting to subconsciously rear itself, and, furthermore, she was enjoying it; this was a side to her nature that he had not yet seen.

'So, what's their penthouse like?' he asked her as they waited for Gray's private elevator to whisk them up directly into their apartment. Adam, it appeared was now anxious to quickly shake off his bad mood before they got to the Gray's home, knowing full well that they needed to show a united front, as he began trying to placate her, if only for that evening. Adam Faris could not take any chances and certainly did not want Konrad Gray to detect any hostility between him and his wife, as he knew just how much the Grays liked and respected Sir Howard and Francine, aware that he would not even be in the ring with such a man if it were not for his fortuitous marriage.

'Actually, I really don't know what it's like, I've never been inside,' she told a very surprised Adam.

'Really, I didn't realise that? I automatically assumed you had been there many times, as I've heard your father talking about Konrad's dinner parties, so I just presumed you went along too?' he remarked.

'Yes, my father has over the years been invited up to Gray's many times, but they were all an older group of people, and from what he told me, they talked mainly of politics and investments, I remember once when I was curious about their home, I did ask him that same question, you know, what's it like? Is it very grand? But he just laughed, telling me it was big, dark, and a bit like a museum. Anyway, I guess we will see for ourselves in a few moments.' she stated, as a matter of fact upon their arrival.

# CHAPTER 35

## Home of Horrors

**B**oth Francine and Adam's jaws simultaneously dropped as they stepped from the elevator into the home of Konrad and Millicent Gray. You just don't realise how big twenty thousand square feet are until you stand inside such a voluminous space, and, it was just for the two of them, plus a small retinue of live-in staff, who were neatly tucked away out of sight. But once Francine's eyes had adjusted to the size, she immediately understood what her father meant when he said it was like living in a museum, except to her it seemed less of a museum and more like a house of horrors.

Even though it was large, it seemed oppressive, and unnaturally dark. Standing in the oak-panelled hallway that was almost the size of a small ballroom, she noticed immediately that it contained no windows to draw her sights to the outside world and the New York skyline, instead your vision was instantly directed towards the centrally placed wide Gothic-style staircase of carved oak that had been polished to a high sheen while adorning those stairs was a stunning royal blue carpet that made you feel you could be climbing up to heaven; maybe that was because the ceiling at the very top had been painted to represent a heavenly sky, where dainty cherubs sat poised on fluffy white clouds, it certainly made an unforgettable psychological impression on the mind. She could see a seemingly hidden world beckoned at the top of those stairs, which branched out onto a wide circular walkway going around the entire top of the apartment. It could be described as a very grand mezzanine that showed off numerous display cabinets, illuminated from the inside.

'Wow', she thought, 'now that really does look interesting, I wonder just what he's got up there?' hoping she might find a way to discover for herself. The dominant sight of metal amour standing to attention along the hallway walls, almost as if the men were still inside, looked fierce and imposing, and at a guess, was probably dated to around the 14th century; because it was obvious that these were no cheap replicas, each having a very distinctive presence about them that was truly compelling. All at once, her heightened sense of imagination kicked into gear as she felt like she was standing among the ghosts of the Knights Templar, who had probably worn these iron cages on the Crusades to the Holy Land, and seen, well, you can only imagine, the blood, the torture, and the sheer terror, that prevailed in the Middle Ages.

The scent coming from the beautiful black and gold flickering candles that were placed on the many small antique tables around the hallway, provoked something in her memory, she recognized the aroma immediately, but couldn't quite put her finger on it; the fragrance instantly transported her yet again to another place so profoundly that she lost herself momentarily before the presence of Konrad made his dark appearance.

'Francine, how splendid to see you,' taking her hand to kiss the back of it, just like they did in the old movies.

'You seem to be far away within your thoughts,' he said.

'Hello, Konrad, yes, you're quite perceptive, I was. I think it's due to the scent of the candles, they are so distinctive, and for some reason, I am reminded of Rome. No, wait, actually it's the Vatican, am I correct?' she wanted to know about this mysterious fragrance he was burning. He was flattered that his candles had made such an impression, as he told her.

'I'm so glad you like them actually, they are hand-poured for me in London by an artisan who ships them over to me; sorry, Francine, but they are unavailable here in New York. Amusingly enough, the brand is called FORGERY X! This one is Fumus Sanctus or Holy Smoke! I

195

believe the story goes that the original candle essence of frankincense and myrrh was created in 1512 for the Holy Roman Pope Julius II to proclaim the completion of the Sistine Chapel,' he told her.

'How wonderful to think it goes back that far, amazing, they certainly create a beautiful atmosphere,' she exclaimed.

Millicent Gray rushed over to kiss Francine on her cheeks, 'Francine, Adam, it's so wonderful you're here, thank you for coming to our little party, I'm just so sorry your father is not here with us this evening, we so miss him, he is an amazingly good company, so cultured and intelligent, and as for that fabulous British accent, well my dear, I don't mind confessing to you that I could listen to it all evening, even if I never understand that naughty English humour of his! Now, let me look at you – gorgeous, so beautiful, I simply love the dress, that emerald green is truly inspiring, you know, I think that's the one I saw at the Dior fashion show when I was in Paris or was it somewhere else? Anyhow, it's just so now, and with those fabulous earrings, darling, it's just utterly stunning on you!' Francine was gloating inside from Millicent's comments, 'Adam, you really are a lucky man to have such a remarkable wife,' Millicent spouted off in Adam's direction with her rapid-fired speech, a habit typical of many New Yorkers, before her mind moved on as quick as a flash, turning the attention back on herself, 'I wonder if that colour would suit me? What do you think, Konrad? Do you like Francine's dress? Do you think I have the right hair colour to suit green?' turning to her husband for his opinion, who nodded in agreement with his wife; his view was purely academic to her, except he knew it was better to agree with whatever his wife thought about fashion, but it wasn't hard to see from the expression on Konrad's face that he really had not the slightest interest in dresses. This was not lost on Francine who couldn't resist giving her husband a sideways glance of glee knowing her choice of the dress had been the right one all along.

Francine congratulated her, 'You must be thrilled about your appointment to the board of the MOMA, well done, that is excellent news,' she told the society hostess, who looked as pleased with herself as a dog with a juicy bone. The sixty-two-year-old was enjoying her moment in the spotlight, and more than willing to soak up as much praise as she could get. Millicent Gray was the perfect example of Upper East Side wealth. Her shoulder-length dyed honey blonde hair was styled into the perfect super rich look that framed an over-made-up face, evidently treated by regular trips to the dermatologists for the customary Botox, fillers, and the obvious one too many face lifts, which could be considered a warning to anyone else who might have desired such procedures. Her look was completed by the abundant flashiness of some brashly large diamonds that made her literally sparkle like a Christmas tree. Millicent's thinness was reminiscent of hunger in the Third World and would be worrying, if it were not deliberate, allowing her to fit perfectly into every new designer outfit that Paris and Fifth Avenue had to offer each season, no matter how ridiculous the style.

'Come on,' she said, taking Francine and Adam by each elbow, 'Let's go into the drawing room and join the other guests as my darling husband wants to make a speech, and we're running behind schedule as you two naughty children were the last to arrive,' Millicent subtly scolded them. They dutifully obeyed their hostess.

Konrad tapped loudly onto his crystal champagne glass with a knife from the table, which immediately gained the attention of their exceedingly wealthy, and a well-connected array of guests; anyone who was anyone was in attendance, paying their due diligence, as the rich always do to each other.

'I would like to thank you all for coming to our little soiree this evening to congratulate my wife Millicent, who I know will bring energy and vision to her new position on the board of the Museum of Modern Art, and make lots of money from her unsurpassed fund-raising skills, which I'm sure will be very welcome! Also, our dear friend and neighbour Francine, or should I say Dr Francine Page-Hamilton, who has joined us here tonight, and I might add will be gracing the cover of Time Magazine this month with the article suitably called, The Woman Who Knows inside the Mind of Leonardo; I would like to include her in our celebrations, so please raise your glass to these two exceptional women. To Millicent and

197

Francine! The crowded room of guests acted in accordance.

'To Millicent and Francine,' they said in harmony. Millicent Gray positively revelled in the admiration, while Francine felt highly embarrassed and amused by all the fuss and attention.

'Francine, now that my speech is over, I would like you to come and meet my brother,' Konrad proclaimed.

'Oh, I didn't realise you had a brother, yes, of course, I'd love to meet him,' she was more than a little curious.

'Edmund, let me introduce you to Dr Page-Hamilton, I believe I've told you about the daughter of our friend, Sir Howard, she's a very clever young lady, do you know she holds the eminent position as head curator of fine arts at Christie's no less, and is in charge of the sale of the Salvator Mundi,' Konrad told his brother who was standing by the fireplace with a drink in his hand. For a few moments, she felt mute, unable to speak from the shock of seeing Konrad's brother.

'I've heard so much about you, it's great to finally put a face to the name,' Edmund said to a silenced Francine, as he took her hand to kiss the back of it. She didn't resist, but her feeling was that it seemed spooky, the way they both did exactly the same thing, kissing the hand like that, and she couldn't fail to notice at the same time that both brothers were wearing identical rings, that consisted of a large black stone with red rubies on either side, firmly attached to their small finger, 'Umm, maybe they are family heirlooms,' she mused. It was a strange experience, watching them as they worked in perfect union like they were just one person who had been divided into two halves.

'Hello, pleased to meet you too,' suddenly finding her voice, the brothers laughed at her reaction, 'It always happens, and it never fails to amuse us.' Edmund said to her. Konrad and Edmund were identical twins, and she really could not tell them apart, their likeness was uncanny, and aside from the different styles of clothes, they wore, every detail of their flesh seemed to correspond with each other, even down to their perfectly matched topiaries manicured black eyebrows. Seeing both standings in front of the mirror above the fireplace, she was almost too afraid to look, wondering if they possessed an image to reflect, before telling herself to stop being so absurd.

'Do you also live in New York? 'She asked Edmund.

'No, I live in LA, Beverly Hills to be exact, I'm a film producer and that's where the work is,' he explained.

'Gosh, that sounds very exciting, after all, who's not intrigued by the magic of the movie industry?' she said, clearly fascinated.

'Trust me, there is no magic, and it's nowhere nearly as interesting as you may think, well at least not for me; you see, I just put up the money for a film, then sit back and wait for the results, and sometimes I make an absolute fortune. When I am not doing that, mainly because I'm waiting for the right project to come my way, I play match-maker.' She looked at him puzzled. Edmund smiled, 'I introduce my Hollywood and Palm Beach friends to Konrad, as most of them like to invest in good quality art, so who better than my brother to advise them? The rich and famous get a bit paranoid about whom to trust, only liking people who come recommended, so it suits me perfectly, acting as an art broker. I'm not artistic in any sense, my background is in economics, I was an investment banker on Wall Street, way back in the day, but decided a long time ago to divert my skills into something else, and went to California, and through contacts began to invest in movies. Then, five years ago, one of the films I was producing won an Oscar for the best film!' Edmund boasted.

'How fantastic, which film was it?' she asked, wondering if she had watched it?

'When Memories Don't Walk Back,' he replied.

'I remember that film, all about surviving a war, it well deserved to win,' she flattered him; in truth, she had never seen it, but fortunately knew what it was about. He took her compliment in his stride as he was so used to the attention that came with the territory of being in the movie industry, everyone sucked up to you, whether you were the actual movie star or not.

'Now, my brother Konrad, well he really does have an eye for fine works of art and antiquities. Have you seen his collection?' Edmund asked her.

'Yes, I can see the amazing collection of paintings on the walls, it looks quite incredible. Max Ernst, Franz Marc, Otto Dix, all very beautiful, simply stunning, and he's so lucky to have those rare and stunning Albrecht Dürer drawings, incredible, and all German artists?' she observed.

'Yes, of course! You see, our mother was German, born in Berlin, and naturally we both have a very strong affinity with our Germanic roots; in fact, we both feel more German than American, if truth be told! See that painting over there of a castle. That our family home in Bavaria, it dates back to the 16th century. Our mother came to America in November 1938 as a very young woman, not that long before the war in Europe broke out. Our father was an American physician doing research in Berlin when they met, and shortly after they were married, he wanted to return to work in New York, so they came back. Our mother never felt at home in New York, always missing Germany and her family over there, and then the war meant there was absolutely no opportunity to go back and see them. At the time she was lonely and friendless, my father was always working to build up his medical practice, and because she was German, he desired to keep her out of sight, he didn't want his patients to discover her nationality, but then she found her purpose when we were born in 1949 and things became a lot easier for both of them as his practice thrived and he made a lot of money. Finally, when the time was right, she took us back to Germany to meet our extended family and visit the castle, our ancestral home that we had heard so many stories about. We were intrigued and enchanted. Always staying for the long summer school vacations. From the very moment, Konrad and I arrived at the castle we both knew we were home. It felt like we belonged. So now we divide our time between the castle and our other family home which is in Argentina.' Edmund told her as he revealed some of their family histories.

'How absolutely fascinating, I had no idea,' she was completely mesmerized by his story, while feeling somewhat freaked out by the fact that, while she often laughed to herself about how Konrad had always reminded her of Count Dracula, the knowledge that he really did have a family castle was just too much. Thinking to herself that if she told someone all this, they simply wouldn't believe her; it was just too bizarre for words. It seemed that fact and fiction had merged into dark matter, a dangerous substance that would swallow you whole without warning because you didn't know it was there.

'Konrad, take Francine upstairs to your gallery and show her your treasures, while I go and talk to her husband, Adam. I want to know all about his gallery,' Edmund insisted to his brother.

'Would you like to take a look?' Konrad asked her. It was the invitation she had been hoping for but never expected, now she couldn't wait to get up there and see exactly what he had in that mysterious space that looked so promising.

'Yes please,' almost leading the way herself in eager anticipation. The ascent up the grand staircase felt exciting with just a hint of danger. And she was not going to be disappointed.

'Take your time, look around, if you want to know anything, just ask,' Konrad insisted. She didn't know quite where to begin; there was just so much. Again, there were no windows to the outside world, this inner temple he had created was all set against a backdrop of crimson silk wallpaper, giving a sense of celestial intensity, almost like you were enclosed in a parallel universe that was devoid of any relationship to real life, but then again, perhaps these artefacts demanded that kind of attention. It certainly captured the imagination. The first thing that caught her eye was an Egyptian Wooden Mummy from 1500 B.C. Then the Egyptian Bronzes of Isis and Horus; she remembered the auction sale for those particular lots, which had taken place at Christie's in London, but didn't know it was Konrad who had purchased them. An extensive collection of several first edition books were on display and included one by William Shakespeare, plus a rare copy of the first Bible printed in English in 1537. A large wooden box that contained possibly hundreds of ancient Roman Imperial coins, all in silver and almost perfect condition, each one fearlessly stamped with the heads of past Caesars, the regal, the glorious, and the bad. This treasure trove was a dream come true. Shifting from one display cabinet to the next she was overjoyed to see such rare items. Her eyes fell onto the white, stark, foreboding unemotional faces of Mary Queen of Scots, Napoleon, and of Horatio Nelson.

'Are they original?' she enquired, wondering if she was staring straight into the death masks of these historical figures.

'Alas no, I did manage to find these first-rate copies, having tried in vain to get the actual ones, but they seem to have eluded me, and my very generous offers to buy them were rejected, I was told in no uncertain terms they were not for sale at any price. They are the only things in my collection that are not original – I utterly detest the idea of one of my pieces being a fake, therefore, I always ensure I only obtain the real thing!' Konrad had a strong distaste that anything he owned should not be wholly authentic, which she could quite understand.

'Yes, I imagine you do, but I must admit I'm really quite fascinated by the Admiral Horatio Nelson mask, just thinking of him has brought back fond memories of my childhood in Greenwich, London. It's where my grandfather Max was born, my father was born, and I was born; it's where Lord Nelson spent much of his time when not at sea, and then of course our family name, Hamilton. You see, we are related to Sir William Hamilton, who was the husband to Lady Emma Hamilton, the long-time mistress of Lord Nelson. Have you ever been to Greenwich Konrad?' she asked him.

'Yes, I have, a delightful little place full of royal naval history. I only spent a few hours there; I may visit again one day. But that's a real surprise, regarding your family history. I had no idea, your father has never mentioned that to me, how marvellous. I wish I'd had the opportunity to have met your grandfather. His reputation and expertise on Italian Art were renowned. He was well-liked and respected within the profession, and from what I understand he built up quite a fortune; I have heard he left you quite a wealthy young woman, you were lucky to have had such a splendid grandfather.' She appreciated his kind words, and of course, knew Adam must have told him of her inheritance.

Turning to examine another intriguing object on display, to which Francine wildly responded, 'Wow, that's incredible,' she stared, 'That is just…well I must confess, I'm more than a little impressed,' she gushed with relish, 'But how…?' 'How did I get it? If you know the right people, as I do, well, it's not that hard; also, its provenance is impeccable. So, you like it?' His face beamed with pride.

'Well, if there was one thing I could take home with me, it would be that! Just imagine the actual palette that belonged to Rembrandt, and was still ingrained with the limited colours he used so well. Words fail me; it must be incredibly valuable. I presume the Rembrandt Museum would bite your hand off to obtain it!' She told her host, who said she wasn't far wrong on that score. Wandering around further, she spotted a very curious-looking ring, she read the description which left nothing to the imagination, boldly stating it was a Death's Head Ring, a silver band engraved with Heinrich Himmler's signature, a ring that was only ever given to the most senior Nazi officers, it carried a skull, the swastika, and the Sig Rune, the instantly recognizable SS symbol. The black and white photograph strategically placed was the bait that made her do a double take; it was the face of none other than the monstrous Adolf Hitler, and there placed next to his image was an elaborate Walther pistol that he had once owned, gleaming under the light, knowing that his fingerprints were most likely still on it made her feel physically ill. Never could she have imagined Konrad's collection was going to contain such lurid items, little wonder it's kept well away from most people. The next to be exhibited were several personal belongings of another infamous Nazi.

These items included a cigar box with the inscription 'Custom made for the Marshall of the Realm, Hermann Göring,' the silver-framed photo of Hitler with Göring together at Carinhall and personally signed by the Führer; a stark reminder of the two monsters of World War II, as was the glass cabinet that resembled a coffin that encased one of the uniforms that Hermann Göring had actually worn; it was as if his body was still breathing inside the pale blue outfit; she wondered if he might have even been wearing it when giving orders to murder people. Francine shivered, recoiling from the thoughts she was having. Hastily redirecting her mind from the man, whom until a few days ago she had no real knowledge of, now it seemed as if he was everywhere she turned. For some inexplicable reason the infamous Göring was becoming a real presence in her life, and one she had no control over, it was as if recent events had taken on a life of their own. All this time she was aware that Konrad was monitoring her, his dark unblinking eyes took pleasure in her obvious aversion at some of the disturbing items on display; her reaction was all he could have wished for, as he vicariously enjoyed her response.

'Something tells me you know precisely what I'm going to ask you?' she said pointedly to him. He grinned, 'Of course, it's predictable, people are predictable, you are thinking, aren't some of these objects controversial? And in very bad taste? Well, yes, you could possibly say that, but let me pose this theory; you need to see it in context. Whether we like it or not, all this is now our accrued history; and the past is dark, very dark, and much messier than most people will ever understand. Real history is not for those of a sensitive disposition! Unfortunately, I'm afraid my brother's industry, Hollywood that is, has done so much injustice to the past, they have romanticised, even glamorised what really occurred in those dim and distant times,' he stated in half amusement.

'My dear, you must separate the issues, I am just the custodian of such relics remember, they are not my crimes, I have no ownership of that labyrinth of ugliness from those terrible days, but I do love the secrets they yield; after all, we all have secrets, don't we, Francine? These objects will, and must be allowed to reveal the deception, lies, and riddles they contain within; their stories have to live on, whether people find them distasteful or not, we don't get to choose our history, we can only make our own, and one day, I hope I will contribute to that myself!' he concluded, as if it were a prophecy. Francine wondered why he had stated so pointedly that everyone has secrets. Surely that was a coincidence, and he was just making an off-the-cuff remark? 'Besides, all these items need to be preserved for future generations. Look, Francine, there are many unsavoury pieces in museums, items that were used for torture in the Spanish Inquisition for example, not to mention the people who visit places like Auschwitz; why do they go when they know perfectly well what happened there? They go because of morbid curiosity; it's the human condition. It's only the distance of time, that is the disparity between them, nothing else.' Konrad enlightened her. Francine nodded her head in a sort of agreement, knowing that everything he said was true. Although seeing these historical items in a museum seemed more legitimate, seeing them in someone's home felt different, although it really wasn't.

'So, tell me, Konrad, is that why you collect them – for those future generations?' she asked him directly.

'No, absolutely not, not at all,' is the honest answer. I buy them because I covet them, they fascinate me like nothing else. I believe they carry the energies of those who owned them, don't you?' he asked her. Again, she had to agree with his statement.

'Yes, I think that there is probably a lot of truth in that sentiment, so I cannot question your motives for wanting them,' she concurred, knowing full well that all historians found their mystic quite compelling.

As she continued her tour around his abundant possessions, she spotted on the wall and placed under slightly tinted glass, two pages of drawings by Leonardo da Vinci 'Good grief, you even have those, I thought it was impossible to acquire his sketches, outside of the Vatican or the British Royal family? How did you manage to get hold of them?' she asked with genuine curiosity.

'Francine, you of all people should know that everything, and especially people, are for sale if the price is right. The art world is a law unto itself, you know that; it's still the most unregulated, secretive, and deceptive business there is, apart from illegal drugs and illegal arms, which just shows you where our profession is pitched, for all its glamour, it has two sides to it, and let's be honest, there's just too much money at stake. Last year the global art market was estimated at over $250 billion, and that was the legal side alone, goodness knows how much went under the table, and when there's that much money around, then, my dear, people are very willing to turn a blind eye to anything, just as long as they are doing nicely out of it themselves. Come on, Francine, be honest, even the auction rooms are required to clean up their mess every so often!' He wasn't wrong.

'Yes,' she said, 'it's sadly all too true, the art market is more corrupt than I care to acknowledge, it's not something I like or want to be part of.' Francine knew that the auction houses had been guilty of many illegal acts over the years; it seemed as if he had an answer for everything. Konrad was enjoying himself, knowing he had forced a bona fide and honest historian to concede to his every point of view.

Scanning the rest of his menagerie, she could see at the far end a large area that stood alone, isolated, and sectioned off naturally, she wanted to know what it was and why it needed to be separate from the rest of the collection. It appeared to be on what looked like an altar. There was no harm in asking, she decided, 'Konrad, may I see what you have down that part of the room, standing by itself?' He stood and contemplated for several moments before he stated that she could, however, it came with the proviso that afterward, they could talk about the impending sale of the da Vinci painting at Christie's.

'Well, yes okay, that's fine, but I'm not sure what I can tell you that's not already in the public domain?' she replied, agreeing to his request.

'Good, then I will take you to see it,' he said as he guided her toward the segregated area; Konrad confessed to her that it was almost his most prized possession of the entire collection, and rarely if ever did he allow anyone near it, let alone cast their eyes onto it; he did not want the energy from anyone else to contaminate it. It was for his eyes only, and something he paid homage to every day.

In a hermetically sealed large glass dome, placed on a stone altar, dimly lit from above and surrounded by candle-light, were the lost pages from a Medieval illuminated manuscript, created in the middle ages at the Benedictine Monastery of Podlazice in Bohemia. Francine studied the pages, which, although beautiful, were written in Latin, leaving her confounded by the obsolete language.

'I can see these pages are magnificent, the decorated soft sheen of the gold leaf is incredible,' her voice trailed off.

'And now you are wondering, what do the words mean? and why are they so special to me?' Konrad casually smiled, but then his face morphed into an almost trance-like appearance as if he was in another world; 'Well, Francine, I will tell you why... You see, these pages come from a book, a very special book, that is as rare as anything that you can dream of, or even believe in your deepest imagination. The book is called Codex Gigas,' he informed her.

She looked even more perplexed.

'What is the Codex Gigas? I have never heard of it,' she said in all innocence, never expecting the reply she was going to hear.

'My dear, quite simply, it is THE DEVIL'S BIBLE...

'The words written here were whispered into the ears of a monk by Lucifer himself, revealing the secrets of the hidden kingdom. His Kingdom. And one day, I pledge, I will find the rest of the Bible, it means more to me than almost anything.'

'But Konrad,' Francine retorted, now scolding him in the manner of an old schoolmistress, sounding older than her years.

'You can't possibly believe in the Devil; do you?'

Towering over her, looking deeply into her eyes, an uncomfortable feeling gripped her, as he said.

'But of course. Don't you, Francine? I think only a fool would not believe in him...'

# CHAPTER 36

## 'Make them an offer they can't refuse'
## – Don Corleone

Konrad's study should not have come as any surprise after seeing some of the most distressing items in existence in his upstairs chambers. The room was enigmatic and just as cryptic as its owner. Completely circular, it was graced by twelve floor to ceiling Roman style columns; his desk sat in the middle of the room, surrounded by signs and symbols that meant nothing to her; the austere feeling was overpowering and oddly cold, considering how the room was warmed by central heating.

'Please, sit down here,' Konrad gestured to a Victorian velvet armchair. Francine sat where she was told to.

'The auction. I want –no, I must – purchase the Leonardo and I want to know, who is in the running? I am an extremely wealthy man, and my pockets are very deep, but I want to know who I'm up against? The Chinese? The Russians? Or the Arabs? I have given it a lot of thought, and my conclusions are that the Chinese and the Russian are now spending vast sums of money trying to buy back works of art belonging to their own past glories. And the Arabs? Well, would the Salvator Mundi really be of any significance to them? 'The Saviour of the World,' is, after all, a Christian religious painting, why would they want it? So, I don't think they could be interested, do you? Although I cannot rule out the possibility that this represents the ultimate prize for any of them, so I need to know how serious any of them might actually be. As for any of the institutions, well, let's face it, most museums are broke, so I believe I'm in the best position and feel extremely confident that I can get the painting. When that happens, I am prepared to donate the masterpiece and allow it to be on permanent loan to the Frick Museum; which, as you can imagine, would be immensely prestigious for our great city. It would then generate huge financial rewards from tourism, and if it were to go on loan to other museums around the world, it would raise vast amounts of money to fund our arts programme for children.' Konrad gave his convincing pitch to Francine.

'Ah, now I see! Finally the penny has dropped.' It all made perfect sense to her. 'So that's why he's taken such an interest in Adam and his gallery, and the sudden invitation to their home to supposedly celebrate Millicent's appointment!' she thought.

'Konrad, as you must realise, it's impossible for me to reveal any of the names, or organisations, of any potential bidder; that would be highly inappropriate. As you know only too well, client confidentiality is paramount in any transactions within the auction house,' she said giving him a gentle ticking off.

'Nevertheless, I will say this, you could be wrong in your assumptions. I don't think I would be breaking any of the rules if I told you that you can expect all the usual runners and riders on the day if that helps?' Not the words he wanted to hear, as it became apparent that he would now be up against the deepest pockets on the planet. This information displeased him immensely.

Not one to give up so easily, Konrad made a proposal, 'Look, I am a practical man, and I understand from what you have just told me that this artwork is going to generate fierce bidding; but, as you know, these things are totally unpredictable! And correct me if I'm wrong, but I understand there is to be no reserve price. Well, that's quite a gamble for the seller. So, I am prepared to make a pre-sale offer. If they would consider it, maybe there's a deal to be done. Therefore, I want to instruct you to make the owners a verbal offer on my behalf.

If they are interested, I can arrange with my lawyers to make the offer in writing.'

'Yes, I can do that, what is the offer you want me to give them?' she asked him. He took a pause.

'Well, after careful consideration, I am prepared to go to the absolute maximum, which is $275 million and that is my one and final offer, which I believe is not an insubstantial amount, I think you would agree? Plus, of course, Christie's fees.' Konrad knew it was a serious amount of money.

'Yes, that certainly is an eye-watering amount of money. How the client will react, I cannot possibly say. But I can assure you that first thing tomorrow morning I will act upon your instructions. Just email me this, I need it in writing that you have instructed the auction house to act on your behalf, and as soon as I get a response from them, I will let you know at once,' she assured him.

'Good, I need you to do your very best. Make them an offer they can't refuse!' Francine laughed, 'Konrad, you sound like the Mafia!' 'Do I? Come on, I think we should go and find that husband of yours.' Konrad opened the door for them to go, but before he could leave the room, she turned to him, 'Can I just ask you a question?'

'What, concerning the sale?' he asked.

'No, not about the Salvator Mundi painting. It was something you mentioned upstairs when you said that your Codex Gigas, the Devil's Bible, was 'almost' your most prized possession, I must confess that after seeing all your unusual and very rare items, it made me think, what on earth could you own that trumps all of those?'

'So, now you want to know what it is? Well, yes, there is something, and, if you knew what it was, I believe it would make your hair stand on end, and besides, if I did tell you, I would have to kill you, so pray that I never do!' he said with a completely dead-pan face. At that precise moment an awkwardness arose between them.

'Was he serious, or was it just a bad joke?' Whatever it was, she now regretted having posed the question.

'How did you like my brother's collection of ... er ... what shall I say, objets d'art? Did you find it amusing?' Edmund asked laughing loudly.

'Amusing? Not exactly the word to describe what she had just seen,' she thought, considering some of the contents of his cabinets. Now looking at both Konrad and Edmund together, she could see quite clearly with 20/20 vision, as she acknowledged to herself, they don't come any more 'unusual' than these two gentlemen; maybe it was because they were identical twins that somehow a strangeness existed between them.

'Yes, indeed, Konrad's does own some truly original and unique pieces,' she told Edmund, choosing her words with consideration, not wanting to sound approving or disapproving. She didn't want to give Adam any more ammunition against her if for any reason, Konrad chose not to invest.

'Adam has been telling me about a very talented young artist you have recently discovered. What's his name again?' Edmund asked.

'Hector August,' she replied.

'Ah yes, such a great name! Well, if he fails to make it as an artist, he can always come to Hollywood, and with a name like that, I'm sure he would become a huge overnight success. But seriously, he sounds promising, Konrad, I think you should look at this young man's work. We both know that talent is a rare commodity,' Edmund quipped. Konrad was seemingly very keen, 'Yes, I will. If Francine thinks he's good, then her judgement is enough for me.' Turning to Adam, he said, 'Could you arrange to bring the young man over here, say Monday or Tuesday evening, with some of his work? Francine, do you have his number?'

'Yes, of course, I can call or message him, but I'm sure he will pop into Christie's tomorrow, as he has done that every day since the da Vinci went on the show. So I will speak to him then, and on that note, I will go and say goodnight to Millicent. Thank you Konrad for a very interesting evening. Edmund, it was fascinating to meet you,' she lied.

'Goodnight, Francine, Adam, remember, we shall be seeing you very soon.' For the briefest moment, when Konrad had praised her judgement over Hector's painting skills, she felt flattered, even validated by him, but that feeling was all too quickly dissolved when she saw the 'knowing glance' that had passed between the twin brothers and her husband, a look that told her something was not right. She could see complicity had been forged between them. Somehow that night a bond had formed. She couldn't understand exactly how, but something was going on, and something told her, that it was bad.

# CHAPTER 37

## Hector's Reversal of Fortune

B ack in their apartment Francine was even more baffled by her husband.

'Sometimes, I really find your attitude difficult to fathom,' she stated.

'What are you talking about? Oh, do you mean about Hector?' Adam said in a casual manner as he poured himself a large nightcap, but he knew precisely to what she was referring.

'Yes, of course, I mean Hector, you know exactly what I am referring to. Earlier this afternoon you were very rude and dismissive to him, which had been totally uncalled for; so, yes, you could say I am somewhat bewildered,' intrigued to know exactly why her husband had apparently done a complete U-turn on the young man.

'Relax, calm down, you're getting all worked up over nothing; what can I say? This afternoon, well, I was feeling pretty tense, I mean, I didn't want to blow my chances, and being invited to a party at the home of the biggest art dealer practically in existence is a huge deal, it was a major breakthrough for me. I overreacted, so what? You should just cool it, I admit, I owe the guy an apology, which I'll give him. When I was speaking to Edmund, he started asking me about my gallery because he is aware that Konrad is thinking of investing, so naturally, he wanted to know about the style of work we are currently showing, and, of course, I showed him our website from my mobile. I was extremely disappointed that he seemed somewhat underwhelmed.

He told me that people in Hollywood were tired of the same type of paintings now on show in most galleries, they wanted something different. They don't like being part of the masses, and that made me think about the work that Hector had just delivered that afternoon, and, I have to admit, his work is very different to be fair to him, so I found myself actually endorsing his talents, telling Edmund what you had told me, that he's practically a genius when it comes to a paintbrush, as it appears he can produce any other artist's work to perfection, from old to new masters, all except of course Pollock, but, then again, I don't think even Jackson Pollock could reproduce one of his own paintings!' Adam's explanation was beginning to sound reasonable.

She asked him, 'Did you know that Konrad wants to buy the Salvator Mundi?'

'Yes, he did tell me, he also told me he wants to create the Konrad Gray Art Foundation, here in New York. He explained it all to me over lunch the other day, just how much he wants to become a philanthropist, like Paul Getty, it's now his life's ambition.

Konrad's belief is that if he can donate the da Vinci to The Frick Museum. It will be his way of being taken seriously.' Adam told her. Francine shook her head.

'Konrad is the walking definition of calculating. The man is just desperate for recognition. My father has always told me of his desire to become immortalized! Konrad Gray is not the altruistic benefactor he's trying to sell himself as being. Quite the reverse.

'I wonder where Edmund fits into all this, you can see that Konrad is the much more dominant twin of the two. All this philanthropic notion is just about him, and his personal glorification, a guaranteed place in history. You have to remember that if he does buy the painting and donates it to say The Frick, let's not forget, it's only on permanent loan, he is not actually giving it to them. That way, he keeps his capital investment, i.e., the painting, and all the while the people of New York will be paying for the very high insurance and the huge security bills via their taxes, while in the meantime, a wing of the Frick would be named after him. So, you see, when you actually analyse his motives, he is not quite as philanthropic as he pretends. He is just playing the New York society game of putting all the pieces into place to secure his permanent legacy.' Francine gave Adam her perspective, and he just shrugged his shoulders, as he told her, 'So, what's the problem with that? I would do the same myself if I was in his position. I admire him, good on the guy.'

'Francine, I think you should come out of that ivory tower. Your problem is you go around with a rose-tinted view of the art world, when in fact the harsh reality is it's cut-throat, and totally ruthless. There's no room for the timid and mild-mannered, or, to be blunt, anyone who's not willing to be economical with the truth from time to time, which makes it no different to any other major business. It's hardball, and if a major player in this game comes along and starts taking an interest in me, then I'll tell you this, I will do whatever is required, and if you don't like it, then that's too bad.' Adam's determination to succeed at all costs was laid bare before his wife, in no uncertain terms.

'But, can I rely on you to speak to August and arrange for him to come over? Edmund is staying with Konrad for ten days or thereabouts, therefore, it's vital to get him over as soon as possible,' he asked her. Although Francine was not in a great mood, she reluctantly agreed. She had no appetite whatsoever to help Adam, but it would be utterly unfair if she allowed her annoyance towards the three men to effectively prevent her from doing the right thing. Hector needed a break. This might be his one and only opportunity. Although, after Adam's treatment of him, she wouldn't blame Hector if he never wanted to speak to either of them again.

# CHAPTER 38

## Post Impressions

The party at the Gray's the previous night now seemed a long time ago. It was amazing what a night's rest can do to restore you, which surprised Francine as she was fully expecting her sleep to be disturbed by vivid nightmares after seeing some of the most controversial items that human history had ever created. Not to mention the meeting the peculiar twin, Edmund.

Looking down the queue she could see Hector as usual standing patiently in line waiting his turn.

'Hello, how are you this morning,' she asked him meekly, 'Oh, hi, yes I'm fine,' he said quietly, 'Can we just go over there and have a quick chat,' she asked, indicating that they go somewhere a bit more private than standing in the queue trying to hold a conversation

'The thing is, I just may have some potentially good news for you, and could we just forget about yesterday and start all over? I spoke to Adam last night and he is very embarrassed about it all,' she told a surprised Hector, who made no mention of their previous encounter at their apartment

'Sure, no problem,' was his easy reply. She assumed for him, that when your mother is so sick, everything else in your world becomes secondary, and the bad behaviour of an arrogant art dealer pales into insignificance.

'Firstly, Adam really liked the painting, which means that he'd probably like the rest of your work. In fact, he liked it so much he told his potential investor about you, who is also in the art business, perhaps you have heard of him, Konrad Gray? Anyhow, Adam must have sung your praises, because it seems Mr. Gray wants to meet you for, well, to be honest, I am not sure why. But I think it's definitely worth your time to check it out, as who knows where it might lead?' Her words gave the young artist a window into a possibility that had so far eluded him.

'Really, he wants to meet me? Okay, yes, that would be great. I can't say I've ever heard of the man you just mentioned, but then, as I told you before, I really don't know anyone in the art world. I just paint,' his answer was to the point.

Unfortunately, by not knowing anything about the art business, Hector could be in for a brutal shock at how it really operates, which was without mercy. The strangest aspect of the profession was that, unlike most other businesses, talent alone will not enable you to survive or thrive, the artists themselves need to be even more cunning at playing the hideous games that are required to succeed, you had to be brash and downright obnoxious. The art world demands a back story, and the more wretched, coked up, and insufferable the artist, then all the more publicity, that's when the artist gets a name and become bigger than their work, a bad reputation is the greatest of all selling points for any dealer. Buyers just love to purchase notoriety. Francine could never contemplate Hector in that vain. His personality was sweet, thoughtful, and stable. She could never see him doing anything that could ever be thought of as notorious. No, that was not Hector's personality, he was grounded and probably quite predictable. He was not the stuff that legends were made of.

Francine was eager to see if she could now broker some sort of deal that would secure Hector some work, whom she believed deserved the luck

'Let me just call Adam and see what I can arrange?' Adam informed her that he would need to phone Konrad to see when would be best for him and Edmund, then call her straight back.'

'Okay, I will ask him. Adam wondered if Tuesday evening around eight o'clock would be good for you. Oh, and Mr. Gray wants you to bring one or two of your current paintings, and they also want to see a couple of the copies of the old masters you have done,' a request that did puzzle her somewhat, but Francine nonetheless relayed the request to Hector.

'Yes, definitely, I will arrange for the sitter to come early to take care of my mother, then I'll be there,' he told her.

'So, Hector, that's all sorted, you're due to see the two Mr. Gray's on Tuesday evening around 8 pm, and Adam said he looks forward to seeing you then. Now I really have to go, I have a lot to do, 'bye for now, and enjoy our Leonardo,' she said before making her way off to her busy day.

Back in her office, she picked up the phone, after consulting with the chairman at Christie's, she had been given the go-ahead to put in a call to the owner of the Salvator Mundi, with the $275 million offer as requested by Konrad Gray. It was the largest sum of money she had ever had to negotiate on behalf of a client and for a single item.

Happy to have now sorted out any misunderstanding between Adam and her new protégé had put her in a good mood. She knew the previous evening had been awful and wanted a truce between her and Adam and she pondered the idea of calling him back and suggesting they go out for dinner that evening. 'Yes, that would be a nice gesture, thinking that somebody needed to become the grown-up in the room.'

'Hi, I won't keep you as I expect you're busy too, I was just wondering if you'd like to go out for dinner tonight?' she asked her husband.

'Sorry, but I will have to say no, Konrad and Edmund have invited me up to the penthouse tonight, hopefully, to talk about the gallery. At least that's what I assume they want?' he told her.

'But I thought you were going to see them on Tuesday with Hector, isn't that what we have just arranged?' Francine said somewhat confused.

'Yes, that's correct, on Tuesday evening I will take Hector and introduce him to the Gray brothers, but tonight, they want to see me alone, as I just explained to you,' he said as he sighed down the phone.

'Oh, okay then, if I'm home before you, shall I make dinner for us before you go to see them?' she struggled to ask. He quickly declined her suggestion of a shared dinner, 'Actually, count me out, I'll come home, have a quick shower then head up to see them, so don't worry about me.'

Entering the apartment Francine saw Adam's coat on the chair. From the quietness, it seemed he had already left for his meeting with the Grays. She noticed on the hallway table an expensive-looking gift bag, thinking to herself that Adam had obviously bought her a present as an apology, but on looking inside, it soon became apparent, it was not from him. It was from Konrad. The black and gold bag contained a beautifully boxed FORGERY X Candle and the handwritten gift card just said simply, 'Enjoy' KG.

I certainly will, she thought lighting it up immediately. FORGERY, that's certainly a provocative name, as she remembered that the brand was from London, where humour, eccentricity and just being out there were synonymous with British culture. It made her realise just how much she missed the country. Life there seemed so much less complicated, and fun. Her thoughts turned to dinner, thinking she might as well just order a takeaway and watch a movie until Adam came back. With her second movie finished, Adam had still not returned, and it was way past midnight. After clearing the remains of her meal, she decided to go to bed, at first, she couldn't sleep, wondering why he was so late. Soon she drifted off, only to be woken by Adam finally creeping into the bedroom as quietly as he could manage before she saw that it was nearly three thirty.

'Sorry, I didn't mean to wake you, go back to sleep,' he told his semi-conscious wife, who did just that.

Francine woke up and made her way to the kitchen where she found Adam who was already dressed, quickly finishing off his coffee. It was obvious to her that he was anxious to leave

'You spent a long time with the brothers last night? 'Francine commented to her husband who was already heading for the front door of the apartment, 'Yeh, sorry, didn't mean to disturb you, well you know how it is, just talking shop, they're both just so interesting, full of stories, really intelligent guys and the time just flew by,' he told her

'And don't forget tonight I'm taking Hector to see them, oh, and I'm going to be away for a few days,' he mentioned almost as an afterthought.

'Going away, where, what for, when?' Francine was surprised, coming out of the blue like that

'Yes, on Wednesday. Konrad and Edmund are going to their castle in Germany. God, did you know they even have a private plane? How cool is that? Anyway, they have invited me to go with them.' Francine could see that Adam had been enticed into the Gray brothers' web. He went on and told her, 'As you may know, Konrad deals in a lot of German art, so he needs to go there every few weeks, and well, he wants me to go and meet their people and see their organization.' For some reason, her husband's explanation sounded rather contrived and very suspicious.

Germany? Until the past couple of weeks, it was a country she had never visited, or even thought about. Still, now it was becoming all-pervading as the forceful personalities of Konrad Gray and Hermann Göring were starting to become very dominant factors in her life. How did this happen? This was a question that was giving her considerable anxiety.

# CHAPTER 39

## When Silence isn't Golden

Everything had gone quiet, too quiet. She had not seen or heard anything of Hector for the last week, almost like he had vanished into thin air. It could be due to his mother's illness. She called him several times, but the phone just went straight to his voicemail. Wondering if she should go to his home, she decided against the idea, as, after all, she really didn't know him that well anyway. He's probably just busy, and come to think of it, so was she, but that did not stop her from pondering as to what had happened during his meeting with the Grays that night, and why he had not let her know the outcome?

Likewise with Adam, who had gone to Germany with Konrad and Edmund. He had not phoned, emailed or texted her. She had no idea where he was, or what was going on, but concluded that if the castle in Germany was in the middle of nowhere, as it probably was, it might have little or no internet reception, which was the most likely explanation. Except of course, there is always a landline, which surely, they must have. However, he said he would be back by Tuesday or Wednesday late evening, so she decided she would just have to wait until then.

With just over two weeks left before the night of the grand auction, which was expected to be the biggest ever to take place, there was still so much to do. One of the tasks was to inform Konrad that his offer of $275 million for the painting had been rejected out of hand. That will not please him. Now Konrad Gray will have to bid alongside those rare individuals who could afford to pay such obscene amounts of money for one very small piece of art.

Francine wondered if Konrad would actually make an appearance and be there in person on the night. This kind of sale almost guaranteed that for the really serious players, bidding would be done by phone, via their lawyers to the auction house staff, who would relay their offer, and those names would remain undisclosed. This would always be the normal course of events.

But, as Konrad was intending to buy the art primarily to donate to the Frick Museum, he might want maximum attention and be seen by New York society. Then at least they would know of his altruistic ambitions for the city. So even in the end if he loses out, all the positive media he would garner will go a long way to enhance his reputation at the very least. Therefore, Francine expected he would be there in a prominent position, ready to lay claim to his prizes and take centre stage in what he hoped would be a public relations masterstroke.

# CHAPTER 40

## Where Art Goes, Money Flows

Francine was used to seeing enormous sums of money being paid in the auction house, but this was going to be on another level entirely. Realising that Konrad felt completely comfortable and at ease with his offer of $275 million made her think. 'Just how did he amass so much wealth?' Everything about him was shrouded in mystery. In the last few days, she had Googled him several times, but there was no real information anywhere. It was all so vague. Yes, there were lots of photographs of him and Millicent attending various gala dinners, and functions. Millicent at fashion shows, and the odd bit of news about Konrad selling a major piece of art for huge sums of money, but nothing remarkable about who he was, and just how he got to where he was today.

But from her research, it soon became apparent to her that he didn't want anyone to know anything substantial about him. That lack of transparency hadn't prevented him from becoming the dominant force he was, and, knowing that nobody ever questioned him or his judgement in the art world, strengthened his influence without question. His clients, some of the shrewdest people around, were now very wary of the volatile stock market after getting their fingers burned in the financial crash. And it did not take long for them to see the high prices being fetched for art, which had now firmly established itself as a 'blue chip' secure investment. They placed their trust in Konrad, to the extent that they would buy from him whatever he told them to, and his 'clients' own judgements were of no importance to him, as their personal tastes were of no consequence. They would buy what he said was a wise investment, without even exactly knowing why, and when one rich client makes a successful purchase, the rest soon come running. In fact, a story going around town was that one unnamed Russian oligarch flew into New York solely to view a large abstract work by Cy Twombly, an artist the oligarch had never even heard of purely on the recommendation of Konrad. The Russian, staring conspicuously at the painting for about fifteen minutes, turned to Konrad and asked him, 'What the hell is this rubbish you are showing me? And how much is it?' Konrad said 'it's an intelligent financial procurement, for a mere $25 million.' The Russian looked at Konrad and said.

'Done! Now ship it immediately to my home in Moscow.' The oligarch walked straight out to his chauffeur-driven car, to whisk the billionaire to his waiting plane and head straight back to Russia.

Konrad's well-established business was the pure envy of every other dealer. His scoops and high-volume sales had become legendary. Francine wondered if many of the high-net-worth clients knew of his predilection for collecting Nazi memorabilia. She doubted it. The fact might raise some eyebrows if they did know, but Konrad would suggest that he just had a keen interest in rare relics from history, whatever era they came from.

Seeing the items in Konrad's collection that had belonged to Hermann Göring, made her think. It was all becoming just too much of a coincidence. It crossed her mind that possibly her grandfather, Max, was trying to reach out to her from beyond the grave, prompting his granddaughter to make her decision. She had conveniently pushed the letter to the very back of her mind, but things kept transpiring, and up until a couple of weeks ago, the only time she had been aware of anything to do with the Nazis was a few lectures she had attended at university on the great art plunder they had committed during the war in Europe.

'What's going on?' she asked

'All these connections to Germany, what with Konrad and

Edmund, Göring, her grandfather's time in Germany, what did it all mean?' It was driving her mad, not knowing what to do, the intrigue, the indecision was pure torment. She had to face the facts that the only way to find out for sure was to open that letter. And it would need to be soon, if only for peace of mind.

Her attention turned to the movie she had watched the previous week, ironically it was The da Vinci Code and made her think. 'Was her life now beginning to imitate art? And if so, would Tom Hanks save the day?' Now there's a nice thought.

'Just landed', the text message said. Finally, Francine had heard from her errant husband. She was not too pleased with his lack of communication over the last week, firmly believing he could have made more of an effort to let her know how things were going. In spite of that, she decided not to say anything or ask him why. In truth, she actually couldn't be bothered. Adam's self-absorption, along with his self-importance had now become his permanent modus operandi. Maybe that's why he admired Konrad and Edmund so much? they were all so alike, real birds of a feather, and that was not a thought she took any comfort from. Swiftly taken aback with an acute suspicion of wondering if in time her fate was to be reduced to becoming the equivalent of a compliant Millicent, the very epitome of a 'Stepford wife', married to a dominating, overbearing, and controlling man

'Was that what lay in store for her with her marriage to Adam Faris? Perish the thought!'

'So, how was Germany?' she asked Adam over dinner

'Amazing, fantastic, it's all just so impressive, you have to see it to believe it, the castle that is. I've never seen anything so old, and it is absolutely enormous. It must cost a small fortune to run, that's for sure. I met the people within their organization, Edmund is a silent partner, so to speak, as it's Konrad who decides everything. During our time in Germany, we had a long talk about Konrad investing in my gallery, but it turned out to be a bit of a ruse because he was not really interested in any investment. It was me he was interested in. So, there's been a major change of plan,' he told her. Francine didn't speak for a few moments. Intuitively, she didn't feel right about what she was starting to hear and didn't like him being mixed up with the questionable Gray brothers in any form whatsoever. Her gut reaction towards Konrad and Edmund screamed warning bells, but she knew only too well that if she questioned her husband about his involvement with them, it would provoke a raging argument, and, besides, he would do whatever he wanted regardless of her opinion.

'Sounds interesting, so what is the new plan?' he asked, anticipating she was not going to like his answer.

'Konrad bought a large building on Fifth Avenue last year which has been undergoing a complete renovation with a specific aim. And now it's ready to be launched in four weeks' time, with a sensational opening night, invitations are going out today. Edmund has arranged for a lot of his showbiz friends from Beverly Hills to fly in, obviously, their expenses will be paid by Konrad and Edmund, then there's the important international collectors, investment bankers, the media, and of course, the other dealers, naturally we wouldn't want to leave them out, who could resist rubbing their noses in our upcoming success. I imagine they will all shut up shop when they see exactly what they are going to be up against in the future. We've got so many plans,' he was certainly high on his own enthusiasm.

'The plan is that Konrad intends to out-do any gallery in New York, it will blow any other place out of the water. And, in due course he intends to rival the likes of Christie's and Sotheby's. If all goes exactly as planned, he will open up an auction house. He is just seeking the right building in the best location. He's looking into all the legalities, then the two arms of the business will run side by side. But this new gallery is going to be the place to buy art of any description, for sure. He has the money, the collectors, the contacts, in fact, he has the whole damned thing, nothing has been overlooked, Konrad has taken care of everything, he's even arranged to negotiate insurance packages, storage, and transportation. I mean, the guy's an absolute genius! It's a huge space where we can hold lavish receptions, stage the best exhibitions, photo shoots for top companies for promotional purposes, such as fashion houses, and collaborations with the music industry, not to mention an exclusive suite of rooms at the back, out of sight for privacy, which will stock only the finest wines, so naturally clients can visit, see anything new, while they have a quiet drink. That's a such great idea, don't you think? I mean, the more you ply them with alcohol…well, anyway, the gallery is on three floors, so, it's going to be called, The Three Floors Gallery. On the top level, we will deal with rare artefacts, and antiques which will be Konrad's domain. On the middle floor we will show only the very best-established current artists who have a good track record of sales, some sculptures, and a few installations, and once a year we will run a competition for the art schools to submit their works and the winner gets the chance to be seen and hang in the gallery for a period of six weeks. Can you imagine the great press coverage that will generate alone? New Yorkers will love that! And then finally the ground floor will be reserved for the very best. The piece de resistance.

'The NAMES! Those rare breeds of artists whom the wealthy get out of bed and compete for,' Adam continued, 'Konrad told me about those kinds of super-rich collectors who are transfixed in a kind of herd mentality, determined, consumed with an absolute need to obtain a trophy piece. So that they can out-do the other guy, it's just about the only thing that excites them anymore, that level of competitiveness becomes their new addiction, and probably borders on an obsession, it's definitely their new drug, flying around the world at a moment's notice when they receive a call from Konrad, telling them he has acquired something sensational, then sitting back to watch as each tries to outbid the other. It's like an exclusive game of 'International Poker' that only a few of the wealthiest can ever get to play. It makes the casino in Monte Carlo look tame.

'And according to Konrad, getting clients to part with their money is the easy part, when you convince them that they are getting something unique, then they just have to have it. But you have to ensure that you always have a constant supply of great works to sell in the first place, which Konrad said has never been an issue, he also said to listen out for the Three Ds, which are apparently, divorce, debt, and death. It's under those circumstances that you can pick up some real bargains. With the reality of inheritance tax, alimony, and gambling debts breathing down their necks, it's so easy to manipulate the price, because most don't want the fuss or publicity of going to auction, or to court. Letting everyone know the state of their financial affairs, then you can really clean up. Why do you think it's called rich pickings!' Adam's delight over the ability to exploit someone at their worst moment was a new low for him. Francine saw how he delighted in this prospect, and it was horrible.

'It's going to be like the Gold Rush all over again. We can't fail. When you think that a Picasso, for example, can fetch $100 million, that's more than you would pay for a luxury yacht or even a palace, it's totally ridiculous,' he laughed

'What is it they now say on Wall Street, that art has become a 'license to print money'? It has gone beyond all recognition. To the well-heeled and moneyed, their art collection reflects their position in the pecking order. It's definitely how they measure up and judge each other, just as long as it's accompanied by the legitimate painter's signature and that all-important provenance. Those two things put together are far more important than the actual twirls of paints on the canvas. That they don't really give a toss about! I doubt they ever bother to look at what's on their walls. And let's face it, the whole art business is like Michael Jackson's Neverland, something that doesn't reflect anything real, at least, to most ordinary people. It's just an opaque world of smoke and mirrors.' Adam waxed lyrical.

'Um,' his wife thought to herself, 'that was just like Konrad, a master of deception'.

'After spending time with Konrad in Germany, I learnt an awful lot, he's actually more of a psychologist than a dealer. He studies people, gets to know their weaknesses, and then he goes in for the kill, it is all quite calculated on his part.' Adam seemed thrilled with his new ideas of the human mind

'Anyhow, he'd been looking for the right person to help run this new venture, so he sounded me out, thinking, I just might be the 'one' as he put it, and made me the offer. When I said yes, he immediately made arrangements for us all to go to Germany, saying it was a sort of initiation, a requirement for me to go and experience inside their operation, I was told it was a ritual that would be essential, allowing me to appreciate fully what I would be getting involved in. They both wanted my absolute commitment. It had to be, all or nothing! And I can tell you, after being with them in Germany, spending time inside their castle, my mind was made up. I wanted in. So, I vowed there and then to Konrad and Edmund, my total dedication.' Adam's choice of words seemed normal to him, but Francine could not understand how he had no insight into just how bizarre it was all starting to sound. She was baffled by his use of language, 'Taking a vow? Initiation?' It sounded more as if the Grays had demanded his very soul and Adam had given it to them willingly. None of this made any sense to her, 'What on earth was he going on about? Perhaps he had drunk too much Schnapps in the Fatherland?' she thought. He should wake up to the fact that they had only employed him as a gallery director, and nothing more. Anyone would think they had become mythical blood brothers the way he was talking. She thought they all sounded a bit off their trolley, an old English expression, that seemed to sum them all up exactly.

Francine was only too well aware from everything he had just told her, that it all stank to high heaven. 'Are you sure about this and thought it all through? Do you think you can trust them? You always made it clear that you wanted to work for yourself. Build up your own business, giving you the freedom to run things the way you wanted to?' she reminded him of his own words.

As soon as those words left her lips, she wished she had kept her views completely to herself, as immediately she saw his raw hostile reaction, 'Yep, and here we go. So, let me ask myself, am I surprised by what you've just said, no! Understand this once and for all: it's my call, not yours. Don't try and control me. If you think I'm going to miss a golden chance like this, then you are truly mistaken and deluded. Do you think guys like Konrad Gray come along every day offering you this? It's one in a million, so get real! The problem with you, Francine, is that your entire life has been so goddamn easy, what with your private education, embassy lifestyle, parties at the White House with daddy, a huge inheritance, waltzing into your precious job as top curator at Christie's, and then, just to top it all, Time Magazine. Well, just maybe I might want my photograph to grace the cover of Time too! Really, you have no idea what it's like in the real world. You have been cosseted by your father and grandfather your entire life, everything handed to you on a plate while some of us have had to hustle and become hard-nosed for all that we get!' His callous shocking resentment of his wife's success had become like an open, festering wound. Adam's loud aggressive voice persisted, 'And besides, unlike you, I happen to like Konrad and Edmund, they live the kind of life I want to live, and with their help, I will get it!' Just like his scorpion birth sign, his words not only stung, but they were lethal.

Not willing to just stand there and take his abuse, she stood her ground.

'So, tell me, what exactly is it they have, that you don't?' she threw back at him.

'To be able to buy my own home for a start. After all, this apartment is yours! Then in time my own private jet, and who knows what else, but for sure, I want it all!' he yelled at her.

Taking a step back, just looking at him, Francine understood precisely, it was now Konrad who was pulling his strings. She could see there was no point in dragging out the disagreement any longer, as she asked him, 'Can we just draw a line under this?' Francine had no more intentions of raising the subject with him again, ever! As far as she was concerned now, he could do as he wished. Their marriage was less than a year old, but she couldn't deny the fact any longer. She didn't like the person he had become. His only priority was money. If she were a lawyer, the evidence presented would be overwhelming. He was not the person she thought he was, in fact, she now believed he had married her under false pretences.

Although she didn't want to continue with their conversation, she had one more question that she did want to ask, 'Have you seen or heard anything from Hector since the meeting you both had in the penthouse?'

'Yes,' Adam said, giving her that look of his, not willing to elaborate.

'So, what happened?' Francine pushed him for an answer

'Well, for your information, Hector went with us to Germany and he's still there,' his attitude to her was abhorrent, but nonetheless, she figured, what the heck, asking him, 'Why is he still in Germany?' 'Because Konrad offered Hector a commission, which he accepted, and that's why he is still there if that is okay with you? Are you satisfied with my answer?' He was becoming more and more annoyed. This new information had completely taken her by surprise. It was all beginning to sound very ominous, asking herself, why take Hector all the way to Germany to paint? 'None of this adds up, what were they up to?' she thought

'Really? A commission, what kind of commission?' trying to sound genuinely interested, and not as if she was prying.

'Look, if you're so goddamned desperate to know Konrad's business, then I tell you what, why don't you jump into the elevator and go and ask Konrad yourself? I'm sure he will be delighted to inform you,' his snide comments to his wife sounded like a determination to be cruel. The atmosphere in the apartment was heavy with his frustrated narcissism, and Francine wanted to escape from it all

'I have some work to do, so I think I will take my laptop to bed and work from there, goodnight,' she told him

'I'm going out for a while,' he mumbled as he slammed the front door behind him.

# CHAPTER 41

## Eye of the Beholder

Francine had overslept, and woke up trying to focus her attention on what she needed to do that morning, and even though it was now nearly nine, she still felt tired due to a poor night's sleep brought on by the stress of the previous evening's argument. The utter cruelty of his words had come out of the blue and had stuck deep in her mind all night. She had had no idea just how much he resented her upbringing and career.

As Adam came into the bed-room she detected he seemed somewhat calmer, even offering to bring her a cup of tea

'What's wrong, you look shattered?' he wanted to know. Replying to his sudden unconvincing concern, 'oh, just feeling a bit tense I suppose,' 'Really, why are you so tense, is there something wrong?' but did he really need to ask? Was there something missing in his thought processes, she wondered. Surely, their harsh exchanges of words the night before were enough to give anyone anxiety. His lack of awareness was alarming, which she knew wasn't right.

'Then why don't you stay in bed with your tea and relax for a while? I'm running late, got a busy morning, then I am meeting up with Konrad this afternoon. We're going to the new gallery, so will probably be very late home, and I'll eat out,' he informed her as he took off.

Francine decided to message her team to let them know she would be working from home that morning. Reaching out to the bedside table for her work phone she discovered it wasn't there, 'Um, what have I done with it?' she said to herself. Hunting around the bedroom it was nowhere to be found, then recalling just before falling asleep she'd sent a message to her assistant to remind her about the seating plan for the sale, she thought it must be around here somewhere

'Of course, I'll just use my other mobile to call the work number to detect it,' immediately it became apparent that the sound was coming from under the bed. She climbed on her knees to peer underneath and saw the light coming from the ringing phone, and noticed something else. 'What is that?' the mobile phone light was showing up a shadow, an image of what appeared to be a smallish cube shaped item wedged under Adam's side of the bed. Going around to his side, she pushed her hand under the space between the bed frame and the floor in an effort to retrieve the item. It was a small ornate leather box with an unusual and ugly-looking clasp

'Well, what do we have here?' she thought, 'this doesn't feel right. Nobody hides things in strange places without a reason?' It wasn't hers, therefore it must belong to Adam. She resisted the urge to open it, initially, but then her curiosity got the better of her, as she conveniently recalled what Oscar Wilde once said, "That you should resist everything…but temptation" and she was tempted. So, believing the Irish always had the right approach, she followed Oscar's wise words. As she opened it, horror swept through her. It was a large gold ring adorned with a black stone and red rubies. It was identical to the ring that Konrad and Edmund Gray both wore. It chilled her to the very marrow of her bones, but she didn't know why. These were definitely not family heirlooms. Francine flopped on the bed quite shaken up by this alarming discovery, but she needed answers. Taking it out of the box she could tell from its weight and general appearance it was obviously old, very old. Racking her brain thinking, 'Who can I ask, who might be able to help me?' Then in a flash, she realised precisely who that person was. William Wallace!

It was nearly 11 am, and rushing to shower, dress and get to work as soon as possible was now her priority, knowing full well that Will always lunched at twelve on the dot, you could set your watch by him, and there was absolutely no point calling him on his mobile as he never answered it. In fact, she believed he never even charged it up. Will, who had never really forgiven his mother for naming him after probably the most famous man ever in Scottish history, got mocked wherever he went. Always dressed in his native tartan in one guise or another, be it a waistcoat, tartan trousers, or even a complete suit, his signature bow-tie completed his striking appearance. He was a proud unconventional Scotsman. But he was, without doubt, one of the nicest, most down-to-earth people she had ever met. As one of Christie's experts on ancient jewellery, going back as far as the Egyptians, what he didn't know about anthropology and ancient cults, you could write on the proverbial postage stamp.

'Is Will here?' she asked, out of breath after rushing all the way trying to catch him.

'Sorry, you have just missed him, he's gone to lunch. Can I give him a message?' his assistant asked.

'No, thank you, just let him know the moment he gets back I need to see him. Don't forget, will you? It's very important I speak with him,' she told the young guy in the ancient relics department

'Sure, of course, immediately he walks through the door, I will let him know,' he reassured her that he wouldn't forget.

How an hour can drag when your clock watching. She needed to get the ring back under the bed as soon as possible, just in case Adam returned to the apartment unexpectedly. Unlikely, but you just never know. And besides, she would feel better, no, safer, with it back in its place

'Were her instincts, right? Did she now have to fear for her safety from her disaffected husband?' 'Hi, Francine, I believe you want to see me. 'Will said as he popped his head around the door of her office.

'Yes, indeed I do. I want to show you something, but not here,' she told him.

'Okay, let's go down to my office. Now, how can I help?' Will was keen to know.

Pulling the leather box from her pocket she handed it to him, 'Um, what do we have here?' taking it from her. Scrutinizing it closely under his eye-magnifier, he asked, 'Gosh Francine, where on earth did you get this from?' 'Well, actually it belongs to a friend of mine who's just moved into an old house, she told me she'd found it when doing some gardening; anyway, when my friend showed it to me, we were both naturally intrigued and thought maybe you might know something about it. I mean, it does look old, don't you think?' Speaking ten to the dozen, the flustered words of her story sounded quite improbable, as it just came spilling out of her mouth, but she didn't want Will to know the truth of where she had found it, and to whom it really belonged.

'Slow down!' he said teasingly, 'Well, if you want my opinion, I think you should tell your friend to throw this ring into the Hudson River and fast!' he laughed, 'Just kidding.' Francine was bewildered by his wry humour

'All joking apart, this is actually extremely valuable, how on earth did it end up in your friend's garden. That is very strange. Anyhow, these were passed down through the centuries, and very few men had a ring like this one, it's incredibly rare, look here at the very distinctive insignia engraved all around the gold band. As soon as I saw that, I realised its importance, it's quite exciting to be able to hold one of them. I've only ever seen photographs of them before in Germany. Actually, the tales surrounding these rings are grim and ghastly.' He continued telling Francine, who was eager to learn more. Will went on, 'The origin of them date back to around the fifteenth century, and they came from Romania, where everyone knew the men who wore them were the chosen few, deemed to be the most loyal, and, they say, the most depraved! They were the fanatical followers of a very famous warlord, or perhaps more accurately infamous, and they all belonged to a cult called, The Eye of Bedim,' he told her.

'Will, really? This all sounds so remote and somewhat far-fetched, and I don't think I have ever heard of any warlord, famous or otherwise in Romania!' she confessed.

'Yes, of course, you have, I think everyone has heard of him. He was known as 'Vlad the Impaler' or by his pet name of Vlad Dracul! He was a local ruler, if you like, and not an especially nice man, whom it was said had a bit of a reputation because whenever he had a temper tantrum, which was often, he was prone to impale anyone who upset him, or, even if he didn't like the look of you on that particular day! So naturally, as you can imagine, he was not that popular. When he finally died in very mysterious circumstances, his devoted followers, who were now fearing for their own lives fled into Germany, taking as much gold and treasures with them as they could get their hands on. The story goes that is where they settled, buying up land and castles, assimilating completely into the Germanic culture, becoming invisible, which enabled them to continue secretly with the adoration of their dead leader.' Will's story was gripping, 'But tell me, I still don't understand. What is the Eye of Bedim? And what exactly do you mean by a cult?' she asked, now feeling anxious.

'Well, when I say a cult, perhaps I should say more accurately Occult. They were Satanists or devil worshippers. You see to them, Vlad was an embodiment of evil, the incarnation of the Devil himself, everyone saw Vlad and the Devil as the same person, and who knows? The story was that Bedim was the Devil's right-hand man, and it was his job to 'vet' anyone who wanted to ingratiate themselves with Lucifer, so Bedim would 'Eye' them to determine who would be allowed to enter into their inner circle, through a portal, which was their allegorical doorway into the underworld, where they could pay homage and be blessed by the Prince of Darkness. Bedim was so revered by Satan, who saw him as his trusty mercenary and disciple, that he honoured him with a special ring that was bestowed with the most despicable powers. They say the black stone represented the dark Soul of Satan and the rubies his pure blood-line, so, you can see Bedim was extremely powerful in his own right when wearing his master's personal gift. The legend also claimed that written in the lost pages of the Devil's Bible which were believed to have been stolen, and, this is where it might be of particular interest to you, supposedly, the folklore goes that Leonard da Vinci was given one of the rings as a gift. It was stated in those lost pages that when Lucifer heard that the artist was the toast of Florence as a result of his divine painting talents, he was so intrigued he paid him a visit and da Vinci was 'invited' to paint a portrait of his most beautiful and adored wife. Well, as you can imagine, Leonardo, realising just how dangerous it would be to take on a task like that, did not want the commission. He loathed the very idea of it, and who could blame him? But then again, who can refuse the Devil? Obviously, the guy is in a real predicament. So not really having any choice in the matter, the Florentine artist reluctantly sets about the painting, taking his time, as he knew there was no room for error, he must get it just right, and you know Leonardo was famous for taking an extremely long time to finish a commission, or even just abandoning a painting half-way through. Anyway, too much time had passed by, and Lucifer had had enough of da Vinci's procrastinations. His patience had been eroded to the point where he was no longer prepared to wait, and he demanded to see exactly what had been done. Then, when he finally saw how the artist had painted his wife, he exploded! They say his rage of fire was like nothing that had ever been witnessed before on earth! He hated everything about the painting, accusing da Vinci of deliberately hiding her breath-taking beauty, even making her look plain, telling the artist he never wanted to see his work again, and ordered him to destroy it. And, da Vinci's life would have ended there and then, if it were not for Lucifer's wife, who adored the painting and begged her husband to let Leonardo live. When the Vatican heard of da Vinci's involvement and discovered that Lucifer himself had dictated to the Benedictine monk Herman the Recluse to write an addition in the Devil's Bible denouncing Leonardo. Pope Julius ll decreed those pages be found and obliterated, but the Bible mysteriously disappeared. When it was found many years later, the pages defaming da Vinci were missing, never to been seen again. I wonder whatever happened to them?' Will commented. She knew what had happened to them, and exactly where those lost pages were. They were in the home of Konrad, where just a few days before she had seen them, but she had no idea what they had said. Will continued his saga, 'The Eye of Bedim became a symbol to the cult, whenever a new recruit joined their ranks, fresh blood, so to speak, a ring would be given to them after their initiation, where they would pledge obedience, secrecy and their utmost loyalty on pain of death, and once admitted, there was no way out!' Will continued with even more revelations of past horror stories. 'It was also believed that several members of the Nazis wore these rings in secret. They know for sure that Heinrich Himmler wore 'The Eye of Bedim' along with the Death's Head Ring, as they found them on the hands of his dead body in 1945: you see, the Nazis were heavily into the occult, although, they would utterly repudiate having any connection to Romania, that would have been conveniently airbrushed from history. But as far as the Nazis were concerned, it went back far enough not to be of any significance, and they truly held Vlad with the highest esteem for his sheer force of personality – something they saw in their own leader Adolf Hitler.'

'Tell me, Will, do you think this cult is still in existence?' she asked

'Who knows? Probably, let's face it, there are more than enough loonies around these days who desire nothing more than to exist within a permanent state of obedience to some higher authority, which usually amounts to the same old thing, a lust for power and money, and then more money. It never changes. Cultists are not very original, are they? Personally, I can't see the appeal, preferring to spend my free time with friends in a bar somewhere having a few cold beers than on my knees worshipping at the high altar of some pompous charlatan! But there you are, I guess I'm not that ambitious. And, if they are still in existence, you can be certain they won't be very nice people, that's for sure. In fact, I imagine they would be positively dangerous, unbalanced, and definitely not all the ticket,' He declared. Then, suddenly taking the palm of her hand, he placed the ring on it, 'Close your eyes, take a minute or two. They say you can actually feel its bad energy?' Will told her. His theory of the terror held within the ring seemed to be true, as suddenly she began to experience a very weird sensation of intense heat that bore deep into her hand. It was almost like it had impaled itself into her flesh

'The mythical painting of Lucifer's wife, I wonder if she existed, and if so, who was she supposed to have been?' Francine considered.

'Um, that's an interesting thought, you know it had never occurred to me before, but seeing as you are the expert on him, what do think, do you have any ideas?

I mean, could it have been the Mona Lisa?' This time Will was looking to her for an answer to a puzzle

'Do you know something, that's precisely what I was thinking because they never knew who exactly the Mona Lisa really was. They have speculated on her identity for hundreds of years, but it's always remained a total conundrum, and another question that should be asked is, why exactly did da Vinci keep her portrait with him until he died? You know he took it everywhere he went. Maybe, when we look at the portrait of the Mona Lisa, we are looking at the face of the wife of the Devil! There is definitely something we don't know about that painting, and why it remained closely beside him right up to the end, you know something, Will, it sends a shiver right up and down my spine just thinking about it.' Francine wondered if her estimation had any truth to it?

'I'm sure your friend will be fascinated when you tell her all about its history, and not to worry, if any of the cult members are still around today, they will probably be living in some Eastern European country, not New York City. That would be absurd, wouldn't it?' Will scoffed.

# CHAPTER 42

## Be Careful What You Wish For

Francine had wanted to find out the truth about these rings. And now she had. Will's expert knowledge, along with all its vivid and gory history, came as a complete shock. Furthermore, it wasn't the kind of thing you imagine your husband to be mixed up in

'Are you busy? If not, can I see you?' she texted her father

'Just on route to my club, arriving in about five minutes, you will find me in the library, come by, and then I'll order us each a club sandwich and some of that tea you like. See you soon,' he replied

'Ok, be there in about 40 minutes,' she messaged him back.

Making her way to the library she found him deeply engrossed in a newspaper. His elegance and calmness, coupled with the familiar scent of his Penhaligon aftershave and the lingering aroma of his freshly smoked cigar were all very reassuring. Looking at her face, and whole demeanour, it didn't take a genius to realise that something was wrong

'I must say you look like you could do with a stiff drink rather than a pot of tea! Whatever's wrong?' Sir Howard asked. Francine sighed, 'You're very perceptive,' as she sank into the armchair

'I really don't want to sound dramatic, but where do I start?' 'At the beginning is usually preferable,' he stated in his usual unflappable manner

'Have you ever seen one like this before?' his daughter asked, as she showed him the ring, 'Maybe on Konrad?' He didn't need to inspect it too closely, as he knew he had, 'Go on,' he said. She began her account of what had been happening, revealing everything to her father, from the party at Konrad's, his bizarre upstairs gallery collection, Adam's odd and hateful behaviour towards her, his treatment of Hector, and the urgent trip to Germany with the Gray brothers, how they had taken Hector with them, finally culminating in finding this ring.

Her father sat patiently waiting until his daughter had finished 'Interesting, unpleasant, and all somewhat sinister. As for the ring, I have noticed Konrad wearing one, it's very conspicuous and hard to miss. If you want my advice, I suggest when you leave here, go straight home, return the ring to exactly where you found it, pack what you need and move back in with me. That's what I think you should do, but what do you want to do. That is, what you have to ask yourself?' Francine was relieved to hear his proposal

'Yes, I would like to do that, but what do I say to Adam?' she asked sounding scared of his response to her decision, 'Don't concern yourself with him, if he tries to cause any trouble, he'll be making a grave error of judgement, trust me, I can make his life a misery if I need to. He would be wise to stay out of your way. Just send him a message or email. Whichever, but do not phone him, just tell him that due to the tensions between you both recently, you cannot concentrate on your work, and as the auction is now imminent, it requires that you be fully focused, therefore please respect my wishes. That's all you need to say.' Like any father, Sir Howard wanted to protect his daughter from what he saw as a verbally abusive thug. His long-held misgivings about Adam were now coming to fruition and so soon after the marriage

'You're right, and that's exactly what I'll do. But what do you think about everything I've told you today? Did you know about any of this?' she asked, keen to hear his opinion. Sir Howard smiled in a kind of philosophical way, 'No, certainly not, I had no inclination of anything like this, but, as I have told you before when you have travelled the world as a roving Ambassador, you come into contact with, not putting it too mildly, the strangest people on the planet. Some, as they say, you wouldn't give house room to, and no, I've never been invited to see Konrad's collection, as far as I know, nobody was allowed up there. So I suspect that he wanted you to see it for a specific reason', his words unsettled her.

'Me? Why choose me, I don't understand?' she was perplexed by the notion that Konrad took her up there for a reason.

'It could be that the brothers were sussing you out? I actually think they have 'recruited' Adam because they want you!' Her father's words made her terrified.

'Me, but why? What could they possibly want from me?' she said, looking horrified at the suggestion

'Look at all the facts. Konrad's world is art, where the obscene amount of money floating around the art market is eye-watering. It's now gone beyond what anyone could have ever believed possible, and you're very well connected with it. However, of much more value to them is the fact that you are trusted, liked, and respected, having established yourself in the finest and most renowned auction house in the world. You are the ultimate insider, something that Konrad has never been. And, for all his money, I know for a fact he's not well-liked. That's why he's trying to find a way in! Underneath all his obvious wealth and bravado, the fact is he is terribly insecure, that is his own personal demon.

'I believe they looked at your husband and quickly realised that he would be easy to manipulate, so they reeled him in. I knew you could not see it at the time, but Adam was transparent and from the start, I was aware he was a person who was no good. And the brothers saw exactly the same thing, that his greed and ambition would be his weakness and his downfall, but they considered that if they could get him, in turn, they could then get you!' Her father's words made her understand that she had just had a near miss

'I believe you. I found to my cost that Adam was going to be hard work when his supposed charm evaporated so soon after the wedding, and it seems we are now in this precarious situation because of him. I'm afraid that Adam and the Grays will come after us, as we know too much', she declared.

'They don't know all that we know, and you are letting your

imagination run away with you, just put the ring back, move upstairs and we both carry on as usual. Let them get on with their nonsense. It's not against the law as far as I am aware to be stupid, although I think it probably should be,' he joked, 'And, as for your husband, well, his so-called charms never existed. He is just a con artist, her father's words were now blatantly obvious to her.

Asking her father what he now thought of Konrad and Edmund, Sir Howard laughed as he rolled his eyes, 'You mean, do I believe that the Gray brothers and your husband can conjure up the 'Devil'? Then, my answer is no, I really don't imagine they can. But that doesn't mean they are not mentally deluded and as such, they are a threat. One thing that I found a bit strange though, is you say that Konrad and Edmund have homes in Germany and in Argentina?' Sir Howard stated.

'Yes,' she confirmed to her father as she mused that it was odd really when you consider that most people from New York have a summer place in either the Hamptons or Palm Springs. The castle is their family home so that you can understand, but Argentina?

That's a bit random, I must admit I wondered, why there?'

'Perhaps it is not quite as strange as you imagine. You see at the end of the war in Germany, Hitler and his new bride Eva Braun, supposedly committed suicide, and then their bodies were burnt, which meant their remains were unrecognisable. However, the talk at the very top, among the British, Americans, the Russians, and French, all strongly suspected that it had been a staged event and that Hitler and Eva Braun had both escaped to Argentina where so many other Nazis had also fled. You see, they would have felt safe and welcomed in that country because of the many sympathizers at that time with the cause of the Third Reich. Hoping that once settled there, they would be able to rebuild again as they planned for the Fourth Reich!' Sir Howard told his shocked daughter.

'What, no, you cannot be serious, can you?'

'That is the strongly held belief, that's all I can say, but I'm aware of the existence of some very large files held by the FBI on what they assume really happened to Hitler. Naturally, I have no idea myself, it's all pure speculation and theory, however…' He shrugged his shoulders as if to say, who knows?

'You say they confessed to you that they felt more German than American. Well, I think that information alone tells me it's probably quite true. However, it's none of our business. It's not illegal to have homes in any country you choose. I know you said you were not going to tell Adam about your grandfather's letter. Is that still the case?' her father asked

'That's right,' she replied, 'I haven't said anything, thankfully. But tell me, don't you think it's all quite strange that since you gave me that letter from grandfather Max, everything just seems to be revolving around the Nazis and Germany, it's starting to feel incredibly odd, and surely too much of a coincidence,' she reflected

'I am not a person who is in the least bit superstitious, but I have to concede it's quite the mystery, very baffling. No doubt, in due course all will be revealed.' Sir Howard remarked.

'Now, go to your apartment, put the ring back in its place, pack your things, and get out of there, once you are settled in, send that rogue husband of yours a message to inform him that you have moved in with me. Then, my dear, put all your energies into making a wonderful success of the Leonardo da Vinci sale.' Her father was right, his reserved common sense was just what she needed to calm herself down and put everything into perspective, which now included the termination of her disastrous marriage to Adam Faris.

# CHAPTER 43

## LOT 9B
## Christie's New York, 15<sup>th</sup> November 2017

The small oil on the walnut panel of 'The Saviour of the World', circa 1500 dominated the room. The accompanying information read: The smoky sfumato technique, that the artist had so ingeniously invented, brought a new, and unique dimension to painting that had never existed before in the Renaissance world. In this painting, the undertones of flesh gradually fade into one another, producing a softened haziness, where the light conveyed is almost luminous, seemingly bringing Christ to life. The dynamic bounce and weight of the cascading ringlets are a classic signature of the greatest old master of them all – Leonardo da Vinci.

The throng gathered in the saleroom that evening displayed an eager and lively manner, hungry for excitement, demanding to be entertained, and there was nothing like the smell of money to entice those so inclined to attend with expected anticipation of being vicariously enthralled. At that moment auctioneer and Christie's Global President, Jussi Pylkkanen, with his usual manner of urbane composure, stood poised behind his podium, ready for the commencement of the bidding. Everyone was in place as Christie's staff, with their hands hovering over the phone's mouthpiece at the ready to be instructed by their anonymous clients, who would direct them from the comfort of their palaces, country estate, or yachts, to do high-stakes bidding for them.

'Good evening, ladies and gentlemen, we begin tonight's sale with

Lot 9B, an Oil on Walnut Panel, known as The Salvator Mundi by Leonardo da Vinci, which has been in the collection of three English kings. So, shall we start the bidding at... $70 million, a phone bid starts us off – $80 – $90 – $110 million – $160 million I am bid, – $200 million... $240,' a tense pause fills the saleroom as the negotiator confers with a potential buyer – 'So, back to you, François, it's with your client... I hear $268 million – now it's with you Alexis and your client? Jamie, are you out?' – Silence grips the room – 'So, now we have two left in the game? $275 million, I am bid' – a long momentary pause fell – 'Are we all done?' Jussi, the President of Christie's, takes a moment or two, scanning the room for any sign of a new bid

'Ah, there's some more talking going on, so maybe we're not all done after all – Alexis, will you give me $300 million? Is that a, yes?' Instantly wild applause broke out from the floor as the onlookers gasped. 'Is that it? I have a bid for the Leonardo standing at $300 million... What? Is that a bid?

'Yes, it is, I hear you – $318 million – it's now at $320 – $328, with your client again now Alexis, selling at $330. No? We have a bid for $332 – Now a further bid at $350 million – another gasp – 'Are we all done, now? No? It seems not, they're still talking to their clients. Christie's auctioneer Jussi jokes along to the audience as he leans over his podium, telling them all, 'I think we can take a minute or two.' François shakes his head as his clients pull out of the race

'The last bid is now at $400 million – we have a bid for $400 million... Alexis, it's with your client,' as Christie's president and auctioneer take a last look around the room to see if there are any more offers. 'No? The sound of the gavel comes thundering down – 'The Piece is SOLD!' With the buyer's premium on top, a small oil painting had cost somebody a staggering $450.3 million!

The rapturous applause from the onlookers that night was hard to contain. A new world record for a single piece of art had been written into the history books at Christie's.

After nineteen minutes of tense bidding, a price had been achieved shattering every expectation. It was all over, and Christie was jubilant. Francine, however, had mixed emotions. She was happy it had sold for such a large amount of money, understanding its high price would protect it for the future, but seeing the painting every day, as she had done for the past month, it was now time to say farewell. After the legal transfer of ownership and the finances were settled, it would be gone forever to its new owner. Now, of course, there would be wild speculation in the media as to who that person was, and where it would be going.

But, in reality, there were only a handful of people in the running. Could it soon be flying off in the private jet of a Saudi Prince? She couldn't possibly comment. Everyone would just have to wait and see.

From the corner of her eye, she could see a very disgruntled Konrad Gray, who obviously didn't achieve his ambition. It must have really stung him, knowing his wealth could not match those of the global elite, who could outbid him in just under twenty minutes flat

'Oh God', she thought to herself, 'I really don't want to talk to him.' Knowing what she did about the Gray brothers, Francine was simply too wary and wanted to keep her distance. Trying to make her way out of the salerooms was proving difficult, as the exodus of the spectators and press were causing a bottleneck at the door, as she waited to get out into the lobby area, Francine began checking the many messages that were beginning to bombard her mobiles, among them was a text from Hector, 'At last,' she thought, keen to know what had been going on with him;

'Hi, Francine – thank goodness I just about managed to squeeze in at the back of the room to see the sale, I expect you feel like me? Guess that's that, never to see the painting again! But hey-ho! Anyhow, I imagine your husband has already told you, but I'm just so excited that Mr. Faris is allowing me to show three of my paintings at the opening of The Three Floors Gallery on Sunday evening. Fingers crossed it will be my big break. Looking forward to seeing you there, wish me luck! Hector.' Still looking at her mobiles she didn't realise that Konrad had crept right up behind her, 'Francine,' he said in his deep slow voice, which made her freeze, 'Oh, Konrad, hello, how are you?' she said as she quickly composed herself, 'So sorry that you didn't get the painting, you must be very disappointed. Did you actually put in a bid?' she enquired, trying to maintain an air of professionalism.

'Well,' he sighed heavily, 'there did not seem any point, the numbers were going up too fast, and you know very well I had my upper limit – obviously, I'm not pleased, but that's the way it goes. It was overpriced anyway if you ask me. Of course, you must have heard, as it is all around town, that the Salvator Mundi is a fake! Naturally, I don't believe that myself, I wouldn't have wanted to buy it if I thought that was true. But I live to fight another day, and you never know, perhaps one day the Mona Lisa will come up for sale, and I can try again,' he said in all seriousness. She found his statement quite bizarre, 'But, Konrad, you must surely know that will never happen, ever, it belongs to France and the French people,' she said completely flummoxed, wondering how he could possibly not understand that.

'Never say never, maybe you could broker a deal for me in the future? You must always be aware, my dear girl, that in life, circumstances often change. What is not for sale today, perhaps tomorrow, who knows? Whatever, I just have a deep belief that one day, and soon, I will come to own a da Vinci painting and not just his drawings!'

'Sure, but only in your dreams Konrad,' she thought to herself. Suddenly his heavy hand landed on her shoulder, stopping her from moving, as his deep unnerving voice whispered into her ear, 'Tell me now Francine, exactly what do you know about the Mona Lisa?' He gave her a look that indicated that he knew something.

'Sorry Konrad, I don't understand what you mean, I don't possess any more knowledge about the Mona Lisa than anyone else does.' Her mind raced considering the possibilities, 'What could he know? What was he talking about, her grandfather's letter? That was a sheer impossibility, there's absolutely no way he could even be aware of its existence, let alone of its contents, as nobody knew what was contained within that sealed envelope!' As they stood close together, the crowd started to move on, 'Thank God, at last,' she thought, as Konrad declared he was going to take himself off for a glass of something to commiserate with, 'Goodnight, well, not a good night for me, was it? However, I will see you on Sunday evening for the grand opening of the gallery, which I know Adam has not told you anything about. He is under strict instructions not to say anything to anyone, including you, to keep up the suspense you understand, and maintain maximum excitement! Although, of course, we had to feed a few crumbs out to those hungry vultures in the media, just to get their taste buds whetted, when you see what I have to unveil, it will easily take your breath away, quite simply it will be a feast for the eyes, my dear girl, a feast for the eyes!' Konrad told Francine as he walked away from the masterpiece he had just lost. It was also glaringly obvious from his sarcastic jibe at the price the painting had fetched that he was a sore loser and bitter at missing out on the chance to make his name in the art world with such a historic purchase. It must have wounded his pride to realise he just did not have the kind of money that the super-rich possessed. It was also clear from their conversation that Konrad had no idea that she had left Adam.

# CHAPTER 44

## Cruel Intentions

Francine was perfectly aware of their grand opening on Sunday night, there had been so much press interest that you would have needed to have been on another planet not to notice. After all, Konrad Gray was a dominant figure in NYC, as well as internationally within the art business. Up until that moment, though, she had had no intention whatsoever of going, as she most definitely did not want to see her husband, but now that Hector was sounding so elated to be at last getting his chance of recognition, something that was all too rare in this business, she knew she couldn't and wouldn't let him down. She would of course just have to go.

So much had happened in the past few weeks that she felt drained by it all, and her father was away again in Washington giving a lecture at the British Embassy. She could have really done with his wise counsel about going to the gallery opening, but instead, she gave herself a good talking to, asserting she could handle any awkward scenario that might occur from seeing her, soon to be ex, husband. But realistically she didn't believe that a confrontation would happen, as Adam would be far too busy fawning over his new business partners, the Gray Brothers, or as she thought of them nowadays, the Brother's Grim. So, he won't give her a second thought, after all, she believed. Since she had left their apartment and moved back in with her father, he had not messaged her once, not even to wish her good luck for the auction. She imagined that she would probably be utterly invisible to him that evening, as his forceful charm would be in overdrive to impress his new-found friends. That is what she hoped would happen, but if on the other hand, they did speak, she was determined to remain cordial. If there is one lesson, she had learnt from being the child of a professional diplomat, it was to always be pleasant. If she did speak to Adam, that is what she would be, polite – at least, that was her intention.

Now Adam Faris had ingratiated himself with his billionaire friends, she was persona non grata, and he had moved on to bigger and better things. Francine now understood she had been but a stepping stone, as he made his way up to wherever he thought the top of New York society resided. When Adam met Konrad Gray, he saw a reflection of what he wanted to achieve for himself, and to be honest, Francine couldn't compete with that. She wasn't even sorry their marriage had not worked out. Within a very short space of time, she discovered to her cost, that Adam was shallow, ruthless, and worst of all, not a kind person. He was just as her father had said, an opportunist, a stereotypical, clichéd con artist. Looking back, it was hard to understand how she didn't see it before. The clues were all there. Francine had just not paid enough attention to her usually pristine sixth sense.

# CHAPTER 45

# Gallery Opening Night

W hat to wear? Black or red?' She didn't need to think too hard about that. Obviously, it had to be red. Defiant! Her mood was certainly that. Even though she didn't want to attend the night's flamboyant show of self-aggrandizement, she was only there to lend her support and advice to Hector. Unaccustomed as he was to the art business, she knew only too well what a vicious and jealous world it was, the competition was ferocious, and rejection was a constant reality. Approaching the well-lit gallery, the floor to ceiling glass façade was certainly a showstopper, and judging from the large crowd inside, it certainly looked like it was going to be a huge success. The canopy perfectly matched the carpet on the ground for the VIP guests as they posed for the cameras, which she thought was a bit over the top, but evidently fitting for the Hollywood crowd that Edmund Gray had flown into town, as hordes of fans had gathered to be in the presence of the great and good, whose fame gave the ultimate kudos to the Gray brothers as they 'kissed the ring', metaphorically speaking, as if the two men were the Pope. Francine wondered which stars of the silver screen who were avid collectors of art, would put in an appearance as they looked to discover the latest, most radical, and provocative contemporary artwork for their homes in the Hollywood Hills while being photographed with their new 'find' giving both the A-lister and aspiring artist several column inches of free publicity, which guaranteed their art would then soar in value: all making them even more money. It saddened her to think how it's never really about the talent, no, it was only ever about the return on investment. That alone was the deciding factor.

Francine looked at her watch again. Hector should have been here a long time ago, she thought to herself, how very late he was for his first ever public viewing. Then she recalled that he had mentioned to her that occasionally, the sitter who looked after his mother was not always the most reliable. Reluctant to go inside, Francine, who had not realised just how cold it had turned when she had dressed that night, started to walk up and down in an attempt to keep warm, but as the time was slipping by, she was concerned that the sitter had not turned up at all, and with no one to take care of his mother, Hector would miss his chance to meet some very influential people who may help him with his burgeoning career, and more importantly, even sell his work. But surely if that were the case, then he would certainly have called or messaged, wouldn't he? At the very least, he could let her know that he might be running a little late. Besides, if the worst came to the worst, he could put his mother to bed and just come down for an hour or so. He needn't stay for the entire evening, just stay long enough to make some all-important contacts.

However, another half an hour had passed, and still, there was no sight of Hector. Sleet was beginning to fall, and it was freezing, she had not brought an umbrella and her hair was getting wet. Francine decided to call him and discover if for any reason he was not going to turn up. And if so, she would go back home, but there was no reply, just straight to voicemail. Possibly he has no battery or was in the subway with poor or no signal, she speculated

'Well, it's no good just standing here huffing and puffing and getting wet, just suck it up and go inside,' she thought, deciding she could not wait outside any longer as her hands were turning blue, and as it was the art scene, she would know half of the people in there anyway, so she would not be short of conversation with anyone.

Approaching the entrance via the carpeted sidewalk, Francine could hear loud, 1940s-style American Jazz emanating from the musicians inside, which created an exciting, but ever-so-cool

253

sophisticated energy. In fact, it provided just the right vibe, allowing the ultimate feel-good factor for the evening, it almost guaranteed the perfect catalyst to encourage several spontaneous buying sprees. A team of young and good-looking attired staff had been hired to serve discreetly, offering up chilled champagne, tiny delicacies of Japanese finger food, White Pearl Albino caviar on blinis, and Moose Cheese on black charcoal crackers to the well-heeled prospective clients, who demand their food to be either organic or exotic, but preferably both. Accepting a drink, as she walked through the door, she could fail not to recognise that the Grays had done it. Francine had to admit to what could only be described as a masterstroke of ingenuity. Konrad and his brother had pulled out all the stops, no expense had been spared in their execution of creating the grandest, most swanky gallery that she had ever seen. Looking around, she had to hand it to them, it was a most extraordinary accomplishment indeed. This will make huge waves in New York, putting a lot of the other dealers' noses out of joint, if not out of business, how were they ever going to be able to compete with such an opulent place?

The gallery was enormous, and the lighting, so important when showing works of art, was perfect, and incredibly flattering. It was arranged over three floors, hence the name, it boasted a round amber coloured smoked glass and brass elevator in the middle that took you seamlessly to each level in absolute comfort, no tiresome steps for those women in their designer heels to concern themselves with. The concept was of the moment, but classic and definitely super stylish and most importantly, it was aspirational, certainly a place to hang out and be seen in. Konrad was a seasoned enough dealer to know it would attract those very difficult, rarefied, and uncompromising contemporary artists whose work now commanded literally millions of dollars, prompting them to sign up with him exclusively, because once they had established a name for themselves, it becomes their turn to call the shots, always threatening to go to more prestigious galleries if they don't get their own way. As their status rises, so do their demands. The art world's premier league of prima donnas. This place will certainly lure those who like nothing more than a shiny new toy while leaving all the other gallery owners scratching around fighting for the leftovers.

Konrad, noticing her walk in, rushed over immediately, 'Francine, at last, where have you been? Never mind, you are here now. So, tell me, what do you think of our little place? Not bad, is it?' Konrad's question did not warrant a reply, as he confirmed his own answer. Taking her firmly by the arm he led Francine around, giving her a personal introduction, as his pride and joy beamed all over his face. The compliments from the biggest names in film history came thick and fast, even she had to admit how thrilling it was to be standing next to her own screen idol, whom she'd had a crush on since she saw him in one of the Godfather movies years ago

'However, Francine, even your fashionable lateness is impeccable, as I was just about to unveil four recently discovered paintings by the most sort after, and desired artist, at this moment in time.' Konrad declared to her with a fanfare of pomp, as if he was Moses himself just returning from Mount Sinai with the holy scriptures

'That sounds intriguing, Konrad,' thinking to herself, 'Okay, now you have me captivated,' as she wondered which paintings could he be talking about.

She was totally puzzled as to what could possibly be that important and new on the market that she hadn't heard of. Walking toward a large roped-off area, Konrad calls everyone to attention with the microphone handed to him.

'Thank you all for being here this evening, I feel blessed and humbled. Well, not that humble!' Konrad laughed at his own fake self-mockery, 'When I tell you all that I can hardly contain my excitement tonight, not just with the new gallery, created by myself and my brother Edmund. Edmund, where are you? You should be here next to me, not drinking all the profits over there, he joked, 'And also a big thank you to our new junior partner, Adam Faris, whom many of you have met this evening. Now, I'm absolutely thrilled to bring to the market for the very first time, four recently discovered paintings by Ernst Kirchner, who, as many of you know, was a leading German Expressionist, whose canvases were branded as degenerate by the Nazis. Sadly, most of his works were destroyed, but fortunately these have survived, and I am proud to be able to show them to you all tonight, so in celebration of not only our splendid opening but to an artist who was ahead of his time.

But do not get overly excited, or even bother to get your money out, as these have already been sold! And that's why they will remain behind the ropes as requested by their new owners. Sorry, but you won't be allowed to get any closer!' Konrad informed them. Those few privileged individuals who had been invited there that evening, all lived and breathed art, and were savvy enough to know the exceptional quality and rarity he was showing them was not only unique but out of even their price range. To say they were impressed was a complete understatement.

Tonight, without fail, Konrad, his brother and, she had to admit, Adam, had sealed tight their future prosperity, along with the outrageous riches soon to be winging their way. And just like a bank heist, they had pulled it off, or so it would seem.

Francine asked herself as she stood there, was it all aided and abetted by the 'Eye of Bedim? The Devil's Bible?' Or was their apparent victory just good luck, fate, or just sheer business acumen, and nothing to do with the occult? The only thing she was sure about was that these three men all worshipped at the temple of greed, where money was the only religion worth dedicating their lives to.

Francine was simply astonished, if not shocked, by seeing these rare works by Ernst Kirchner. In recent times his paintings had risen to the top of the most desired canvases in the world, due in part to the notoriety that surrounded his back story, every collector and museum was desperate to get their hands on them, so much so that the price had sky-rocketed out of all proportion, even surpassing many old masters. Any painting whose provenance carried that degenerate tag was definitely now one of the 'new kids on the block'. There was certainly no doubt in her mind that these would fetch tens of millions. She was aware that just one of Kirchner's paintings Christie's had sold eleven years ago in 2006, had fetched $38 million, so, goodness only knows what price they might reach today. And Konrad has four of them! 'Wow, that must be, taking a rough guess, more than $150 million. No wonder Konrad Gray looked so pleased with himself. And how on earth did he manage to acquire those? What a coup in finding them, but that was why he was so successful, I guess,' Francine reasoned.

'Adam, come over here and say hello to your wife,' Konrad shouted out to her husband in the distance, trying to get his voice heard above the music. Within a second Adam had done as he was told, making his way towards them both

'Now, take care of your lovely wife, I need to find Millicent and that stray brother of mine. I want him to introduce me to all those exceedingly rich A-listers to get them to part with some of that money. After all, we have been plying them all evening with Krug champagne, as we don't want them to think too hard about the price when they tap in their exclusive American Express Centurion pin numbers! And Adam, once you have shown your wife around, don't forget, we are here to do a lot of business.' Konrad gave Adam his orders. Greeting each other with an awkward peck to the cheek, Adam asked her, 'So, what do you think of our enterprise, bet you are quite shocked?' 'Congratulations, I hope it all works out for you,' she replied politely.

'No need to concern yourself about that, it will definitely work out for us. We really can't fail, I mean, look around you, we've smashed it,' he boasted

'I really didn't expect you to be here tonight, what happened? A change of mind about Konrad and Edmund. Have you conceded that you were utterly wrong about them?' Adam's compliant deference towards the brothers was obviously unshakeable, as he continued, 'You see, through them more than anybody else, I've discovered that when you get to the very top, well, it's only then that you see the way the world really is, and how it must remain for those who reach that glorious height!' The sneer on his face left no room for doubt in her mind that he was enjoying what he believed was his triumphant victory over his wife.

'Actually, I came here to support Hector, it's an important night for him, so maybe you'd be kind enough to show me where his paintings are hanging. I would like to see them while I wait for him to arrive. I guess he's having a problem getting here on time,' she said. Adam looked at her in a kind of delighted way, before he burst out laughing. It was a cruel, snide type of laughter. Francine was perplexed by his reaction, asking him, 'What's so funny?' failing to understand, as he held up his hands in a juvenile gesture. 'I have to admit, I'm guilty.' 'Guilty of what?' Francine, still bewildered. Adam grinned again, obviously highly amused, 'I led him on deliberately, and I have to say, it was with the greatest of pleasure! I told him I'd hang three of his painting at tonight's opening, also, just to rub salt into the wound, I actually believe he would have got some brilliant reviews in the press, his work is good, in fact, I would even go as far as saying it is exceptional, his canvases would have sold for thousands, he is, without doubt, one of the best young artists I have seen in a long time, and as you know, I'm very hard to please. So, with our endorsement, and the right PR behind him, in time I think his work could have sold for millions. Your protégé, as they say, would have been on a roll, I could, if I had chosen to, made him very rich. But I'll let you into a little secret, that's presuming you want me to be entirely honest? I actually sacrificed making a huge profit out of your young friend, and instead, used Hector to get back at you. So there you have it!'

Adam, along with his callous smug condescension felt invincible as he continued his malicious explanation, 'I knew you felt sorry for him, and championed his work, so I set him up, which he completely fell for. You know the type? Desperate, but always needing others to set the agenda for them. Then this morning he sent several distraught-sounding texts, concerned about why he had not heard anything about bringing in the paintings for hanging. What an idiot, I mean, come on, couldn't he take the hint? That alone should have told him the score, but obviously not, it seemed he needed to have it spelled out to him in black and white! So, I put the poor guy out of his misery and informed him that, 'I'd changed my mind, nothing doing pal,' he must have just accepted it because he never responded. He didn't even try to argue his case. I'll tell you this much, Francine, he has no backbone, no fight in him. What kind of an artist is that? No edge to him, the art market demands a 'personality', can you imagine Picasso or Jackson Pollock taking that lying down? Pollock would have come staggering into the gallery, drunk, completely off his head, and demanded my attention, not sitting back waiting for a text message. A dangerous element is precisely what is expected of the modern artist, that chutzpah and audacity, and your guy has none of that!' Adam was not only indifferent to how this would probably affect Hector. He was celebrating his demise

'You mean, you actually intended to be that vicious to him? Just to seek some irrational revenge against me?' Francine was horrified by that admission.

'Well, let's just say he was collateral damage, and do I care how he might feel, really Francine, need you ask me that? Is that likely?' Adam continued to bask in his own glory.

'Tell me, Adam, just out of interest, did Konrad approve of your actions, you know, allowing you to discard such a potentially lucrative artist, one that would have been so profitable for the business?' she asked, daring to make him realise his own short-sighted stupidity, and curious to understand if Konrad had sanctioned his behaviour. Momentarily the smile disappeared from the face of Faris, his pernicious power had clouded his judgement, and he suddenly knew it. Looking flustered, his face took on an appearance of pure, unadulterated hatred towards her, as his obvious blunder was laid bare to them both.

'Look, Hector did what was asked of him in Germany and got well paid for it, and nothing more was ever guaranteed,' he snapped back at her, trying to cover his conspicuous ill-judgement over Hector's potential worth, as Adam quickly insisted that Konrad had given him total latitude when it came to the middle floor of the gallery and that he had full control over the abstracts, installations and any of the new upcoming artists. It was his domain to run his way. But her thoughts were now about Hector, as Francine raises her voice in disgust, 'How can you be so...' Adam jumped in, 'Spiteful, vengeful, ruthless? Blah...Blah...whatever, take your pick, who knows honey, and what's more, who gives a damn, but I guess that's something I've just managed to cultivate along the way, we all have our natural talents! Anyway, got to go and press the flesh as they say, lots of very important people who want to meet me.' Walking away, Adam turned and called out her name slowly, 'Hey, Dr – Page – Hamilton,' his disrespectful and childish dig at her title was deliberate. 'Catch – you can have these – oh, and thanks for the free board and lodgings! Just send my stuff on, because, as of tonight I will be staying in the lap of luxury, I have a suite at the St Oliver Hotel, for the time being, until I buy my own apartment on Park Avenue. You never know, we might become neighbours. Oh, and do try the canapés, I hear they are rather good! 'He left her standing there holding the keys to their apartment, thinking he had had the last laugh.

# CHAPTER 46

## Hector – The Underdog

Leaving behind the razzmatazz of the gallery opening, Francine made her way to the exit, she felt deflated and angry in equal measure, recognizing once and for all that Adam Faris really was rotten to the core, but the noise of a loud scuffle at the entrance grabbed her attention. All at once she saw that it was Hector who was causing all the hassle as he tried unsuccessfully to gain entry and was being told in no uncertain terms to leave. He was obviously unfamiliar with gallery opening protocol that require you to show a personal invitation card to get in. Francine swiftly went to speak to the security guards, who were only doing their job, 'It's okay, he's with me, I'm Mrs. Adam Faris,' she told them, and although saying the words 'Mrs. Adam Faris' stuck in her throat, it was a necessary evil at that precise moment. Immediately, she saw how much thinner he'd become

'Hector, why are you here? I have just heard what Adam has done to you, I'm so sorry, you didn't deserve that and must be feeling absolutely furious with him. I know I am. He had no right to treat you that way. Let's get out of here.' Francine, trying hard to mitigate the situation, could see from the sheer anger in his eyes that he was not ready to be pacified, and it concerned her. He looked unstable if she was being truthful, like a man who had been pushed too far to the edge, 'Come on, let's go, there is nothing to be gained from staying here. Just let them get on with it. They're really not worth the trouble,' she pleaded with Hector.

'No! I came here for a purpose, and I intend to fulfil that purpose,' his voice was filled with total determination. She quickly reasoned that perhaps it would be better to let Hector go and give Adam a piece of this mind and get it out of his system, as it wasn't fair or right to keep it all bottled up, even if it really wasn't the time and place. But then again, Adam had it coming to him, the way he pushed people around, what did he expect.

'Okay, but I'm going with you,' she insisted

'When I left him, he was on his way up to the middle floor so let's take the elevator,' she said, leading Hector towards the glass cylinder.

As the doors of the lift opened, Hector stepped out, and there, in full sight, was his nemesis, Adam Faris. Posturing, and confidently dressed in his expensive designer suit he stood as large as life, surrounded by his new clientele, as he sucked up to them for all he was worth, brazenly self-satisfied in his new empire.

'Excuse me, there's something I have to deal with,' Adam told his guests, walking over towards the elevator, Hector could see straight away that Faris was far from pleased to see him standing there as he challenged him, 'What are you doing here?' Adam said to him before he saw Francine standing behind him

'Oh, you again? I should have guessed you would be involved in this, well, you can both turn around, get back into the elevator, then get the hell out of here! Neither of you is welcome, and if you don't leave now, I'll call security to escort you both out of the building, and I don't think that sort of image will go down well with your boss at Christie's, Dr Page-Hamilton!' Faris said, being hateful to her once again.

Hector squared up to him.

'Faris, don't pretend to be surprised. You know exactly why I'm here. You have treated me like a complete fool,' Hector shouted at Adam, as his new influential gallery patrons that circled around him were taken off guard by the animosity between the two men, but before Hector could finish what he wanted to say, Adam, now fuming by this unwanted person invading his refined territory, waded in with

262

a caustic avalanche of abuse forgetting the bearings that allowed his streetwise character, so ingrained in him, to come right to the surface, letting everyone witness his true nature, 'Look chum,' poking his finger violently into Hector's shoulder, 'Go take a walk downtown to some of the lesser galleries, who just might take your work, because, let's face it, you're not up to the mark for this kind of establishment, let me put it this way, in case you don't understand, your work is just not good enough, Pal! Failing that, why don't you try and sell on eBay?' Adam quickly attempted to regain the composure he had been cultivating all evening. Acutely aware his guests were all watching the acrimony unfolding between them. Turning to apologise to his guests for the incident, Adam tried to laugh it off, putting it down to an artist's temperamental nature. It was impossible for Francine not to see the intense volcanic rage that was festering within the young artist, as she realised it was now out of her control to prevent whatever was going to happen next. Hector stared hard at Adam as he told him, 'Now it's my turn, and you won't shut me up. All you people here have absolutely no idea what's going on, and what these so-called dealers are up too. Take my word for it, you're all being conned, just like I've been conned' then suddenly, without any warning, Hector pulled out a knife. The already horrified onlookers gasped in total panic, 'No! Hector, don't do anything stupid, he's not worth it, think of your mother, who'd look after her?' Francine pleaded.

'My mother died this morning, and she died believing I was finally getting the opportunity to become a professional artist,' he blurted out, as the two men stood face to face, like wild animals preparing for combat. Hector's destructive despair was dangerous, like somebody who had nothing to lose, as he told Adam, 'It's just one big game to you, treating me like garbage, something that can be disposed of at will. Then maybe Mr. Faris you can put this in your trash can as well' then swiftly and without any hesitation, Hector, with one stroke of his knife, cut off a large chunk of his own ear, yelling at Adam Faris with the full force of his pent up rage as he thrust his amputated body part into Adam's face.

'Is this what you want? Sorry, it's not quite a pound of flesh! Tell me, is this what you need to do to get noticed? It worked for Vincent van Gogh. Will it work for me?' Now, as Hector's blood spurted in all directions, the queasy guests were repelled by the sight of the claret-colored carnage now splattered all over Adam's face and his Tom Ford attire. The dramatic gesture produced frantic screaming from those gathered watching the calamity unfold before their eyes. One woman vomited in full sight of everyone, nobody could believe what they had just witnessed, while some less squeamish purposely took out their mobiles, as they recorded the mayhem of the two men unravelling in front of them, ready to instantly upload onto their social media for likes, and then all too soon, for it to go viral. This will be like a gift from the gods for Konrad Gray's competition! By now, everyone in the gallery was aware of what had happened and, to put it bluntly, it was going to be a public relations disaster for them. Adam screamed at Francine, 'Get that maniac out of here now!'

'Come on,' she said to a disorientated Hector, who was bleeding profusely, telling him to put his jacket firmly against his head, as she handed him some tissues from her bag instructing him to wrap his discarded flesh inside

'Let's get you out of here,' guiding him by the arm towards the lift, leaving everyone in complete shock at the nightmarish fiasco that had just occurred.

Their grand opening night had certainly been a complete sensation, that was for sure, but just not the kind of sensation that the three men had planned so meticulously for. It was an evening in New York that nobody would ever forget, but for all the wrong reasons.

# CHAPTER 47

## Becoming Vincent

Outside the gallery the narrative and hype were being debated furiously, some appalled, but plenty were revelling in the hysteria, enjoying every minute of the freak show they had just witnessed by the apparently 'unhinged artist,' an expression overheard from one of the guests nearby. Francine finally managed to hail a cab to take Hector to the emergency room and away from the prying eyes, who wondered what had possessed him to take such an action. Francine realised he might be in a state of delayed shock at his mother's passing away that very day, and this more than likely motivated him to confront Adam, 'I'm so sorry to hear about your mother, I can only but imagine just how upset you are, 'she offered her condolences, knowing that Adam's unforgivable behaviour and dishonesty about showing his paintings must have pushed Hector over the edge 'I just don't know what to say? But firstly, let's get you some medical attention,' she told him, taking charge.

'Do you think Konrad or Adam will call the police?' a worried Hector asked her, now slowly regaining some common sense.

'No, I doubt that, it's not in their interest, and I can assure you, they'll be far too preoccupied with the fall-out from the media coverage they are likely to receive. They will be spending all their time and resources trying to limit the negative publicity, and besides, what could they have you arrested for? Crashing into a private party? Impersonating Vincent van Gogh? Anyway, you only harmed yourself, and, hopefully, their reputations,' she reassured him.

Sitting together in the chaotic atmosphere of accident and emergency waiting to see the doctor, Francine strongly advised Hector to say he had been attacked, 'Whatever you do, don't say you did this to yourself, otherwise, they will detain you for psychiatric evaluation, and I really don't think you need that kind of intervention'. Hector agreed.

'So, the wound to your ear, you were very lucky that you managed to retrieve what was cut off, now there's every possibility we can reattach it, don't worry too much, it looks worse than it is. I must say, it's a strange injury to sustain from an attack, I don't think I have seen that happen before, did you see who did it?' Hector told the triage nurse that he didn't; 'The doctor will be with you shortly, she'll take a better look and decide what needs to be done, and you will have to give the details of your health insurance or credit card,' the nurse told Hector.

'Don't worry I will take care of the bill,' Francine told the nurse. Francine considered it the least she could do to help him under the circumstances.

'How are you feeling now, any better?' she asked, concerned

'Yes, I'm okay, such a dumb thing to do really; it won't get me anywhere, all I've done is make myself look ridiculous,' he said

'Hector, can you tell me what has been going on? The last I heard was that you went to Germany to do some work for Konrad, which I imagine you were happy about. Then tonight you made a very strong statement in front of everyone about how they were all being cheated. What did you mean when you said that?' she said, treading warily. Hector paused before he asked her.

'Are you sure you really want to know? Because, you might not like what you hear, as it involves your husband?' he stated.

'Yes, I do want to know, and as you saw for yourself tonight, the explosion between Adam and myself, well I think that was self-explanatory, now I'm just determined to get to the bottom of all of this, so tell me everything,' she insisted.

'Okay, here goes, it all began that night Adam took me to meet with the two brothers in their apartment. Before they even said anything, I had to sign something they called an NDA, which at the time I'd never heard of, but I'm sure you know what that is. A 'Non-Disclosure Agreement', they explained to me the full consequences if I were to ever break my silence and reveal anything they said, and it was legally binding. Francine knew exactly what it was. Hector continued, 'Konrad and Edmund were exceptionally nice to me, in fact, so was your husband, believe it or not. Anyway, the three of them scrutinized every detail of the paintings they had asked me to take along; they said I was very talented and displayed a great eye for fine detail and were impressed that I was able to adopt any style or brushstroke at will. I was completely surprised and really flattered to hear such praise from people like them, as it was not something I was expecting. Then Konrad Gray showed me some high-resolution photographs and asked me if I could paint in that style. After I studied them for a few moments I knew it wouldn't present any problem, so I said I could, and it wouldn't be difficult. Edmund then asked me if I had a passport, and if was I prepared to travel and paint four canvases exactly in the style that he had just shown me, if so, they were willing to pay me $10,000 to do the work, but I had to be ready to leave very early the next morning; they said I would be gone for roughly ten days or so. I told them that I would like to, but I had to care for my mother who was terminally ill, they said not to worry as they would pay for a private nurse to live in and tend to all her needs. I didn't have to think about it. And I certainly didn't ask any questions! Can you imagine just how much I needed that money? I was blown away; I knew instantly that I could use it to help pay for my mother's medications and when the time... Hector hesitated, pay for her funeral. So, I agreed.' Hector continued with his story, 'By the time I got back home from seeing the Grays, a nurse had arrived at the house and was ready to look after my mother, incredible how fast money works! Anyway, very early the next morning, before it was even light, I was collected and taken to Mr. Gray's private plane. The very first thing I had to do was to hand over my mobile phone, it wasn't allowed. I had no idea where we were going, they didn't say, and I didn't ask. Everything was pleasant enough on the journey, with no problems, but when we landed, I had a hood placed over my face and put into the back of a vehicle. After about an hour, maybe more, we arrived, and then they removed the hood, imagine my surprise to find out I was now standing in a castle! And I mean a real castle, can you believe that? I soon discovered I was in Germany.' Hector's experience had started to sound like something straight out of a James Bond novel. Francine listened intently, 'Go on,' she told him.

'They took me down into what I assumed had once been dungeons or maybe wine cellars, but it ran under the entire castle, anyway it was a huge space; one thing for certain, it was absolutely freezing cold, but the real shock was to come. I couldn't believe what I was seeing; it turned out they were producing fake works of art on an industrial scale!

'The so-called respectable Konrad and Edmund Gray are just common hoods! That's how they've made their fortune, and now your husband is in it up to his neck. It was then I understood the reason for the NDA, taking my mobile and putting the hood over my face so I wouldn't know exactly where I was, but the castle was in the middle of nowhere, so I had no idea anyway. Then these two older guys gave me some food; after I'd eaten, they took me to a tiny room which was very basic, there was no outside communications, no phones or tv set, nothing, and they told me to get some sleep because I would need to work eighteen hours a day, which was okay with me, and, besides, there was no natural light so you lose all sense of time anyway. It was hard to believe so much criminality was occurring down in the depths of such a grand old castle. I saw a lot of machines which I soon learnt were scans, x-rays, infra-red and ultra violet lights, and other types of technology; things I'd never heard of; there were teams of expert forgers, all creating works of art, another team who were painstakingly concocting the most authentic provenances; to be honest, I had no idea about provenances, what they were, or how vital, I was totally ignorant about them, but now I know just how much value they add; it can make or break a work of art, it's what museums and auction houses crave for, I soon had my eyes opened about that;

well, you know all about provenances'. Hector continued with the most unbelievable expose of just how much attention to detail they went to in order to deceive the art world, 'They paint mostly what they term as second tier old masters, because, although they are worth a lot of money, they don't attract too much publicity in the auction rooms like the big names do, it's much more low-key, and I can tell you, it gives the forgers in the castle a real laugh when they hear about it, as they know the truth. Their research is spot on because when these guys create a forgery, they ensure that if the artwork is x-rayed, or undergoes chemical analysis, or whatever other testing they do, they make sure that these fakes reveal precisely what the 'skilled eye' of those so-called experts would expect to see; the Gray brothers also have scientists who reproduce pigments identical to the ones used by the old masters; they can also age canvases, and so many other procedures, truly, there's nothing that is overlooked in their process; it is meticulous, I discovered that every time a new piece of technology comes onto the market to confirm the age or authenticity of these things, they circumnavigate a way round it! Some of the old guys who worked there spoke English, and that's how I learnt what was going on, there were also Russians, men from Poland, Bulgaria, and others, mainly Eastern Europeans who said they were all leaving soon as now it's winter they go back home to their families until the spring.' Francine couldn't take it all in, as she asked him.

'So, they know full well they are producing fake works of art?
'Yes, of course, they know, but they don't think about it anymore, and what's more, they don't really care. They know the brothers are making a lot of money out of them, but what can they do about it? They all told me the same tale, that they wanted to be either artists or artisans, but all too soon discovered it was impossible to make a living and feed their families doing that type of work; then years ago each of them was approached by 'agents' who were on the look-out for their kind of skills, offered them the work, and that's how it all began. When I listened to their stories, I came to appreciate how different our two worlds are; where they come from, it's so much harder to get money, and then, once you do get the money from the fakery, you

become trapped. Their desire to provide for their families is far more real than any piece of art.

And, I suppose, at least they get to use their talents, but it's certainly not an easy life being stuck underground, it is damp and cold even in the summer, they said, and they are unable to see their families for months at a time.' Hector told her.

'Did you see any other work being produced there?' she probed deeper.

'Yes, for sure, marble sculptures, old coins, the paintings, of course, all sorts of stuff, oh yes, and an old Russian man was making these really beautiful and delicate looking Eggs, called Fabergé. I felt sorry for them, some of these guys are worn out and weary from the conditions, and they look a lot older than they really are, just living on coffee, and endless cigarettes and the food wasn't great either, mainly stews they cook themselves, but they just quietly get on with it, and they know they have to keep their mouths shut.' Hector finished his shocking tale of the underground forgers whose lives were so far removed from the exciting world of the expensive fine art market as could be imagined.

By now Francine was dumbstruck, in almost total disbelief by what Hector had revealed to her, 'It's all so hard to take in', she asked him.

'Exactly why were they scared?' Hector sighed, 'It's because they all know that if they ever speak out about what they are doing to anyone, their families will disappear! It's that simple; it's not a game, they understand that these people are ruthless. Besides, what would they gain from informing the authorities? And who could blame them? Put yourself in their shoes, they are powerless,' he told her the stark dangerous reality of the situation.

'It is a well-organized art mafioso; do you know what artist you were told to fake?' she asked, keen to find out. Hector conceded that at first, he had no idea, but one of the Polish guys who was very knowledgeable told him it was by someone called Ernst Kirchner.

'I'd never heard of him, and couldn't Google anything either, as I said, they'd taken my phone away, so I just got on with what they wanted from me, and they seemed very pleased with the work I'd produced.'

Francine exclaimed, 'Oh my God, of course! Now it all makes sense,' telling Hector that the paintings he had done were on show that night at the gallery and that's why at the opening Konrad had put the display of the four paintings, supposedly by 'Ernst Kirchner,' concealed far away behind the rope, telling everyone that they had all been sold, and it had been requested by the buyer they remain that way

'You see, Hector, the work would have been only surface dry as you had only just painted them, and I presume, they didn't want to take any chance of damaging the paintings by drying them artificially; so, because his ego got the better of him, and he wanted to show them off, but couldn't take the chance of someone noticing, hence the rope trick, you have to credit Konrad, he thinks of everything! And what's more, you would never have known they were fakes, I took a good long look at them, simply because his works are so rare, and even from a distance I could see that vital and absolute essential flow of energy within the paintings that only the actual artist can ever normally achieve; so, they would have passed with flying colours, not many forgers have that ability,' she said cynically.

Hector went on 'As soon as I landed, I was handed back my mobile, instantly I found I had received several messages informing me that my mother's health had deteriorated drastically. I got back home as fast as I could, and thank God, I was in time,' Hector's words trailed off, but Francine didn't pursue it.

'Then out of pure curiosity, I wanted to know all about Ernst Kirchner, who I learnt had been a German Expressionist painter whose work was branded as 'Degenerate' by Hitler in 1937. After his public humiliation at the hands of the Nazi regime, along with the destruction of most of his works of art, it culminated in him committing suicide a year later. His story was tragic. You know Francine, it makes you wonder if it's worth it, all that struggle, being constantly rejected, your work ridiculed; sometimes I believe we are cursed with a wretched talent, only to be exploited by others. I must confess, I did think about Vincent van Gogh, who made nothing from all those great paintings of his. It's just about the dealers, the collectors, and the all-important provenance, and which wealthy person had owned the goddamn art before! So, what happened tonight at the gallery, you know, the ear thing, I just saw red; some stupid form of revenge for myself, Vincent, and for poor Ernst Kirchner!'

She had to admit Hector's words were sadly very poignant and all too true.

# CHAPTER 48

## Twenty-Four Hours...

After most of the night at the hospital and successful minor surgery, Francine told a bandaged Hector to get some sleep as she dropped him off at his home, while the cab took her back to Park Avenue.

At 8 a.m. she was woken by her mobile going off with messages galore. Every media outlet was vying for the story, which was being dubbed, 'Art Wars in Manhattan.' And now it was Hector on the phone.

'I'm being bombarded by the press non-stop. I have them all outside my home, they're banging on the door. I don't know what's happening or what to do, are the police going to arrest me?' he sounded frantic.

'No, they are not going to arrest you!' she said as she picked up the remote to put on the TV; it's all over the television now.

'Listen, stay calm and leave it to me, don't go outside your home or talk to anyone, and keep the blinds closed, I will get back to you,' she promptly hung up and quickly made some calls to the many contacts she knew in the media. Within half an hour she called him back

'Hector, do you want the good news, or the very good news?' She could hardly contain her excitement. He was puzzled by her statement.

'What, I don't have a clue what you mean?' was his natural response to a delighted Francine.

'It would seem you are about to become very famous because, not only are most of the TV networks wanting to interview you about last night, also, it seems that most the contemporary major art dealers in New York are desperate to get hold of you and are all bidding for exclusive deals to represent your work; and they haven't even seen any of it! It's ridiculous, but you have crossed the Rubicon Hector!' she laughed.

'The what? What's a Rubicon?' he asked her, not having a clue what she was on about – 'Oh, don't worry about that, it's just an old saying, forget I said it! So, I have arranged everything, a car will pick you up at 10 am to take you to the TV studio, I will meet you there, also, take four, no make it five of your paintings along with you; do you think you can handle an interview?' she was concerned he might find the prospect daunting.

'I'm not sure, and I just don't get it. How can these galleries be interested in me and my work, when they have no idea what I even paint; that's crazy!' His head was spinning with the madness of it all. Francine understood exactly what he was saying;

'Yes, I agree it is a kind of madness, I realise it does all sound very strange, but that's the way the art world works, there is nothing they like more than notoriety, and that is what you gave them last night!' she laughed.

'What do they want to ask me? What should I say? Suppose they ask about how I know Adam, and should I tell them about Germany and the fake paintings and what if they ask me about...' He went and on getting himself in a state.

'Stop! You are getting yourself worked up, look, Hector, chances like this rarely, if ever, come along, so grab it, remember this, keep it very simple, you tell them you know Adam through me, and he had promised you the opportunity to hang your paintings at the gallery's opening night, then at the last minute he reneged on you, just as your mother had passed away; and the incident with your ear happened because you were emotionally overwrought and not thinking straight, and how you bitterly regret your actions; keep to that script, and Hector, listen to me, whatever happens, do not mention Germany, or the fake paintings you did for Konrad that were on show there last night, whatever you do! Firstly, we have no proof whatsoever, and if you say anything, he will sue you for slander, trust me on this, and besides, he would have removed them all by now,' Francine had to drum it into his head to remain in control for the questioning he was about to undergo.

'Okay, I understand I won't say a word it,' he promised her

'Remember, Hector, the media know nothing about any of that. Their angle is just about how the 'struggling young artist' is exploited by the mega-rich gallery. It's one of those stories that the press and social media just love. There is nothing they like more than the 'underdog' – sorry, that sounded awful the way I said that,' Francine apologising for how it might have come across.

'No, that's okay, I know what you are saying, and it's true, but will you be there with me? If you are, I'll be okay,' he asked her

'You'll be fine, look how you stood up to Adam in front of all those people last night, you have inner resources that you don't realise. I have complete faith in your abilities,' her reassurance was just what he needed as he reflected on the course of events of the last twenty-four hours, first with the death of his mother, then his showdown with Adam Faris at the gallery, his moment of insanity that led to him cutting off part of his ear, and now, all this totally unexpected, overwhelming attention. How your life can change in just one day!

# CHAPTER 49

## The Renaissance of Konrad Gray

Francine was relieved that the TV interview was over. Hector had surpassed himself, coming across as genuine, talented and likeable. His art spoke for itself as demonstrated by the phone calls flooding into the television studio with offers to buy his paintings. Francine was pleased that Hector could now go forward with the career he was fated to have. However, not all was good. The fallout from the previous night hadn't abated, quite the reverse. Francine knew only too well that when the media sniff the scent of blood they go all out, and Konrad, his brother and Adam were now the in the firing line, ready to be taken down.

From New York to Beverly Hills the gossip and acrimony showed no signs of lessening. In fact, it had now gone International as her father had confirmed in a text message saying it was all over the BBC and Sky News in London. Jealousy, hostility and rivalry were now the heady mix of what ailed the other dealers and gallery owners, whose hatred motivated their need to ruin the wholly tarnished reputations of the Gray brothers once and for all. Now back home after the frenzy of the past twenty-four hours, the calm interior was just what she wanted. It was bliss, such a welcome relief. That was until, suddenly, a violent hammering on the apartment door made her jump out of her skin, 'Who on earth could be pounding on the door like that, what do they think they are doing?' Francine was not expecting anyone, and for protocol and security reasons the doorman would always call

276

through on the intercom to inform a resident if somebody had arrived unexpectedly. Nobody was ever allowed to just come up. Looking through the spy-hole she was aghast to see the back of Konrad's large head. Immediately her heart rate shot up, she really didn't want to face him, 'Why was he at their door in any case? She presumed it was not to borrow a cup of sugar! There's an unwritten rule in Manhattan, that neighbours, and especially on Park Avenue, simply do not visit each other without the requisite prearranged appointment, it's just not the done thing! 'I'll just pretend I'm not here,' she thought. After a few minutes of hardly breathing in case his apparent supernatural powers heard her, Francine assumed he had left. Tempted to look again through the spy-hole, she saw those wild menacing eyes staring straight back, as if able to penetrate right through the heavy wooden door, even though Francine knew rationally that he couldn't, but fear took over as she stumbled backwards and accidentally knocked a delicate porcelain vase from the hall table onto the black and white marble floor, which echoed loud enough that Konrad heard it.

'Francine, open the door, I know you're in there. I want to talk to you, and I want to talk to you now', he demanded.

'How does he even know I'm living here? Had Adam finally told him?' Against her better judgement, Francine nervously unlocked the door to admit Konrad, who was dressed from head to toe in black, making his body look like a solid dense mass as he walked in passed her.

'Oh dear, made a bit of a mess there haven't you? How unfortunate,' Konrad reprimanded her just as his highly polished shoes trod deliberately and slowly over the shattered ornament, crushing the broken pieces almost into a powder, 'Tut…tut…tut… what a pity, I expect it was quite valuable, knowing, as I do, your father's excellent taste in antiques? You seem to be making a mess everywhere you go these days,' he said as he made his way into the elegant sitting room and deliberately made himself comfortable in Sir Howard's dark blue winged armchair, crossed his long legs, while simultaneously his large hands gripped the arms of the furniture so intensely, she could see the whites of his knuckles as he assumed full ownership.

'What can I do for you, Konrad?' she enquired, wanting to sound polite, not wishing to antagonize him, 'Where are your manners, dear girl? Aren't you going to offer me a drink?' His tone of voice had set the icy atmosphere. 'Yes, of course, what can I get you?' she asked the uninvited guest

'For a start, I think I would enjoy some of your father's superb single malt whiskey. Umm, yes, that's what I'll have to start with!' he declared. Pouring from the heavy decanter into the glass, Francine quickly picked up his ominous statement, along with his pernicious energy as it began to fill the whole apartment. Handing him the drink, she glanced at his ring, the evil 'Eye of Bedim' prominent on his small finger, before asking him, 'What else do you want, one of my father's cigars?' Konrad didn't respond as he allowed several awkward minutes to pass, his uncompromising body language had become oppressive. She knew he was taking control, but was unsure of how to respond;

'You're amusing Francine, just so amusing, you really are quite the comedian, tell me, does it come from that famous English eccentricity we hear so much about, um, I wonder? But I think we both know exactly what I want,' his fixated stare remaining on her as he swallowed down the large whisky in one go, then forcefully banging the empty whisky tumbler onto the small lamp table next to him. The tension emanating in the room was palpable, as he went on, 'because of those outrageous, unforgivable and heinous antics of that reprehensible, contemptible husband of yours, who, no longer serves any purpose and is therefore of no use to me whatsoever, I will not be content until I see him where he belongs, which is in a cesspit of his own making, along with that unbalanced Hector August. They have both openly discredited me and my brother, Edmund, who has had to remain in hiding at my home because he cannot face going back to Beverly Hills and confronting the backlash. I don't need to tell you of the damage that has been done to our impeccable reputation that we have nurtured and painstakingly built up over decades, because that is abundantly clear from the ugly, wild accusations being reported in the press, not to mention the stench being created via social media, it's all over the city. The respect we have earned has gone, vanished overnight!

Do you know that Millicent was called into MOMA this morning? No? Of course, you don't! Well, my girl, because of your husband's shameless behaviour, and the ensuing scandal, Millicent has been asked to 'temporarily' stand down from the board she has just managed to get herself onto, while 'things' settle down! MY WIFE! My dearest Millicent, has NOTHING...to do with any of this, but your husband has in one evening managed to drag her good name down into the gutter at one stroke! The gutter is just where he belongs and that's precisely where I intend to see him. I won't stand for it!' With the deafening and frightening sternness of his voice, she knew he meant business. Konrad went on with his castigations in full flow one after the other, 'I want – no, I demand – how shall I put it, full compensation for all my losses, and one that will be a big enough gesture to restore my great name and reputation once again. Only this time, it will be something that will guarantee that I come back even bigger than before! And you, my dear Francine, have just the very thing I need to make that happen, you will facilitate my own personal Renaissance, the Rebirth of Konrad Gray! And I want it within the next forty-eight hours, and there will be no second chance!' His words were forceful and uncompromising.

'I really do sympathize Konrad for what has happened, it's just awful and so unfair to Millicent, but I have no idea what you are talking about?' she said as she struggled to placate him.

'Francine, Francine, please, look at me, do I look like a fool to you? Do you really believe I don't know what you are in possession of?' Konrad sighed heavily as he rose from the comfort of the chair, stating with exasperation, 'I'm getting rather tired of this silly game,' then, picking up a silver-framed photograph from the side table of her father with Barack Obama at the White House, his following comments were blatant, 'Um, that is nice, I hope you're looking after him, you just never know... Well, what can I say, unexpected things can happen.' The threat from Konrad's statement was clear and unmistakable, as he replaced the frame back onto the table. She understood exactly the implications.

Francine wanted him to leave. His controlled antagonistic, but deliberate overpowering choice of words and continued presence made her feel extremely distressed, 'Konrad, I'm sorry, but I really don't know what you're talking about, or imagine I have possession of that you want me to give you?' her voice almost pleading with him. As Konrad made his way towards the door, he turned in his customary slow, snail-like manner and told her, 'What I want Francine, is the letter.

The one written by Leonardo da Vinci.

The one that contains 'The Secret'.

That's all...'

His mouth, all at once twisted into an imbecilic grin, but his eyes remained lifeless and dead, resembling those of a shark circling its prey. His departure left Francine struggling to fully absorb all that had just occurred. It was utterly impossible for him to be aware of the letter, as she knew absolutely for sure, that the only two people in the world who had any knowledge of its existence were herself and her father. It was therefore incomprehensible how he had found out, but evidently, he had. Feeling shaken up by the intimidating scare tactics from Konrad, Francine immediately called her father in London to tell him what had just happened, 'I'll be back very soon, we won't discuss it now, let's wait until I return home, then we can take this further, if you feel unsafe in the apartment, stay with a friend tonight?' he suggested, extremely concerned for her. She reassured her father, 'I'm okay, now I've told you, but to come here and threaten us like that. And how can he possibly know about the letter, what is happening? Is he capable of causing us harm? I just worry because it's impossible to fathom what is going on in his mind.' My advice to you is, don't even try, you will never unravel the mind of a man like Konrad. He operates on an entirely different level altogether. Now, as I have just said, let's wait until I return home to talk about this situation, okay?' Her father's words were wise and to the point.

It was now nearly 10pm and the afternoon and early evening had faded into dimness. The past few hours had been spent thinking of nothing other than Konrad's brazen threats that culminated in a dire warning that she had just forty-eight hours to hand over the letter or else, to face exactly what? Francine could not have asked him what would happen if she did not give him what he demanded, because that would have been tantamount to admitting that she had guardianship of it. The thought of going to the police was a non-starter as she played out the scenario in her head, 'So, Dr Page-Hamilton, you say it's all about what, The Eye of Bedim? A Crazed Billionaire Art Dealer? Leonardo da Vinci? And a Secret?' It wasn't hard to imagine precisely how it would look to the officer at the front desk of the precinct, who would probably then simply ask the name of her current psychiatrist, 'Or believe she was high on some narcotics. No! That was definitely not a great idea'.

Francine entered her bedroom and switched on the lamps which reflected the soft pale green wallpaper that was a nostalgic throwback to the 1930s, ideally complementing the walnut veneer furniture. The room was a haven of tranquillity, the perfect therapy to the noisy and brash life of the New York City streets that continued relentlessly round the clock. After spending the entire evening in pensive thoughts about the nature of the Cult that the Gray brothers and Adam were all embroiled in, she recalled what Will Wallace, her friend from Christie's, had said, concerning its members ruthless endeavour to thrive,' it was his throw-away remark of, 'Once you were in, there was no way out', that struck her. Konrad had said that he 'wanted to see Adam in the gutter'. What did he mean by that? Literally, or just metaphorically? You simply couldn't tell with Konrad, he was so opaque, and, quite possibly, genuinely evil

'Oh, for heaven's sake, listen to what you are saying! Pull yourself together! Stop it now and get out of the apartment before you send yourself round the bend,' Francine remonstrated with herself, as she promptly grabbed her coat and left.

Francine had not eaten since early that morning and was not even sure if she could summon up an appetite, but she hoped that, once out of the apartment, the sight of one of Joe's burgers or bowls of spaghetti, just might sufficiently tempt her to indulge.

Joe's was a diner she often went to, liking its warm relaxed atmosphere. It was a family-run business where she knew everyone, and trusting it would provide a respite from the obsessive introspection and alarming thoughts, that both she and her father were in danger, after her shocking encounter with Konrad. The parallel of her grandfather's lucid words of warning, and how he and his family's lives would have been at risk, if it was ever known exactly what he had discovered about the Mona Lisa really struck home to her. As likewise did the motto, 'damned if you do, damned if you don't!'

Leaving Joe's diner, Francine couldn't fail to see a large cluster of people gathering at the top of the block. Curiosity being part of her nature, and also, since it was on her route home, Francine decided to go and look for herself. The harsh burst of car horns as traffic came to a standstill added to the sense of a drama unfolding as Francine furtively made her way through the crowd to reach the very front, all vying to see exactly what had just happened. The numerous police cars and ominous yellow taped off area, along with the morbid sight of the open doors of a black mortuary van, suggested that someone had come a cropper. Francine suddenly realised she is standing right outside the Five-Star St Oliver Hotel, the one that Adam had bragged he had just taken up residency in: all at once a deep unsettling sensation washed over Francine as she asked the young woman standing next to her, 'Do you know what happened?' The young girl replied, 'Yeh, they said some guy jumped from the balcony of the hotel. You've just missed them putting his body into that death wagon over there. Funny isn't it, you would think that someone who could afford to stay in the St Oliver, wouldn't have any problems, would you? Still, that's New York for you, money or no money, everyone's got problems!' she said, sounding cynical, but resigned to the harshness of life. The speculation that it might be Adam had crossed her mind for the briefest of seconds, but that was just a ludicrous idea, as he thought far too much of himself to ever consider that course of action. Francine now wanted to remove herself from the chattering crowd as they began to consider as to all the possible reasons behind the man's apparent suicide. It was definitely time to leave she surmised as she turned to make her way home, instantly she became frozen to the spot, unable to move a muscle, because there, lurking in the shadows, towards the back of the crowd, was none other than Konrad, calmly watching. 'Was that a coincidence? Or had he been to the hotel for a showdown with Adam?' She knew that he wasn't simply out for a casual evening's stroll to take in the night air. Konrad Gray didn't walk anywhere. She deduced intuitively that something was not quite right. It was just too circumstantial for Konrad to be present right outside the hotel that Adam had booked into. It began to nag away at her as she immediately reached into her pocket and pulled out her mobile to capture his image. Francine's gut reaction was now on full alert as she started to piece together the known facts: 'Adam's Hotel – the dead body of a man – and Konrad's presence.' She was disturbed by a realization that it must have been Adam who had lain on the sidewalk. Adam knew far too much about their cult, and the workings of Konrad's organization, he had become just too much of a liability to the Gray brothers, who would not allow themselves to face any more unnecessary risks. As such, he needed to be disposed of, Francine presupposed. The brothers' ruthless personas finally hit home, with a fear that surged full throttle as she ran all the way back to her apartment to arrive rushing into the foyer totally frazzled.

'Are you okay? You seem panic-stricken,' Seamus, the doorman, asked her. Francine, not wanting to cause undue alarm, replied, 'No, I'm fine thank you, I just got a bit spooked because I thought someone was following me, probably just being overly precautious, but all the same would you be kind enough to see me up to my apartment? I know I'm being silly, but...'

'Of course, I will, you can't be too careful these days, and you are not being silly, don't you go worrying yourself, I'm here all night, you can call on me anytime,' he told her in his reassuring mellifluous Irish accent. Thank goodness for Seamus.

How the darkness intensifies an already overactive imagination. So it was a relief to Francine to finally see the daylight once more when she opened her curtains and allowed the sunshine into her bedroom, bringing with it the welcome of a new day. As she examined her watch, she knew her father would be arriving in about an hour as he had caught the red-eye flight from London.

'I'm so glad you're finally home,' she told her father as he dropped down his suitcases and greeted his daughter with a kiss to the cheek, 'Yes, me too, and now I want to get to the bottom of all this unpleasant business with Konrad Gray,' he told her.

Immediately her father made a phone call, 'Good, I will expect you within the next hour,' she heard him remark, then wondered who he had been talking too, and why had he insisted they come to their apartment straight away

'I could do with some coffee, and it's not too cold for the balcony,' her father insisted.

'OK, I will bring some out', she told him.

'Now, let me get this straight, you informed me last night when you phoned me in London, that Konrad has full knowledge of your grandfather's letter. Am I correct? 'Sir Howard wanted to make absolutely sure of all the facts.

'Yes, that's right, he does,' she confirmed.

'Well, I think I know how he does, and that is why we are sitting out here!' Sir Howard told her.

'You do? How exactly?' she was more than surprised by her father's statement.

'Let's just wait, we will know soon enough,' her father stated, then asking her, 'You also said last night that you believe it was Adam who was found lying outside the St Oliver Hotel?

'I have had the night to think about it and in the cold light of day, well, now I'm not so...' her voice trailed off

'Let me see the mobile photos you took. um... These are quite blurry, and inconclusive,' her father said as a matter of fact, 'Although, I must say it certainly does resemble Konrad, it's a shame you didn't take a better picture. I think our best chances lie in Germany.' She knew her father's judgement of the photos were accurate, somehow, in her nervous haste she had failed to capture a clear and distinct image of a suspected murderer.

# CHAPTER 50

## Friends in High Places

'Your assumptions were correct Sir Howard, but it's all sorted now. If there are any more problems, just call,' the two middle-aged men said.

'Well, actually, there is something else, but it's a lot more involved, and it is in Germany.' The retired ambassador proceeds to give them full details of the scale of what was occurring in the bowels of a certain residence that belonged to Konrad and Edmund Gray. Sir Howard's reputation was impeccable, and he knew this request would be taken with the utmost seriousness and dealt with at the highest level.

'Consider it done, Sir, we will inform Interpol, it certainly won't be difficult to locate the castle,' they reassured him. Sir Howard expressed gratitude to them both as they left.

'Who were they?' Francine asked curiously. He smiled, 'Well actually, and between you and me, they were from Intelligence. When you have been an ambassador to Moscow, Saudi Arabia, and Washington, well, let's just say it comes with some special perks, you know, friends in high places who can get things done!' he grinned.

'So, now we know! Konrad Gray had our apartment bugged!

Well, all except the balcony of course. I have given them the spare keys to sweep your apartment, as I expect they will find the same there. Now, for how long he had been listening in is anybody's guess, but I'm assuming it was probably sometime before the Christie's auction of the Salvator Mundi. I expect he was basically just trying to obtain insider information to allow him to gain the upper hand in his fanatical quest to buy that painting – but then he couldn't believe his luck, when he heard us discussing the legacy your grandfather had left you! So, we now know, he didn't use any mumbo jumbo or supernatural powers of his misguided cult. It was just plain old-fashioned criminality, and from what I'm starting to discover, I think very little in Konrad's life leans towards the legitimate!' Her father had solved that mystery. Francine stood opened mouthed, 'I don't know what to say! All that would never have occurred to me, but how did he even get into the apartment? And, what's more, you don't even seem surprised!'

'Well, that's because I'm not, you see, when I was an active ambassador, our homes were swept monthly for bugs, of course, you wouldn't have been aware of it at the time, it's all done very discreetly, but now I'm retired, they don't sweep nearly so often, only twice a year, and, I guess, Konrad just got lucky with his timing, because they were due to come in next month,' he told her.

'You mean to say, people still might bug your home?' Francine was astonished. Her father laughed, 'Of course, they do! Actually, they discovered a device in my study in 2014, when I had been due to meet President Obama at the White House. In fact, quite often, whenever a monitoring device was found, we would often just leave them in place, and feed them false information. you see, fake news has been around for a very long time. But that's the life of international diplomacy and politics, there are too many interested parties always hoping to hear something they can use to their advantage.

It's one big international surveillance game of chance, you know. They do this... and we do that! Just plain old-fashioned spying in the traditional sense, you know, wire-tapping, surveillance, taking compromising photographs that can then be used as leverage, the old tactics continue to work amazingly well, not everything is done by cyber and high-tech satellites, as Konrad's actions prove, listening in and trying to use blackmail. As you see, nothing changes, my dear, and that was my first assumption after you told me what he knew, but I wished I had known earlier what he was doing, I could have had some fun with him. And I would have thoroughly enjoyed it! Oh, and

Konrad didn't get in or even get his own hands dirty. He would most certainly have used professionals to carry out such a job. It's ingrained in me now to react the way I do, once you have worked in the Foreign Office, all this becomes a normal instinctive way of thinking. You really get used to it, and there's very few surprises left anymore.

So, not to labour a cliché, but it just goes with the territory! Now we must go down to the precinct and inform them that you suspect it might be the body of Adam. If it is not, then so be it.

Anyway, we will show them the photos, but too be honest, I don't expect much will come from that, it's not really any hard evidence, and as for the apartment being bugged, I think we will keep that between ourselves.

Right now, I'm going to call Amos, and tell him to meet us there, it's best we have our lawyer present,' her father asserted, firmly taking control of the situation.

# CHAPTER 51

## Mistaken Identity?

'I'm Detective Roy Egan – is it Mrs. Faris, or is it Dr Page-Hamilton?' he asked her, she replied it was the latter.

'You must be quite intuitive as we were just about to pay you a visit. Now, would you care to explain precisely why you've come here?' The New York detective's demeanour came across as sardonic while waiting for her explanation. It didn't take her long to tell them all she believed and suspected.

'So, although you say you didn't know for definite anything had happened to your husband, Adam Faris, your assumption was based on the facts of last night. Namely the dead body of a male on the sidewalk of the St Oliver Hotel, and the seeing Mr. Konrad Gray among the crowd, of whom you took photos. And so you put the two facts together and come up with a murder. The St Oliver Hotel has confirmed that a man booked into the Prestige Suite under the name of Adam Faris, and identification to that effect was found in that suite. Therefore, I ask you, Dr Page-Hamilton, if you believed that it was your husband lying there last night, why have you left it until this morning to come here?' The detective asked her in an interrogatory manner, as her father's lawyer Amos Woolf stepped in, ready to protect the rights of his client.

'Look, Dr Page-Hamilton has come here of her own volition, and, as she has already told you, she and Adam Faris were no longer living together, so now you have this information, maybe you could use your time better and go pay a visit to Mr. Konrad Gray, who might like to explain just what he was doing there at the same time as Mr. Faris supposedly jumped to his death. That, Detective Egan, is where I suggest your line of questioning should be directed, and, considering the irreparable damage done by Adam Faris to the Mr. Gray's business and reputation, there, I would suggest, is your motive!' the lawyer told Detective Egan.

'And that, Mr. Woolf, is exactly what we are doing! Mr. Konrad Gray is in an interview room down the hall with his lawyer, you don't need to tell me how to do my job! Let me see the photos you took last night,' requesting her to hand over her mobile phone for evidence. Francine immediately complied and, after close examination, Detective Egan, with his brusque manner, ordered Francine, her father and Woolf to remain in the room. Within a short space of time Detective Egan returned looking none too pleased.

'Dr Page-Hamilton, not only are these photographs very ambiguous at best, but it seems you have failed to mention to us that Konrad Gray has an identical twin! I heard he had a brother, but as I don't get around to following the art scene much these day's I was unaware of that fact! Egan's sarcasm was evident in his voice.

So, how on earth could you possibly know for certain who you thought you saw last night? Consequently, the improbability of a positive outcome of any formal identification is almost impossible. Therefore, seeing as there is apparently no credible evidence linking the death of Adam Faris to Mr. Gray, who said he spent the night at home with his brother, Edmund and his wife, Millicent, we have told him he is free to leave, at least for now. We will be going through all the CCTV of the hotel, and will question the on-duty doorman to your apartment block for last night.' Egan informed them.

Detective Roy Egan continued, 'We are aware of the incident that happened at the gallery on Sunday evening between your husband and Hector August. And it must have been quite a spectacle, no surprise then that the press has had a field day with their coverage of the behaviour of the gallery towards the young artist, who had just lost his mother. And I have it on good authority that the entire art establishment has acted to distance itself from Mr. Gray, who I gather is none too popular with many of the other dealers,' the hard-nosed detective informed her.

'Earlier this morning, Mr. August was interviewed, and it seems he has a watertight alibi. He spent last night talking with his priest, Father O'Rourke about his mother, like a good Catholic boy, which puts him in the clear. So, although you have stated that you and Mr. Faris were no longer living as man and wife, did you know what the state of his mind was?' he quizzed her.

'If you are asking me, do I believe Adam would take his own life? No, absolutely not, he wasn't the type. Yes, of course, the trouble at the gallery was undeniably devastating for all of them, and it would have finished Adam's career in the art business, but to kill himself because of that? No, never, he just wouldn't do that,' she insisted to the detective.

'What makes you so sure? I mean, after all this gallery was a huge financial investment and...' Francine interrupted, 'Detective Egan, Adam, I can assure you wouldn't take his own life, for one thing he was just far too arrogant. I don't mean to sound cruel, only accurate, he was not a sensitive man, I'd even go as far as saying he carried within him a dangerous level of self-belief, in fact, both sides of his Jekyll and Hyde character were convinced of their own greatness, if I can put it like that. So, you see, without reservation, I would say he was a survivor. Something as drastic as taking your own life would never even have occurred to him. Adam's death was not the result of an accident or suicide, I am convinced, which just leaves the one alternative. It was murder...' Francine concluded.

'Um...I understand you are English, and, perhaps, you Brits do things a bit different in the UK, but with all due respect, this ain't no Agatha Christie movie, so if you don't mind, we'll do the detective work around here. You can keep your amateur sleuthing theories to yourself! Tell me, doctor, did you and your husband sign a pre – nuptial agreement?' Egan said, quizzing her further. Amos Woolf jumped on this as fast as lightening.

'What's with that line of questioning, my client is not here as a suspect in her husband's death.'

To which the stern-faced Egan fired back, 'I think it's quite relevant under the circumstances. It certainly provides her with a strong motive, if in the event of a divorce or death...' Woolf cut in again, 'Detective Egan, let me put this to bed for you. Yes, my client did have a pre-nup, I should know, I drew up the agreement myself.

Neither party would have gained financially from a divorce or death, as Dr Page-Hamilton's assets would have been distributed to her various charities, and as my client is independently wealthy, and Adam Faris was not, his death would not have advanced her in anyway, so does that answer your question?' Therefore, unless there is anything else I think we are finished here. Any further questions, contact my office, here's my card,' Amos Woolf's reputation as one of the sharpest lawyers in New York was clearly well deserved. Egan knew there was nowhere else to take the interview, so he conceded, 'You are free to go!'

'I guess Detective Egan's engaging charm comes from spending all his time among the low life and criminal fraternity!' Amos commented with a cutting disdain as they exited the precinct. Sir Howard nodded his head in agreement before commenting to his lawyer. 'Yes, that's probably quite true, but can you imagine what he has to contend with every day? Don't misjudge Egan's caustic exterior. He can't afford to be any different, not if he wants to survive in that kind of tough violent setting, his hard shell is the only thing that prevents him from being swallowed up and spat out by the system.'

# CHAPTER 52

## Downfall

The grim and depressing experience of spending several hours inside the police precinct prompted Sir Howard to suggest they go and have a late lunch. 'Would you like to join us, Amos?' 'Thank you, but no, I must get back to the office. Francine, don't concern yourself anymore, apart from the identification of Adam's body as his next of kin, put all of this out of your mind. I think they will now start to look a lot closer at the Gray brothers because that's where they will find the murderer, or murderers, of Adam Faris,' Amos Woolf said as he took off in a cab.

'Let's go to Morton's, I don't think we are in the mood for the Metropolitan's formality today.' Francine readily agreed.

The smiles from the staff at the front desk of Morton's was a pleasant sight as Sir Howard and Francine entered the restaurant without having time to make a reservation.

'It's a bit late but can you accommodate us for lunch?' he asked

'Of course, Sir, may I take your coats?' the young girl asked them both.

'Yes, thank you, oh wait a moment, I think that just might be the phone call I've been waiting for,' Sir Howard said as he pulled out his mobile from inside his heavy tweed overcoat before handing it to the cloakroom attendant.

'Excuse me, Francine, but I need to take this call...Yes, um, yes, I see, very good, excellent, no, that's fine, great job, and thank you.'

Sir Howard was extremely satisfied with his phone conversation. It had been less than twenty-four hours since he made his request and now Interpol had issued a RED NOTICE on behalf of a member country, Germany: For the provisional arrest of Konrad and Edmund Gray for International Art Fraud. Astounded by the speed of events, Francine asked, 'How did they know where to find their castle, and so fast?' 'That was not difficult, quite the contrary, all that blindfold nonsense they used on Hector was just a form of intimidation and served no real purpose. You see, Konrad and Edmund always made sure the only people they brought in were not in any position to take action against them. Hector, I believe, was just a one off. You know, in the right place at the right time, they could see he was extraordinarily talented, and the young man was very desperate, therefore he was easy to exploit, and so with the upcoming opening of the gallery they seized an opportunity to make a huge amount of money with the four fake paintings of 'Ernst Kirchner'. It was something they just couldn't resist. But the Gray twins made some fatal errors of judgement. Firstly, with Adam, although they quite rightly recognized his greed and ruthlessness, but then seriously misjudged his weaknesses and his uncontrollable petty jealousies. As far as Hector goes, well, let's face it, artists have always been erratic, shall we say. And Hector has had a lucky escape! I am not trying to pervert the law, just stretch it a bit in favour of somebody who deserves a second chance, because as far as I can see, there is nothing to be gained from telling the police about Hector being at the castle. His life has been tough enough already. I do believe the downfall of the brothers is now imminent and that's not before time. They have worked in the shadows, maintaining low profiles, always in the trenches and just coming up when the situation demanded their presence. When all this comes out, my god, it's going to be like the Bernie Madoff financial Pyramid Scandal all over again!

'All those clients who have invested billions of dollars into worthless art are not going to take this lying down, I can tell you. If it were still the days of the Wild West, there would be lynch mobs out in droves. I wouldn't want to be in the shoes of either Konrad or Edmund Gray when all this stinking detritus washes up at their feet. They won't know what's hit them!' Sir Howard's prediction now seemed inevitable and fully justified.

# CHAPTER 53

## Divine Inspiration

With lunch almost over, Sir Howard hoped their exhaustive talks about the events of the past several weeks would produce some kind of resolution, but Francine's mood was stubbornly subdued.

'You know, until now, art has been my whole life, but all this has made me question just about everything involved within that culture. I really don't know how I feel about it anymore, or even if I still want to work at Christie's.' Francine's sudden unexpected confession mystified her father, 'Why? It's not Christie's fault, they had nothing to do with any of this! Heavens above, you can't let what's happened affect you in such a negative way, as hard as it may sound, life throws curve balls at us all sometimes. You shouldn't give up on what you love because of this, don't be defeated, this is just a setback, in a few weeks' time you will feel completely different, you just need a good holiday and things will start to improve and look very differently. As for Adam, I can only but imagine the situation must be extremely difficult, but he was wrong for you from the start, you see that now for yourself. And as for the world of refined beauty – Art, well, isn't it estimated that up to forty percent of the art market consists of fakes... You told me that! Therefore, what the Grays have been up to, cannot really come as any surprise, can it? Admittedly, you don't expect to find it on your own doorstep, so to speak! Also, now I come to think of it, I do recall one Sunday in London, many years ago while consuming a delicious roast dinner, a heated debate on whether Michelangelo was right or wrong when he committed an act of art forgery because he was poverty stricken and needed to eat. It is not, of course, that the Grays were ever going hungry, but you get the point I am making. You see, whether you like it or not, forgery is a historical activity, in fact it's found everywhere, and in many guises, not just in the world of art, and I don't suppose that it will ever change!' her father affirmed. Francine conceded to her father's accurate knowledge and his elephant-like memory of a Sunday dinner long ago about which she had totally forgotten. As the waiter brought over the coffee, Sir Howard could see just how deep in thought she still appeared to be, before he recognized that familiar, determined and tenacious expression as it emerged. He had seen so many times before as it began to radiate her face, 'I know that look. Something is going on in that mind of yours, tell me, what you are thinking?' Her father was astute enough to notice an insightfulness when he saw one, as Francine raised her hand slightly indicating for him to wait.

'Just a moment, let me just clarify my thoughts,' then, suddenly, grabbing her mobile from the table in an obvious haste to make an exit from the restaurant, Francine accidentally knocks over her cup of coffee spilling most its contents over the white tablecloth, apologizing profusely to the baffled waitress, and her father, who is now confounded by this obvious change in mood, as he asked, 'What on earth is it?' trying to fathom out her outburst.

Francine was experiencing a perception that she knew only too well, that familiar, inexplicable knowing. She told her father, 'I really don't know what it is myself, it's incomprehensible, except to say, I have a very strong sense of purpose,' before insisting with total conviction, 'Sorry, but I just have to go!' The staff looked at her as if she had taken leave of her senses, while trusting it was not as a result of the cuisine? Sir Howard sat there bemused by his daughter's behaviour.

Rushing out the door of Morton's restaurant, Francine blocked her mind completely to any possibility that she would, or even could now alter her decision, due to her inherent obstinacy, accompanied by that rush of pure adrenaline, giving her the courage to pursue what she saw as an urgent mission that simply must be accomplished. Francine knew it was now or never

'Come on… come on… hurry up…' she groaned, hitting the elevator button hard again, displaying an uncharacteristic act of impatience

'At last,' she mumbled getting in. Throwing her coat, bag and door keys onto the hallway floor, Francine lost no time in reaching her destination: Sir Howard's study. And now she was there, standing in front of the Dutch old master that concealed the safe. Removing the painting, she hesitated, fixed to the spot, paralyzed as if set in aspic jelly. She questioned herself again, 'Do I really know what I'm doing? Well do I? Suddenly uncertain, she knew that doubts were closing in on her, as she thought she heard the words, 'the devil is at your elbow,' whispering in her ear.

Was her mouth bone-dry because she had run all the way from the restaurant or because of a fear of the unknown? Squeezing her eyes tightly shut, Francine asked her grandfather for assistance, 'Well, you got me into this mess!' From nowhere, a calmness and tranquillity replaced any sense of inner turmoil and restored her composure, as she opened her eyes, the trembling in her hands had ceased, the safe was now open, and she could see the buff-coloured envelope that held her grandfather's personal covering letter to her, the one she had previously read that day over lunch at the Metropolitan Club, an incident which now seemed like a lifetime ago. There, staring her in the face was that bold red seal daring to be opened, and she understood that its magnetic power had finally won.

The uncanny silence of the room told her unmistakably, 'Go on, don't quit now' and she was not about to, Francine finally broke the seal of the bulky envelope that contained firstly, several pages of slightly yellowing paper, which she could see were obviously extremely old. Carefully unfolding them, at once she knew there was no mystery about the author. It was by none other than Leonardo da Vinci himself. She was more than familiar with his renowned back to front mixture of Latin and Italian words as evident from his famed journals, his writing was as commonplace to her now as her own personal scribble. But, unable to translate its contents, she gently lay them aside, as she started to open up the rest of the other pages containing the easy-to-understand words emblazoned on the top of the embossed-gold-leaf letterhead, which read:

## The Reichsmarschall Hermann Göring
## Carin Hall
## 1940

Francine understood enough to recognize that the pages were written in German, French, and then, thankfully English, and presumably each contained all the same words.

The first few lines she read from the English version, explained that this had been penned by Dr Otto von Becker, a German scholar and authority on Leonardo da Vinci, who then went on to testify that on this day in 1940, he had transcribed the following words from an authentic document that had been discovered by Hermann Göring himself, hidden in the back of the original frame of the Mona Lisa. The letter went on in much detail to state that Reichsmarschall Göring had been personally gifted the Mona Lisa painting by the Vichy Government and was now the legal owner of the Masterpiece

'Umm...?' She read on, it continued to recount that the transcription had taken place at Carin Hall, in the presence of Göring, and that copies were produced in German, French and English, affirming that each of the person so named on the transcription would be handed copies personally by the Reichsmarschall, at a meeting to take place at the Ritz Hotel, Paris on an elected day, unspecified at present. These persons will be: Professor Charles Jardin, Head Curator of the Louvre, Monsieur Pierre Guyon, Director of the Musée National, and Philippe Pétain, Head of the Vichy Government.

The fact that Hermann Göring was involved had not come as any surprise to Francine, as her grandfather had already said as much. But it was entirely new information that the Reichsmarschall had had actual legal ownership of the Mona Lisa. That was altogether another level of intrigue, and it blew her mind. She was confounded by this knowledge for a split second before realizing it was just so blatantly obvious. Of course, how stupid not to suspect, because the more she thought about it, the more it seemed so utterly plausible, if not downright evident, after all, everyone knew how the Nazi's stole almost all of Europe's finest art, so, why not take possession of the da Vinci masterpiece? It made complete sense that this painting would be top of the list, Göring's prime target.

But, as it now appears he really did take the Mona Lisa back in 1940, why then did France keep that fact undisclosed to the nation? Francine vividly recalled seeing black and white photographs during one of her university lectures on the plunder of European art during World War two. One of those photographs was of the Mona Lisa 'supposedly' being removed from the Louvre. This must just have been French propaganda they staged, showing that the da Vinci painting had been safely hidden for the French nation, hastily done before Göring arrived in Paris, knowing full well what was on his agenda. Was this the 'secret,' that would have proved so catastrophic to certain people, if it had been revealed that Jardin and Guyon's subterfuge to hide Göring's theft had been nothing more than a pack of lies?

Now, after such a time lapse, this information would be completely unremarkable in today's world. She thought about it for a few minutes, and could see how at the end of the war, it would have been extremely shocking for the French to have found out that their national treasure had been in the possession of The Third Reich for several years. It would have been akin to Winston Churchill admitting to the British Nation, that Hitler had taken the Crown Jewels from the Tower of London, even if only for a short time. Those dilemmas put a totally different perspective on events during wartime, and trying to compare those days to now was unreasonable and futile. But, in this day and age? it would hardly make a footnote in the history books. So, was that it? Was that really what all the fuss was about? Had her grandfather, Max, unwittingly exaggerated this whole entire melodrama? She smiled to herself thinking, then all this had been about something and nothing after all! Taking an enormous sigh, she felt completely deflated. What a tremendous disappoint it had turned out to be!

Curled up on the winged brocaded chair, Francine glanced at the photo of her grandfather on the desk, thinking of him as she stared at his face, she couldn't help but observe that it looked different, but how, and why? Unable to quite put her finger on it, as she asked herself, had one of his eyebrows always been that much higher than the other, making him look exasperated? 'Odd, I've never noticed that before!' Suddenly, from absolutely nowhere a chill factor had penetrated the room, Francine sensed a presence, as she imagined his very distinctive voice speaking from behind her, too scared to turn her head, she listened intently to the words.

'Francine, my dearest darling granddaughter, for heaven's sake child, read the rest of letter!' The spectral voice became the spark that brought her abruptly back to reality, in realisation that her determined train of thoughts had been momentarily diverted. She now believed that the essence of her grandfather, Max, was in the room with her, scolding her for reaching a premature conclusion. Now feeling seriously rebuked, she did as she was told and read on, which was precisely what she should have done in the first place.

# CHAPTER 54

## Let Sleeping Dogs Lie?

Nothing could have prepared her for the words that were written on the pages. It was so far beyond anything that she could have imagined in her wildest fantasies that she needed to read it over several times to fully absorb every incendiary word of da Vinci's testament. It was electrifying, as if the great man had struck at her central nervous system with bolt of lightning, catapulting her into action with a gravitational force over which she had no control. It set her on a clear path that she knew she had to follow. Thinking of her grandfather, she could now understand exactly the reasons why he had locked the document away. Without doubt, Francine knew only too well the outrage, the anger and the sheer hostility, that she was about to provoke if she were to charge headlong into making an explosive public exposure and dramatically release it onto the world stage. Even if it was at her own personal cost, aware of the backlash and abuse that she was about to inflict on her life.

'Francine, she heard her father shout out, what on earth is going on here? I nearly tripped over your bag and coat that you have just left lying on the floor as I came through the door, anyhow, I've just received news of the Grays. Actually, where are you?' her father calling out again, as he made his way along the hallway.

'I'm in your study,' she called back. Entering, he immediately saw the oil painting propped up against his desk and the safe wide open. He didn't need to ask.

'Ah, I see, so you finally decided to take a leap of faith? And from the lack of expression on your face, you are either terribly disappointed, or suffering from shock, and now I guess I'm about to discover for myself,' he noted as his daughter handed him the letter. Sir Howard, ever the cool reserved diplomat, was always in control of a situation, and any response would be in his typical fashion, which was naturally understated, therefore, Sir Howard knew his matter-of-fact reaction would not come as anything unexpected to Francine.

However, for once, her usually composed, impassive father displayed a reaction that took her completely by surprise as his animated voice reacted to what he had just read. 'Good god, what a shocker, an absolute total mind-blowing seismic shocker, and I must confess, that for once, I'm really taken aback, I certainly didn't see that one coming, but, first, do you think it's genuine? I admit, it does look real. However, this transcription was done such a long time ago, how do you know if it's even accurate? Remember, it was written by this Dr Becker, who might have been under acute pressure, can you just imagine having to write this with an ogre like Göring breathing down your neck? And, then again, it is quite possible the Nazi dictated all this to him, making wild accusations for his own reasons, we just don't know. You can see precisely why your grandfather hid it though. My advice to you would be to put it back into the bank vault and forget entirely all about it. Francine, surely you must understand that this is an impossible situation to remedy, there is nothing to be done, there is no satisfactory solution for this.' Her father's deep reservations were bona fide, and his concerns for her wholly justified. Nevertheless, it would appear his advice had fallen on deaf ears as she quickly changed the topic of conversation.

'You said you had some news about the Grays?'

'Yes, I do, I have it on very good authority that Konrad, Edmund and Millicent have left New York. It seems they were given a tip-off, by who, we don't yet know, but the Grays were told by the informer of what was about to occur at their castle at the hands of Interpol, and that they were going to be pulled in again for questioning as suspects in the death of Adam. God only knows what people they have on the payroll who have been keeping them that well informed, but Konrad and Edmund knew the game was up. It seems they transferred all their money from their New York bank into their Swiss bank accounts and took off on their private plane, and, from the reports I have been privy to, headed in the direction of Argentina, no doubt clutching new identities, and passports. Now it's up to the FBI to contact the government of Argentina to try and locate them, which evidently won't be easy. With their financial resources, and I suppose a network of like-minded contacts based there, it will be a very difficult task indeed. I imagine they'll just disappear into the ether. It's quite funny when you consider the lengths to which Konrad and his twin had gone in their fanatical desire to be immortalised. Now their faces will be plastered over the International Most Wanted List for all the world to see! Just not the kind of recognition they anticipated. How far the mighty have fallen. A kind of rough justice after all, don't you think? Oh, I nearly forgot, and goodness knows what you will think of this, but when Interpol was searching their castle, they discovered behind an enormous medieval tapestry that covered an entire wall, a door that led into a room that was used for, well rituals, I suppose you'd call it. And there in the centre of that camouflaged sanctum was a shrine.

'Anyway, upon this shrine was a reliquary casket that contained two very rotten looking teeth, and according to the script written beside it they belonged to none other than Adolf Hitler!'

Francine gasped in disbelief.

'No? Is that for real? The thought of that disgusts me, it's actually quite repulsive, what is wrong with these people? You know something, now I come to think of it, when I went to Konrad's apartment and he showed me his collection of the most extraordinary artefacts, not to mention the pages from the Devil's Bible, my impression was that this was all extremely weird, interesting, but truly strange things to want to own on a personal level. Nonetheless, he mentioned that the pages from the Devil's Bible was his 'almost' prized possession, when I asked him what then his most cherished artefact? he stated cryptically.

'If I told you that, I would have to kill you,' I thought at the time he was just teasing me, now it looks as if he really meant it!' she recalled.

'Is there any evidence that they really can be attributed to Hitler?' Francine asked, not sure she really wanted to know.

'I have no idea, and unless there's any DNA of Hitler's still in existence, which I very much doubt, to compare it with, then I don't suppose we'll ever know, unless of course his dental records prove otherwise? Though, it does beg the question, if they really are the remains of Hitler, where exactly did Konrad Gray get them from, and even more disturbing, what did they intend to do with them, especially today, when genetic cloning is becoming a real possibility! A most disturbing thought, don't you think? Can you imagine the horror and scandal it would unleash if this information ever got out into the public domain?'

Francine was curious over the whereabouts of the teeth

'I have no idea, or who now has possession of them, I imagine they're still in Germany, but I really don't know, obviously, it's all highly sensitive, as you can imagine, but it is no longer our problem.' Sir Howard assured her, before he reminded his daughter that their conversation was naturally, 'off the record.' Of that, she perfectly understood.

Sir Howard tried again, 'You seemed to have skilfully avoided my suggestion about putting the da Vinci pages back into the vault and let sleeping dogs lie, as they say. So – and I am almost afraid to hear your answer to my question – what are you intending to do?' Francine concurred with her father.

'I absolutely agree with you, we don't know if these pages are genuine, especially now I know so much about fakes, I cannot just take this on face value. Fortunately, at Christie's we do have access to one of the world's top Lab's, which is in Arizona, and does carbon-14 dating work for most of the auction houses and museums around the world, and its fool-proof. In fact, they did the carbon dating on, not only the Turin Shroud but also the Dead Sea Scrolls, so they are just about as good as you can get, and even Konrad, with all the equipment they had under the castle would not have had anything like this kind of superior technology. Anyway, I have called and explained what I require from them, I didn't go into too much detail, as there was no need. I know this process takes a few days to obtain the results, and I am sending it by the special couriers we use at Christie's to ensure utmost security, they will be coming here shortly to collect the package; I am going to carefully cut off this extremely small section at the bottom of the paper with this ink splatter on it, they only need the tiniest piece for the carbon dating, that way they can test the age of the paper and the ink; and will give us a very accurate date; and, as for the translation, I have spoken to Jonathan Bayeswood, he's a Latin scholar, I don't know if you remember him? We became friends when we were working together on the Leonardo da Vinci exhibition at the National Gallery, and I know I can trust him implicitly, he's currently ensconced in the Bodleian Library at Oxford, so I have uploaded high-resolution photographs of the original da Vinci pages along with the translation that Göring supposedly had carried out by Dr Otto Becker, and he's working on it as we speak. Jonathan said it won't take him very long, so we should hear from him quite soon,' Francine was putting all the pieces into place.

'Do you know if you can really trust your friend, Jonathan Bayeswood?' her father was naturally apprehensive, given the sensitive nature of the issue.

'Yes, I have no doubt whatsoever that I can trust Jonathan. Don't forget I have the original da Vinci writings here with me, besides, Jonathan's reputation is solid, he worked for quite some time at Windsor Castle when he was asked personally by the Queen to transcribe some of her collection of da Vinci's works, which is precisely why she awarded him an MBE, so, if Her Majesty can trust him, then so can I.' She made a good point to which her father was unable to argue.

'Now, all we can do is wait for the results to come back and then we will finally know the truth.' They both acknowledged this.

# CHAPTER 55

## 'The Truth Will Out...'
## William Shakespeare

The large hotel conference room was packed to the rafters, as the assembled journalists avidly consumed the warm, freshly baked croissants, washed down with endless cups of Nespresso and bottled spring water, as they speculated as too why they had been invited to attend this event. After all, nobody calls a press conference in New York without an extremely good reason. As Francine quietly took a sly peek at the attendees who had gathered, she could feel the excitable atmosphere growing as they waited with animated impatience, all champing at the bit, ready for the off and eager for yet another news sensation to come onto the horizon for them to exploit. The sheer intensity of the moment was all too nerve-wracking, as she quipped to lighten her burden, by saying, 'I understand now how poor Anne Boleyn must have felt as she was about to put her head on the block!' Her father considered that remark under the circumstances to be in very poor taste. But Jonathan Bayeswood, who had flown to New York from the UK the day before, could sense the irony in her humour and tried to hide a wry smile from Sir Howard.

'Francine, you know full well I never, ever interfere in your life, and especially when it comes to your career, but I feel it is my duty as your father to urge you to pause, and think very carefully before you go ahead and do something you may come to regret. Have you really thought all this through properly? You know there's still time to change your mind. It's not too late,' Sir Howard needed to be convinced that his daughter fully appreciated just exactly what she was about to do, along with all the undeniable repercussions it will have, not only on her career, but on France!

'This is going to be like throwing a metaphorical 'Molotov cocktail' at the art world, who will loathe this kind of disruption, and once out, you cannot put the genie back into the bottle, this will go down like a lead balloon, and you might never be forgiven, do you really have any notion of the hostility you can expect to receive, especially in this age of social media?'

'I understand completely what you are saying, and I can assure you that I have thought long and hard about all the chaos it's likely going to create? But sometimes life presents you with very uncomfortable truths, and when it does, should we pretend differently, look the other way and ignore it? Don't think for one moment I'm finding this easy, but for some inexplicable reason I have a strong conviction that I simply must do this, to do what is right, and remember, this is precisely what da Vinci wanted. And now we have absolute, definitive, and unequivocal proof to back up what I am about to reveal to the US and the international press that have amassed outside in that conference room, all waiting anxiously. So, can you imagine if I were to cancel at the last moment, I think they would hang me out to dry! Anyway, you know what they say, 'they always shoot the messenger,' therefore, I won't be surprised after this when the art establishment turn their back on me and do everything they can to try and dismiss this truth. I believe the shock will give them a unified nervous breakdown.

Most are snobs of the highest order, and will stamp their feet kicking and screaming blue murder. They won't be able to cope with it, I know precisely their mindset, which is completely fixed, but, on my side is something that Leonardo would have thoroughly loved and completely approved of... and that is science! Our evidence cannot be challenged, because, we have the hard facts to back it up, and that is all there is too it! It is, as they say a *fait accompli*, so they will just have to get their intransigent minds around it', she replied in absolute seriousness.

'No, there is no turning back now. This whole thing has taken on a momentum all of its own. As I've now terminated my contract at Christie's with immediate effect, at least I don't have to worry about involving them in a scandal. So, here's goes. Let's hope I survive in one piece?' Francine told her father, while walking out with Jonathan Bayeswood towards the podium and into the unknown.

# CHAPTER 56

## Shock and Awe

'Good morning, and thank you all for coming here today, and at such short notice. At the end of this briefing press packs will be available, which will contain detailed copies of all the documentation of the many varies high specification tests carried out, including among others, Carbon-14 timeline and QDE testing, known as forensic handwriting analysis, which I am pleased to say have all been fully appraised and validated, confirming the information we are about to reveal. I would like to introduce you to Dr Jonathan Bayeswood MBE, a reputed Italian and Latin scholar, who has recently been working for Her Majesty Queen Elizabeth. His full resume you will find in the pack. Being here today was a decision I did not take lightly, because, what I am about to disclose is something that has been hidden for over five hundred years, and the term 'let sleeping dogs lie,' would have been a far easier option, and a natural, conservative one to take, however, I feel that now we are in the 21st century, and with our enlightened times, if not now, then when? I will just give you a brief introduction to the timeline, but, as I have said, everything has been laid out in full for you to read in the information pack that you can collect at the end.

'So, where do I begin? It starts with my Grandfather, Special Officer Max Page-Hamilton, who was a British art historian and went on to become one of the Monuments Men during the Second World War. But to be brief, at the end of the war in Europe, he found himself in the partially bombed out home of the leading Nazi Reichsmarschall Hermann Göring, and, just by good fortune he discovered in that home, the painting of the Mona Lisa, that Göring had taken from the Louvre in 1940. Miraculously it had survived unscathed, and had not been damaged in any way by the bombing. However, what he also discovered on that day was an envelope, firmly attached to the back of the Mona Lisa frame, and carried the official waxed seal of the Reichsmarschall. My grandfather proceeded to open that envelope. Of course, we can go into the rights and wrongs of that decision, but we were not there, or in his shoes, so I am not here today to discuss that action or to defend it.

But what did come to light on that day back in May 1945, was so profound that my grandfather felt the need to shield it away from the world, and subsequently he placed it within a bank vault in London, where it remained for many, many decades. In fact, it did not see the light of day again until now. When he died some years later, he had bequeathed it to me, his only grandchild, and, as I was still quite young at the time of his death, he had left it at the discretion of my father as to exactly when I should receive it. I should also mention that my father, Sir Howard Page-Hamilton, had no knowledge of the contents of my sealed legacy, which my grandfather had decided, in his wisdom, to pass on the baton to me, so to speak, where it's fate would now lay in my hands. And that is why we are all here today. Am I braver than my grandfather for standing before you now with this disclosure? I think not, it's just different times we live in. Everything I am about to tell you has been authenticated by those distinguished and leading institutions cited in the documents.

'So, as I stated, my grandfather opened that sealed envelope, and too his complete shock he found original papers belonging to Leonardo da Vinci, as an art historian himself, he recognized the left-handed idiosyncratic writing style of the old master, it was apparent that Hermann Göring had had these pages translated into German, French and English and these copies of that transcription were also included within this large envelope. So, you may say, the old master wrote thousands of pages, and you would be quite correct, nothing new or unusual about that. However, it is the contents of precisely what he wrote on those pages that are now about to rewrite art history. And the world has a right to know. I will put up on the screen for you to compare the two transcriptions taken from the original da Vinci pages that had been attached to the back of the Mona Lisa frame. One transcription was completed a few days ago by Dr Jonathan Bayeswood, and the other one completed by da Vinci scholar, Dr Otto Becker in 1940 at the request of Hermann Göring. And as you can see, both the transcriptions of Dr Becker and Jonathan Bayeswood are identical. That is, word for word, exactly, what Leonardo da Vinci himself wrote, it is his voice that now reaches out to us from the past.'

Francine continued to the hushed tone of the audience within the large conference room, 'before I begin, I would just like to bring to your attention, the language used in Renaissance Italy was quite different to the way we communicate with each other today, so please bear that in mind.

Leonardo, was now aged 65 at the time of writing this, and was living as the permanent house guest of King Francis I at his Chateau in Amboise.

'I will now read out what Leonardo da Vinci wrote in the year 1517, two years before he died.'

# CHAPTER 57

## THE MAESTRO
## LEONARDO DA VINCI
## CHÂTEAU DU CLOS LUCÉ
## AMBOISE

France – November 1517

*The Château is still, all are asleep, and only the ghosts are here to keep me company. These days much of my attention leans towards one thought, should I have done things differently? How much that question vexes me with its endless torment as I sit here night after night by the fire, which, like me is slowly burning out. Once I raged full of energy, bold and bright. Now, I quietly observe the passing of my years, all the time becoming ever more dispirited, lamenting in the darkness as the spitefulness of age comes ever closer, destroying and consuming everything with relentless jaws, bringing its slow and certain death.*

*My thoughts are my friend and my fiercest enemy, conscious of past sins committed, and sins unknown. Where once the holy sacrament was dismissed, now I seek it daily, to ease my mind – but has it come too late? The weakness of my flesh provokes an urgency over a wrong I wish to redress while still having all my faculties intact. It is time to confess that I am guilty of many things.*

*I constructed a deliberate veil to separate me from other human beings, always seeking solitude to pursue only those flights of fancy which inspired me each waking day. My lack of discipline and attention to the mundane, could, perhaps be ascribed to the lowly position of my birth. By resenting being denied a formal education, while delighting in*

312

the freedom it permitted, I was fully aware of my contrary, unemotional state of being, even at a young age. It is a truth I perceive, that when you are born illegitimate and legally prevented from carrying the name of your father, while never really fully knowing the mother who bore you out of wedlock, you are barred admission into the respected distinguished Guilds that would allow a certain status denied to me, it fosters a profound sense of inferiority within, leaving a permanent scar that never heals.

I was, nevertheless, allowed entry into Verrocchio's studio in Florence as a young apprentice, and my eyes were opened wide as to how, through the beauty of art, and the patronage of powerful men, I could finally achieve a position in society I had long coveted, and then enter the Guilds.

With my exceptional abilities, it was quickly accepted that I was the most gifted of all the students, as my skills soared far above theirs. Where I questioned all things, pressing for answers, always searching for reasons, the others did not. At first, it was a novelty to them, this handsome talented loner. I was much applauded, but all too soon the responses to my remarkable gifts in all things began to turn sour, and without doubt, they bore resentment towards me.

In the year 1476, the initial admiration, so enjoyed, turned to envy, when anonymous, unfounded, unspeakable acts of heresy saw me accused and stand trial of the vilest of crimes, and had I been found guilty, a death sentence could have been my fate – naturally no evidence could be presented to the court since I was innocent.

The case was dismissed, but the damage to my carefully cultivated reputation inflicted a lasting damage as still cautious eyes looked suspiciously upon me. I sought sanctuary within myself, the one person I could trust, as I became wary of my fellow human beings.

In 1481, I received my first important commission from the Augustinian monks of San Donato A Scopeto in Florence to paint the Adoration of the Magi, which I readily accepted. In work I could immerse myself. But an unyielding malaise began slowly to dominate my senses, and my intellect came to recognise that I now lacked any real passion to paint, and although I considered painting to be the highest *form of art, nonetheless, the fire of inspiration had died within me, and it pains me to admit, it no longer stirred any motivation in me. Feeling like a bird trapped within a cage, my only desire was to escape.*

*I knew on occasion a commission would necessitate that I be required to pick up the brush, but only for the prudent reason of the financial reward that provided for the smooth running of my household. It was just a pragmatic activity, akin to any common labourer using his skills, and never, out of love of the art, because that demanded far too much of my time, time better employed with my real passion, the pursuit of science, the art to be found in nature, and so much more.*

*But now, pressed with a sense of urgency, my brain full to bursting with many new ideas and experiments on my horizon, I hastily departed Florence, and conveniently dismissed what I had left behind.*

*In 1500, and with nearly five decades of age, I found myself consumed by a long period of ardent reflection that led me to visit the Convent of San Marco. I returned home with a new addition to my household, a young girl of eighteen years, who was hired to cook, mend, and attend to the general household chores.*

*I was not quite sure when I noticed just how intelligent a person she was, the kind of intelligence rarely seen in anyone, let alone in a naïve young female. Her boundless energy and inexhaustible curiosity were much like my own, which naturally I much admired. Her questions, I eagerly encouraged, although they often left me exhausted. She was, without doubt, a challenge. But her simple innocence acted as a natural antidote to the toils of my day. It was during our many varied conversations, where I would often be a passive listener, she confessed, with my full approval, of her desire to paint – something she knew would be denied to her, because, being a female, and, furthermore, one born out of wedlock, which fate was worse, she didn't know? However, she understood and accepted that her high-minded dream would die with her. How much I appreciated the predicament of illegitimacy. Of all people, I knew the impact of this only too well. It intrigued and amused me when I would often find her late at night, supposedly cleaning the studio, examining the dormant dusty jars of pigments, while grasping my unused stiff brushes in her hands as she traced them over an imaginary wooden panel or canvas, living out her lofty day-dream of painting. She never saw me watching her. It fascinated me to observe somebody compulsively wanting to do something so strongly, but due to their place in life, knew it remained unavailable to them. This stirred within my mind.*

*One late spring day it occurred to me how much she presented me with a real living experiment. I, the Maestro, would teach her how to paint. She laughed at first, thinking naturally I was only jesting with her. Then her mood turned to happiness. It was a test I welcomed; to be able to take somebody with no knowledge and see just how much the conscious brain, especially that of a female, might be encouraged to reach for more than they ever could imagine possible.*

*Yes, I looked forward immensely to undertaking this living observation – up until now, I had only ever been able to dissect and experiment on corpses in the morgue. But now I was compelled by the potential of how much a living human being might be shaped under the right instruction, and, if this was so, the prospects for humanity would hold no bounds. Could it even be proven that a woman just might be equal to that of a man intellectually? It was fascinating, to discover if there was even the remote possibility that a woman would be able to apply herself to become as single-minded as a man in pursuit of a goal.*

*It was an intriguing prospect, and a noble ambition.*

*In the utmost secrecy, as it was essential that nobody knew of the clandestine tutoring, we began. We would spend many months in the pursuit of her learning how to sketch, understanding perspective, and then to draw in much more depth and skill. Her quickness to master this work took me totally by surprise. With the sharpest of eyes, absolutely no detail was lost on her, she had mastered the task within a heartbeat. Before I knew it, she was ready to move on. We discussed many subjects for her debut at great length. I suggested that she should draw her own portrait – her modesty protested but I took the final decision that this should be so. The precise use of mirrors easily facilitated her ability to observe her own reflection without any hindrance, first she sketched her face before progressing onto finer details, after many months she had managed to perfectly capture the truth of her inner being. This experiment with my young prodigy was deeply engrossing to me.*

*However, it was now more than one year, and progress was insufficient, often due to my other preoccupations, and sometimes because she had little time and energy after her exhausting household chores. Fortunately, she had youth on her side.*

*And slowly it started to emerge, layer by layer the thinly applied transparent pigments, painted only when the light was just right, to produce a smoky atmospheric mystique. Her interpretation and ability to take my instruction reminded me how patiently I had listened to my master, Verrocchio. But her natural dexterity with the brushstrokes now needed little guidance from me, except where the background was concerned, there she struggled, but my suggestions soon came into perfect fruition.*

*But once again, other matters distracted my attention, and much of my time was devoted to more pressing issues.*

*The seasons would come and go, and I would resume periodically with my observations and instructions. Late one evening, after she had retired to her room, and aware that she had been working for several months without my supervision, I undertook a thorough inspection of the portrait. I had initially anticipated from the start a limited positive result, in consideration of the fact that she was a gentle female with only domestic abilities. But any notion of how it would unfold was certainly not this. She had by far exceeded all expectations, and had, without a shadow of doubt, completely transcended me – Leonardo da Vinci, the Maestro. But my reactions now were not those of umbrage or jealousy, just a sense of pride.*

*Now it was time to finish the last few brush strokes.*

*The harshest of all winters descended that year of 1505 as the rumours began to spread fast, but it was no rumour. All too quickly the feared sweating sickness had returned with its violent, merciless, and deadly wrath.*

*That evening she did not possess her usual keenness as she entered the studio.*

*The next morning the house was devoid of warmth, there was no* burning fires, and the smell of freshly baked bread that usually greeted my day, was absent.

The illness had taken hold of her during the night, and the decline was rapid as she began to fade. Before dawn the next day the sickness had taken her.

This humble, eager to learn young girl had disrupted all my state of loneliness. Now she was gone. It was almost as if she had never even existed.

I ordered 3lbs of wax for the torches, four priests, four pall bearers, four acolytes, bell, book and sponge. A fitting burial outside of the city took place.

Much time has since passed.

I await the arrival of Piero, the master craftsman I will instruct to make a special frame for the portrait that I will keep beside me in my room, where her presence will bring a lightness to the remaining days of my existence.

But, before he completes the task, I will place this letter I have documented within the back of the frame that I have designed, as the safest place I can conceive of.

The outcome of the experiment I soon came to accept could never be written or referred to in my journals.

I am a man of science, logic and deduction – therefore, it is only reasonable, I would argue, that a woman does possess the prerequisite abilities for an apprenticeship and, subsequently, be allowed to eventually enter the Guilds in the same way as any man, this I have proved. However, this truth I know would be deemed a profanity by the Vatican, a most serious accusation of ungodliness and a violation of the church, her soul would be damned for all eternity as immoral. Alas, in the eyes of the church, a female is either a respected wife and devoted mother, a servant, or a woman of ill repute and low morals. No alternatives are permitted for them.

But I have a strong and deep belief within me that in the future, not only will man fly like the birds in the sky, and explore the ocean floor in machines, but a female will be equal in all things. This I predict will become a truth.

317

*But that time is yet to arrive.*

*Therefore, the knowledge of her accomplishments must remain hidden until such a day exists when the truth will linger upon the eyes without fear of persecution, and it will no longer be declared as heresy.*

*Her loss has affected me much more than I ever expected, and it is not unlike the day her mother Agnese passed away in Florence.*

*Agnese, a young orphaned girl offered me a deep friendship that I eagerly took, but which I ultimately rejected – because, by admission of my deep ever-present vanity, ambition, temperament, and disdain for commitment to another person, for which I was ill-equipped.*

*Out of fear I fled the city, leaving behind not only the unfinished work of the Adoration of the Magi, but also a damaged reputation. That day in 1482 I collected monies from the monks for the work I had done in the San Donato A Scopeto. Those gold florins I gave to the Convent San Marco which I visited before taking my leave from Florence. My departure from that city was as rapid as my horse could manage. I would return to the Convent several times over the coming years – with many more florins.*

*As I gaze at the portrait of her in my bed chamber, the resemblance is all too clear, with her dark hair, grace and intelligence, her endless ever-present curiosity matched the smile she crafted so well. Now, as her knowing eyes stare back at me, I can reveal here in this letter the secret I have carried with me for all these years. But I pray she will forgive an old man for the wrong he did her that day when her mother, Agnese, who had favoured me, died in childbirth, and out of desperation I left the tiny crying infant female in the care of the Sisters of the Convent San Marco, whose shock was equal to their forgiveness and compassion, vowing to take care of the child out of a love for Agnese, the Novice Sister in their charge. Now, all I have left is this painting that will remain with me until the day I depart this place. Then I will join her.*

*The day after her burial, along with so many other desolate souls encased in their own grief, I registered her name in the Book of the Dead – nobody noticed – but it is there for all to see. . . Lisa da Vinci.*

*My beautiful daughter – Her masterly painted self-portrait I shall call – Mona Lisa.*

*Will my earnest confession ever be found? And if so, allowed to be known? I don't know. And although many will question and doubt my words, they should not. But with patience and endurance her brilliance will somehow eventually find its way into the world, and upon that day she will be held in the highest esteem.*

*Until then, we wait for the truth to enable Lisa da Vinci to take her rightful place beside me, her father – Leonardo da Vinci. . . where she belongs.*

*On this day I declare that... "Truth was the daughter of time."*

Leonardo da Vinci
1517

# CHAPTER 58

# Chain Reaction

Francine stood braced, waiting for all the questions and recriminations to begin, not to mention conspiracy theories, and ridicule but instead, she was met with an uncomfortable, ubiquitous silence from all of them. Both she and Jonathan looked at each other in total disbelief. This was not the reaction either had expected. But then slowly, one by one, the journalists started to applaud, within seconds the whole room was shaking to the sound of the audience clapping and cheering so loud it was quite deafening, it had reached a crescendo, from one extreme to the other. The journalists were now starting to shout out, all vying for her attention, the room was in utter chaos with excitement, a scene that was so far removed from the hostile reactions they had anticipated and prepared for.

Within hours the news had gone global. The world had seen nothing like it. The revelation was unparalleled. Every television network was talking incessantly about nothing else from New York to Beijing, Moscow, London, Riyadh, and naturally to Paris. The interest was phenomenal.

'Francine,' her father shouted, 'Quickly, come and see the TV news coverage. Look at Paris, it's incredible, they have gone wild, the queues, the excitement is almost contagious, people are flooding into the capital from all over the world. It was reported that every hotel room is taken, people are renting out their spare rooms, such is the demand, all flights are booked solid, everyone, from everywhere wants to pay homage saying they will queue for days, or, for how long it takes. Now they just want to see her with 'new eyes', and from listening to those being interviewed by the journalists outside the Louvre, I think it's fast becoming accepted that the Mona Lisa has been transformed from a French icon into a global icon. One young man summed it up perfectly when he said, 'Of course, how could we have all been so blind? For years, academics have pondered and argued about who she was, because nobody ever really knew. Da Vinci, by his own words was not a sentimental man, yet he kept her beside him until he died, now we know precisely why, and if you really look into those eyes, and that mischievous all-knowing smile, the truth was there all the time, right in front of our noses, we just didn't see what da Vinci wanted us all to know when he encouraged her to paint her self-portrait, he really was quite the rebel.' Francine's observation was spot on, telling her father, 'This enigmatic Master of the art world produced only a handful of paintings in his lifetime, and now we know why. Driven by his utter fascination of all the natural sciences, Leonardo was able to predict back in the 16th century that one day man would fly like birds in the sky, and now we do. So, when da Vinci cited at the bottom of his confessional letter that, "truth was the daughter of time" his quote was pure genius, and as we can see, the time was just right. The world was ready to embrace his daughter with open arms. It was a shame that Professor Jardin and Pierre Guyon, didn't fully grasp this miracle of a painting they had in their midst. I think their insecurity over the potential negative reaction, or scandal it might create if the world ever found out literally terrified them and clouded their judgement, and therefore decided it was just too precarious to ever be known. They would not allow themselves to ever take that chance, so fear drove them to hide the truth, convinced it was the right thing to do. It must have tormented them, there was no precedence for this situation. It would have been a massive gamble for them to risk France's most valued asset, because, if they had got it wrong, then what? And as for the Maestro, well, it's nigh on impossible these days to entirely appreciate in our enlightened times just how advanced da Vinci's mind really was. His ingenuity justified him in ignoring all the dangers and natural instincts of the men of his era, permitting him to think way outside the box when he decided to teach her to paint. He also had an ulterior motive, because he must have seen in her the perfect example of how an apple never falls too far from the tree. No wonder he wanted to perform his experiments, it was borne out of pride and much vanity, something Leonardo confessed to having in abundance, but which he viewed as neither a negative nor a positive, just a scientific observation that compelled him to understand.'

'My dear, I think your critique of the whole scenario is probably just about as near as we will ever get to an intelligent insightfulness as is humanly possible to achieve!' Sir Howard concluded.

# CHAPTER 59

## When Life is Stranger Than Fiction

The people of France, and the Louvre Museum, were now the custodians of the most precious, the rarest of all paintings, and without question, the most valuable piece of art on the entire planet.

Lisa da Vinci had surpassed the Master, her father, Leonardo da Vinci – and he thoroughly approved.

'If you don't hurry up, we will miss our flight,' Sir Howard said, trying to get his daughter and her suitcases out of the door and into the cab that was waiting outside their apartment

'At last, we can finally leave – good grief, Francine, just how many bags do you need?' he asked her baffled why she had packed so much.

'You never know?' she responded.

'It's quite an honour for you to be invited by the French President to attend an official reception at the Elysée Palace to hand over the da Vinci letter, I expect they cannot wait to receive such a unique piece of history. I think the president must be absolutely delighted by just how much the French economy is going to benefit from all that has occurred lately.' Francine was overjoyed that it had all worked out for the good.

'Because of everything that has happened, we never got around to celebrating your seventy-fifth birthday, so I have arranged for us to have dinner after the reception at the Ritz. What do you say to that?' she surprised him.

'Oh, that sounds like a wonderful idea,' Sir Howard replied.

'Actually, I was thinking that after Paris, I want to return to Britain. It was exceedingly nice of Christie's to ask me back, but London is where I feel I now want to be,' she confessed to her father, who admitted he also liked the idea of staying put in their London townhouse, as he asked her.

'What would you do?' She laughed.

'Well, actually, believe it or not, but with all that's happened, it has given me an appetite for writing.' Her father, somewhat amused, 'Really, dare I ask what about?'

'You know, that's the thing about art,' Francine declared, 'there's always something new to discover. Just think about it, all those famous artists with their sordid scandals, salacious secrets and irredeemable sins, hidden, still waiting to be unearthed. I have a feeling that their life stories will be far more interesting, outrageous and stranger than any work of fiction could ever possibly be, that much I sense. And now I've thought about it, I cannot wait to get started...!'

# AFTERWORD

1. All details of artworks, paintings and architecture are factual and as described.
2. Coco Chanel's relationship with the Nazi spy, Baron Hans Günther von Dincklage is well documented.
3. Chanel was personally involved with Nazi missions and had her own secret agent number (F – 7124) code name Westminster.
4. Chanel lived openly with the Baron in their suite at the Ritz Hotel in Paris throughout WWII.
5. It was established that Chanel was addicted to drugs and injected herself daily until she died.
6. The conversations between Göring and Chanel are imagined, but Göring did, on a personal level, have an intense dislike for women like Chanel.
7. All descriptions and the timeline with regards to Leonardo da Vinci are fact.
8. All references to WWII are factual.
9. The sale of the Salvatore Mundi at Christies is a fact.